H

DON'T SHOOT YOURSELF IN THE FOOT

"A highly practical approach to helping people solve their most frustrating problems. There is not a physician or patient in this country who would not benefit from reading the book."
— **George Robert Simms, M.D., Ph.D., professor of Family and Community Medicine, Penn State University College of Medicine**

✔ ✔ ✔

"Good reading for anyone . . . essential reading for us hard-charging Harvard Business School types."
— **Fran and Heather Kelly, co-authors, *What They Really Teach You at the Harvard Business School***

✔ ✔ ✔

"Very readable and workable . . . offers a systematic, effective approach to stopping self-sabotage. Don't let your Internal Saboteur talk you out of reading it!"
— **Martha Baldwin, M.S.S.W., author of *Self-Sabotage: How to Stop It and Soar to Success***

✔ ✔ ✔

"An upbeat book . . . one can trust because it is grounded in reality."
— **Milton R. Cudney, Ph.D., Emeriti Professor, Western Michigan University Counseling Center and co-author of *Self-Defeating Behaviors***

✔ ✔ ✔

"A book written by a great man with a keen insight . . . a wonderfully practical book that helps readers determine how they are sabotaging themselves—and how to stop it."
— **Joel Dreyer, M.D., The American College of Forensic Psychiatry**

more . . .

DR. DANIEL G. AMEN, a board certified child, adolescent and adult psychiatrist, is the Medical Director of The Center for Effective Living in Fairfield, California. Widely published in the professional and lay press, Dr. Amen has won writing and research awards from the United States Army, The American Psychiatric Association, and the Baltimore-D.C. Institute for Psychoanalysis. He is the author of *The Sabotage Factor*, a correspondence course designed to uncover the barriers holding people back from success, and he wrote and produced "An Intimate Parent-Child Talk," a two-hour videotape for parents and children. Dr. Amen lives in Fairfield, California, with his wife Robbin and their three children Anthony, Breanne and Kaitlyn.

DON'T SHOOT YOURSELF IN THE FOOT

DANIEL AMEN, M.D.

WARNER BOOKS

A Time Warner Company

Confidentiality is essential to psychiatric practice. All case descriptions in this book, therefore, have been altered to preserve the anonymity of my patients without distorting the essentials of their stories.

Warner Books, Inc., 1271 Avenue of the Americas, New York, NY 10020

W A Time Warner Company

Printed in the United States of America
First printing: November 1992
10 9 8 7 6 5

Library of Congress Cataloging-in-Publication Data

Amen, Daniel.
  Don't shoot yourself in the foot / Daniel Amen.
      p.   cm.
  ISBN 0-446-39373-8
  1. Success—Psychological aspects.   2. Success—Problems, exercises, etc.   3. Self-defeating behavior.   I. Title.
BF637.S8A464   1992
158'.1—dc20   92–6630
                                                      CIP

Cover design by Diane Luger
Book design by Giorgetta Bell McRee

To Robbin

my teacher
my partner
my best friend
my lover
my wife

ACKNOWLEDGMENTS

I would like to thank the many people who have encouraged me and helped me through the process of putting together this book. Specifically, these people include Ken and Chris Roberts, whose support made this project possible; Stanley Wallace, M.D.; Lois Fishler, M.D.; James Collins, M.D.; Edward Mervis, M.D.; James Bowen, M.D.; Jeanne Sharpe; Melissa Barrow; Bob Gessler; Fran Franklin; James Taylor; Judy Moretz, the editor for the course version; and my editor from Warner Books, Tracy Bernstein. In addition, a very special thanks to my agent Carl De Santis, who continually encourages me. We are relational people and I appreciate your support.

Also, my deepest gratitude goes to my parents, Lou and Dory Amen, who have taught me by example and word that we are what we make of ourselves. What we do in life is up to us. Mixed with love and kindness, it is the best lesson a child can learn.

And, my warmest love to my children Antony, Breanne and Kaitlyn. They are the reason to study and write about success, to give them a map to make their way easier.

NOTE: To avoid awkward sentence construction, I use the pronoun "he" to mean both "he" and "she." No sexual bias is intended.

CONTENTS

DON'T
SHOOT
YOURSELF
IN THE FOOT

Introduction

Self-sabotage. We all do it. Unfortunately, some of us make a habit of it, destroying our chances for getting what we want out of life. This book is designed to help you specifically uncover the ways *you* hold yourself back and give you an individualized prescription for overcoming those obstacles. The principles in this book apply equally to your relationships, your work life and your personal life outside of relationships or work.

This book is based on my course "The Sabotage Factor: Find Out What's Holding You Back (And Exactly What To Do About It)," which is an interactional correspondence course that I have been conducting out of my private practice office for a number of years and that includes students from thirty-seven states and seven countries.

This is not another success book. This is a book about you. Most how-to articles, positive thinking manuals, and self-help books on success don't work. They offer only simplistic and general principles that may have little if anything to do with you as an individual. They often tell you how someone else achieved what they wanted and imply that if you only do the same thing you can have your dreams come true as well. Not true. *Success is a complicated and very personal phenomena.* It is wise to understand how others became successful, but it is foolish to assume that you can clone their formula and get the same results.

This is not a self-help book. Self-help books deal with other people's successes and failures; they promise you everything; and they are generally easy to put down after reading only a few chapters. These books may sell by the millions, but they change few lives.

This is an interactional process, a study, in which you are the main character. This process is similar to studying a subject in school, except that here the subject is you. Since this is a process, much is expected from you. You cannot just passively read the book and expect to get the most out of it. Change requires action. And, since the change is to occur in you, *you* need to take the action. This point cannot be overemphasized. The people who received the most benefit from The Sabotage Factor course were those who worked the program. I'm convinced that, at a minimum, those patients of mine who diligently worked through the material saved themselves at least several thousand dollars in therapy.

In going through this book it is important to personalize it and make it your own. Mark it up (unless you checked it out of the library); circle ideas that apply to you, and refer to it often. This is your bridge to where you want to be. Don't try to read it as a novel. Think of it as a workbook. Work through it at a pace that allows you to understand and assimilate the material. The most effective results will come if you read and absorb a section at a time. There is so much material that you could become overwhelmed if you tried to read it all at once. Remember the first time you drove a car, and how overwhelmed you felt? There seemed to be so many things to think about and do at the same time. This process is similar; take the time you need.

Section One in the workbook will help you define what you want out of life. In order to uncover what is holding you back, you must first be able to spell out your dreams and goals, those things that would make you feel successful. This section illustrates how your stage of life, family background, social status, and psychological makeup influence your goals, and it offers nine rules to help you define personal success. At the end of the section you'll find a worksheet designed to help you clarify your own definition of success and what you're doing to attain it.

Section Two identifies twenty-six major self-sabotaging characteristics. Each chapter begins with a quiz, where you plot your score on a master graph to eventually give you an overall comparison of your strengths and weaknesses as they relate to self-sabotage and success. This personal "Sabotage versus Success" profile will clearly identify your strengths and the areas holding you back and give you direction for change. After each quiz I then define the individual self-sabotaging characteristics and give practical examples of them.

Section Three takes an in-depth look at the process of change. You will learn how to go from holding yourself back from your goals to getting what you want out of life. It discusses the ten steps involved in change and shows you how to measure your progress in removing the roadblocks from your life.

In Section Four the twenty-six necessary ingredients common to successful people are identified and explored. For the most part these ingredients are the flip side of the "hallmarks of self-sabotage." After I discuss each characteristic there is a series of practical exercises designed to help you strengthen the areas that were identified as a problem by the quizzes in Section Two. Section Two helps you identify areas that are holding you back from reaching your goals and Section Four tells you what to do about it! Taken together these sections will give you what I call your "Individualized Prescription for Success (IPS)." Sections Two and Four are detailed and intensive. They may require several readings.

This book concludes by emphasizing living in "real time," which is a daily process of focusing and working toward your goals. I'll show you how "real time" living prevents burnout.

The uniqueness of this book is that it is tailored to you. It will help you find out what has been holding you back and exactly what to do about it. As a psychiatrist, I know that all people are truly different, with different genetic structures, different social backgrounds, and different psychological makeups. Any effective program for change needs to be individualized as much as possible.

This process has been developed out of many years of observing people who repeatedly put themselves in the way of their dreams. As a psychiatrist who cares for children, adolescents and adults, I have evaluated and treated many people whom society would classify as failures. Although there was an enormous range to their problems, the common themes outlined in this book occurred again and again. I have watched and participated in many of their transformations. I know that lasting change can take place, and I know the ingredients involved in change.

I have not, however, only studied and observed success from the negative side—from human suffering and failures. I have observed the quest for success and its ingredients firsthand.

To begin with, I am the son of a man who embodies the American Dream. Coming from very poor immigrant parents, my father found and developed the self-directed talents to become one of southern California's most successful grocery chain owners. Several years ago he was president of the California Grocers' Association.

In many ways this course parallels my own life, for I have gone from feeling very unsuccessful to feeling that I can get anything I want out of life. In order for you to be able to identify with me as a companion on this road of life, not just as a psychiatrist or an author, I will share some personal experiences. My hope is that you'll be able to see yourself in the journey I have made and am still making, and that this will help motivate you to press on with your journey.

Despite my father's influence, I spent the early part of my own life floundering in mediocrity (we'll explore the pitfalls of being a child of a successful person). I was a very average student in high school, graduating with a C+ grade point average. In athletics, it seemed I could never overcome being five foot six inches. I always tried hard, only to end up sitting on the bench. And, in love, things also developed very slowly.

However, it is in love that I learned my first success lesson: persistence. I fell in love with Robbin the first day I met her (this is not something I generally recommend). No one had ever made my heart jump with excitement, or my eyes light up with anticipation, as she did (and does). The only problem was that she was in love with Bob, who happened to be tall, good looking, smart, and a starter on the football team. The thought of her possessed me, however, to the point where I decided to overcome my fears of rejection and failure, and changed my ways to win her love. It took many months, serious planning, rejections, and persistence. In the end, she fell in love with me—the sweetest success I have ever known.

And, as you will learn, success begets success. Having her love, I felt better about myself, more confident and more assured. Looking back, I realize that was one of the pivotal steps in my life. After some time in the army, I went to college as a pre-medical student. Some said it was a crazy choice, given my previous grades, but through the things I learned (and will measure in you and help you change), I was able to graduate from college with a 3.93 grade point average (on a 4.0 scale) and go on to medical school, where I graduated magna cum laude and second in my class.

Several years after I wrote the Sabotage Factor course, I started a private psychiatric practice. I utilized the principles outlined in the course and here in this book to guide my business. They work. My schedule was full in less than three months and within a year I had ten other clinicians working with me. This is in an area where several other psychiatrists had left town due to a lack of business.

I know what transformations are all about. In my life I have gone from mediocrity to success, and have studied the process in my patients, in successful people, and in myself along the way.

In choosing this book you have taken the very important first step toward establishing your own success story. You have not only recognized that there are problems with your life (a crucial first step); you have, more importantly, taken an active role in changing your life's direction. Deciding to do this may very well be one of the most important steps you ever take.

You are the key to your life and your success, if you can stop putting yourself in your way. This book is certainly not a magical cure that will solve all of your problems. It offers a process that will teach you about yourself and give you the tools you need for success as you define it. It is up to you to use these tools.

Defining Your Success

Your Success Is Yours

One person's success may be another person's failure.

Most people want to be a success without ever knowing exactly what that means for them, without having a personal definition for success. It's ironic and a bit sad to think about all the people who feel bad about themselves for not being successful when they are not even sure what it means. They are not sure what they are missing, but they know they are missing something.

When pushed to define success, most people equate it with happiness, wealth, recognition, independence, friendships, achievement, or inner peace—all very vague concepts. Even most dictionaries define success in ways that have little specific meaning: common phrases used are, "a favorable result"; "the gaining of wealth, fame, etc."; or "a successful person or thing."

Does this mean that success is ambiguous? Not at all. It simply means that success is a very personal thing. And it needs to be defined in the context of individual lives. What may be one person's success might be another person's failure.

Defining success depends on many factors in an individual's life. Let's look at some of them.

DEVELOPMENTAL STAGE OF LIFE

Success for a sixteen-year-old is often having enough money for a car, making the team, and having a date every Friday night. A person in his thirties may measure success by being on the right career track, having a home and a mortgage he can afford, and being able to give his kids the piano or dancing lessons they want. These are both markedly different from the way a sixty-five-year-old might look at success. To him success might involve security, health, contentment with his life, and being able to share the joys of his children's lives.

FAMILY BACKGROUND

Family of origin is one of the most important influences on how people define individual success. Family values, traditions, religious orientations, and goals serve as the backdrop against which success is often measured. What is measured as success in one family may mean little, or may even be seen as failure, in another family. For example, one family might put a high emotional value on education and academic accomplishment, while another family might put it on athletic success. Some families may define success in group terms, for the married couple or for the family as a whole, while others have more individualistic definitions.

Success messages are given to children even before birth. It is not uncommon to hear parents voicing aspirations for their children during the mother's pregnancy. As the child grows, these messages may be subtle: excitement when a child pretends to be a doctor or picks up his first football, or apathy when he bangs on the piano or takes an interest in classifying bugs. Or the messages may be overt: ridicule when a good student brings home four As and three Bs, indicating that acceptance only comes with perfection; or praise when a child dates the culturally acceptable person and disdain when he does not.

Initially, most children are very much interested in getting their parents' attention, and they are constantly on the lookout for ways to gain favor. If the parental messages are too harsh, however, it is not uncommon to find children defining success in ways opposite to the ideas of their parents, setting up conflict.

Unfulfilled goals or dreams of parents are also transmitted to children. A parent who always wanted to go to college but could not afford it may put a strong emphasis on education. A mother who felt trapped or tied down by her marriage and children will encourage her daughters to have careers and make something of themselves, so as not to repeat her unhappy scenario.

Several other important factors originate from family background. These include: identification with parents or grandparents; the wish to please, hurt, or compete with parents; and the desire to give their children things they felt were lacking in their own childhoods. Someone raised in the turmoil of an alcoholic home might define success in terms of having a loving family life and being able to give his children the stability and emotional security he never had.

Competition with siblings is often an important factor in how a person defines success. A person may believe he is successful only if he is more successful than his siblings.

In my clinical experience, I have found that if a child grows up in an approving and loving environment, success is much easier to find in whatever way he chooses to define it. But if a child grows up in a household where the parents are never satisfied no matter how hard the child tries, success is likely to be defined in unreachable terms.

SOCIOECONOMIC BACKGROUND

A person's social base plays a fundamental role in determining his individual definition of success. Someone from an impoverished background often defines success in terms of material things and being able to give his children a better chance in life than he had. Conversely, a person from an economically comfortable family does not worry so much about survival and may turn his attention to humanitarian or service goals.

PSYCHOLOGICAL MAKEUP

How a person is put together psychologically also has a great impact on how he views success. Character structure, inner life, relationships, and psychological health interact to give him feelings of contentment or turmoil. A person who has a great need to be loved and admired will feel more successful with fame and achievement as opposed to wealth. Someone who is a loner will feel more successful with individual accomplishments than group ones. Likewise, an antisocial character will feel more successful breaking the law and getting away with it rather than living by the rules.

One of the most successful people I have met was a patient of mine who had a serious, psychotic illness: chronic schizophrenia. Almost every aspect of a schizophrenic's life is affected by this devastating illness. For Beth, however, it was different. She sought the treatment she needed, took responsibility for taking her medicine and keeping her therapy appointments, and trusted the husband who loved her. Success for her was different than it is for most people. It was defined as staying out of the hospital and being able to raise her children in a sane environment, one that was different from the torture of her own early youth. I never saw her more proud than the day she walked into my office and said she had gotten a job all by herself at a doughnut shop. Success is individually defined according to the circumstances of your life.

INTERACTION OF ALL OF THESE, AND MORE

You are a complicated person. How you define success will depend on all the factors listed above, along with many others that go into making you the unique individual that you are.

Your success can only be defined by you. But in order for me to help you think about it, we need a working definition that you can apply to your own life situation. In general, then:

Success is
1. Getting to do what you really want to do in your love, work, and personal life
2. Doing it well
3. Being rewarded for it
4. Feeling good about yourself in the process of doing it

2

Nine Rules for Defining Success

Defining success for yourself is key to getting what you want. It takes your life out of the realm of the unconscious programming from your past and puts it square in the present. In order to define success, we need to define ourselves. This is a complicated process and involves knowing ourselves and what we want out of life. As already mentioned, stage of life, family and social background, and psychological makeup go into making us who we are. Therefore knowing more about ourselves helps us to define our success goals.

At the end of this Section you will find a worksheet designed to help you think about what success means to you as an individual. In defining success for yourself, here are nine rules to keep in mind.

Rule #1: YOUR SUCCESS IS DEFINED ONLY BY YOU

Unfortunately, most people look to others for examples of success. Statements such as, "He must be successful because he is a surgeon," or "drives a Mercedes," or "lives in a rich neighborhood," are very misleading. Unless you know how other people define success, you have very little idea whether they consider themselves successful. It's clear from my clinical work that many, many people who others would classify as "successful" are unhappy. They lack the feeling of success. Only we can author our success, and we need to personally define its parameters.

Along a similar line, if you let someone else define your individual success, you're likely to be very unhappy. You may even feel as though you are living out someone else's life, not your own. Pat, a patient of mine, was an example of this.

Pat had wanted to be a grammar school teacher since the fourth grade, and she entered college with that in mind. However, Pat let her father, an executive at IBM, talk her out of it. Low pay, disruptive kids, and waning social status for teachers were the reasons he gave her. He told her that she should enter the business world to make a more successful way (actually, to follow his way).

Pat followed her father's advice, but she always felt unfulfilled in her job at IBM, and found that she longed to work with kids in a classroom. This conflict between what she wanted and her desire to please her father led to sleepless nights, frigidity with her husband, and decreased productivity at work. After all, if she was no good at IBM, her unconscious mind told her that she might have to be relegated back to the classroom. In order for her to do what she wanted to do, which was to be a teacher, she first had to appear to be a failure at IBM.

Rule #2: SUCCESS IS A FEELING

Success is nothing until you feel it. I once heard a story about three umpires on how they call balls and strikes. The first one said, "I call them the way I see them." The second umpire said, "I call them the way they are." And, the third one said, "They ain't nothing until I call them."

Success is a feeling, a perception on your part. Most people think of success in terms of symbols, not feelings. In the final analysis, however, it is how we feel about where we have been and where we are going that is the ultimate measure of our success in life.

We all know of people who had all of the success symbols—social status, wealth, possessions, outstanding achievements, admiration—but who considered themselves failures. The symbols did not prevent Elvis Presley, Marilyn Monroe, Freddie Prinze, Jimi Hendrix, Janis Joplin, John Belushi, and countless other so-called successful people from feeling like failures who needed drugs or alcohol, or who turned to self-destruction, to be rid of the painful feelings. I call this the *Empty Success Syndrome:* the outward appearance of success without any of the positive feelings on the inside.

Farther back in American history, think of the multitude of suicides on Wall Street during the stock market crash of 1929. The feelings of success for those who killed themselves were attached to the symbols, and when the symbols were gone, so was their success.

I am not saying that there is anything wrong with having the symbols of success. Being rewarded for your efforts is essential to the feeling of success. I am certainly very proud of the M.D. after my name. But if your internal perceptions of success do not match the symbols, watch out! Your success may be an empty one. A word of caution: Sometimes feelings lie to you. If all evidence points to success in your life, but you feel unsuccessful or like an impostor, there may be a problem in how you perceive yourself. More on this later.

Rule #3: SUCCESS AT ANY PRICE MAY NOT BE SUCCESS

Since success is a feeling, the means by which the symbols of success are obtained may be important. For most people (not everyone), the ways in which they reach their goals have an impact on how they feel about themselves in the process. If goals are reached in ways contrary to individual belief systems, conflicts over the reality or value of the success may arise.

For example, if an executive made it to the top by using his friends as stepping stones, he may feel loneliness later on that could ruin his feelings of accomplishment. Or, consider the situation of someone who gets ahead by lying or cheating. People who build a career on a foundation of dishonesty may temporarily enjoy their achievement, but after a short while they are likely to feel doubt about their ability and self-worth, and end up feeling more like criminals than success stories.

Similarly, success at any price is not worth it for me. I love my family. And, if doing things to enhance my professional career led me to neglect them or estrange them from me, I would feel regret, not success.

King David in the Old Testament illustrates the dangers of getting what you want at any price. David fell in love with Uriah's wife, Bathsheba. Uriah was one of David's key generals. When Uriah was off fighting a war, David got Bathsheba pregnant. To hide his guilt, and also to free Bathsheba to marry him, David had Uriah murdered. He sent him to the front line of the battle, and then in the heat of the fighting had the other troops withdraw from Uriah, who was quickly killed.

After David married Bathsheba, the Lord, who was upset by this whole chain of events, sent the prophet Nathan to tell David a story about a rich man who had stolen a precious little lamb from a poor man's house. Incensed at the story, David vowed to have the rich man killed. When Nathan explained that David was the rich man who had taken Uriah's only treasure, his wife, tremendous guilt overcame David. His suffering increased when the baby he had with Bathsheba died. (As an aside, the power of forgiveness is also illustrated by this story, for the next child born to David and Bathsheba was Solomon.)

Rule #4: SUCCESS IS A PROCESS

Success is not a static entity, a gold watch at the end of thirty years. It is a process of defining and redefining, struggling toward and reaching the goals you set for yourself. It is the day-to-day feeling that accompanies your efforts, that drives you on.

Most people think of success as an end point, the pot of gold at the end of the rainbow. The end of the rainbow, however, may be a dangerous place to be. There are many examples of people who reach their pinnacles only to develop serious illnesses or depression shortly thereafter.

Executive promotion depression has been known to behavioral scientists for some time. This occurs when a person has reached his major goal in work, say to become a company's chief executive officer, and then becomes depressed. Unless he immediately sets new goals for himself, the feeling of "Is this all there is?" may set in, leading to depression.

I have known several medical students who experienced similar feelings. Their only goal in life was to get into medical school, and they worked day and night for years to make themselves acceptable to medical school admissions committees. Acceptance to medical school gave them a profound sense of success. But they did not develop new goals once in medical school, and this lack of goals contributed to a deterioration in their attitudes as they wondered why they had worked so hard for admission just to have to work even harder once they started medical school.

More insight into the dangers of reaching goals comes from the research of Dr. E. K. Gunderson and Dr. Richard Rahe, who correlated life events with the development of physical illness. Surprisingly, they found that not only did stresses such as death of a spouse, divorce, job loss, and detention in jail correlate with greater physical illness, but so did positive events such as marriage, outstanding personal achievements, graduating from college, job promotions, and retirement.

If success is viewed as a goal to be reached, what happens after that? Feelings of success live only for a short while after goals are reached. The ultimate satisfaction comes from attaining, not from attainment. Successful people are not *there;* they are in the process of *getting* there, wherever *there* may be for them.

Rule #5: SUCCESS OCCURS IN STEPS

No one is born with the feeling of success. In fact, we are all born a bit confused and soon learn that we are very small in a very big world. It is hard to have much sense of self-esteem and mastery when you have to crawl, or walk along the furniture, to get anywhere. With loving and encouraging parents, however, our sense of mastery grows day by day, not in leaps or giant steps, but in small baby steps. We hope that our progression will always be forward, but there will always be days when we slip back a step or two. With support, we learn that these setbacks are part of the process, and we continue along the road of self-development.

Early successes bring positive feelings, which encourage children to want to do more to obtain more positive feelings. If the child builds up enough positive feelings about himself, he will begin to believe in his abilities and be able to achieve—not to prove himself, because he already knows inside that he is OK—but because it feels good to be successful. This process does not happen overnight and will not change overnight. Expecting to find success in instant solutions (instant wealth, instant relationships, instant recognition, or instant achievement) invites lifelong disappointment. Success, like learning to walk, is a process that occurs in tiny steps.

Rule #6: SUCCESS IS A BALANCING ACT

Balance is just as important to feelings of success as to a ballet dancer. We all have a personal life that no one else sees, a relational life with others, and a work life. It is very possible to feel successful in one of these areas while feeling like a failure in the others. Very few people I know have it all. But if your life becomes too unbalanced, you may find that your non-success areas drain energy from those areas you feel good about.

Balance, perspective, and trade-offs are necessary for success.

What good is it to make all the money in the world if the person of your dreams leaves you?

You decide how much weight to give to each area of your life. This varies for all of us, and it even will be different at different stages in your life. When you think about defining success, don't unbalance your act.

Rule #7: SUCCESS CAN BE LEARNED

Success is not something that you're born with, or something you inherit. It is something you learn. In fact, as we will see in Chapter Three, being born into a successful family may have more drawbacks than advantages.

One of the most intriguing questions that has arisen in my clinical practice is why some children from the same family grow up to feel successful while others do not. You can probably think of many families in which this is true.

In the chapters that follow, we will explore in detail the traits of the successful and the unsuccessful. As you examine these you will find that all behaviors, successful and unsuccessful, can be taught and learned; indeed, that is the major premise underlying this book. All behaviors also can be unlearned. If you are willing, this book will help you learn the ones you need and discard the ones that stand between you and your goals.

Rule #8: DEFINING SUCCESS TOO HIGH OR TOO LOW IS A NO-GO

When I was in basic training in the army, a trainee was classified as either a "Go" or a "No-Go." Go meant he had successfully completed his task and could move on to the next step. No-Go meant he had failed. Anyone who received too many No-Gos was in danger of having to repeat basic training—and this threat provided significant motivation to do your best.

Many No-Gos failed at the rifle range, and they generally did for one of two reasons: setting the sights on their rifles too high or too low. Either way, they were bound to miss the target.

The same is true in defining success for yourself. If you start too high and too fast, you'll quickly feel overwhelmed, and your goals will dissolve into daydreams. Expecting to make a million dollars on your first real estate deal after the seminar, or expecting your chronically conflicted marriage to turn around in a week, only sets you up for failure. Change, success, and fulfillment take time.

On the other hand, if you start too low and too slow, your patience and endurance may run out before you get the positive feelings necessary to motivate you to go on. The best way to start defining and experiencing success is to set up reasonably realistic goals that can be obtained in a foreseeable period.

Rule #9: SUCCESS IS HAVING THE ABILITY TO BE HONEST WITH YOURSELF

In order to feel successful, you must be able to be honest about the things that are really important to you. Whether it has to do with acquiring money, changing careers, becoming involved in a new relationship, or discarding a destructive one, being truthful with yourself is the only way to allow the inner sense of contentment and success to exist without feeling like an impostor. Persistent dissatisfaction and frequent mind changes are clues that you aren't being honest with yourself.

As you go through this book look at your life, your desires, your work, and your relationships as honestly as you can. You probably bought the book because you were dissatisfied with some aspect of your life. Dissatisfaction, if it leads to action, is the first meaningful step toward change. Take the next step and be honest with yourself about what you want and what would truly give you the feeling of success in your heart.

3

Five Things Not Necessary for Success

The notion that one can be born into success is a myth.

Myths surround the idea of success. Foremost among these is the myth that it takes high intelligence, formal education, a successful family background, money, and luck to be successful. In upcoming sections we will look at your recipe for success and what is holding you back, but first let's dispel these myths.

INTELLIGENCE

Intelligence is a very misleading concept. Some people, particularly parents, place high value on it. Many parents of preschool children have asked me to have their children's I.Q. tested by the psychologist who works with me. Unless I suspect a problem with mental retardation, I decline, because if the child tests out in the average or below-average range, parents might not expect much from him; if the child has a good day and tests in the high range, parents might always be disappointed if he doesn't live up to their expectations. Psychiatrists have found that if you treat a child as though he is gifted, he will perform better, while if you treat him as though he is stupid, he is more likely to act that way.

I think most of us have known very bright people who, for one reason or another, felt that they were failures. I have had many intelligent patients who felt like that, and I have also known many physicians who would put themselves in the same category. Intelligence did not make the difference for them. Too much intelligence may cause things to come too easily to a developing child and thus impair his need and desire to work in order to achieve.

Also, people with learning disabilities are thought by many to be intellectually inferior and to have more trouble succeeding. The fact is that many people with learning disabilities are highly intelligent and have acquired the will to work and overcome adversity.

George, a physician, is dyslexic, which means it is hard for him to understand what he reads. Many have asked him how a learning disabled student could finish medical school. He replies, "I am an auditory learner. So, I had all the medical textbooks put on audio cassettes and learned by listening to the tapes."

An astonishing story? Yes. But true. In fact, Albert Einstein, Winston Churchill, Thomas Edison, and Nelson Rockefeller, to name only a few, overcame significant learning disabilities to become more than successful.

FORMAL EDUCATION

Along similar lines, formal education is not essential to obtaining the feelings of success. There are countless examples of people with little or no formal education who have gone on to achieve great success in their personal or work lives. At the same time, you probably know someone with a great deal of formal education who acts or feels like a failure.

My father, about whom I wrote in the introduction, is a tremendously successful man. Yet he only graduated from high school. He couldn't afford to go to college. I have also known people with advanced degrees who hoped their diplomas would lead them on the path to success—to feeling good about themselves. Unfortunately, the degrees did not give them what they were looking for. Too much formal education costs a lot in time that may be better spent gaining experience in the real world.

Don't get me wrong, education is very important and I'll encourage all of my children to go as far as they can in learning. Education increases the odds for success, but by itself it guarantees nothing.

SUCCESSFUL FAMILY BACKGROUND

A successful family background may be a help, but it is often a hindrance. On the surface, it seems helpful to come from a family of successful people: after all, you can learn the ingredients of success firsthand.

When we delve further into successful families, however, a disturbing fact emerges: Many children of successful people have a terrible time in life. Numerous examples of suicide, severe drug abuse and antisocial behavior exist among children of very successful people. Many children of successful parents feel that they can never live up to the image of their parents, and they give up in despair. This is especially true if the "successful" parent never admits to or discusses his failures and faults.

As I mentioned earlier, another curious fact about family background is that some children in a family may grow up to be successful while others in the same family do not. Coming from a particular type of family no more guarantees success than does a high I.Q. or extensive formal education. It is what you do with what you have that makes you successful or not.

MONEY

I have heard it said many times, "If only I had money, my troubles would be over." At times, when I was a student, I was tempted to believe this but, even though money is necessary in life, having a lot of it is not a prerequisite to success. Again, you can probably think of many people who had all the money they could ever want, yet who despaired in life and turned to drugs, alcohol, or crime.

LUCK

Many successful people attribute their success in life to luck. They deny their abilities. Put these people in almost any situation, however, and they will come out on top. They have the ingredients of success, but luck is not one of them. Chance favors the prepared mind. I think they give luck as a reason for their success because they are afraid of being envied by others, and afraid that they might be jinxed if they become prideful or boastful.

In summary, possessing a high I.Q., having extensive formal education, coming from the right family, starting with lots of money, or being lucky may have little to do with success. In fact, it is dangerous to rely on these things alone on the road to success.

4

Your Individual Definition of Success

With the principles from the preceding chapters in mind, the following questions are designed to help you clarify exactly what success means to you at this point in your life, and what path will produce feelings of success. Remember, success is a process, and the answers to these questions will change over time. Answer the questions as honestly as you can, and be prepared to be surprised by your responses.

This chapter builds on itself. Answer the questions in sequence. It will take some time to complete, and the material it will generate is crucial to helping you define your goals for success. When you finish, go over your answers at least twice to reflect on their significance. Make it count!

1. Rank the following ten items in order of their importance to you (1 = most important, 10 = least important). Write each item on the line after the appropriate number.

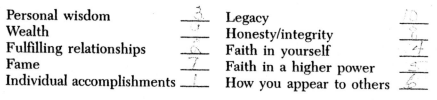

Personal wisdom	3	Legacy	
Wealth		Honesty/integrity	
Fulfilling relationships		Faith in yourself	4
Fame	7	Faith in a higher power	
Individual accomplishments	1	How you appear to others	

2. With the above ranking in mind, what are you now doing to accomplish or enhance the first five items you placed on the list? (Success is a process. What are you doing to help that process along?)

1.

2.

3.

4.

5.

3. Think of yourself reading the story of your whole life. What was really important to you in your life? What really mattered to you? What has eternal value for you?

4. Are you giving enough time and effort to those people or things that really matter to you? Or are you spending the bulk of your time on things of lesser personal value?

5. What developmental period of life are you in (adolescence, young adulthood, middle age, etc.)? How have your personal goals changed from the previous period? How do you think they'll change ten years from now? (Thinking ahead prevents things like mid-life crises, empty nest syndrome, etc.)

6. Reflect on your emotional development as a child in your family. Do you think it has impaired or enhanced your chances for success?

In what ways? Be specific.

7. Name five people whom you look up to and admire. Describe the specific traits you admire and the ways you would like to be like them.

8. Name five people you know whom you do not admire. Describe the specific things about them that turn you off. Be as specific as you can.

9. List five experiences in which you felt like a failure. Are you more likely to repeat your failures or your successes?

10. List five experiences in which you felt successful in the past. Remember them, dwell on them.

11. There are three major areas in your life:

a. relationships (with spouse or lover, children, family, friends)
b. work/finances (your job, school if you are a student, or tasks at home if you're a homemaker, current and future finances, etc.)
c. personal life (the part of your life that applies just to you outside of relationships or work: physical and emotional health, spirituality, interests, intellectual growth, etc.)

How significant/important is each to you? Rank each area on a one-to-ten point scale, giving ten points to areas that are all-consuming and one point to areas that have little significance to you.

Relational life   _____
Work/Financial life   _____
Personal life   _____

How much time do you give to each area? Does this reflect its importance to you? Explain.

12. With the above information in mind, list at least three specific one-year, five-year and ten-year goals in each area below (be positive in stating your goal, and be as specific as possible). After each goal list what you are specifically doing to accomplish it.

Relationships: Include what you want from them and what you can give to them. (spouse/lover/children/family/friends)

One-Year Goals
1.
2.
3.

Five-Year Goals
1.
2.
3.

Ten-Year Goals
1.
2.
3.

Work/Financial life: Include such things as what you want to be doing, hours willing to work, salary and plans for advancement. List timetables for accomplishment where appropriate.

One-Year Goals
1.
2.
3.

Five-Year Goals
1.
2.
3.

Ten-Year Goals
1.
2.
3.

Personal life: Include here what you want for your physical and mental health, spirituality, interests and intellectual growth; and the time each week you are willing to give solely to yourself.

One-Year Goals
1.
2.
3.

Five-Year Goals
1.
2.
3.

Ten-Year Goals
1.
2.
3.

5

The One-Page Miracle

One way to solidify this personal information is a powerful, yet simple exercise I call The One-Page Miracle. It will help guide nearly all of your thoughts, words, and actions. I call it The One-Page Miracle because I've seen this exercise quickly focus and change many people.

Directions: take one sheet of paper and clearly write out your major goals. Use the following main headings: *Relationships, Work/finances,* and *Self.* Under *Relationships* write the subheadings of spouse/lover, children, family, and friends. Under *Work/Finances* write current and future work and financial goals. Under *Self* write out physical health, emotional health, spirituality and interests. Self is that part of you outside of relationships or work. Often it is the part of you that no one sees but you.

Next to each subheading succinctly write out what's important to you in that area; write what you want, not what you don't want. Be positive and use the first person. Also, write what you want with confidence and the expectation that you will make it happen. Keep the paper with you so that you can work on it over several days. After you finish with the initial draft (you'll frequently want to update it), *place this piece of paper where you can see it every day,* such as on your refrigerator, by your bedside or on the bathroom mirror. In that way, *every day you focus your eyes on what's important to you.* This makes it easier to match your behavior to what you want. Your life becomes more conscious and you spend your energy on goals that are important to you.

I separate the areas of relationships, work and self in order to encourage a more balanced approach to life. Burnout occurs when our lives become unbalanced and we overextend ourselves in one area while ignoring another. For example, in my practice I see that a common cause of divorce is a person working so much that little energy is left over for his or her spouse.

EXAMPLE: Evan is a thirty-nine-year-old attorney who is married with two children. He came to see me because of frequent mood changes.

THE ONE-PAGE MIRACLE
WHAT DO I WANT???
WHAT AM I DOING TO MAKE IT HAPPEN???

EVAN

RELATIONSHIPS

Spouse/Lover: Enjoy time together, rather than feel time-pressured
I treat her as special as she really is to me
I'm improving our communication which means I clarify things I do not understand, before reacting
I support her in whatever she chooses to do for herself

Children: I am involved in their lives
I notice their good behavior
I am firm and fair with them
I am a good listener to them

Family: I am involved with members of my family in a positive way
I stay out of the politics of the moment and am less reactive to the buttons my younger sister pushes in me

Friends: I spend time with special friends
I nurture new friendships as I meet special people

WORK/FINANCES

> I do my best for my clients
>
> I engage in activities that generate future clients to keep my business healthy
>
> I continue professional education and develop my professional interests
>
> I do charity work to give back to my profession
>
> I save fifteen to twenty percent of net income to invest
>
> I am accumulating enough money to live in the specific area that is best for my family
>
> I am investing in a retirement fund that will allow me to retire by the age of sixty, maintaining our current life-style

SELF

Physical: I eat a diet that helps me feel better and live longer

I walk 30 minutes a day for exercise

I maintain weight between 160 and 165 pounds

Emotional: I am more even-tempered and do not allow little things that are not important to upset me

I am more positive and optimistic

Spirituality: I continue to search for meaning in my everyday world

I to go church to have a group of people with whom to worship and pray

Interests: I enjoy keeping up on current events

I continue to enjoy working on restoring old radios

THE ONE-PAGE MIRACLE
WHAT DO I WANT???
WHAT AM I DOING TO MAKE IT HAPPEN???

YOUR NAME:

RELATIONSHIPS

Spouse/Lover:

Children:

Family:

Friends:

WORK/FINANCES

SELF

Physical:

Emotional:

Spirituality:

Interests:

How is it going to be at the end of your life? Will you have worked toward goals that were important to you? Or will you have worked toward other people's goals? It is up to you. Many other people are happy to decide what you should do with your life. Use The One-Page Miracle to help you be the one who has the say.

What's Holding You Back: Characteristics of Self-Sabotage

6

The Sabotage Versus Success Profile Introduction

We have met the enemy, and he is us.
—Pogo Possum

In this section of the book you are going to develop your own "Sabotage Versus Success Profile." With this information you'll be able to take an in-depth look at your strengths and weaknesses. I'll then help you develop a focused plan to overcome the barriers holding you back.

This is going to be a hard section for many of you to read and work through, because if you're honest in answering the quizzes you'll see yourself in much of what is written. You have several choices in how you handle the upcoming discomfort. You can say, "Yes, that's me. Now I know part of why I've had trouble succeeding, and *I can do something about it.*" Or you can build up your defensive walls and deny that any of this applies to you, saying things like "I'm just unlucky," or "I wasn't born at the right time," or "Success is beyond my control. It is something that happens to other people." Finally, you can put this book aside, telling yourself you don't have time for it right now, or that you don't believe it can really help you improve. Which of these choices do you think is most effective—and which are simply more self-sabotage?

> *Self-examination is difficult,*
> *but it is necessary for change.*

Later, in Section Four, we will look closely at the ingredients in the recipe for success. I call it a recipe because we need all of the ingredients, in the right amounts, to make it work. Too much or too little of something will spoil the final product. But before we get to the recipe, it's important to look at those things that will spoil the soup outright. Most of the hallmarks of self-sabotage are actually the flip side of success ingredients. As you will notice in the "Sabotage Versus Success Profile," many of the concepts overlap. The overlapping will serve as reinforcement for you.

Initially, place a minus sign (—) by the areas you can immediately identify as a problem for yourself and a plus sign (+) for the areas you see as strengths.

HALLMARKS OF SELF-SABOTAGE

ATTITUDES OF SELF-SABOTAGE | SUCCESS

1. blames others — personal responsibility
2. lacks focused goals — focused goals
3. expects to fail — expects to succeed
4. counts on luck — prepared for luck
5. repeats mistakes — learns from mistakes
6. rigid/inflexible — creative

WORK HABITS OF SELF-SABOTAGE | SUCCESS

7. unobservant — observant
8. uninformed — informed
9. unprepared/unorganized — prepared/organized
10. trouble making decisions — able to make decisions
11. inability to delegate — delegates
12. impulsive — disciplined
13. overly cautious — takes reasonable risks

INTERACTIONAL SELF-SABOTAGE	SUCCESS
14. inability to communicate	good communication skills
15. surrounded by negative people	surrounded by positive people
16. unable to learn from others	teachable
17. shies away from competition	sees competition as win-win
18. insensitive to others	empathic toward others
19. dependent on others	independent

PERSONAL SELF-SABOTAGE	SUCCESS
20. stinking thinking	accurate perception
21. fear of success	motivated for success
22. emotional disorders (depression, anxiety, drug/alcohol abuse, attention deficit disorder)	mental health
23. lack of energy	energetic
24. lack of integrity	integrity
25. lack of self-confidence	self-esteem
26. gives up easily	persistent

Try not to feel overwhelmed by this list. No one has all of the sabotage traits listed. You have many strengths as well as weaknesses. We all do. It is not the strengths, however, that are holding you back.

It's important to fill out the quiz at the beginning of each of the following chapters before reading the chapter. After you determine your score on each quiz place it in the appropriate slot on the Sabotage Versus Success Profile Sheet, found at the end of this section. Once that sheet is completed you'll have a comprehensive, personalized profile that you can use to shape a positive direction for change.

7

The Attitudes of Self-Sabotage

The following characteristics are basic attitudes that seriously undermine a person's ability to get what he wants out of life. Attitude encompasses so much of our reality that if we allow our attitude to be eroded by the following self-sabotaging characteristics, there is little hope that we'll be able to get what we want for ourselves.

Quiz #1: The Attitudes of Self-Sabotage

Read the following statements carefully and respond to them by placing the number from the answer key that most closely reflects how the statement applies to you. Respond to the statements as honestly as possible; anything less is a waste of your time.

key:
0 = false
1 = mostly false
2 = more false than true
3 = more true than false
4 = mostly true
5 = true

_3_ 1. I often see myself as a victim of circumstances.

_____ 2. I just take life as it comes, rather than planning my life out.

_____ 3. I often anticipate that I'll be unable to learn something new, even before I try it.

_____ 4. I often don't try my best, yet hope things will work out for me.

_____ 5. I have a tendency to make the same mistakes over and over again.

_____ 6. I resort to handling problems in old ways even when they haven't worked in the past. For example, I fight with my spouse or parents in the same way as always.

_____ 7. When I experience a problem in relationships, I often think about how I might have contributed to the situation.

_____ 8. Before I do something important, I most often have in mind a clear set of objectives that will be accomplished by the task.

_____ 9. I often visualize myself succeeding at an important task before I do it.

_____10. Before I come to an important situation (a special social occasion, a speech), I take time to think about it and prepare for it.

_____11. Failing at something most often stimulates me to try again until I get it right.

_____12. When a problem arises with someone, I am able to compromise.

_____13. My mood is most often tied to how others treat me.

_____14. I have trouble deciding what work deeply interests me.

_____15. When I have a new idea for something (at home, work, etc.), I often keep it to myself because I think that others are not likely to be interested in it.

_____16. If I took a class, I am the type of person who would not read the assigned material before the class.

_____17. When I make a mistake, it causes me to shy away from similar situations in the future.

_____18. I have trouble initiating changes that are good for me.

_____19. I work on changing myself, instead of trying to change those around me.

_____20. I have taken the time to think, plan, and write down my life's goals.

_____21. When I shop for something like a car, I expect to get the best deal available.

_____22. One way I handle anxiety about upcoming tasks is by adequately preparing for them.

_____23. The fear of failure does not paralyze me from reaching toward my goals.

_____24. I have the ability to look at common things in an uncommon way.

_____25. I realize that I have many choices and options in life and I am able to take advantage of them.

_____26. I lack clear focus and direction for my personal, work, or relationship life.

_____27. Even when I know an answer to a question, I expect that when I'm asked I'll mess it up.

_____28. I often do not deal with important issues, hoping they'll take care of themselves or that others will decide for me.

_____29. The fear of failure prevents me from trying to make my dreams come true.

_____30. I am unable to solve problems in a creative or novel way.

_____31. I have a tendency to focus on how others have contributed to my problems.

_____32. I spend my time working toward goals that stimulate and excite me.

_____33. I have hope in my heart.

_____34. Before I attend a meeting with someone important to me, I spend time laying the groundwork for the meeting, including writing down the important points I wish to cover.

_____35. I do not make the same mistakes over and over.

_____36. I look for new ways to solve problems.

_____37. When problems come up in my life (e.g., marital problems, work problems, weight problems), I usually spend my time and energy looking for solutions, instead of blaming someone else for them.

_____38. I spend too much time working for other people's goals.

_____39. When I go into a new situation with someone, I often expect that it won't work out.

_____40. I often don't do as well as I am able because I put off my work until the last minute.

_____41. When I make a mistake I berate myself for it, rather than learning from it.

_____42. I usually get upset when something unexpected changes how my day is scheduled.

_____43. I have a tendency to blame others when things go wrong.

_____44. The goals in my life are balanced between my personal, relational, and work life.

_____45. I believe that this book will help me.

_____46. If I really want to do something well (athletic sport, work task, etc.) I am the type of person who will spend the necessary time practicing and rehearsing it until I get it right.

_____47. When I make a mistake, I analyze what went wrong.

_____48. In doing things that many other people do, it appeals to me to try to invent my own way of doing it.

_____49. For the most part the way my family and friends treat me depends significantly on how I act toward them.

_____50. I often act impulsively or say things I regret later on.

_____51. I usually expect to be disappointed.

_____52. I find that when something is expected of me, I often forget about it until the last minute.

_____53. When I fail at something, I try to forget about it, because it hurts too much to think about it.

_____54. In my work, I rarely ask myself how things might be done in other ways.

_____55. When something goes right for me, I think that I'm just lucky and that things will turn back to the way they usually are.

_____56. My time and energy is focused on my goals.

_____57. I expect to accomplish what I set out to do once I have researched and prepared for it.

_____58. I prepare myself for luck by being well educated in the necessary tools for my goals.

_____59. It is OK for me to make mistakes because I know that I can learn from them. I do not have to be perfect to feel good about myself.

_____60. When I have decided on a course of action, I reconsider it if unforeseen disadvantages are pointed out to me.

"It's Your Fault!": BLAMES OTHERS WHEN THINGS GO WRONG

Permitting your life to be taken over by another person is like letting the waiter eat your dinner.
                                                    —VERNON HOWARD

A. Add up your answers to questions 7, 19, 25, 37, and 49 and place your answer here: _____

B. Add up your answers to questions 1, 13, 31, 43, and 55 and place your answer here: _____

C. Subtract the smaller number from the larger number and place your answer here: _____
If A is greater than B place a + sign in front of the answer.
If B is greater than A place a − sign in front of the answer.

Place your score on Line 1, "Personal Responsibility," on the Sabotage Versus Success Profile Sheet, page 129.

The first and most devastating hallmark of self-sabotage is the tendency to blame others when things go wrong in your life. People who sabotage themselves generally take very little responsibility for their lives. When something goes wrong at work or in their relationships, they often find someone to blame. They rarely own their individual problems. Typically, you'll hear statements from them such as:

"It wasn't my fault that..." (that I wasn't prepared for the meeting, they never give enough notice, etc.)

"That wouldn't have happened if you had..." (I wouldn't have had the affair if you'd been better to me, etc.)

"How was I supposed to know..." (that the boss wanted the reports in two days. He should have told me, etc.)

"It's your fault that..." (that you got pregnant, you should have protected yourself, etc.)

"If it was so important, why didn't you remind me?"

"That's not my job."

The bottom-line statement goes something like this: "If only you had done something differently I wouldn't be in the predicament I'm in. It's your fault, and I'm not responsible."

We all do some blaming. It's part of our nature not to take the rap when things don't turn out as planned. There are not many Saint Christophers around to carry the burden of the world on their shoulders. However, if you are a self-saboteur who carries blaming to an extreme, you need to address this serious problem.

Blaming others for your troubles, or making excuses when things don't go as you would like, is the first step in a dangerous downhill slide. The slide goes something like this:

Blames others
"It's your fault."

|

Sees life as beyond personal control
"My life would be better if it weren't for..."

|

|

Feels like a victim of circumstances
"If only that didn't happen, then..."

|

Gives up trying
"Nothing will ever go right for me. Why try?"

Blaming others serves the purpose of temporarily ridding ourselves of feelings of guilt or responsibility. However, it also reinforces the idea that life is out of our control, that others can determine how things are going to go for us. This causes much inner turmoil, leading to anxiety and feelings of helplessness.

Psychiatrists have known for some time that the patients who do the worst in psychotherapy are the ones who take no personal responsibility for getting better. In fact, as early as Freud (1927), the patient's increased sense of personal responsibility has been a major goal of psychotherapy. Dr. Carl Rogers went so far as to develop a "personal responsibility" scale to predict those who would get better with treatment and those who would not.

Sally came to see me for work-related stress. She had been in psychotherapy with another psychiatrist for more than three years but seemed to be getting nowhere. She complained that her boss was a sexist and treated her as an inferior person. She was often tearful and depressed and had problems concentrating. In our initial interview it was clear that she took no responsibility for how her life was turning out. She blamed her boyfriend for getting her pregnant at age nineteen. She then had felt "forced" to marry him, but complained that he was unmotivated so she divorced him. Then in succession she impulsively married two different men who were alcoholics and were physically abusive toward her. At the time of our first session she was married to a man who was also an alcoholic and not working. Tearfully, she expressed her feelings of being continually victimized by men, including her current husband and her boss.

At the end of the session I asked her what she had done to contribute to the problems she had. Her mouth dropped open. Her other psychiatrist had been a good paid listener but had never challenged her notion of helplessness. At the beginning of the next session she told me that she almost hadn't come back to see me. She said, "You think it's all my fault, don't you?" I replied, "I don't think it's all your fault, but I think you've contributed to your troubles more than you give yourself credit for, and if it's true that you've contributed to your problems then you can do things to change them. As long as you stay an innocent victim of others then there's nothing you can do to help yourself."

In several sessions she got the message of personal responsibility and made a dramatic turnaround. As a child she had grown up in a severely abusive alcoholic home where she really was a victim of her circumstances, and unfortunately for her she maintained that role in her adult relationships and work. Her unconscious continuation of her abusive childhood was ruining her ability to have control in her life and be happy.

The reason I put "blaming others" at the top of the "Hallmarks of Self-Sabotage" list is that if you don't take personal responsibility for changing your life, for changing the downward slide, no one will be able to do it for you. Other people and other things, including this book, will be able to help, but only with your permission and your active participation.

Invariably, in classes where I teach this concept I'll have a person tell me that his problem is not blaming others, but blaming himself for the difficulties in his life. One woman who had been sexually abused by her father said that for many years she had blamed herself for the abuse and was now learning not to blame herself. I told her that these two concepts, blaming others versus blaming yourself, are not mutually exclusive. She was certainly not responsible for her father's abuse and there are things that have happened to you that aren't your fault. It is possible to go overboard blaming yourself for troubles and getting stuck in such a mire of guilt that you become powerless to change your life. A good "personal responsibility" statement goes something like, "Bad things have happened in my life, some of which I had something to do with and some I was a victim of. Either way I need to learn from these experiences and be responsible to find ways to overcome the difficulties and bad feelings that resulted."

When you are faced with sabotage, the first place to start looking for answers is within yourself.

Additionally, people who lack personal responsibility very often live in the past. You will hear them saying, "If only I had done so and so, things would be different."

If only:
I hadn't married that good-for-nothing husband of mine.
I had finished school.
My parents hadn't gotten divorced.
The company hadn't changed hands.
I had made that sale.
I hadn't forgotten my diaphragm.
I'd chosen a different career.
I had rich parents.
Etc., etc., etc. . . . .

For some reason, the past continues to haunt these people even when it has no relevance. A tremendous amount of emotional energy is invested in things that cannot be changed. I had a patient, Kathy, who had an encyclopedia of "If onlys."

"If only I finished college. If only I hadn't married David. If only we didn't live in Washington, D.C. If only I could find a good day care center. If only we lived in a different neighborhood." And on and on.

When I pointed out to her how much energy it must have taken to come up with this list, Kathy said, "If only I didn't worry so much." I was about to pull out my hair with her. But after several months she learned to rechannel that energy into "What do I want now, and how do I get it?" This is a much healthier approach to life.

"I'm lost!": LACKS FOCUSED GOALS (the hallmark of unconscious living)

A. Add up your answers to questions
   8, 20, 32, 44, and 56 and place your answer here: _____

B. Add up your answers to questions
   2, 14, 26, 38, and 50 and place your answer here: _____

C. Subtract the smaller number from the larger number
   and place your answer here: _____

If A is greater than B place a + sign in front of the answer.
If B is greater than A place a − sign in front of the answer.

Place your score on Line 2, "Focused Goals," on the Sabotage Versus Success Profile Sheet, page 129.

As I mentioned earlier, it is ironic that many unsuccessful people feel like failures but, at the same time, they have no idea what would make them feel successful. They have no plan for their life and no idea where they are headed. For them long-range planning is making the grocery list before driving to the store or studying for the next test a week ahead.

These people generally have not studied themselves and do not have a grasp of what is important to them. It is not that they are incapable of self-knowledge; they are. It is because a dangerous seven-letter monster holds them back: comfort.

Comfort is one of the most demotivating forces on earth. It stops people from going farther, from pushing themselves to their limits. Barry was an example of this. He was a pre-law student who was at the top of his class at a Pittsburgh university. During the summer between his junior and senior years he got a job at a steel mill and was quickly promoted to assistant foreman.

When it came time to go back to school, Barry found that the regular paycheck, good working hours, and not living from test to test were too tempting to pass up; he lost sight of his goal. Eight years later, however, he said that opting for comfort had been the worst mistake of his life. He saw his friends go on to large law firms and much bigger paychecks than the steel mill offered. He had lost his vision for comfort—a very common occurrence.

I spent seven years as a U.S. Army psychiatrist and saw this same scenario played out by many military and government employees. They would start out excited about their jobs, but as the years wore on they became frustrated and disgruntled with the bureaucracy. Still they stayed with jobs they hated, in order to get their government check. After so many years they rationalized, "Only ten more years and I can retire. I can't wait till then. I hate this job, but who can give up the security?" Unfortunately, they failed to realize that the stress of staying in a job they hated could take years off their lives, making the retirement check worth far less.

You will sabotage yourself in every aspect of your life if you do not ask yourself what's important to you. If you can be clear with what is really important in your life, then you are better able to focus your actions to get what you want and match your behavior to your goals. This applies to your personal life, your work life and your relationships. For example, if you are not clear about your work goals you'll probably waste a lot of time in low-priority activities or on goals that have more value to others, such as attending meetings that have little to do with your direct work. Staying focused is key.

In raising my children it is very important for me to think about what I want in my relationship with them. When I was young my father worked all the time. It seemed the only time I saw him was when he took me to work with him. The message I was given about what men do is that they work all the time. Even to this day, if I don't really think about my goals then I'll work all the time as well. I love to work and my unconscious programming is set on work. I have to look at my One-Page Miracle goal sheet every day to keep myself focused, because at the end of my life work will not be nearly as important to me as my relationship with my wife and children. Many, many people, however, never ask themselves what is really important to them and they end up living the unconscious programming from their childhood.

"I Can't Do That": EXPECTS TO FAIL

A. Add up your answers to questions
9, 21, 33, 45, and 57 and place your answer here: _____

B. Add up your answers to questions
3, 15, 27, 39, and 51 and place your answer here: _____

C. Subtract the smaller number from the larger number
and place your answer here: _____
If A is greater than B place a + sign in front of the answer.
If B is greater than A place a − sign in front of the answer.

Place your score on Line 3, "Expectations," on the Sabotage Versus Success Profile Sheet, page 129.

Having negative expectations is another way people hold themselves back. These people often feel they are going to fail even before they start something, that they are doomed to failure no matter what they do. For example, a man who expects to be turned down for a job is more likely to blow an interview; a patient who doesn't expect hypnosis to help him quit smoking is likely to get little benefit from it; and a person who expects to have trouble getting to sleep often worries so much about it that he actually does have difficulty falling asleep.

Unconsciously, negative expectations often cause people to sabotage their own chances for success. This is commonly seen in medical practices; when patients do not expect their medicines to work, they do not take them as prescribed, lessening the chances that they will work.

Another example of this form of sabotage is seen in relationships. Jane's father left her at an early age. Subsequently, her ability to trust men was very low. She thought that all men, at some level, were like her father and would leave her. Whenever a strong relationship with a man began to develop, she would do something to undermine it. She would forget dates, become insanely jealous or be rude to the friends of the men she was dating. When they became upset with her, she accused them of being impatient and oversensitive. After they stopped coming around, she would tell her friends, "See, I told you men were no good. They can't be trusted."

Our expectations are based on the myriad experiences we bring from the past, and, even though they are often based on distorted material, these expectations have a profound influence on the process of our lives. Eric Berne, M.D., the founder of Transactional Analysis, went so far as to say that we are all born with life scripts (expectations) which are only changed by a great amount of directed effort. I wouldn't go so far as to say that our life scripts are written from birth, but the plot is set very early, along with the main characters and major themes. I believe with all my professional knowledge, however, that the process and ending are up to us and can be changed.

Sometimes negative expectations are programmed into our minds at a point along the developmental trail. Statements made by powerful people in a child's life (parent, teachers, etc.) have a hypnotic quality. They become firmly embedded in the unconscious and drive the individual in that direction. If you are always told that "you can't," where do you learn you can? Other common negative programming statements are:

"You'll never amount to much."
"You can't do that."
"Why do you try so hard?"
"If you're not perfect, you're no good."
"You're stupid. Why can't you do anything right?"
"You are a disappointment."

These statements don't even have to be made directly; they can be conveyed by tone of voice, facial expressions, or behavior. Either way, the child gets the message. If the programming is strong enough, children who receive messages such as these become caught in a negative mental set that is very hard to break. The unconscious mind, like one in a hypnotic trance, takes the negative programming as fact. Children are unable to objectify the input, so it becomes a part of their belief system.

Since the notions become unconscious, I often find thirty- and forty-year-old people thinking the same way about themselves as they did when they were five or six—the same "I'm not good enough" attitude. This book will teach you how to dehypnotize yourself and free yourself from this distorted web of false beliefs.

"I Hope I Get Lucky Today": COUNTS ON LUCK INSTEAD OF ABILITY

A. Add up your answers to questions
10, 22, 34, 46, and 58 and place your answer here: _____

B. Add up your answers to questions
4, 16, 28, 40, and 52 and place your answer here: _____

C. Subtract the smaller number from the larger number
and place your answer here: _____
If A is greater than B place a + sign in front of the answer.
If B is greater than A place a − sign in front of the answer.

Place your score on Line 4, "Prepared for Luck," on the Sabotage Versus Success Profile Sheet, page 129.

There are two ways you can think about luck. The unsuccessful person views it as something that happens to him. The successful person sees luck as something he *makes* happen.

Now you might be asking, "What about people who win the lottery, or are discovered by a producer on the street, or are left a million dollars by their rich uncle?" It is true that lady luck shines on some, but in order to win the lottery you have to be willing to lose your money over and over again (and be very, very, very lucky); if you're discovered by a Hollywood producer, you have to at least have some measure of talent (pretty faces don't last too long); and if you have a rich uncle who happened to think of you, it is certainly better to know what to do with the money instead of squandering it. Luck, unless you are prepared for it, may sneak by you.

The fact is, you have to be prepared for luck if you are to recognize it. John McKay, the great football coach of the national champion University of Southern California Trojans, said, "If you are prepared for luck, you can take advantage of it. If you are not, it will usually pass you by."

Most people think that when Sir Alexander Fleming discovered penicillin in 1928 at St. Mary's Hospital in London, it was a freak or "lucky" accident. It is true that by chance he noticed a mold contaminant on a culture plate of staphylococci, which had resulted in a killing zone in the bacteria. But without his previous foundation in microbiology, the organization of his laboratory, and his discipline to follow through on his discovery, that chance accident might have gone unnoticed for fifty more years. In actual fact, that accident of nature must have occurred many times before, but no one had been prepared enough to discover it.

· I have a friend who is a very competent and successful contractor. He is often lucky in getting good contracts even during the recession. This friend is upbeat and fun to be with. He has a brother, however, who is chronically unhappy and unsuccessful in his work. I often wonder why two people from the same family can have such different outcomes in life. They have the same parents, basically the same childhood atmosphere and the same opportunities. I'm sure the answer is complicated but a significant part is the attitude they have toward luck. My friend is prepared for luck; he doesn't expect it to find him but rather goes looking for it with good skills. His brother has a sense of entitlement and expects luck to come his way. He waits and waits for something that might never come.

If you are waiting for the day you hit the lotto or a rich uncle leaves it all to you, it may be a long wait. Being prepared for luck will help you to recognize it when it comes your way.

Stopped by Mistakes: SEES FAILURE AS DEFEAT

A. Add up your answers to questions
11, 23, 35, 47, and 59 and place your answer here: ———

B. Add up your answers to questions
5, 17, 29, 41, and 53 and place your answer here: ———

C. Subtract the smaller number from the larger number
and place your answer here: ———
If A is greater than B place a + sign in front of the answer.
If B is greater than A place a − sign in front of the answer.

Place your score on Line 5, "Learns from Mistakes," on the Sabotage Versus Success Profile Sheet, page 129.

The perspective one takes toward failure will most always separate the successful from the unsuccessful. Unsuccessful people see failure as a defeat, as a reaffirmation that they cannot succeed, that they will never succeed. Failure is very discouraging to them, and often causes them to quit striving toward their goals.

Successful people see failure as an opportunity, as a challenge, as a chance to learn. You will hear many of them say, "Each failure is one step closer to success. Never waste your failures. Learn all you can from them."

I have seen children illustrate this difference many times. After trying once or twice at a task such as learning to play checkers or to throw a ball accurately, some children give up if they don't do it perfectly. Some even throw away the ball or overturn the checkerboard in frustration.

Other, more successful children handle the same situation much differently, even if they have the same ability as the unsuccessful children. Trying and failing at tasks does not discourage them, it actually encourages them to overcome a new challenge. I find that these kids want to practice and practice at the thing they failed at until they get it right. And you can bet that more often than not, they finally get it right.

William is a great example of this. When he was seven, his father taught him how to play chess (a hard game for a seven-year-old). But William had a strong will to achieve. And even though he lost all the games for the first year, he did not give up. In fact, he actually taught other children in the neighborhood how to play chess so that he would have others to practice with when his father could not play. When he finally won a game against his father the following year, his success was felt deep within, where he knew he could turn his failures into strengths.

In business, Anthony was the opposite of William. Anthony, a bank employee who wanted to be financially independent, went into business for himself and purchased a franchised clothing store. After six months when he was only breaking even (on target with projections from the franchiser), Anthony became nervous and sold his interest in the store. He was so devastated by the experience that he would never again venture into a business for himself. He stayed with a secure bank job until retirement. Even though he was unhappy at work, he felt safe.

How do you handle failure? Does it stop you from pursuing what you want, or does it challenge you to look deeper within yourself and work harder? Does it stimulate you to find new ways to master your goals? Most of us look at success in the same ways; it is how we take our failures that separates those of us who consider ourselves successful from those who don't.

When the space shuttle *Challenger* exploded on January 28, 1986, killing the seven astronauts on board, many said that would be the end of the shuttle program, that we should not tolerate such tragic failures. President Ronald Reagan, however, came on national television shortly after the tragedy and said, "The space shuttle program will continue. The future does not belong to the fainthearted. It belongs to the brave."

To the schoolchildren across the country who had a special interest in that flight because one of its crew members was Christa McAuliffe, the first schoolteacher astronaut, the president continued, "I know it's hard to understand, but sometimes painful things like this happen. It's all part of the process of exploration and discovery. It's all part of taking a chance and expanding man's horizons." Failures are a part of life. It is how we deal with them that determines what we get out of life.

Along similar lines, it's also critical to be able to learn from mistakes and not repeat them. Mistake repeaters often unconsciously sabotage their chances to achieve their goals. You will find a strong emphasis in this book on breaking patterns of the past, patterns that keep you from fulfilling your goals. There are many dramatic examples of how our past influences our present. People who were abused as children often grow up to abuse their own kids; girls who saw their mothers abused by their fathers often grow up and marry men who turn out to be wife abusers; and people who get divorced often remarry the troubles they tried to get rid of. Unless the reasons behind mistakes are understood, the same errors are very likely to be repeated.

How could this be so common in such an intelligent species? Many psychiatrists explain this repetition-compulsion as conflict within the unconscious. Psychiatrists have written millions of pages on the unconscious, but boiled down, all this means is that unknown baggage from the past is interfering in our present life, causing a repetition of things that are not good for us. The source of this baggage is most often, at least initially, unknown. It resides in the unconscious. We all have some baggage that interferes with our present functioning. The self-saboteur's baggage seriously interferes with his progress toward his desired destination. Identifying and challenging unconscious sabotage is key to accomplishing your goals.

Same Solutions to Old Problems: LACK OF CREATIVITY/ADAPTABILITY

A. Add up your answers to questions
12, 24, 36, 48, and 60 and place your answer here: _____

B. Add up your answers to questions
6, 18, 30, 42, and 54 and place your answer here: _____

C. Subtract the smaller number from the larger number
and place your answer here: _____
If A is greater than B place a + sign in front of the answer.
If B is greater than A place a − sign in front of the answer.

Place your score on Line 6, "Adaptable/Creative," on the Sabotage Versus Success Profile Sheet, page 129.

Another significant hallmark of self-sabotage is a lack of creativity and adaptability—an inability to look at common situations a little bit differently. I've found that people with this trait often approach a recurrent problem in a way that has failed for them in the past.

It doesn't make much sense, but I've seen unhappily married couples have the same argument in the same destructive way over and over for many years. I see many parents who deal with unacceptable behavior in their children in exactly the same way (usually spanking), despite the fact that the behavior has not changed, or has gotten worse, every time the parents used this method. I have seen business executives, as well, who, despite poor productivity, refused to look at their mode of operation from a different angle. They appeared to fear newness and change. But I think they should fear failure more.

True, many "creative" individuals are looked upon as eccentric, but it is their ability to look at life in unorthodox ways that helps them to reach higher. Many, many millionaires do not make their fortunes with new inventions. They take an old product and re-do it from a different angle. Mrs. Fields' Cookies, Cabbage Patch dolls, and McDonald's restaurants are just three of the many, many examples.

Many people claim they are not creative. The truth is that these people are afraid to look at their world differently. Although their world may be unsuccessful by their standards, it is what they are used to, and it is comfortable. As we will see, change occurs only when a person is uncomfortable with his world. Creativity takes energy and grows out of a need to see things differently, an inner drive to express other parts of one's individuality. For many, unless they feel a motivating inner source, the comfort of even an unhappy existence is too great to allow them to explore new inner worlds.

Often in combination with a lack of creativity there is an excessive resistance to change. It is not uncommon to hear of businesses going under because they did not "change with the times." They were not flexible in a fluid marketplace. It is also not uncommon to hear of marriages breaking up because of an inability to change: "They just grew apart," is the reason given. One partner was unable to adapt to the changes made by the other. We also see a resistance to change in those with serious addictions (smoking, alcohol, food, cocaine, etc.). Even though these people know on an intellectual level that their addictions are harmful to them, they cannot take action that will help them change.

Decisions are based on the information known when the decisions are made. As the information changes, so must the decisions. Pilots who fail to alter their courses after takeoff often do not reach their destinations. Driving a car requires constant adjustments. Remember how difficult these adjustments were to make when you first learned to drive? You needed to pay attention to where you were and where you were going every minute.

Rigidity prevents the fine-tuning and flexibility needed to be on target for your goals. Rigidity and lack of creativity are very similar negative characteristics. They prevent a person from changing as his environment changes and as his wants and needs change.

In children, we call this inability to change "developmental arrest." Something happens at one stage of development that prevents them from moving on to the next stage; even though they grow in size and years, they lag behind emotionally; they rigidly adhere to immature behavior patterns of the past.

An example of this is how people deal with authority issues. It is typical for adolescents to have some difficulty with authority (parents, teachers, etc.). After all, the emotional tasks of adolescence are to figure out one's identity and to become a more independent person, two difficult jobs. When the adolescent does not adequately work through his identity and independence, he may carry the subsequent authority conflicts with him into adulthood. Most of us know several adults who have trouble with authority (bosses, the law, etc.). This defiant behavior is a remnant from the past, and does not do the individual much good.

Insecurity, fear of change, and comfort are other reasons people find themselves stuck in failure patterns they dislike. For six months I treated a woman whose chief complaint was unhappiness in her marriage. When I asked her why she stayed with a husband who physically abused her and cheated on her, she replied, "I have invested eleven years of my life in this marriage." I answered, "From everything you've told me, it sounds like a bad investment. What do most people do with bad investments?"

Another form of inflexibility that sabotages success is inflexible goals. Some people think that in order to be successful, they have to be successful in a very specific way—that there is only one road to success. This is illustrated by statements like:

"My life is a failure if she won't marry me." (Be careful what you ask for; you may get it.)

"I'll never be happy if I don't get into Harvard Law School."

"If I don't make that sale, I'll never be able to live with myself."

"If I don't get an A on the test, I'm no good."

"If that stock doesn't do well, I'll never invest again."

These statements rigidly limit success. The fact is, there are many avenues to success. Limiting yourself to one of them is like having a road map of California with only one street listed.

8

The Work Habits of Self-Sabotage

The next group of behaviors and characteristics directly reflects work habits that overtly undermine and discourage success. These characteristics occur almost automatically and are continually working against a successful life. Becoming aware of these reflexive behaviors is the first step toward changing them.

Quiz # 2: The Work Habits of Self-Sabotage

Read the following statements carefully and respond to them by placing the number from the answer key that most closely reflects how the statement applies to you. Respond to the statements as honestly as possible; anything less is a waste of your time.

key:
0 = false
1 = mostly false
2 = more false than true
3 = more true than false
4 = mostly true
5 = true

_____ 61. It seems that I do not observe many things that others do.

_____ 62. Often, the fear of appearing stupid prevents me from asking the questions that I have.

_____ 63. I often do not schedule similar tasks together and end up backtracking through the day.

_____ 64. I am just as happy to let circumstances decide a matter for me.

_____ 65. I have do-it-yourself-itis. That is, I have to do everything myself.

_____ 66. Taking the easy road gets in the way of going after my goals.

_____ 67. I am overly cautious.

_____ 68. Before I come to a conclusion about something, I take the time to closely observe the situation.

_____ 69. When I have an important task to accomplish, I often ask experienced people for help. For example, if I wanted to learn a new skill, I would ask someone who knows the skill how to go about learning it.

_____ 70. When I start a rather large project that is due in a few days, I take the time to list the separate things that need to be done in the order I will do them.

_____ 71. Before I make an important decision, I gather as much information as possible about the decision, including finding out most of the options that I have.

_____ 72. When I delegate something I allow the other person to offer his or her input into the task.

_____ 73. I have harnessed my impulses, and work in the best interest of my goals.

_____ 74. I am able to take risks that may lead to increased personal strength. For example, I am the type of person who would seek out counseling if I had an emotional problem.

_____ 75. The emotional turmoil in my life often prevents me from objectively looking at or observing things in my life.

_____ 76. I expect myself to know things before I have gathered information. For example, I expect that I should know how my spouse or a friend feels before he or she has told me.

_____ 77. I often lose ideas or important thoughts because I fail to carry writing materials or a tape recorder with me.

_____ 78. When I have a serious decision to make between two alternatives, I find it so hard to decide that I do not wholeheartedly follow up either choice.

_____ 79. If I want a job done right, I _have_ to do it myself.

_____ 80. It seems that I waste time and effort on things unrelated to the goals I have for myself (e.g., excessive TV, unimportant meetings, small talk).

_____ 81. Almost always I make safe investments rather than putting any of my money on higher-yield, more risky investments.

_____ 82. I take time to observe people who have accomplished the goals I am interested in to see how they did it.

_____ 83. Before making a major purchase, I take time to research the products and the best buys.

_____ 84. When I am in a situation where I might have to wait (e.g., at the doctor's office) I bring along something to do so that I can utilize that time to my advantage.

_____ 85. When a decision I make affects other people, I try to consult with them to get their input before I make it.

_____ 86. If possible, I stay away from repetitive tasks that others can do.

_____ 87. I have the discipline to follow through with what I start (e.g., diets, quitting cigarettes, promises to others or self).

_____ 88. The risks I take are consistent with my goals.

_____ 89. I find it difficult to take the time to spend time alone with myself, observing and listening to what is going on inside of me.

_____ 90. I have often not gotten the information I needed because I was afraid I might be a bother to the other person.

_____ 91. I waste a lot of time looking for things because I didn't initially take the time to put them in their right place.

_____ 92. After I decide something important I often have second thoughts or regrets about the decision.

_____ 93. I spend a good deal of time doing things that others could do better for me.

_____ 94. It seems that I start many things with enthusiasm, but I become bored or disappointed with them in a short period of time.

_____ 95. I generally predict things will turn out poorly and I plan for the worst.

_____ 96. After watching an expert do something I want to do (tennis pro, gourmet chef, expert at work), I find that my ability to do the same thing is improved.

_____ 97. When I have a question, I find a way to ask it.

_____ 98. I often ask myself, "What is the best use of my time?"

_____ 99. I do not have trouble making decisions.

_____ 100. If I want others to do things for me, I will first take the time to clearly teach them how I want it done.

_____ 101. I put in the time and effort to get things done right the first time rather than just quickly doing them to be done with them.

_____ 102. I enjoy the challenge of some risk.

_____ 103. I often assume things to be true before I observe the actual evidence.

_____ 104. I get myself into trouble by thinking or assuming that I know something when I really don't.

_____ 105. Before I do my taxes (or similar tasks) I spend a lot of time going through all of my papers from the previous year at the last minute, organizing what I wish I had done previously.

_____106. When a new opportunity comes my way, I miss out because it takes too long for me to decide.

_____107. I spend a good deal of time doing things that have little meaning toward my major goals in life (e.g., I spend a lot of time compulsively cleaning the house or yard when keeping these perfect is not at the top of my list).

_____108. I do impulsive things that I later regret.

_____109. The fear of failure prevents me from trying to make my dreams come true.

_____110. When someone is talking to me, I make an effort to really hear what they are trying to tell me.

_____111. Before I make an important decision, I gather as much information as possible about the decision, including finding out most of the options that I have.

_____112. I organize my work area (desk, kitchen, garage) so that I can easily find things, and I put the high-priority items where I'll see them first.

_____113. I have a systematic approach to making important decisions.

_____114. I concentrate my efforts on the projects that have the most payoff for me (emotional, financial, relational), rather than spending my time doing low-value activities.

_____115. I am the type of person who asks questions before I act.

_____116. I accept the risk of failure as a condition of succeeding.

_____117. Important people in my life have told me that I don't pay much attention to their needs.

_____118. I find that when I really want something, I'll act impulsively to get it before appropriately researching it.

_____119. I rarely make out a To-Do list, hoping that I'll remember what needs to be done throughout the day and week.

_____120. I often feel confused when I have an important decision to make.

_____121. I believe that I should be able to do everything myself.

_____122. I work just hard enough to get by.

_____123. I generally refuse to take chances, even when the odds are on my side.

_____124. I do not place value judgments on things before I have the facts I need.

_____125. When in doubt, I ask others for help.

_____126. I know how I spend my time, and use it in the best interest of the goals I have for myself.

_____127. I make decisions that are consistent with my goals.

_____128. I often use other people's time, energy, and expertise to help me with my goals.

_____129. I can wait if that means having better things down the road.

_____130. I do not have problems taking reasonable risks once I have weighed the possible consequences for it.

"I Didn't See That Train!": UNOBSERVANT

A. Add up your answers to questions 68, 82, 96, 110, and 124 and place your answer here: _____

B. Add up your answers to questions 61, 75, 89, 103, and 117 and place your answer here: _____

C. Subtract the smaller number from the larger number and place your answer here: _____
If A is greater than B place a + sign in front of the answer.
If B is greater than A place a − sign in front of the answer.

Place your score on Line 7, "Observant," on the Sabotage Versus Success Profile Sheet, page 129.

Paying attention to your goals is necessary for success in any endeavor you undertake. From the spouse who wants a fulfilling marriage to the parent who wants to raise healthy kids, and from the waitress who wants to make the most she can in tips to the psychotherapy patient who wants relief from inner turmoil—actually for anyone, achieving success depends on how well we attend to our tasks.

The waitress who doesn't pay attention to the needs of her customers will not find her tips very rewarding. The psychotherapy patient who refuses to look at how he contributes to his life situation will not gain much insight or make many changes. The spouse who claims to want a good marriage but fails to observe and understand the needs of his partner will always be frustrated. And the parent who wishes to raise healthy children but takes no time to find out what is happening in their lives may be devastated when a child becomes involved with drugs.

Observing the things and people that are important to you and asking goal-oriented questions of yourself and others is a key to success that cannot be overlooked.

The reason many seem oblivious to their own success goals is that it's easier: the comfort trap again. It is easier to work from nine to five and think about relaxing activities after work than it is to observe how things might be done more productively. It is easier, when you do not understand something at school, to not ask questions for fear of appearing stupid. It is easier in a relationship to blame the other person when things go wrong than to try to observe your own behavior. And, it is easier to not pay attention to the details of your goals because that takes constant effort and you're feeling just "too" tired.

In order to change, you need to be curious and pay attention to yourself, your interactions, and the world around you. Chess players would never win if they did not pay attention to the board. Golfers would never improve unless they had someone observe what they were doing wrong. Businesses would fail if they did not pay attention to the needs of their customers. If you wish to be successful, learn to observe.

"I Don't Know": UNINFORMED

I have no data yet. It is a capital mistake to theorize before one has data. Insensibly one begins to twist facts to suit theories instead of theories to suit facts.
　　　—SHERLOCK HOLMES in *A Scandal in Bohemia*

A. Add up your answers to questions
69, 83, 97, 111, and 125 and place your answer here: _____

B. Add up your answers to questions
62, 76, 90, 104, and 118 and place your answer here: _____

C. Subtract the smaller number from the larger number
and place your answer here: _____
   If A is greater than B place a + sign in front of the answer.
   If B is greater than A place a − sign in front of the answer.

Place your score on Line 8, "Informed," on the Sabotage Versus
Success Profile Sheet, page 129.

At no other point in history has information been more readily
available than it is right now. Information abounds on everything
from commodities and computers to modeling and marriage. Yet one
of the most common ways people sabotage themselves is by not
accumulating enough information on their tasks or goals, by being
uninformed or misinformed. Many people will blame others for this
lack of knowledge—"He should have told me"—or for misinformation—
"You can never believe anyone."

There are a number of reasons self-saboteurs do not become
adequately informed, including failing to ask the appropriate questions, not knowing how to gather accurate information, magical
thinking that says, "I should know all," fear of the truth, and a desire
(often unconscious) to perpetuate helplessness.

Asking the right question is the most important step to getting the
right answer. It is a sign of curiosity and indicates a willingness to
learn. The fear of appearing stupid, however, often prevents questions and stifles the learning process. This fear, for those who hold
themselves back, outweighs the fear of ignorance—which should be
a much more frightening prospect.

How many times have you wanted to ask a question, yet, when it
came to saying the words, fear of embarrassment kept your mouth
shut? How many times have you not gotten the information you
needed because of the fear that you would be a nuisance to the
other person? You may be the victim of misconceptions.

First, many people see those who asks questions as interested and
willing to learn, not stupid. Second, many people feel good if they

can help others and enjoy sharing their knowledge. If you're bothering them, you will probably be able to tell, and you can ask them another time. Even better, you can start by asking if this is a good moment for them to answer a question.

In a classroom, if you are reasonably prepared and you begin to feel lost in the material, most likely others share your feeling and appreciate your questions. I have found that most professors also appreciate questions, because it indicates students are paying attention and helps the professors to improve their job of teaching.

Likewise, in business, if you do not have all the information you need to do your job, but you are afraid to appear stupid by asking questions, think of how much worse you'll feel when it's discovered you're not doing the job right. Most supervisors wish to share information because they, like most of us, get satisfaction from helping others to do something well—especially if they're held responsible for the kind of job you do.

There is no doubt that the failure to ask questions and gather information damages many relationships. When we are confused about others' behavior or think we may have gotten the wrong information from them, it is crucial to clarify the meaning of their behavior. Without clarification, our assumptions take over, and little things may turn into monsters.

The worst thing that can happen when you ask a question is that someone may refuse to answer it, give you an answer you don't like, or make you feel stupid for asking. I think ignorance is worse than those three things. You can lessen the chances of a negative response by asking questions in an appropriately respectful way at the right time. But when you have questions, ASK THEM! They will get you more information, which in turn will bring you closer to your goals.

Not knowing *how* to get information will also hold you back from your desires. The best remedy for this, however, is to ask the right questions of the right people. When that is not possible, there are other ways to gather information. In a public or university library you can get information on almost anything. They have professional information gatherers. Yet many people do not know how to use libraries. If you are one of them, learn. Where do you learn? Ask a librarian. The library is a great information source, and you can't beat the cost.

Expecting yourself to know something without being taught is what psychiatrists call magical thinking. It is like a person who has never been somewhere before refusing to ask for directions when he is lost. This magical thinking of "I should know the answers" occurs in many situations. I see it most frequently with parents who expect themselves to be good parents despite never having had a good role model to teach them. Pride is often an excuse to cover ignorance. Be kind to yourself and don't expect more from yourself than is reasonable. If you don't know something, admit it and find the answer to it.

A fourth reason people don't ask questions or become informed is that they are afraid of the answers. I see this most commonly in people who marry after knowing each other for only a few weeks. They are generally tired of being alone and want to be in a relationship so badly that they leave common sense behind. Ignorance, they think, is better than information.

But this usually backfires. Often, hidden information surfaces, and one or both parties feel betrayed. Some are too eager to trust before finding out if a person is trustworthy. This may also be true in business or personal issues when something is wanted so much that denying reality is preferable to denying the opportunity to obtain the desired goal. For example, a hospital corporation really wanted to open up a new hospital in a northern California market despite a very difficult medical reimbursement climate. In their expansion enthusiasm the planners overlooked this critical point and the hospital was in serious financial trouble just two years after it opened.

The last common justification for a lack of information comes from dependency needs. The unspoken statement that operates here is something like, "If I don't know, then you have to stay and take care of me." This is commonly seen in people who never learn to drive, husbands who never learn to cook, and wives who never learn about financial matters. The dependency ploy often backfires, however, because the other person feels put upon. Dependency fosters closed-in trapped feelings on both sides. Independence fosters intimacy.

Current information is essential to every task or goal. How informed are you in the areas of your goals? What can you do to improve the situation?

"I'm Too Scattered": UNORGANIZED

A. Add up your answers to questions
   70, 84, 98, 112, and 126 and place your answer here: _____

B. Add up your answers to questions
63, 77, 91, 105, and 119 and place your answer here: _____

C. Subtract the smaller number from the larger number
and place your answer here: _____
If A is greater than B place a + sign in front of the answer.
If B is greater than A place a − sign in front of the answer.

Place your score on Line 9, "Organization," on the Sabotage Versus
Success Profile Sheet, page 129.

Nothing is more frustrating to a boss, coworker, family member—
anyone—than to be associated with someone who is poorly organized or unprepared for his daily tasks. You've probably felt the
irritation of having to wait for a task to be done later than planned,
or having to change plans because of somebody's poor organization.
The irritation can linger for some time.

Billie was a bright, articulate and energetic administrative assistant. She rose quickly in a small computer company because of her
verbal skills. Yet her disorganization became a glaring deficiency
when she was promoted to office manager. The smooth-running
operation began to sputter as many of the small details were
ignored. At first Billie's boss was going to fire her for her deficiencies.
After he talked to a consultant, however, he realized that he had
promoted her because of the abilities she had shown in the previous
position but that they had little to do with what he expected from
her in her current position. Instead of firing her he sent her to
several "organizational" workshops, and she dramatically improved.

How do you match up on being organized and prepared? Psychiatrists say that someone who is chronically unprepared for tasks or
always late to appointments is manifesting underlying hostility. Such
people get their anger out in passive-aggressive ways; instead of
telling someone they're mad, they act it out by being late or
sabotaging their task. It has been my experience that many people
who sabotage themselves are hostile underneath, for whatever reason, and this gets in the way of how they approach an important
task.

Being unorganized is another symptom of the "Unconscious Life,"
where no real thought or planning is present. Living this kind of
life, a person will go from crisis to crisis or deadline to deadline

without taking full control of his life. Getting well will include some organization and prioritizing of life, time, and effort.

"I Can't Make Up My Mind!": TROUBLE MAKING DECISIONS

A. Add up your answers to questions
71, 85, 99, 113, and 127 and place your answer here: _____

B. Add up your answers to questions
64, 78, 92, 106, and 120 and place your answer here: _____

C. Subtract the smaller number from the larger number
and place your answer here: _____
If A is greater than B place a + sign in front of the answer.
If B is greater than A place a − sign in front of the answer.

Place your score on Line 10, "Decision Making," on the Sabotage Versus Success Profile Sheet, page 129.

Patient waiting and researching information can be carried to an extreme, endangering chances for success. Some wait forever, letting many exciting and challenging opportunities pass them by, or they remain in unhealthy jobs or relationships far past the time that is good for them.

Indecisiveness can either mean that someone has trouble making decisions, or that he needs to have others make decisions for him. Either way, the net result is little self-motivated action. And successful people are action oriented (although not impulsively, of course).

Do you have trouble making decisions? Do you always worry excessively over the decisions you have made? Is procrastination part of your middle name? Do you fall apart if your decision maker goes away for a few days? Problems like these often come from an internal sense of not being "good enough." People who have this trouble may have been ridiculed for the independent decisions they tried to make as children, or they may have been dominated by parents who had to be in control, who never helped the child make decisions for himself.

Karen is an example of this. She was born two months premature and was a very sickly child. Her mother, from the time Karen came home from the hospital, got into the cycle of always worrying about and overprotecting her daughter. Karen's mother made all of the decisions for her.

At forty-two, Karen is still allowing Mom to make her decisions. No man has ever been good enough for her, so she hasn't married. The jobs she could get were beneath her, so she didn't work much. And since Mom still worries about her health, Karen does not go out much. God only knows how Karen will make decisions after Mom is dead.

In business there is a corollary to Karen's case. Often if a young executive is thrown into a situation before he is ready and he makes a mistake, he becomes much more reticent about making independent decisions in the future. Early decisions that turned out poorly often set the stage for paralysis in decision making.

Granted, Karen's case is extreme, but I have seen many cases in which indecisiveness paralyzed any chance the individual had for success. This process, like many of the others we've looked at, started in childhood and will remain in force until some action is taken to correct it.

"Do-It-Yourself-Itis": INABILITY TO DELEGATE

A. Add up your answers to questions
   72, 86, 100, 114, and 128 and place your answer here: _____

B. Add up your answers to questions
   65, 79, 93, 107, and 121 and place your answer here: _____

C. Subtract the smaller number from the larger number
   and place your answer here: _____
   If A is greater than B place a + sign in front of the answer.
   If B is greater than A place a − sign in front of the answer.

Place your score on Line 11, "Delegation," on the Sabotage Versus Success Profile Sheet, page 129.

Details are important to the successful person; repetitive tasks are not. Success takes time, but unsuccessful people often get bogged down doing things that are unnecessary for their goals, or doing things others could do better. The inability to delegate stops many from success; they are so busy handling routine chores that they don't have time to accomplish the important steps that could bring them closer to their goals.

Overmanaging is often listed as one of the top ten fatal flaws that derailed executives from moving up the corporate ladder. Henry Ford said it succinctly, "I don't have to know how to do it. I need to know who does it best."

Linda, an attorney for a large law firm, was a perfectionist. Her strong suit was courtroom work, but she often became so bogged down on law research that her cases took too long to prepare. This inefficiency was noted by her partners, who tried to find her good assistants. She made little use of her assistant, insisting on doing most of the work herself. Her law firm let her go because of a lack of performance. Her inability to delegate cost her a job she loved.

Delegation is important in all aspects of life. In family life, it is important to delegate and share tasks around the house. This not only cuts down on the parents' workload and gives them more time for pleasurable family activities, but it also teaches children the lesson of responsibility. There is strong evidence from many studies to show that children grow up to be healthier and happier when they are made responsible for jobs when they are young. It increases their sense of belonging to the family.

Are you too busy earning a living to make any money? Are you so busy that you don't have time for yourself? Do you spend too much time doing things you don't have to? Time and energy are needed for success. Don't waste them on things that are not in your plans. Look at how you spend your time. Is it moving you closer to, or farther from, your goals?

"I Must Have It Now!": IMPULSIVE

A. Add up your answers to questions
73, 87, 101, 115, and 129 and place your answer here: _____

B. Add up your answers to questions
66, 80, 94, 108, and 122 and place your answer here: _____

C. Subtract the smaller number from the larger number
and place your answer here: _____

If A is greater than B place a + sign in front of the answer.
If B is greater than A place a − sign in front of the answer.

Place your score on Line 12, "Discipline," on the Sabotage Versus
Success Profile Sheet, page 130.

People commonly sabotage themselves through impulsiveness.
They do not wait until the right moment to act; they act when the
impulse arises. If they are tired of being single, they may impulsively find someone to marry (ever heard of a person who married
someone after only knowing them for a few days?). Or, if they want
to open up a new business, instead of doing a market survey or
thoroughly researching their venture, they may impulsively make a
bad business deal or go into a poor location.

Advertisers and salespeople depend on impulse buying for much
of their business. That is why some packaging actually costs the
company more than the actual product. Labels, slogans, and logos
are carefully designed to appeal to the impulse dollar.

Have you ever noticed the merchandise around the checkout
stands at your local grocery store? In most cases they display items
you passed up when going through the aisles. But as you stand
waiting to pay for your groceries, the store bets you will have the
urge for some candy or gum or whatever they may be displaying.

Advertising slogans put pressure on your impulses. They use
phrases like:

Buy it now.
Don't wait any longer.
For a limited time only.
Don't put it off. You deserve it.
There'll never be a better time.

That is why many state legislatures have given consumers a
three-day cooling off period to change their minds after signing
purchase contracts: to prevent buyers' impulses from causing them
to go broke.

As we'll see a little later on, impulsiveness is one of the major
symptoms of a disorder termed Attention Deficit Disorder. This is a
learning disorder that affects every aspect of a person's life. Typically, people afflicted with Attention Deficit Disorder are impulsive,

have difficulty concentrating, and are distractible and disorganized. They start many projects, yet complete few of them. They say impulsive things and often go from job to job because of inconsistent work performance. More on this later.

Along with impulsiveness often comes a lack of commitment. Unsuccessful people often jump from project to project, from relationship to relationship, or from hobby to hobby. They find it very hard to concentrate their efforts on specific goals for prolonged periods of time, often starting with high hopes and promises but becoming quickly disillusioned or bored. In a word, they lack commitment.

Commitment is the will, the desire, the drive to carry through to the end, to be there when needed, and to be totally involved in the process. For many different reasons, unsuccessful people have trouble with total commitment. The task that they started with enthusiasm becomes boring, the lover who would make their life complete becomes disappointing, or their new-found interest in their physique does not become important below fifteen hundred calories. They find that they start many things and finish only a few. This lack of commitment or inner drive may come from being "burned" too many times, having too few successes to believe the effort is worth it, or from not having a clear picture of who they are and what they want.

It is clear that there are different levels of commitment. The amount of commitment necessary depends on your goals. If you want to become a doctor, you won't get very far without total commitment. If you want to learn golf, the commitment depends on how well you want to play. If you wish your marriage to be fresh and stimulating, your commitment needs to be on a daily basis.

Also, it is obvious that you can be committed to one area of your life and not to the others. One of the most frequent complaints I hear from married women is that their husbands are committed more to their work than to their families. In many cases, employers will not hire women with small children because they know that moms are usually more committed to their kids than to their jobs, and the employers know that if the kids get sick, mom may be absent.

I like the phrase "balanced commitment" better than total commitment. It implies that there are several different areas in your life that need attention.

"I'd Rather Be Safe Than Anything": UNWILLING TO TAKE REASONABLE RISKS

A. Add up your answers to questions
74, 88, 102, 116, and 130 and place your answer here: _____

B. Add up your answers to questions
67, 81, 95, 109, and 123 and place your answer here: _____

C. Subtract the smaller number from the larger number
and place your answer here: _____
If A is greater than B place a + sign in front of the answer.
If B is greater than A place a − sign in front of the answer.

Place your score on Line 13, "Reasonable Risk Taking," on the
Sabotage Versus Success Profile Sheet, page 130.

Unwillingness to take reasonable risks may lead to a safe, predictable, and comfortable life, but also to one that may not be very
satisfying or very successful. Some risk-taking is necessary for any
success—not the lottery kind of risk-taking, where the odds are
never with you, but the kind of risk-taking where you objectively
evaluate the action, and decide that the likely benefits outweigh the
possible negative consequences (positive benefit-to-risk ratio).

People hold themselves back by being overly cautious, by being
afraid to take risks. They have been "burned" before, or they are
convinced that nothing will turn out right for them. They often live
in predictable mediocrity, staying in a job they dislike rather than
risking starting over, staying in destructive or stale relationships
rather than risking new relationships, and being overly cautious in
investments because they are afraid to trust their financial advisors.
No risk equals little gain, in many aspects of life.

Without thinking about it, we take risks every day. We drive our
cars on Saturday night even though the Department of Transportation estimates that one out of ten sets of headlights coming toward
us is in the hands of a drunk driver. And by the millions each year
we fly on airplanes. We just don't think about all the risks we do
take. If we did, we might become agoraphobic and never leave the
safety of home. Living involves risks, sometimes dangerous ones.

There are many reasons some people avoid taking risks toward their success. Most often these reasons involve fear, remembering past failures (letting failure defeat them), and unwillingness to risk their comfort. There is that word "comfort" again. It continues to interfere with success.

Some risk taking is clearly not worth it. When I was a medic in the army, I remember going through a combat casualty course at Fort Sam Houston. At one point we were taught how to traverse a ravine using a double rope bridge. We were harnessed to the bridge by a Swiss rope seat that the instructor tied around us. In order to see how safe the seat was, we were encouraged to let go of the rope bridge and fall back when we were over the middle of the ravine with a forty-foot drop below us onto the rocks.

I watched several people who went before me test the rope seat. When it was my turn, I felt very uncomfortable about falling back. I got out to the middle of the ravine and thought to myself: "With everyone watching, do you want to be a man and fall back the way the others did, or do you want to make it safely to the other side and risk looking like a coward?" The coward in me won out, because worrying about what other people think of me is not one of my primary goals.

When I reached the other end, I turned around to watch a friend of mine fall back. But, to my shock and horror, his safety rope was tied incorrectly and he fell to the rocks below. The accident broke many bones, ruptured his spleen and collapsed his lungs. It was a horrible event to witness.

I have learned to trust my hunches. We need to take risks, but only if they are reasonable and related to our goals.

9

Interactional Self-Sabotage

The next six hallmarks of self-sabotage are interactional in nature. We will look at how problems with our personal interactions can get in the way of our goals, be they personal, relational, or in business.

Quiz # 3: Interactional Self-Sabotage

Read the following statements carefully and respond to them by placing the number from the answer key that most closely reflects how the statement applies to you. Respond to the statements as honestly as possible; anything less is a waste of your time.

key:
0 = false
1 = mostly false
2 = more false than true
3 = more true than false
4 = mostly true
5 = true

_____131. Getting my point across in a discussion is so important that I often do not fully hear the other person or I have trouble understanding his point of view.

_____132. I continue to spend time with people who put me down.

_____133. I often act like a know-it-all.

_____134. The fear of losing often prevents me from trying.

_____135. I often come off as critical of others.

_____136. I need the approval of others to feel good about myself.

_____137. When I do not understand something someone else has said I ask them to repeat or clarify their words.

_____138. I gravitate toward people who make me feel good about myself, rather than those whom I can never please.

_____139. I take time to observe people who have accomplished the goals I am interested in to see how they did it.

_____140. Competition spurs me on to be as good as I possibly can be.

_____141. I can get outside myself to see the emotional needs of others.

_____142. I most often feel free to express my opinions.

_____143. I either clam up or become very emotional in an argument.

_____144. I often feel negative about myself after visiting close friends.

_____145. In a discussion, I have to be right or I feel bad.

_____146. I feel that when someone I know succeeds at something, I've lost out in comparison.

_____147. I find myself saying insensitive things to others, then regretting my words.

_____148. I depend a lot on other people.

_____149. I establish frequent eye contact when I talk with other people.

_____150. I teach the important people in my life to treat me with respect.

_____151. I am able to get the other person's point of view.

_____152. Even when I lose, I learn from competing with others.

_____153. Before I take it too personally when someone dumps on me I ask myself, "I wonder what's going on with them that makes them act that way."

_____154. I have the internal OK to be who I want to be.

_____155. When I'm listening to someone talk to me I often become distracted and will let my attention wander to outside things, such as the TV, magazines, or the mail.

_____156. I feel that I have to fight the primary people in my life in order to feel good about myself.

_____157. If I don't like something that someone else says, I turn him or her off completely.

_____158. Competition makes me very nervous.

_____159. I criticize people close to me (spouse, children, employees) in front of others.

_____160. It seems my life is spent on other people's goals.

_____161. I am able to keep quiet long enough in a discussion to get the other person's point of view.

_____162. The three people with whom I spend most of my time behave toward me in a positive, encouraging way.

_____163. When I have an important task to accomplish I often ask experienced people for help. For example, if I wanted to learn a new skill, I would ask someone who knows the skill how to go about learning it.

_____164. I encourage others to win.

_____165. I treat others the way I'd like them to treat me.

_____166. I would characterize myself as an independent person.

_____167. I often jump to conclusions before I completely hear out the other person.

_____168. The people close to me treat me like I'll never amount to much.

_____169. I get caught in the "Yes, but" syndrome of having to counter advice that others give me.

_____170. Whenever possible, I stay away from competition.

_____171. I am so involved with my own problems that I find it hard to understand or care about the problems of others.

_____172. After I make a decision, I often spend a good deal of time thinking about what so-and-so would say about it.

_____173. When I have important talks with others I will decrease the distractions in the room.

_____174. I spend time with people who bring out the best in me.

_____175. When I have trouble in an area, I seek out the help of others.

_____176. In competing with others, I think there are many times when both parties can come out ahead.

_____177. I am often able to put myself in other people's shoes to understand how they feel.

_____178. I am able to pursue my own dreams, despite what others think of me.

_____179. I'm often not clear in my communication with others. For example, if someone asks me where I'd like to eat for dinner I'll tell them it doesn't matter to me even when I do have a preference.

_____180. Many people who grew up in families where they felt frequently put down surround themselves with the same type of negative people as adults. I am that way.

_____181. Getting my point across in a discussion is so important that I have trouble understanding the other person's point of view.

_____182. I have to win in order to feel good about myself.

_____183. People close to me tell me that I'm insensitive to others.

_____184. I feel more comfortable when someone tells me what to do, rather than making my own decisions.

_____185. I often repeat back what others have told me in an effort to truly understand the other person's point of view.

_____186. I do not tolerate being put down by others.

_____187. I possess a teachable spirit.

_____188. I actively seek win-win situations, where both parties benefit from a situation.

_____189. I make an effort to get along with the people who are important to my loved ones (in-laws, children's friends).

_____190. I am able to make my own decisions.

"You're Not Listening to Me": POOR COMMUNICATION RUINS RELATIONSHIPS

A. Add up your answers to questions 137, 149, 161, 173, and 185 and place your answer here: _____ *20*

B. Add up your answers to questions 131, 143, 155, 167, and 179 and place your answer here: _____ *9*

C. Subtract the smaller number from the larger number and place your answer here: _____ *+11*
   If A is greater than B place a + sign in front of the answer.
   If B is greater than A place a − sign in front of the answer.

Place your score on Line 14, "Communication," on the Sabotage Versus Success Profile Sheet, page 130.

Poor communication is at the core of most relationship problems. Jumping to conclusions, mind reading, and "having to be right" are only a few traits that doom communication. When people do not connect with each other in a meaningful way, their own minds take over the "relationship" and many imaginary problems arise. This occurs at home, with friends and at work.

Donna was frequently angry at her husband. She would often spend the day imagining the upcoming evening together. In her imagination, they would spend time talking and her husband would be very attentive to her needs. In fact, he usually came home tired and preoccupied after a hard day at work, and Donna felt very disappointed and reacted angrily toward him. Her husband felt bewildered. He was unaware of his wife's hopeful imaginings during the day and didn't know he was disappointing her. After six couple sessions Donna learned how to express her needs up front and she found a very receptive husband.

Too often in relationships we have expectations and hopes that we never clearly communicate to our partners or colleagues. We assume they should know what we need and we become disappointed when they don't accurately read our minds. Clear communication is essential if relationships are to be mutually satisfying.

Here are ten ways that communication is sabotaged in relationships.

1. Poor attitude. This is where you expect the conversation to go nowhere and subsequently you don't even try to direct it in a positive way. Negative assumptions about the other person feed into this poor attitude. Up front you don't trust the other person and you remain stiff and guarded when you are together.

2. Unclear expectations and needs. Do you expect people to guess what you want or need? It is great when others can anticipate our needs, but most people are so busy that it's hard for them to see the needs of other people. That does not make them good or bad; it simply means it's important to speak up about what you need.

3. No reinforcing body language. Body language is so important because it sends conscious and unconscious messages. When you fail to make eye contact or acknowledge another person with facial or body gestures, he or she begins to feel lost, alone and unenthusiastic about continuing the conversation. Eye contact and physical acknowledgment is essential to good communication.

4. Competing with distractions. Distractions frequently doom communication. It's not a good idea, for example, for my wife to talk to me about something important during the fourth quarter of a Lakers' basketball playoff game. Decrease distractions to have clearer communication.

5. Never asking for feedback on what you're saying. You might assume that you are sending clear messages to the other person when in fact what they understand is completely different from what you meant. Feedback is essential to clear communication.

6. Kitchen sinking. This occurs in arguments when people feel backed into a corner and bring up unrelated issues from the past in order to protect themselves or intensify the disagreement. Stay on track until an issue is fully discussed.

7. Mind reading. This is where you arbitrarily predict what another person is thinking and then react to that "imagined" information. Mind reading is often a projection of what you think yourself. Even after couples have been married for thirty years it's impossible for them to always be right about what is going on in the other person's head. Checking things out is essential to good communication.

8. Having to be right. This destroys effective communication. When a person has to be right in a conversation there is no communication, only a debate.

9. Sparring. Using put-downs or sarcasm or discounting the other's ideas erodes meaningful dialogue and sets up distance in relationships.

10. Lack of monitoring and follow-up. Often it takes repeated efforts to get what you need. It's very important not to give up. When you give up asking for what you need, you often silently resent the other person, which subverts the whole relationship. Persistence is very important to getting what you want.

A Draining Environment: SURROUNDED BY NEGATIVE PEOPLE

A. Add up your answers to questions
138, 150, 162, 174, and 186 and place your answer here: _____ 22

B. Add up your answers to questions
132, 144, 156, 168, and 180 and place your answer here: _____ 1

C. Subtract the smaller number from the larger number
and place your answer here: _____ ×21
If A is greater than B place a + sign in front of the answer.
If B is greater than A place a − sign in front of the answer.

Place your score on Line 15, "Surrounded by Positive People," on the Sabotage Versus Success Profile Sheet, page 130.

Another disturbing hallmark of self-saboteurs is that they have a tendency to surround themselves with negative people—that is, with people who do not believe in them or their abilities, people who put them down, people who discourage them from success, people who treat them as though they will never amount to anything. If you are surrounded by these types of people, you soon get a clear message that you are no good, that you can't succeed or that you shouldn't succeed because you don't deserve it. So why try?

You might be asking yourself, "Now who would spend time with people like that? Those people must be hard up for friends, or have a need to punish themselves."

Before we look at this question, I want you to examine your own situation. Are you surrounded by people who believe in you, people who make you feel good about yourself? Or do you spend time with people who are constantly putting you down or downplaying your ideas? Who are the five people you spend the most time with? What category do they fit into?

Surprised? Most people who sabotage themselves are.

Why would some people surround themselves with such negative influences? Isn't it a bit odd?

Yes, it is odd, but it is also easy to understand. People who grow up in negative environments grow up to be negative. It is what they are used to and, in a strange sort of way, it is what they are comfortable with.

Let me explain. If an insecure parent continually belittles his youngster to make himself feel better, the child grows up believing that he is no good and that he is not worthy of being around people who make him feel good. In addition, if something bad happens in a family when the child is young (such as a divorce or death) the child often erroneously believes he was at fault and carries around tremendous guilt for a long time.

Some children who witnessed parents struggle through a difficult marriage, subconsciously get the message that relationships are inherently problematic and get involved with others who are not compatible with them.

Adults, as well as children, can be beaten down after years of living through a difficult marriage or being in an abusive job situation. Many people will stay in a job they hate, for example, because their boss leads them to believe that no one else would hire them and they are lucky to have that job. Just as in an abusive marriage, these employees have their self-esteem beaten down to the point where they believe that they cannot go beyond their abusive environment.

Past relationships have a real impact on present ones. If your past relationships were filled with negativity, chances are the present relationships will be the same unless you make a conscious effort to overcome the past. It takes great effort to overcome difficult foundational relationships, but I see people doing it daily. Changing the people you spend your time with may be an important step in changing your chances for success.

Acts Like a Know-It-All: UNABLE TO LEARN FROM OTHERS

A. Add up your answers to questions
139, 151, 163, 175, and 187 and place your answer here: _____ 15

B. Add up your answers to questions
133, 145, 157, 169, and 181 and place your answer here: _____ 8

C. Subtract the smaller number from the larger number
and place your answer here: _____ +7
If A is greater than B place a + sign in front of the answer.
If B is greater than A place a − sign in front of the answer.

Place your score on Line 16, "Learns from Others," on the Sabotage Versus Success Profile Sheet, page 130.

It is reasonable to think many unsuccessful people would be hungry to learn all they could about what holds them back. Yet, in many cases, I have found the opposite to be true. Despite their own admission of failure in certain areas of their life, they remain set in their ways, making excuses for their failures and being unable to learn from those who might prove helpful. They are unteachable, unable to learn from others. They often have a know-it-all attitude, an irritating self-assuredness in the face of obvious failure.

The willingness to learn, to be teachable, is found in successful people. They ask questions and learn from failures. People who sabotage themselves often do not ask many questions. They attribute their failures to bad luck and reason, "If only something different had happened, I wouldn't be in the mess I'm in."

Psychiatrists see many examples of this in their practices; even though these patients pay a sizable sum to consult with us, they negate what we have to say and continue in their set ways. The most striking example I've seen of this occurred in a consultation with Mrs. Joseph, mother of eleven-year-old Charles. Mrs. Joseph brought Charles in to see me because he had run away from home on two occasions. Charles told me he ran away from home because his parents were always telling him he was no good and that he was a burden to them. "Who wants to live with people who don't want you?" he asked.

I spoke with the mother about this, and she said she and her husband were tough on Charles because they wanted him to work harder; that was how their parents had treated them when they were growing up, so it was good enough for Charles.

When I told her how destructive that kind of treatment is to a child, and how to take a more positive approach with Charles, she said that she and her husband would think about what I said. But she abruptly took Charles out of therapy with me and continued treating Charles in the same way until he ran away again.

The Josephs were unable to learn even when the situation was out of control. They wanted me to change their son, but they did not want to take my advice for changing their interactions with him. They took no personal responsibility for the problem.

Being unteachable will harm you in all aspects of your life. People who are unable to learn from supervisors at work do not get promoted and people who are unwilling to learn different ways in relationships often find themselves drifting apart from their partners.

How teachable are you? When things go wrong, do you look for someone to blame, or do you look for answers from someone who might know? Successful people possess a humble and teachable spirit.

A Game of Winners and Losers: SHIES AWAY FROM ANY COMPETITION

A. Add up your answers to questions
140, 152, 164, 176, and 188 and place your answer here: ___22___

B. Add up your answers to questions
134, 146, 150, 170, and 182 and place your answer here: ___12___

C. Subtract the smaller number from the larger number
and place your answer here: ___+10___

If A is greater than B place a + sign in front of the answer.
If B is greater than A place a − sign in front of the answer.

Place your score on Line 17, "Competition," on the Sabotage Versus
Success Profile Sheet, page 130.

Competition occurs in all aspects of life: competition for certain
relationships (I'll take her away from Bob); competition within
relationships (I'm a better tennis player than you); competition
within the individual (I'm going to lose ten pounds in two months);
and competition in business (our designer jeans will outsell all
others).

Competition is a fact of life. Many self-sabotaging people, however, shy away from competition, thinking that there is something
inherently dangerous about it. I hear them say things like:

"I always lose."

"In competition, there are winners and losers. I don't want to be
the loser."

"Competition makes me so nervous that I have to stay away from
it."

"I don't like to win, because that means someone else loses."

They see competition as a game with winners and losers, instead
of something that can have winners and winners. It depends on how
one plays the game. People who hold themselves back often see
competition in a negative light.

Successful people usually thrive on competition, and even if they
"lose," they see the loss as something they can learn from. They
often see competition, however, as a game where two can win.
When I was in medical school, I always competed with Alan for the
top spot in my class. This competition was a special one, and even
though he ended up coming out on top of the class, we both
benefited from it immensely. We studied together, encouraged each
other, and became very good friends in the process. We drove each
other to higher accomplishments. And even though I would rather
have been first in the class, I can say that I share some of Alan's
accomplishments and he shares some of mine.

Many business people have seen the benefit of helping each other
and have formed trade unions and trade associations to further each
other's ability to compete. Competition can be a very positive force;
its usefulness depends on your frame of reference for it.

Unable to Get Outside of Themselves: INSENSITIVITY TO OTHERS

A. Add up your answers to questions
141, 153, 165, 177, and 189 and place your answer here: ____7____

B. Add up your answers to questions
135, 147, 159, 171, and 183 and place your answer here: ___20___

C. Subtract the smaller number from the larger number
and place your answer here: ___-13___
If A is greater than B place a + sign in front of the answer.
If B is greater than A place a − sign in front of the answer.

Place your score on Line 18, "Sensitivity to Others," on the Sabotage Versus Success Profile Sheet, page 130.

In several studies about why executives fail, "insensitivity to others" was cited more than any other flaw as the major problem area. Phrases like the following were typically used about those who did not succeed:

"He never negotiated; there was no room for any views contrary to his."

"He could follow a bull through a china shop and still break the remaining china."

"He made others feel stupid."

"She was always talking down to her employees."

"Whenever something went right, he took all the credit. Whenever things fell through, heads would roll."

"It was her way or no way. If you disagreed with her, you were out."

Insensitivity to others can cause failure in almost any endeavor. A lack of interpersonal skill not only causes others to avoid you, it can make them "mad as hell" and cause them to feel active ill will toward you. Coworkers may look the other way if you are making serious mistakes; lovers may start finding fault in any area they can to retaliate for their hurt; and acquaintances may start making excuses to decrease the time they spend with you.

Being insensitive to others has a serious isolating effect that not only causes loneliness, but also decreases the "reality" feedback from others and cuts you off from coworkers' or friends' creativity and knowledge. Insensitive people are unable to learn from others because others usually don't want anything to do with them.

Being sensitive to others opens many doors for you. It allows you to develop positive relationships. According to Jules Masserman, M.D., past president of the American Psychiatric Association, this is one of the three great needs in life, the others being health and faith.

Sensitivity allows you to learn from others, because they will be more willing to give to you. Henry Ford emphasized this point when he said, "If there is any one secret of success, it lies in the ability to get the other person's point of view and see things from his angle as well as your own." Being sensitive to others will make it more likely that they will want to share their point of view with you.

Being sensitive to others also decreases the likelihood that you'll misinterpret their behavior. As a psychiatrist, I spend much of my time helping patients depersonalize the behavior of others. This means that patients need to realize that when someone dumps on them, it may actually have nothing to do with *them*, but rather what is going on in the dumper's life.

For example, a supervisor comes back after being chewed out by the owner of a company. She snaps at her assistant for not having a report ready. The assistant has just returned from taking her child to the emergency room because he cut his head open falling against the corner of a table at day care. She starts crying and runs into the bathroom. The supervisor and assistant don't speak to each other for a week and the assistant finally quits a job she needed. If, instead of thinking only of their own trying days, each had taken a minute to think about what was going on with the other (to be sensitive), this fight would have been avoided.

Taking someone else's behavior too personally is also a form of being insensitive. We all act out of our own backgrounds. So if I get mad at you, it may actually have nothing to do with you, but everything to do with me and my expectations, which are based on my past and present situation. Unfortunately, when you are insensitive to others, most people do not ask themselves, "I wonder what is going on with him today that he needs to treat me like dirt?" They just get mad and find ways to get even.

How sensitive are you to others? Do you get the most out of your relationships? Or, do you sabotage them by being insensitive? Do you take the behavior of others too personally? Or, when someone dumps on you, do you wonder what might be going on with him that caused him to act that way?

Of course, you can carry that last question to an extreme and attribute any negative criticism directed your way as someone else's problem. Balance is the key. When negative stuff comes your way, you always need to ask yourself two questions. First, did I do anything to bring this on myself? Second, what is going on with him to cause him to act that way? Those two questions will help you to be more sensitive to other people and increase your chances for success. We live in a relational world. Relational failures generally do not feel very successful.

"You Have to Tell Me What to Do": DEPENDENCE ON OTHERS

A. Add up your answers to questions
   142, 154, 166, 178, and 190 and place your answer here: _22_

B. Add up your answers to questions
   136, 148, 160, 172, and 184 and place your answer here: _12_

C. Subtract the smaller number from the larger number
   and place your answer here: _+10_
   If A is greater than B place a + sign in front of the answer.
   If B is greater than A place a − sign in front of the answer.

Place your score on Line 19, "Independence," on the Sabotage Versus Success Profile Sheet, page 130.

Following and pleasing others without regard to your own personal values and goals is a trap in which many people fall victim. Because of their own insecurity or low self-esteem, they encourage others to direct their life, even though they often feel stuck and resentful. These people lack sufficient internal strength to make their own decisions and "be their own person." This dependence on others stifles individuality and prevents emotional growth.

Some common symptoms of excessive dependency include:

• needing the approval of others to feel good about yourself
• spending a good deal of time worrying about what other people would say about decisions you make
• looking for approval from others before you approve of yourself

- feeling more comfortable when someone tells you what to do than making your own decisions
- often feeling resentful toward others
- being unable to express your opinion for fear of what someone else might think
- choosing a career or project based on what someone else thinks rather than using your own judgment.

Parents breed dependence in children by doing everything for them, by making decisions for them and by even choosing their friends. Overmanaging a child gives him the message that he is not competent and that he must look to others for support. Children reared in this way are often insecure and afraid.

The same metaphor applies to work situations. When a supervisor "overmanages" and makes all the decisions on a project, the employees feel incompetent and of little use to the job. Subsequently, they look to management to make all of their decisions and their productivity and creativity drops to very low levels. Little incentive is given to actively contribute in an independent way.

Bill was a federal employee at a Navy Shipyard for seven years. He said it was the most frustrating job he had ever had. He felt constantly micromanaged. "I couldn't order three pencils without someone looking over my shoulder," he complained. He felt tense and irritable a lot of the time, but he believed that he had to stay in that job for security. With therapy he was able to change to a job in the private sector where he felt his knowledge was appreciated and he operated more independently.

Are you dependent on the thoughts and feelings of others in order to feel good about yourself? Do you make your own decisions? Can you risk appearing stupid by stating your opinion even when it may be unpopular? Who do you get your self-esteem from: others or yourself?

Along similar lines, it's also important to stay away from "following the crowd." Peer pressure affects adults almost as frequently as it does teenagers. Mindlessly following trends, be they sexual, relational, or financial, may have devastating consequences that include getting a number of sexually transmitted diseases (these get more deadly all the time), divorce and loneliness, and, obviously, financial ruin. No doubt there is always a great deal of pressure to "go along with the crowd" (peer pressure, national public opinion polls, sophisticated advertising), but this pressure must be resisted at every turn if one is to be successful.

10

Personal Self-Sabotage

The final seven hallmarks of self-sabotage are personal in nature. We will look at how these qualities seriously impair your ability to get what you want. Even if you are almost to your goals, these seven traits will prevent you from reaching the top.

Quiz # 4: Personal Self-Sabotage

Read the following statements carefully and respond to them by placing the number for the answer key that most closely reflects how the statement applies to you. Respond to the statements as honestly as possible; anything less is a waste of your time.

Key:
0 = false
1 = mostly false
2 = more false than true
3 = more true than false
4 = mostly true
5 = true

_____ 191. I tend to make things out to be bigger than they are.

_____ 192. Looking back, I have often set myself up to fail.

_____ 193. I am bothered by many aches and pains in my body for which no physical cause has been found.

_____ 194. I am often restless or irritable.

_____ 195. I sometimes neglect my family or social obligations because of drinking or drug use.

_____ 196. I have trouble sustaining attention.

_____ 197. I often find myself saying, "I don't feel up to it."

_____ 198. I tell lies in order to appear more important than I feel.

_____ 199. I feel like an impostor, even when things are going well for me.

_____ 200. I often give up easily on things.

_____ 201. I look for the positive in a situation.

_____ 202. I am someone with initiative.

_____ 203. I often feel tense and nervous inside.

_____ 204. I often have trouble concentrating or trouble with my memory.

_____ 205. I feel guilty about my alcohol or drug consumption.

_____ 206. I have difficulty completing projects. I start many things I don't finish.

_____ 207. I focus my energy on the things that are important to me.

_____ 208. I am honest in my dealings with others.

_____ 209. I am on good terms with myself.

_____ 210. When I establish a clear goal for myself, I will continue to fight for it during difficult times.

_____ 211. I have a tendency to take innocuous events too personally.

_____ 212. When something good happens in my life (promotion, new relationship, etc.) I often respond by getting depressed or doing something to ruin the feeling.

_____ 213. I am an anxious person who often anticipates the worst.

_____ 214. My mood is most often sad, blue, or depressed.

_____ 215. In my heart I worry that I may have a problem with drugs or alcohol.

_____ 216. I am easily distracted and often find my mind wandering.

_____ 217. It seems that things build up because I just feel too tired to get to them.

_____ 218. I spend time covering up lies.

_____ 219. I often wish that I were someone else.

_____ 220. It is too difficult to follow through on the dreams I have for myself.

_____ 221. I am careful to avoid labeling myself or others with derogatory terms, such as jerk, idiot, bitch, etc.

_____ 222. I have a clear sense of purpose in my life.

_____ 223. It seems that fears dominate my life.

_____ 224. I often find myself feeling lonely or isolated, or withdrawing from others.

_____ 225. My spouse, parent, or significant other worries or complains about my use of drugs or alcohol.

_____ 226. I have trouble maintaining an organized work/living area.

_____ 227. Whenever possible I maximize my energy cycle. That is, if I am a night person, I do the things that are important to me at night.

_____ 228. I am able to match my words and beliefs with my actions.

_____ 229. I feel that people usually have a good time when they are with me.

_____ 230. I continue to work on my dreams, even though reaching them might be years away.

_____ 231. I am often bothered by guilt.

_____ 232. Guilt is a major motivator of my behavior.

_____ 233. I experience panic attacks with my heart racing, chest pain, muscle tension, shortness of breath, and sweating, feeling a need to leave the situation or I'll go crazy.

_____ 234. I feel worthless, hopeless, or bothered by feelings of guilt.

_____ 235. I need alcohol or non-prescribed mood-altering drugs to function.

_____ 236. I often lack close attention to detail.

_____ 237. I perform many important tasks when I am tired.

_____ 238. I often lack a solid sense of integrity.

_____ 239. My self-confidence is very low.

_____ 240. The fear of failure often causes me to quit soon after I start things that are important to me.

_____ 241. I am careful to avoid jumping to conclusions without adequate information.

_____ 242. I am able to go after what I want instead of just daydreaming about it.

_____ 243. I become anxious if I don't do certain things in very specific ways (food preparation, washing, dressing, etc.)

_____ 244. I feel tired most of the time.

_____ 245. There have been several times that I blacked out after using drugs or alcohol.

_____ 246. I often act impulsively or without thinking.

_____ 247. I am an energetic person.

_____ 248. I live up to my commitments.

_____ 249. I feel that I am a very competent person.

_____ 250. I see projects and promises through to the end.

_____ 251. I have a tendency to overgeneralize (i.e., if someone turns me down for a job, I think that no one will ever hire me).

_____ 252. I feel that I often need someone else to push me to do the things that are in my best interest.

_____ 253. Anxiety often paralyzes me from adequately preparing for my tasks. For example, if I have to give a speech, my anxiety about it would prevent me from practicing it beforehand.

_____ 254. I have difficulty falling asleep, or I wake up in the middle of the night and am unable to go back to sleep.

_____ 255. I have experienced physical problems caused by drinking alcohol or using drugs (e.g., accidents, or memory difficulties).

_____ 256. I often feel restless or fidgety.

_____ 257. I feel blocked or slowed down in getting things done.

_____ 258. I do not live up to my own beliefs.

_____ 259. All of us have inner voices that run a dialogue on how we feel about ourselves. My inner voices sound more like a critics' committee than a cheering section.

_____ 260. I start many things that prove too difficult to finish.

_____ 261. I check out my feelings before I act on them.

_____ 262. I most often work in the best interest of the goals that I have set for myself.

_____ 263. I often feel scared for no apparent reason, and subsequently have trouble catching my breath.

_____ 264. I have recurrent thoughts of hurting myself.

_____ 265. I drink alcohol or use prescription or non-prescription drugs frequently to get to sleep.

_____ 266. I'm impatient and easily frustrated.

_____ 267. I have the energy to accomplish my goals.

_____ 268. I teach others that I am trustworthy by my actions.

_____ 269. I have the internal OK to be who I want to be.

_____ 270. I would describe myself as someone with stamina.

_____ 271. I have a tendency to think in terms of black or white.

_____ 272. Often, I have to be motivated by other people.

_____ **273.** I avoid what most people would consider normal things, places, or activities because they frighten me (e.g., plane flights, driving, crowds, open spaces).

_____ **274.** I get little pleasure out of activities I used to enjoy.

_____ **275.** If I stop drinking alcohol or using drugs now, I may experience withdrawal symptoms.

_____ **276.** I often make comments without considering their impact on others.

_____ **277.** I have little energy to get through the day.

_____ **278.** I'm often more dishonest than I'd like to be.

_____ **279.** I feel that I get pushed around more than others.

_____ **280.** Self-help programs have not worked for me because I have failed to follow through with them.

_____ **281.** I am able to perceive when someone's difficult behavior is not personally directed at me.

_____ **282.** I am motivated to do more than just get by; I want to be everything I can.

_____ **283.** I am often bothered by recurrent and repetitive thoughts intruding in my mind.

_____ **284.** There has been a marked increase or decrease in my appetite that is not related to a weight-loss diet.

_____ **285.** One definition of an alcohol or drug abuser is someone who has gotten into trouble because of alcohol or drugs and then continues to use these substances. They didn't learn from the previous experience. That definition fits me.

_____ **286.** Unless I really concentrate on it, my handwriting is very messy.

_____ **287.** I have a bounce in my step.

_____ **288.** I am able to be honest with those closest to me.

_____ **289.** I believe that I can have a positive impact on others.

_____ **290.** I refuse to use excuses to quit.

_____ **291.** I grew up in a home where alcohol and drugs were abused, and subsequently I have found that I have trouble trusting people, expressing myself, or talking about my feelings. Growing up in that environment had a significant impact on me.

Perceiving the World Through Dark Glasses: STINKING THINKING

A. Add up your answers to questions
201, 221, 241, 261, and 281 and place your answer here: _____

B. Add up your answers to questions
191, 211, 231, 251, and 271 and place your answer here: _____

C. Subtract the smaller number from the larger number
and place your answer here: _____
If A is greater than B place a + sign in front of the answer.
If B is greater than A place a − sign in front of the answer.

Place your score on Line 20, "Perception," on the Sabotage Versus Success Profile Sheet, page 130.

Unsuccessful people often display negative thought patterns, or what many therapists call "stinking thinking." They do this by making situations or people out to be worse than they really are. The last twenty years have seen the development of cognitive psychotherapy, which emphasizes correcting these cognitive (thought) distortions. Research shows that these distortions contribute to some types of serious depression and anxiety disorders.

Every time you have a thought your brain releases chemicals that help electrical transmissions cross through your brain, so you become aware of what you're thinking. These brain chemicals influence every part of your body. Whenever you have an angry thought, a hopeless thought, a depressing thought or a frightening thought, your brain releases a certain set of chemicals that cause your whole body to react and feel bad. Think about the last time you were really angry. What happened in your body? If you're like most people you probably noticed that your muscles become tighter, your breathing rate increased, your hands began to sweat and become colder and your heart rate increased. This is the operating principal behind polygraphs or lie detector tests: your body reacts to what you think.

On the other hand, every time you have a positive thought, a happy thought, a hopeful thought or a successful thought, your brain releases a set of chemicals that cause your body to feel more relaxed and settled. What you think has a huge impact on how you feel! It's critical not to just accept what you think. Recognize the thoughts that go through your head and correct them when they are distorted or replace them with positive thoughts when they are negative. You are what you think!

Here are ten types of common "thought" distortions in which the situation is made out to be worse than it really is. Check those on the list that apply to you.

1. *Black-or-white thinking:* Everything is all good or all bad. "If I make the sale, I'm the best salesman in the world. If I don't make it, then I am no good." Thinking is in absolute terms: "She either loves me or she hates me. There is nothing in between."

2. *Overgeneralizations:* One event is viewed as something that will always repeat itself. I have a friend who asked a girl out in college. She turned him down. Later that night he told me that no one would ever go out with him again. What a negative thought! Because of that powerfully negative thought he did not ask anyone else out for the rest of the year. People who use overgeneralizations think that just because something happened once, it is bound to happen over and over again. "My boss got mad at me today. Why does everyone treat me like a doormat?" Whenever you find yourself thinking in words such as always, everyone, never, every time, you are overgeneralizing.

3. *Negative filter:* Everything is filtered through negativeness: only the bad in situations is focused on. I once had a patient who had recently moved to the area. She had 80 percent of her household put away from the move. She didn't focus on that, however. The only part she could think about was the 20 percent that wasn't put away. She told me that she was 100 percent inadequate, 100 percent inferior, and 100 percent disorganized. Even though she was caring for three small children, she could only see what she hadn't done rather than what she had done.

4. *Disregarding the positive:* Any successes or positive experiences are discounted, given over to chance or gained "because someone else helped out." I once treated a very bright woman who returned to college after many years. She worked very hard to get an A in statistics. When I congratulated her she downplayed the A, saying that anyone could have done it. I asked her how many people were in her class. She said forty. I then asked her how many people had earned As. She answered four. Then a light went on for her. She said, "I see what you're saying: maybe not everyone could have done it. I need to appreciate the good things about myself, not discount them."

5. *Fortune Telling:* This is where you arbitrarily predict things will turn our badly even though you have no definite evidence. I once had a patient, Bill, who saw his urologist because of back pain. The urologist wanted him to have an IVP, a kidney X ray. Bill's thoughts were as follows: "I have to have this X ray. The doctor is going to find out I have cancer. I'm then going to have chemotherapy. Be in a tremendous amount of pain. Lose all my hair. Vomit my guts out. And then I'll die." In the span of less than 30 seconds, in Bill's head, he went from X ray to coffin predicting the worst pain and torture. Bill then had a panic attack. I actually went with him to help calm him during the X ray. He had kidney stones, which, although painful, would not kill him or require chemotherapy. Unless you're a contract lawyer there is no good reason to focus on predicting the worst.

6. *Mind reading:* Similar to fortune telling, this is where you arbitrarily predict what another person is thinking before you have checked it out. Even after couples or working partners have known each other for twenty or thirty years they still cannot read each other's minds. This is an emotionally dangerous practice because if you are feeling bad, you have a tendency to assume others feel negative toward you as well. I once knew a minister who told me, "Someone fell asleep during my sermon. I must be a boring speaker." (The person who fell asleep was an intern who had been kept awake all of the previous night.)

7. *Thinking with your feelings:* Assuming the way you feel about something is really how it is. "I feel bad, therefore, I am bad." Feelings, which are based on very complex information from the past and the present, can sometimes lie. In a stressful situation with the boss you might feel unappreciated, but that may have nothing to do with how he really feels about you. He might just be overwhelmed and too busy to verbalize his feelings.

8. *Guilt reasoning:* Motivation comes from moral beatings. "I should have done that. I ought to do this. I mustn't think like that ever again." Canadian psychologist Albert Ellis calls this type of thinking "Musterbation." This moral reasoning generates a significant amount of unnecessary emotional turbulence that holds you back from achieving the goals you want.

9. *Labeling:* Attaching negative descriptions to certain behaviors. "I didn't make the sale. I'm a loser." "She wouldn't make love with me last night. She's frigid." (Or if it was your first date and she did make love with you: "She must be loose.") Whenever you label yourself or someone else with a negative term, you inhibit your ability to take a realistic look at the situation. For example, whenever you call someone a jerk, you lump him with all the people in your life who you've labeled as jerks and you become unable to deal rationally with him.

10. *Personalization:* Innocuous events are taken to have personal meaning. "The boss didn't talk to me today. He must be mad at me." Or, one feels he or she is the cause of all the bad things that happen, "He died while I was nurse on duty. It must be my fault." An extremely important rule I teach my patients (and children) is the 13/40/60 Rule, which says: when you're 13 you worry about what everyone is thinking about you (remember eighth grade); when you're 40 you don't give a damn what anyone thinks of you; and when you're 60 you realize that no one has been thinking about you at all. Don't spend a lot of time worrying about what they think of you, they are probably thinking of their own troubles.

Recognizing these distorted thought patterns is the first step to overcoming them and getting a more accurate picture of your situation. In Section Four I'll teach you how to specifically overcome these negative thought patterns. Your thoughts may be holding you back. Fight them when they are out of line.

Feels Guilty About Success: UNMOTIVATED TO SUCCEED

A. Add up your answers to questions
202, 222, 242, 262, and 282 and place your answer here:_____

B. Add up your answers to questions
192, 212, 232, 252, and 272 and place your answer here:_____

C. Subtract the smaller number from the larger
number and place your answer here: _____
If A is greater than B place a + sign in front of the answer.
If B is greater than A place a − sign in front of the answer.

Place your score on Line 21, "Motivation," on the Sabotage Versus
Success Profile Sheet, page 130.

Believe it or not, many people are actually afraid of success, or at
least they act that way. Before I treated several patients like this I
thought, "You must be kidding. Who fears success? That is what we
all want."

My thinking has changed through the years as I have seen people
get close to success, only to sabotage their efforts. I knew an intern
who went through eleven and a half months of the most strenuous
year of our lives, then quit with two weeks to go. I also knew a
psychology student who had only to finish her dissertation to
graduate with a Ph.D. She couldn't do it in the seven years I knew
her. And then there was a lawyer I treated whose dream it was to
head a large law firm. Within two weeks of being promoted to the
position, however, he was caught stealing sixty cents from the office
coffee fund and was voted out of his job.

As far as I can tell, Freud was the first to write about those
"wrecked by success." He described the surprising and even
"bewildering" discovery that people occasionally fall ill precisely at
the time they reach their goals. He writes, "It seems as though they
could not endure their bliss."

Many others have written about those who have a fear of success
or feel guilty if they near it. There are several underlying reasons for
the fear of success:

1. "I do not deserve success. I am bad inside."
2. "Winning makes me feel guilty. So I won't win."

3. "Winning is dangerous. So why try?"
4. "If I'm too successful, others won't want to have anything to do with me."

The most basic reason people fear success is that they feel they don't deserve it. If it comes within their reach, they begin to feel guilty and find ways to sabotage it. Where do these thoughts come from? Since they are obviously not rational thoughts—everyone deserves success, after all—they must come from a time before we can remember: our early childhood.

As children between the ages of two to five, we thought in magical terms. We thought of ourselves as the center of the world. Anyone with young children knows how they think they can control the world, as evidenced by their play. If something good happens in the family, they think it is because of them, and they feel pride. If something bad happens, they think it is also because of them, and they feel guilt. And if something terribly bad happens, a child may carry around the guilt for that event for the rest of his life.

Julie carried around a sense of never being good enough, despite being a competent and dedicated nurse on a surgery ward. When she was promoted to chief nurse, she became suicidally depressed. Through therapy, it was learned that her mother had become an alcoholic when Julie was about three years old. Julie had always felt that if only she were a better daughter, her mother wouldn't drink; she felt she was the cause of her mother's problems and that therefore she didn't deserve anything good in life. If something good came along, such as the promotion, she had to punish herself or get rid of it (she had been married three times).

The second reason people fear and sabotage success is that it reminds them of early "dangerous" struggles with important people, such as parents or siblings.

Another reason people fear success is that they are afraid of becoming the object of hostility, jealousy, or envy of others. These in fact are the very feelings they themselves have for the successful.

Envy and jealousy are two of the most powerful human emotions—emotions that we are all capable of possessing and fearing. We have all, at one time or another, been the object of someone's envy or jealousy, and it was probably a very uncomfortable experience, especially if the opinion of others is too important to us. Fearing others' reaction to success keeps many people from trying to attain it.

Bill was a welder for a foundry. After twenty years he was promoted to shop foreman. Shortly after that he became very depressed. He loved working among his friends and doing things with them after work, but as shop foreman he would be the boss, inviting hostility from these same people. He felt very isolated and was subsequently depressed. After Bill's boss figured this out, he returned Bill to his former job, where almost immediately Bill's mood returned to its pre-promotion level. Success for Bill was being with a group of friends.

In mestizo villages in Colombia, the townspeople habitually make a pretense of being poor, ill, and downtrodden in order to avoid being thought enviable. In the effort to avoid the evil eye of envy in relation to children, Tzintzuntzan women bind their abdomens tightly for as long as possible during pregnancy. Once exposed as pregnant, they refer to the condition in terms of illness and as one not to be envied.

In the United States, there is an emphasis on modesty in receiving compliments. One doesn't want to appear too successful. If one person attains too much success others often wish to see him fall back to the ranks of the average.

The revised Diagnostic and Statistical Manual of Mental Disorders (DSM IIIR) published by the American Psychiatric Association in 1987 proposed a new diagnostic category that is very similar to these fear-of-success characteristics: the "Self-Defeating Personality Disorder." The major features of this disorder include a pervasive pattern of self-defeating behavior beginning early in adulthood. The individual avoids or undermines enjoyable experiences and is drawn into situations or relationships in which he is likely to suffer, and in which he prevents others from helping him. Here is a list of the hallmarks of this disorder (at least five are required to make the diagnosis):

1. Chooses persons and situations that lead to his failure, or disappointment, or mistreatment, even when better options are clearly available.

2. Incites angry rejecting responses from others and then feels hurt, defeated, or humiliated (for example, makes fun of spouse in public, provoking an angry counterattack, then feels devastated).

3. Is bored with or uninterested in people who consistently treat him well; for example, is unattracted to caring sexual partners.

4. Turns down opportunities for pleasure and is reluctant to acknowledge enjoying himself (despite having adequate social skills and the capacity for pleasure).

5. Fails to accomplish tasks crucial to his personal objectives despite demonstrated ability to do so; for example, helps fellow students write papers, but is unable to write his own.

6. Following positive personal events (for example, new achievement) responds with depression, guilt, or a behavior that brings about pain (for example, an accident).

7. Engages in excessive self-sacrifice that is unsolicited and discouraged by the intended recipient of the sacrifice.

8. Rejects or renders ineffective the attempts of others to help him.

The fear of success, from whatever cause, may have been realistic in its origins. It is not, however, realistic in its maintenance. Overcoming the guilt and fear associated with success is a major goal of this book.

The Chains of Emotional Disorders: ANXIETY, DEPRESSION, ALCOHOL/DRUG ABUSE, ATTENTION DEFICIT DISORDER

I once had a phone call from a very close friend whom I hadn't heard from in years. He sounded different. When we had lived close together he had been energetic, positive, outgoing, funny, and fascinated by the world around him. As I listened to him on the phone, however, his voice was flat and his thoughts were very negative. He told me his life had no meaning and he would much rather "see heaven" than struggle through any more days. My friend was sleeping a lot, had problems concentrating and even had lost interest in sex, which was a real change for him. He suffered from a clinical depression. He was the last person in the world with whom I expected to be having that kind of conversation.

But, mental illness is extremely common. A recent study by the National Institute of Mental Health demonstrated that 23 percent of the population will suffer from a mental illness during some point of their life. Anxiety problems, depression, and alcohol or drug abuse are the most common problems. Mental illnesses strike the rich and the poor, the successful and the not so successful. They devastate individuals and families, and they most often go untreated because of the stigma our society attaches to them. My friend had postponed calling me for more than nine months. It was not until his wife threatened to divorce him that he called me.

Many uninformed people have the erroneous idea that people with emotional illnesses are strange, scary or way out. It is true that some people with mental illnesses have delusions or are violent, but the vast majority of people who suffer from anxiety, depression, or drug use are more like you and me than they are different.

If you or someone you know has persistent symptoms, it's important to have a psychiatric evaluation by a competent professional. Too often, because of the stigma, it takes a broken marriage, a job loss or a life at the brink of suicide before a person seeks help. Our society needs to think of emotional problems the same way as we think of medical problems and teach people to seek help for them much like we would do if we found blood in our urine.

Here are the five most common psychiatric illnesses that I see in my office. When left untreated, they seriously undermine a person's ability to achieve. These include anxiety disorders, depression, alcohol and drug abuse, growing up in an alcoholic or dysfunctional family, and attention deficit disorder.

The Paralysis of Fear: ANXIETY DISORDERS

A. Add up your answers to questions
193, 203, 213, 223, 233, 243, 253, 263, 273, and 283
and place your answer here with a $(-)$ sign in front: _____

Place your score on Line 22a, "Anxiety," on the Sabotage Versus Success Profile Sheet, page 130.

There are four common types of anxiety disorders that hold people back from their goals: panic disorders, agoraphobia, obsessive-compulsive disorders and post-traumatic stress disorders. I'll briefly discuss each of these so that if you recognize symptoms in yourself, you can get further information.

PANIC DISORDER

All of a sudden your heart starts to pound. You get this feeling of incredible dread. Your breathing rate gets faster. You start to sweat.

Your muscles get tight. And your hands feel like ice. Your mind starts to race about every terrible thing that could possibly happen and you feel as though you're going to lose your mind if you don't get out of the situation. You've just had a panic attack.

Panic attacks are one of the most common psychiatric symptoms. It is estimated that six to seven percent of adults will at some point in their lives suffer from recurrent panic attacks. They often begin in late adolescence or early adulthood but may spontaneously occur late in life. If a person has three attacks in a three week period, psychiatrists make a diagnosis of panic disorder.

In a typical panic attack a person has at least four of the following twelve symptoms: shortness of breath, heart pounding, chest pain, choking or smothering feelings, dizziness, tingling of hands or feet, feeling unreal, hot or cold flashes, sweating, faintness, trembling or shaking, and a fear of dying or going crazy. Many people, when their panic attacks first start, end up in the emergency room because they think they're having a heart attack. Some people even end up being admitted to the hospital.

Anticipation anxiety is one of the most difficult symptoms for a person who has a panic disorder. These people are often extremely skilled at predicting the worst in situations. In fact, it is often the anticipation of a bad event that brings on a panic attack. For example, you are in the grocery store and worry that you're going to have an anxiety attack and pass out on the floor. Then, you predict, everyone in the store will look at you and laugh. Well, pretty quickly the symptoms begin. Sometimes a panic disorder can become so severe that a person begins to avoid almost any situation outside of his home—a condition called agoraphobia.

Panic attacks can occur for a variety of reasons. Sometimes they are caused by medical illnesses, such as hyperthyroidism (so it's always important to have a physical examination and screening blood work). Sometimes panic attacks can be brought on by excessive caffeine intake or alcohol withdrawal. Hormonal changes also seem to play a role. Panic attacks in women are seen more frequently at the end of their menstrual cycle, after having a baby, or during menopause. Traumatic events from the past that somehow are unconsciously triggered can also precipitate a series of attacks. Commonly, there is a family history of panic attacks, alcohol abuse, or other mental illnesses.

AGORAPHOBIA

Agoraphobia is a greek word meaning "fear of the marketplace." In psychiatric terms, agoraphobia is the fear of being alone in public places. The underlying worry is that the person will lose control or become incapacitated and no one will be there to help.

People afflicted with this phobia begin to avoid being in crowds, in stores or on busy streets. They're often afraid of being in tunnels, on bridges, in elevators or on public transportation. They usually insist that a family member or a friend accompany them when they leave home. If the fear establishes a foothold in the person, it may affect his or her whole life. Normal activities become increasingly restricted as the fears or avoidance behaviors dominate the victim's life.

Agoraphobic symptoms often begin in the late teen years or early twenties, but I've seen them start when a person is in his or her fifties or sixties. Often without knowing what's wrong people will try to medicate themselves with excessive amounts of alcohol or drugs. This illness occurs more frequently in women, and many who have it experienced significant separation anxiety as children. Additionally, there may be a history of excessive anxiety, panic attacks, depression or alcohol abuse among their relatives.

Agoraphobia often evolves out of panic attacks that seem to occur "out of the blue," for no apparent reason. These attacks are so frightening that the agoraphobic begins to avoid any situation that may be in any way associated with the fear. I think these initial panic attacks are often triggered by unconscious events or anxieties from the past. For example, I once treated a patient who had been raped as a teenager in a park late at night. When she was twenty-eight, she had her first panic attack while walking late at night in a park with her husband. It was the park setting late at night that she associated with the fear of being raped and that triggered the panic attack.

Agoraphobia is a very frightening illness to the patient and his or her family. With effective, early intervention, however, there is significant hope for recovery.

OBSESSIVE-COMPULSIVE DISORDER

This disorder, almost without exception, dramatically impairs a person's functioning and often affects the whole family. The hallmarks of this disorder are recurrent thoughts that seem outside a person's control, or compulsive behaviors that a person knows make no sense but feels compelled to do anyway. The obsessive thoughts may involve violence (such as killing one's child), contamination (such as becoming infected by shaking hands), or doubt (such as believing to have hurt someone in a traffic accident, even though no such accident occurred). Many efforts are made to suppress or resist these thoughts, but the more a person tries to control them the more powerful they become.

The most common compulsions involve hand-washing, counting, checking, and touching. These behaviors are often performed according to certain rules in a very strict or rigid manner. For example, a person with a counting compulsion may feel the need to count every crack on the pavement on his way to work or school. What would be a five-minute walk for most people could turn into a three- or four-hour trip for the person with Obsessive-Compulsive Disorder (OCD). He has an urgent sense of "I have to do it" inside. A part of the individual generally recognizes the senselessness of the behavior and doesn't get pleasure from carrying it out, although doing it often provides a release of tension.

Over the years, I've treated a number of people with OCD, the youngest of whom was five years old. He had a checking compulsion and had to check the house locks at night as many as twenty to thirty times before he could fall asleep. The oldest person I have treated with this disorder was eighty-three. She had obsessive, sexual thoughts that made her feel dirty inside. It got to the point where she would lock all her doors, draw all the window shades, turn off the lights, take the phone off the hook and sit in the middle of a dark room trying to catch the abhorrent sexual thoughts as they came into her mind.

If you have symptoms of OCD or know someone who does, it's important to seek early treatment. The longer this illness continues the more entrenched it becomes and the harder it is to treat.

POST-TRAUMATIC STRESS DISORDER

Joanne, a thirty-four-year-old travel agent, was held up in her office at gunpoint by two men. Four or five times during the robbery one of the men held a gun to her head and said he was going to kill her. She graphically imagined her brain being splattered with blood against the wall. Near the end of this fifteen-minute ordeal they made her take off all her clothes. She pictured herself being brutally raped by them, but they did not in fact rape her.

Since that time her life has been in turmoil. She always feels tense. She has flashbacks and nightmares of the robbery. Her stomach is in knots and she has a constant headache. Whenever she goes out she feels panicky. She is frustrated that she cannot calm her body: her heart races, she is short of breath and her hands are cold and sweaty. She hates how she feels and she's angry about how her nice life has turned into a nightmare. What is most upsetting is that the robbery has affected her marriage and her child. Her baby has picked up her tension and is now often fussy. Every time she tries to make love with her husband she begins to cry and gets flashbacks of the men raping her.

Joanne is experiencing symptoms of Post-Traumatic Stress Disorder (PTSD). PTSD is a psychological reaction to severe traumatic events such as a robbery, rape, car accident, earthquake, tornado, or even a volcanic eruption. Her symptoms are classic for PTSD, especially the flashbacks and nightmares of the event.

Perhaps the worst symptoms, however, come from the horrible thoughts about what never happened, such as seeing her brain splattered against the wall and being raped. These thoughts were registered in her subconscious as fact, and until she entered treatment she was not able to recognize how much damage they had been doing to her. For example, when she imagined that she was being raped, a part of her began to believe that she actually was raped. The first time she had her period after the robbery she began to cry because she was relieved she was not pregnant by robbers, even though they never touched her. A part of her even believed she was dead because she had so vividly pictured her own death.

A significant portion of her treatment was geared to counteract these erroneous subconscious conclusions. This included hypnotic exercises, in which she repeated over and over to herself that she was indeed alive and had not been raped. She focused on how fortunate she was to have escaped these horrible events and on the fact that she could continue to enjoy her husband and watch her daughter grow up.

Post-Traumatic Stress Disorder has a serious effect on a person's life and certainly holds one back from one's goals. In Joanne's case she was unable to make love with her husband, she was an emotional wreck and she was unable to work. Getting treatment is essential for recovery.

Feeling Lost in the Hole of Depression

A. Add up your answers to questions
194, 204, 214, 224, 234, 244, 254, 264, 274, and 284
and place your answer here with a (−) sign in front: _____

Place your score on Line 22b, "Depression," on the Sabotage Versus
Success Profile Sheet, page 131.

Janet, a forty-two-year-old lawyer, wife, and mother of three, was
referred to me because she was tired all the time. Her family
physician ruled out the physical causes of fatigue and thought she
was overstressed. Additionally, she had trouble concentrating at
work and experienced difficulty sleeping. Her sex drive was gone,
her appetite was poor and she had no interest in doing things with
her family. Janet would start to cry for no apparent reason and she
even began to entertain desperate suicidal thoughts. Janet had a
serious depressive illness.

Depression is a very common mental illness. Studies reveal that
at any point in time, three to six percent of the population have a
significant depression. Only twenty to twenty-five percent of these
people ever seek help. This is unfortunate because depression is a
very treatable problem.

The following is a list of symptoms commonly associated with
depression:

• sad, blue or gloomy mood
• low energy, frequent fatigue
• lack of ability to feel pleasure in usually enjoyable activities
• irritability
• poor concentration, distractibility, poor memory
• suicidal thoughts, feelings of meaninglessness
• feelings of hopelessness, helplessness, guilt and worthlessness
• changes in sleep, either poor sleep with frequent awakenings or
  increased sleep
• changes in appetite, either marked decrease or increase
• social withdrawal
• low self-esteem

Whenever I evaluate a new patient who has depressive symptoms such as Janet's, I take a bio/psycho/social approach. That means I look at the biological, psychological, and social causes of depression.

There are several important **biological factors** to look for in depression:

- It's necessary to look at the **family history.** We know there is often a genetic link to depression and it commonly runs in families where there is alcohol abuse.
- It's also important to evaluate patients from a **medical** point of view, as there are a number of illnesses that can cause depression. These include thyroid disease, infectious illnesses, cancer, and certain forms of anemia. A heart attack or stroke can also leave a person vulnerable to depression. Periods of dramatic hormonal shifts (postpartum or menopausal) often precipitate problems with depression.
- Additionally, certain **medications** can cause depression. Most notable among these are birth control pills, certain blood pressure or cardiac medications, steroids, and chronic pain control medicines.
- In evaluating depression it's essential to take a good **alcohol and drug abuse** history. Chronic alcohol or marijuana use often causes depression, while amphetamine or cocaine withdrawal is often accompanied by serious suicidal thoughts.

The **psychological factors** to look for in depression include:

- major losses, such as the death of a loved one, breakup of a romantic relationship, loss of a job, self-esteem, status, health, or purpose.
- multiple childhood traumas, such as physical or sexual abuse.
- negative thinking that erodes self-esteem and drives mood down.
- learned helplessness, the belief that no matter what you do things won't change. This comes from being exposed to environments in which you are continually frustrated from reaching your goals.

The **social factors** or current life stresses to evaluate in depression include:

- marital problems,
- family dysfunction,
- financial difficulties, and
- work-related problems.

In Janet's case, her physical examination was normal, but her father had periods of depression and her uncle had killed himself. Her psychological evaluation revealed that she had a very critical mother and subsequently she was extremely self-critical. In the social category, her marriage had been difficult for the past several years and she was often fighting with her teenage son.

The best results in treating any emotional illness occur with a bio/psycho/social approach. Janet was placed on antidepressant medication and learned to be significantly less critical of herself. In ten weeks she felt more energetic and was able to concentrate. Her mood was good. She slept well and her appetite returned.

Depression is a very treatable illness. Early detection and treatment from a bio/psycho/social perspective is important for a full and complete recovery.

An Altered Brain: DRUG AND ALCOHOL ABUSE

Drunkenness is nothing more than voluntary madness.
—SENECA
When the drug trip or alcohol binge is over the problems will have remained the same or have gotten worse.
—A RECOVERED SIXTEEN-YEAR-OLD MALE

A. Add up your answers to questions
195, 205, 215, 225, 235, 245, 255, 265, 275, and 285
and place your answer here with a (−) sign in front: _____

Place your score on Line 22c, "Drug and Alcohol Abuse," on the Sabotage Versus Success Profile Sheet, page 131.

Drug or alcohol abuse is a clear way many people hold themselves back from reaching their goals. All mind-altering drugs have an effect on the brain and in many cases it can be a permanent effect. Drug abuse often has a serious impact on relationships, work, and health. In relationships, many people complain that their partner who is abusing these substances is emotional, erratic, selfish, and unpredictable. It is very common in my practice to see relationships break up because of alcohol and drug abuse. The list of health problems from alcohol and drugs fills volumes of books. Suffice it to say that many of these substances are poison to your system, and using them amounts to voluntary self-destruction. The most common problems in the workplace include erratic job performance, absenteeism, tardiness, work accidents, and decreased job performance.

I have never seen the use of denial stronger than in alcohol- or drug-related problems. The person with the problem is usually the last one to recognize that a problem exists. Alcohol- and drug-related problems are similar in many ways. I have chosen to lump these two groups together for simplicity.

Note: Alcohol means any beverage or medication that contains any alcohol—from beer to wine to hard liquor, or even some cough preparations; drugs mean any mind-altering substances that produce stimulant, depressant, or euphoric effects—amphetamines, barbiturates, marijuana, cocaine, heroin, PCP, and so on.

Go through the following list of symptoms of excessive alcohol or drug use and check off those that apply to you. This will give you an idea if this area is a problem for you or someone you know.

1. Increasing consumption of alcohol or drugs, whether on a regular or sporadic basis, with frequent and perhaps unintended episodes of intoxication.

2. Use of drugs or alcohol as a means of handling problems.

3. Obvious preoccupation with alcohol or drugs and the expressed need to have them.

4. Gulping of drinks or using large quantities of drugs.

5. The need for increasing quantities of alcohol or the drug to obtain the same "buzz."

6. Tendency toward making alibis and weak excuses for drinking or drug use.

7. Needing to have others cover for you, either at work or at home.

8. Refusal to concede what is obviously excessive consumption and expressing annoyance when the subject is mentioned.

9. Frequent absenteeism from the job, especially if occurring in a pattern, such as following weekends and holidays (Monday morning "flu").

10. Repeated changes in jobs, particularly if to successively lower levels, or employment in a capacity beneath ability, education, and background.

11. Shabby appearance, poor hygiene, and behavior and social adjustment inconsistent with previous levels or expectations.

12. Persistent vague body complaints without apparent cause, particularly those of trouble sleeping, abdominal problems, headaches, or loss of appetite.

13. Multiple contacts with the health care system.

14. Persistent marital problems, perhaps multiple marriages.

15. History of arrests for intoxicated driving or disorderly conduct.

16. Unusual anxiety or obvious moodiness.

17. Withdrawal symptoms on stopping (tremors, feeling extremely anxious, craving drugs or alcohol, vomiting, etc.); most alcoholics or drug abusers who seek treatment have tried to stop many times but have been unable to withstand the symptoms of withdrawal.

18. Hearing voices or seeing things that aren't there is not uncommon.

19. Blackouts (times you cannot remember).

20. Memory impairment.

21. Drinking or using drugs alone; early morning use; secretive use.

22. *Denial* in the face of an obvious problem.

My definition of an alcoholic or drug addict is anyone who has gotten into trouble (legal, relational, health, or work-related) while drinking or using drugs, yet who continues to use them. They did not learn from the previous experience. A rational person would realize that he or she has trouble handling the alcohol or drugs and would stay away from them. The alcoholic or drug abuser denies any problem exists and continues to use these substances.

Unfortunately, many people with these problems have to experience repeated failures because of the substance use, and thus hit "rock bottom," before treatment is sought.

There has been a very helpful trend in medicine over the last ten years to classify alcoholism and excessive drug use as illnesses, instead of morally weak behaviors. The American Medical Association, the World Health Organization, and many other professional groups regard these as specific disease entities. Untreated, these diseases progress to serious physical complications that often lead to death.

Here are some important facts you need to know about alcohol and drug abuse:

1. These addictions often run in families. The more relatives a person has who are alcoholics or addicts, the more likely he or she is to be or to become dependent on these chemicals.

2. Alcoholism or drug addiction shortens life expectancy by an estimated ten to fifteen years.

3. Alcoholism and drug addictions occur in about fifteen million Americans. If this problem applies to you, you are not alone.

4. There is no typical person with alcoholism or drug addictions. These diseases affect people in all socioeconomic classes.

5. Drunken driving or driving under the influence of drugs is responsible for well over fifty percent of the highway traffic fatalities.

6. Alcoholism and drug addictions are treatable. Treatment for alcohol or drug abusers and their families is widely available today in all parts of the country.

The Impact of Growing Up in an Alcoholic or Drug-Abusing Home

A. Place your answer to question 291 here
with a $(-)$ sign in front: _____

Place your score on Line 22d, "Adult Child of Alcoholic/Drug Abuser," on the Sabotage Versus Success Profile Sheet, page 131.

The pains of our childhood always haunt us, even if we've forgotten them, and even if it felt as though we were never a child.

Consider these facts:

- an estimated twenty-eight million Americans have at least one alcoholic parent.
- more than half of all alcoholics have an alcoholic parent.
- in up to ninety percent of child abuse cases, alcohol is a significant factor.
- children of alcoholics are also frequently victims of incest, child neglect, and other forms of violence and exploitation.
- the majority of people served by Employee Assistance Programs are adult children of alcoholics.
- children of alcoholics are prone to experience a range of psychological difficulties, including learning disabilities, anxiety, depression, attempted and completed suicides, eating disorders, and compulsive achieving.

Many people are held back from their goals by their early emotional programming. For those who grew up in an alcoholic or drug abusing family, the unpredictability and high level of emotional turmoil filled their minds with obstacles that they face all of their lives.

There is a good deal of current medical literature, backed up by clinical experience, to suggest that growing up in an alcoholic or drug-abusing environment has long-lasting and often devastating effects on how a person functions in the world. In my clinical practice, alcoholism or growing up in an alcoholic home is *the* most prevalent problem. That past environment seriously affects self-esteem, the ability to parent, and the ability to love.

For those who grew up in an alcoholic or drug abusing environment, consider the following generalizations and see if they apply to your life.

- Difficulty trusting others: the environment where one should learn trust was not trustworthy.
- Difficulty feeling strong emotions: denial of feelings. Denial is one of the major hallmarks of an alcoholic home: "After all, we don't talk about such things."
- Difficulty expressing feelings: will not talk. How could one talk about what happened at home? It was too embarrassing.

In essence, children who grow up in these homes:
    don't trust,

don't feel, and
don't talk.

Researchers have found that the following perceptions are often seen in children who have grown up in alcoholic homes. Circle those that apply to you.

1. guess at what normal behavior is

2. have difficulty following a project through from beginning to end

3. lie when it would be just as easy to tell the truth

4. judge themselves without mercy

5. have difficulty having fun

6. take themselves very seriously

7. have difficulty with intimate relationships

8. overreact to changes over which they have no control

9. constantly seek approval and affirmation

10. usually feel they are different from other people

11. are super-responsible or super-irresponsible

12. are extremely loyal even in the face of evidence that the loyalty is undeserved

13. are impulsive

14. feel that other people may be talking about them, which, growing up, may have been the case

15. have a sense of being inferior or damaged in some way

16. often feel that they are not important enough for others to want to talk to them

Certain other facts are also clear: Children of alcoholics tend to marry alcoholics. They rarely go into the marriage with the knowledge, but we see this phenomenon occur over and over again. They may have a suspicion or a thought that their fiancé drinks, but they overlook it. There is also a much higher incidence of depression in women who grew up in an alcoholic home.

Recognizing these tendencies common to adult children of alcoholics is the first step to changing the negative programming from the past.

Adult Attention Deficit Disorder

A. Add up your answers to questions
196, 206, 216, 226, 236, 246, 256, 266, 276, and 286
and place your answer here with a $(-)$ sign in front: _____

Place your score on Line 22e, "Adult Attention Deficit Disorder," on the Sabotage Versus Success Profile Sheet, page 131.

Do you often feel restless? Have trouble concentrating? Have trouble with impulsiveness, either doing or saying things you wish you hadn't? Do you fail to finish many projects you start? Are you easily bored or quick to anger? If the answer to most of these questions is yes, you might have the adult form of Attention Deficit Hyperactivity Disorder (ADHD), what used to be called hyperactivity in children.

ADHD is the most common psychiatric disorder in children, affecting three to five percent of all children, with boys having it three to five times more than girls. In the 1980s the name of this disorder was changed to Attention Deficit Hyperactivity Disorder because mental health professionals realized that there was more to this disorder than just hyperactivity. The main symptoms of ADHD are a short attention span, easy distractibility, impulsiveness and hyperactivity or restlessness. In fact, only about fifty percent of these children have the hyperactive part.

Until recently, most people thought that children outgrew this disorder during their teenage years. This is false. While it is true that hyperactivity lessens over time, the other symptoms of impulsivity, distractibility and a short attention span remain for most of these children into adulthood. Current research shows that sixty to eighty percent of these children never fully outgrow this disorder.

In my clinical practice I see many children who have Attention Deficit Hyperactivity Disorder. When I meet with their parents and take a good family history I find that there is about a forty percent chance that at least one of the parents also had symptoms of ADHD as a child and may, in fact, still be showing symptoms as an adult. Many of the parents were never diagnosed.

Not infrequently I learn of ADHD in adults when parents tell me that they have tried their child's medication and that they found it very helpful. They report that it helped them concentrate for longer periods of time, that they became more organized and were less impulsive.

Common symptoms of the adult form of ADHD include: poor organization and planning, procrastination, trouble listening carefully to directions, and excessive traffic violations. Additionally, people with adult ADHD are often late for appointments, frequently misplace things, may be quick to anger and have poor follow-through. There may also be frequent, impulsive job changes and poor financial management. Substance abuse, especially alcohol or amphetamines and cocaine, and low self-esteem are also common.

Many people do not recognize the seriousness of this disorder in children and just pass these kids off as defiant and willful. Yet, ADHD is a serious disorder. If left untreated, it affects a child's self-esteem, social relationships, and ability to learn. Several studies have shown that up to forty percent of these children are arrested by the time they reach age sixteen.

Many adults tell me that when they were children they were in trouble all the time and had a real sense that there was something very different about them. Even though many of the adults I treat with ADHD are very bright, they are frequently frustrated by not living up to their potential.

According to Russell Barkley, Ph.D., of the University of Massachusetts, in order to make the diagnosis of adult ADHD a person must have at least three of the following twelve symptoms (five or six symptoms makes this disorder very likely). These symptoms must not be part of another psychiatric disorder, such as substance abuse or depression, and they must have been present since childhood.

1. trouble sustaining attention

2. difficulty completing projects

3. easily overwhelmed by tasks of daily living

4. trouble maintaining an organized work/living area

5. inconsistent work performance

6. lacks attention to detail

7. makes decisions impulsively

8. difficulty delaying gratification, stimulation seeking

9. restless, fidgety

10. makes comments without considering their impact

11. impatient, easily frustrated

12. frequent traffic violations

Recently, it has become clear that ADHD is a neurological disorder with a biological basis. Metabolic brain studies reveal that when a person with ADHD tries to concentrate, the front part of the brain, which controls concentration levels, goes slower rather than faster. In a sense, the brain deactivates when the person tries to use it. Stimulant medication is the treatment of choice for this disorder, which makes sense because the brain is understimulated.

If you think that you or someone you love has adult ADHD, it's important to have a thorough evaluation by a psychiatrist, and if possible by a child psychiatrist because they have the most experience with this disorder. Many adult psychiatrists and family physicians have very little experience with adult ADHD.

There are usually three components to treating adult ADHD. The first component involves medication. Many adults respond to the same stimulants, such as Ritalin, that are prescribed for children. For those who don't or who have high levels of anxiety or depression, we often use an antidepressant, such as desipramine. But as with children, medication alone is never adequate treatment. Therefore, the second component includes relationship counseling and anger management, and the third involves time management and problem-solving skills.

With good treatment ADHD is a very treatable disorder in children or adults. Without treatment there are potentially serious consequences in a person's ability to work and to love. I believe this disorder is the underlying reason for a great many people sabotaging their lives.

"I'm Too Tired": LACKS ENERGY

A. Add up your answers to questions
   207, 227, 247, 267, and 287
   and place your answer here: _____

B. Add up your answers to questions
   197, 217, 237, 257, and 277
   and place your answer here: _____

C. Subtract the smaller number from the larger number
   and place your answer here: _____
   If A is greater than B place a + sign in front of the answer.
   If B is greater than A place a − sign in front of the answer.

Place your score on Line 23, "Energy," on the Sabotage Versus
Success Profile Sheet, page 131.

One of the major complaints of depressed people is that they have
no energy. They wake up feeling tired and often feel that they won't
be able to drag through the day. Their lack of vigor causes them to
get behind in their tasks and to isolate themselves from others. They
begin to withdraw into themselves, feeling hopeless and helpless.

I'm not trying to imply that all self-sabotaging people are depressed (although fifteen percent of the population will experience a
major depression in their lifetimes), but many people lack the
physical and emotional energy to accomplish their goals. Sayings like
those listed below have become standard reasons for not working
toward set goals:

"I'm too tired."
"I don't feel up to it."
"Maybe I'll get to it tomorrow if I have more energy."
"I just can't go on."

This lack of energy causes postponements, allowing things to
build up. Thus the tired person has more waiting for him, which
may be a depressing thought that further overwhelms him.

The lack of energy may be from a physical cause (e.g., hypothyroidism or diabetes), or it may be that the sufferer feels emotionally
overwhelmed. Poor diet, erratic sleep patterns, and poor physical
conditioning may also contribute to low energy levels.

Whatever the cause, if you notice that you never have enough get-up-and-go, you need to learn why, because it will hold you back. The first step to overcoming low energy is examining your lifestyle (diet, exercise, and sleep patterns). If they are not healthful, work on changing them. If the problem persists, see your doctor and get a physical examination: real physical illnesses may cause you to feel washed out. If, after all of that, you still feel out of it, you may need to investigate the possibility that emotional turmoil is draining your energy stores: depression is a very common illness. Fight the low-energy feelings, and the fight alone will bring you strength.

Dishonesty Destroys Trust: A LACK OF INTEGRITY

A. Add up your answers to questions
   208, 228, 248, 268, and 288
   and place your answer here: _____

B. Add up your answers to questions
   198, 218, 238, 258, and 278
   and place your answer here: _____

C. Subtract the smaller number from the larger number
   and place your answer here: _____
   If A is greater than B place a + sign in front of the answer.
   If B is greater than A place a − sign in front of the answer.

Place your score on Line 24, "Integrity," on the Sabotage Versus Success Profile Sheet, page 131.

A lack of honesty and integrity breeds guilt and mistrust and has destroyed people's success through the ages. One of the most precious things each of us has is our word. When we say something is true and we have integrity, people believe us. Without integrity people always look at us and wonder.

Jack, a forty-two-year-old vice president of a computer software company, was on the fast track. He had worked for his company for five years and was gaining more control within the company. However, many of the people who worked with him saw that he took shortcuts and that he was not always honest with his customers. It seemed he would do anything to gain more power and success. Jack's behavior began to isolate him from his colleagues, who were never sure if he was being "straight up" with them. Finally, an irate customer complained loudly to the company's president, who looked into the matter. The president was saddened by what he heard from Jack's peers, because he had high hopes for Jack. No one stood up for him. Because he could no longer trust Jack, the president fired him.

Most people told their first lie when they were less than three years old. It is a normal part of a child's development to discover that other people cannot read his mind and he can have secrets all to himself. When lying, cheating, and stealing persist, however, the behavior becomes a problem. The age of seven is a critical point when children begin to comprehend the difference between a story and a lie.

There are many reasons behind a lack of integrity. Briefly these include wanting to avoid consequences, wanting to appear better than you feel inside, and a lack of bonding with others. Avoiding consequences is the major reason children lie. If a child wants to get out of trouble or conflict it's a natural instinct to say what he thinks his parents want to hear.

Many people who feel inferior to others lie to build themselves up. They believe if they can get others to think that they are impressive people, then they might begin to feel good inside. However, even if they succeed in getting others to think highly of them, they often feel like an impostor and never really take themselves seriously.

A lack of bonding or closeness with significant people in childhood causes many people not to care about others as adults. People who do not care about others have no qualms about lying to or cheating others.

Every day we are faced with issues of honesty and integrity, including issues with relationships, work, taxes, speed limits, etc. There is comfort in honesty and integrity and there is tension, guilt, and fear in dishonesty.

"Am I O.K.? Did I Do the Right Thing? What Do You Think?":
LACK OF SELF-CONFIDENCE

A. Add up your answers to questions
   209, 229, 249, 269, and 289
   and place your answer here: ———

B. Add up your answers to questions
   199, 219, 239, 259, and 279
   and place your answer here: ———

C. Subtract the smaller number from the larger
   number and place your answer here: ———
   If A is greater than B place a + sign in front of the answer.
   If B is greater than A place a − sign in front of the answer.

Place your score on Line 25, "Self-Esteem," on the Sabotage Versus
Success Profile Sheet, page 131.

There comes a time in relationships, personal life, or business
when we have to stand on our own two feet and make decisions for
ourselves, to be independent. Some people have a lot of trouble
with this. They are very dependent on others, not only for their
self-esteem needs, but also for advice on small and large decisions.

Now, I know I said that successful people are teachable; but they
are also able to act independently once they have the appropriate
knowledge. Asking the opinion of people you trust is always a good
idea, but being dependent on them is dangerous. What happens
when they are not there any more? What happens when they start
giving you bad advice? Trouble, that's what happens.

No one is totally independent. We all depend on others to some
degree or, indeed, our lives are sad and isolated. But being able to
think for oneself is key to success. After all, if you only followed the
advice of others, how could you feel like a success inside? You'd feel
as if you had a "coattail success."

Dependent people are always asking others what they think, how
they would handle certain situations, and what is the next step to
take. They are lost without others to guide them, and never grow
out of this adolescent stage. There has to be a balance between
being a know-it-all and an I-know-nothing.

Along the same lines as being too dependent, unsuccessful people are often preoccupied with what others think of them. Every time they do something, they ask themselves:

"What would so-and-so think about it?"

"How will this action make me look in front of my peers?"

"Will I gain the recognition I want by doing this?"

Unfortunately, these people are often disappointed and unsure of who they are as individuals. Their lives have a certain "as-if" quality, acting as if they were someone different in different situations to gain approval.

Ironically, I find the people who do things to please others could never please important people in their own early lives. In a sense, they are still trying to please their highly critical mother or father from the past. Teri was like that.

Growing up, Teri could never please her mother. It didn't matter that she got all As in school, or that she was the state speech champion; her mother was never satisfied and often said Teri could do better if she applied herself. The more Teri achieved, the more her mother expected. It seemed to Teri that she had to work harder and harder to get her mother's approval. Subsequently, she always worked hard, but it was a joyless effort.

Later on, Teri achieved to get approval from her husband (who was much like her mother and was never satisfied) and from her boss, who likewise always wanted more. The effort finally overcame her, and she became seriously depressed. Success without joy or the feelings of success is no success at all.

Stop to think about why you do the things you do. Do you act to please yourself, or other people? Do you live trying to gain the approval of others? That is different than living to serve others! Is your self-esteem dependent on what others think of you?

Please don't misunderstand. I'm not advocating a self-centered society. Actually people are usually happier when they are helping other people, but the motivation behind your actions is crucial to understand. If you live trying to please other people, you will always be disappointed.

"I Quit!": LACKS PERSISTENCE, GIVES UP EASILY

A. Add up your answers to questions
210, 230, 250, 270, and 290 and place your answer here: _____

B. Add up your answers to questions
200, 220, 240, 260, and 280 and place your answer here: _____

C. Subtract the smaller number from the larger number
and place your answer here: _____
If A is greater than B place a + sign in front of the answer.
If B is greater than B place a − sign in front of the answer.

Place your score on Line 26, "Persistence," on the Sabotage Versus
Success Profile Sheet, page 131.

All roads of self-sabotage culminate in this final trait, giving up.
For twenty-six and perhaps a thousand other reasons, unsuccessful
people find reasons to quit:

"It's his fault."
"I always fail."
"No one believes in me."
"I keep making the same mistake. I'll never learn."
"If only I had started when I was younger."
"I never get the breaks."
"I just can't commit myself to it."
"I have no energy."
"I know I'll fail if I try."
"I get caught up in the details."
"I can't change."
"I want it now, but now never comes."
"I just can't decide."
"It's too risky."
"No one knows any more than I do."
"What do you think? I just never know."
"You'll hate me if I do that, won't you?"
"I'm just going along with everyone else."
"It's too hard. I give up."

Unsuccessful people spend far more time on excuses than on
effort achieving their goals.

Without persistence, the recipe of success will fail. It would be
like buying, cleaning, chopping, cutting, and mixing all of the
ingredients for a stew, placing them in a pan to cook, and then
forgetting to turn on the stove, or cooking it for too short a period of

time. It won't taste right. Without persistence, plans won't work.

I had two favorite stories as a youngster, "The Little Engine That Could" and "The Tortoise and the Hare." These simple stories of persistence epitomize real-life success stories. It is not your overt talent and charm that pull you through. It is *you* that pulls you through. If you quit, you are finished. As long as you keep trying, you have a chance. By staying with this book to this point, obviously you haven't given up. You're on your way. Stick to it. Exciting things await you.

11

The Sabotage Versus Success Profile Sheet

Place your scores from each area of the Sabotage Versus Success quiz below. A higher score in a positive direction indicates strength in an area, while a lower score in a negative direction indicates weakness in the area.

Generally, a score of 15 or above in an area indicates strength, while a score below 7 indicates weakness. If you score below 0 in an area, significant problems may exist and it's especially important to pay attention to the exercises in that area in Section Four.

The mental health areas (anxiety, depression, adult attention deficit disorder, drug and alcohol abuse and growing up in a drug- or alcohol-abusing environment) are only negatively scored. The farther away from 0 your score is, the greater the magnitude of the problem. Generally, a score more negative than -15 indicates a significant problem. This does not apply to the section on growing up in a drug- or alcohol-abusing environment which is only a single-question area; in this category, a score more negative than -2 indicates a problem.

Be sure to look over your areas of strength and strive to keep those areas strong.

Also, every day, look over the areas that may be holding you back and continue the work to strengthen them, especially using the exercises in the book.

ATTITUDES OF SELF-SABOTAGE VERSUS SUCCESS

SABOTAGE   SUCCESS

1. Personal Responsibility
blames others   personal responsibility
-25 . . -20 . . -15 . . -10 . . -5 . . 0 . . 5 . . 10 . . 15 . . 20 . . 25
2. Focused Goals
lacks focused goals   .   focused goals
-25 . . -20 . . -15 . . -10 . . -5 . . 0 . . 5 . . 10 . . 15 . . 20 . . 25
3. Expectations
expects to fail   expects to succeed
-25 . . -20 . . -15 . . -10 . . -5 . . 0 . . 5 . . 10 . . 15 . . 20 . . 25
4. Prepared for Luck
counts on luck   prepared for luck
-25 . . -20 . . -15 . . -10 . . -5 . . 0 . . 5 . . 10 . . 15 . . 20 . . 25
5. Learns from Mistakes
repeats mistakes   learns from mistakes
-25 . . -20 . . -15 . . -10 . . -5 . . 0 . . 5 . . 10 . . 15 . . 20 . . 25
6. Adaptable/Creative
rigid/inflexible   creative
-25 . . -20 . . -15 . . -10 . . -5 . . 0 . . 5 . . 10 . . 15 . . 20 . . 25

WORK HABITS OF SELF-SABOTAGE VERSUS SUCCESS

SABOTAGE   SUCCESS

7. Observant
unobservant   observant
-25 . . -20 . . -15 . . -10 . . -5 . . 0 . . 5 . . 10 . . 15 . . 20 . . 25
8. Informed
uninformed   informed
-25 . . -20 . . -15 . . -10 . . -5 . . 0 . . 5 . . 10 . . 15 . . 20 . . 25
9. Organization
unprepared/unorganized   prepared/organized
-25 . . -20 . . -15 . . -10 . . -5 . . 0 . . 5 . . 10 . . 15 . . 20 . . 25
10. Decision Making
trouble making decisions   able to make decisions
-25 . . -20 . . -15 . . -10 . . -5 . . 0 . . 5 . . 10 . . 15 . . 20 . . 25
11. Delegation
inability to delegate   delegates
-25 . . -20 . . -15 . . -10 . . -5 . . 0 . . 5 . . 10 . . 15 . . 20 . . 25

12. Discipline
impulsive   disciplined
-25 . . -20 . . -15 . . -10 . . -5 . . 0 . . 5 . . 10 . . 15 . . 20 . . 25
13. Reasonable Risk Taking
overly cautious   takes reasonable risks
-25 . . -20 . . -15 . . -10 . . -5 . . 0 . . 5 . . 10 . . 15 . . 20 . . 25

INTERACTIONAL SELF-SABOTAGE VERSUS SUCCESS
SABOTAGE   SUCCESS

14. Communication
inability to communicate   good communication skills
-25 . . -20 . . -15 . . -10 . . -5 . . 0 . . 5 . . 10 . . 15 . . 20 . . 25
15. Surrounded by Positive People
surrounded by negative   surrounded by positive people
people
-25 . . -20 . . -15 . . -10 . . -5 . . 0 . . 5 . . 10 . . 15 . . 20 . . 25
16. Learns from Others
unable to learn from others   teachable
-25 . . -20 . . -15 . . -10 . . -5 . . 0 . . 5 . . 10 . . 15 . . 20 . . 25
17. Competition
shies away from competition   sees competition as win-win
-25 . . -20 . . -15 . . -10 . . -5 . . 0 . . 5 . . 10 . . 15 . . 20 . . 25
18. Sensitivity to Others
insensitive to others   empathic toward others
-25 . . -20 . . -15 . . -10 . . -5 . . 0 . . 5 . . 10 . . 15 . . 20 . . 25
19. Independence
dependence on others   independent
-25 . . -20 . . -15 . . -10 . . -5 . . 0 . . 5 . . 10 . . 15 . . 20 . . 25

INDIVIDUAL SELF-SABOTAGE VERSUS SUCCESS
SABOTAGE   SUCCESS

20. Perception
stinking thinking   accurate perception
-25 . . -20 . . -15 . . -10 . . -5 . . 0 . . 5 . . 10 . . 15 . . 20 . . 25
21. Motivation
fear of success   motivated for success
-25 . . -20 . . -15 . . -10 . . -5 . . 0 . . 5 . . 10 . . 15 . . 20 . . 25

22. Emotional Disorders

a. anxiety   no anxiety

-50 . . -45 . . -40 . . -35 . . -30 . . -25. . -20 . . -15 . . -10 . . -5 . . 0

b. depression   no depression

-50 . . -45 . . -40 . . -35 . . -30 . . -25. . -20 . . -15 . . -10 . . -5 . . 0

c. drug and alcohol abuse   no alcohol/drug abuse

-50 . . -45 . . -40 . . -35 . . -30 . . -25. . -20 . . -15 . . -10 . . -5 . . 0

d. adult child of alcoholic/drug abuser

$\qquad\qquad\qquad\qquad\qquad\qquad\qquad\qquad\qquad\qquad$ -5 . . 0

e. adult attention deficit   no adult attention deficit
disorder   disorder

-50 . . -45 . . -40 . . -35 . . -30 . . -25. . -20 . . -15 . . -10 . . -5 . . 0

23. Energy

lack of energy   energetic

-25 . . -20 . . -15 . . -10 . . -5 . . 0 . . 5 . . 10 . . 15 . . 20 . . 25

24. Integrity

lack of integrity   integrity

-25 . . -20 . . -15 . . -10 . . -5 . . 0 . . 5 . . 10 . . 15 . . 20 . . 25

25. Self-Esteem

lack of self-confidence   self-esteem

-25 . . -20 . . -15 . . -10 . . -5 . . 0 . . 5 . . 10 . . 15 . . 20 . . 25

26. Persistence

gives up easily   persistence

-25 . . -20 . . -15 . . -10 . . -5 . . 0 . . 5 . . 10 . . 15 . . 20 . . 25

Add up the number of areas where a problem exists (areas in which you have a score below 7). Then refer to the appropriate paragraph below.

0–6: Your questionnaire results indicate that you have a high level of emotional maturity, and, more often than not, you already work in your own best interest. You have a positive orientation to life's challenges and opportunities. A fine-tuning adjustment to the way you currently approach your life will do wonders for you.

7–14: Your questionnaire results indicate that you have many strengths. As listed above, you also have areas that hold you back. Any work in these areas will have beneficial implications for you in terms of reshaping your life. You are closer than you may think. All it will take is some directed effort on your part.

15–21: Your questionnaire results are concerning, but you are not alone by any means. It is time to take action, for these areas are holding you back and preventing your overall success. You didn't get this way overnight; so expect that changing these areas will take time. If you stick to the exercises in the book, however, life-changing results await you.

22–30: No question about it, you are categorically sabotaging yourself in a major way, perhaps to the point of being at or near bottom. This is probably your reason for choosing this book, so there is hope. You need to stop the slide immediately and turn your life around before you start losing options. Dramatic life changes await those who can honestly say, "I've had it!" You have a lot to do, but no doubt, you can do it if you stick to it.

In order to help *you* strengthen the areas listed above, I have designed a series of exercises specifically for each in Section Four. For the exercises to be effective, *you* must first want the success that these weaknesses are denying you. Otherwise, you will not pay the price that change asks in return, and this book will find its way to your shelf, never to be heard from again.

Nobody ever said change was easy. Change is worth the effort, but it is not easy, especially because it involves working on areas of your life that are probably the most uncomfortable for you. I understand that. The exercises that follow are carefully structured to help you through these areas as simply and quickly as possible.

The Process of Change

12

You Are Not a Grasshopper

Even a journey of a thousand miles must start with a single step.

—ANCIENT HEBREW PROVERB

If you place a grasshopper in a jar with a lid, you can learn a powerful lesson. Grasshoppers in this kind of captivity behave as many people do throughout their lives.

At first, the imprisoned grasshopper tries desperately to escape from the jar, using its powerful hind legs to launch its body up against the lid. It tries and tries, and then it tries again. Initially, it is very persistent. It may try for several hours to get out of its trap.

When it finally stops, however, the grasshopper's trying days are over. It will never again try to escape from the jar by jumping. You could take the lid off of the jar and have a pet grasshopper for life. Once the grasshopper learns that it cannot change its situation, that's it. It stops trying.

In a similar way, many circus trainers teach elephants as babies to stay in one place by placing a strong chain around one ankle. Like the grasshoppers, the elephants initially struggle and struggle to get free until they cannot struggle any more. Once they stop the struggling they will never again try to break loose from something holding them by the ankle. Powerful adult elephants can be held in place by just a thin rope around one of their legs.

It is easy to see the parallel between grasshoppers and elephants, and people who sabotage themselves; once they believe they are defeated, that they cannot do things to change their situation, they stop trying—they give up, never to try again. Even if the lid is removed from their traps, it doesn't occur to them to leave; even if success or happiness is within their grasp, they are unable to reach out and grab it.

You are not a grasshopper. And you are not an elephant, You are a human being. You are separated from these life forms by your ability to think, you ability to reason, and, most importantly, your ability to adapt and change as the environment dictates. Adaptability is the reason human beings, despite being smaller and weaker than many animal species, have come to rule the world.

This section of the book looks at the processes of change and adaptation as they relate to you. In the previous section we looked at the characteristics of self-sabotage. In the next section we'll examine what it takes to have success in your life. But somehow you need to go from holding yourself back to getting what you want.

How do you do that? I like to compare the process of change and adaptation to a chess game. In chess, there are certain rules players must follow: rules for the game's setup, rules for how and in what direction individual pieces may move, rules for how pieces are captured, and rules for how the game is won.

Even though there are rules to the game, no game is ever played in exactly the same way. There are billions of ways to win and billions of ways to lose. The outcome depends on an interactive process between the two players.

Similarly, there are rules and very specific steps that occur in the process of change and adaptation. But there is no one way that people move along the path toward change. No two people, even if they are identical twins, are the same person. The path toward change is an interactive process between the person, his biology, his psychological makeup, and his environment. With this in mind, let's go through the steps toward change, realizing that this is a road map, or general scheme, that you have to individualize to yourself.

As a psychiatrist, my job is to help people change. They come to me with some complaint about themselves and elicit my help in changing. True, sometimes they want me to change someone else (a child, a spouse, an elderly parent, etc.), but at bottom they come to me because of their own discomfort. Through the years, I have observed ten consistent steps leading to lasting change and adaptation.

Ten Steps Toward Change

1. CHANGE REQUIRES DISCOMFORT—A REASON TO CHANGE
2. DECIDE TO CHANGE THE DISCOMFORT
3. DELINEATE SPECIFICS OF THE DISCOMFORT
4. UNDERSTAND THE REASONS FOR THE DISCOMFORT
5. DETERMINE HOW MUCH CONTROL YOU HAVE OVER THE DISCOMFORT
6. DEVELOP A PLAN TO CHANGE
7. CHANGE OCCURS IN STEPS
8. CHANGE REQUIRES AN INWARD LOOK
9. PRACTICE WHAT YOU'VE LEARNED
10. CHANGE NEVER STOPS

STEP ONE: CHANGE REQUIRES DISCOMFORT—A REASON TO CHANGE

First, there must be a reason to change: something that bugs you, something that makes you uncomfortable. No one changes for the fun of it: it takes too much effort. The first step toward change is feeling uncomfortable with something in your life.

This discomfort occurs in one of two ways: naturally, without any conscious effort, without us being aware of it; or through volition, by a conscious act of will. Naturally, we unconsciously become uncomfortable with our stage in life and move toward more mature ways of interacting with the world. This is called development.

Most of us move from stage to stage in our lives, accomplishing the developmental tasks necessary to move on. For instance, when we were less than eighteen months old, we saw ourselves as a part of our mothers; our mothers and ourselves seemed basically the same person. After all, if we felt hungry, they fed us, if we were wet, they changed us, if we cried, they comforted us.

As we learned to walk and talk, however, each of us began to realize that we were separate from our mother, and the "terrible twos" was a great time for us to prove it. We said no to any demands she made on us, thereby saying to her, "See, I'm separate from you." We continue to develop and change throughout our lives. All the time as we go through this development, we are driven by a natural internal time clock toward change, toward evolving as a person. Rarely do we think about the discomfort that drives us on through the stages of development. Yet it is there pushing us along all the time.

When I treat children and adolescents in psychotherapy, the major goal of the treatment is to get them back on the developmental track. For some reason they have veered from a normal developmental progression and their discomfort begins to show itself. My job is to get them back on the right path, whatever that is for them.

The second way our discomfort moves us toward change is conscious. That is, something in our life disturbs us enough so that we consciously set out to change it. Unfortunately, because of comfort, it often takes a crisis to precipitate steps to change. For example, a job crisis may precipitate a long overdue career change, marital separations or affairs may lead a couple into marriage counseling, a heart attack may cause a person to look at his diet and activity level. In the first step of Alcoholics Anonymous' Twelve Step Program (one of the most successful life-changing programs in history), an alcoholic must admit that he is powerless over alcohol and that his life has become unmanageable; the discomfort must be profound before many alcoholics will even think about changing.

The discomfort can arise in any aspect of life. How many times have you heard someone say, after a catastrophic event, that his perspective on life has changed and that he will now take time to "smell the roses"? It doesn't always take a crisis to precipitate change, but for most people to expend the necessary time and resources to change, they must feel significant motivation or discomfort in their present circumstances.

This notion of discomfort remains crucial throughout the change process. Becoming content causes many people to stop the process. This is readily seen in many psychotherapy cases. A person comes in with a complaint, such as depression, and is given some medicine and started in psychotherapy. He begins to feel better in a couple of weeks, thanks to the antidepressant medicine. After he feels better, he has no burning desire to look into the reasons why he became depressed. After all, those reasons are generally depressing. So he stops his therapy. Several months or years later, however, the depression is apt to return, only this time the reasons behind it are a bit more obscure and a bit more resistant to change.

This same principle holds true for business changes, relational changes, and personal changes. Becoming comfortable again after minor adjustments will stop the process of change cold! If you are uncomfortable enough with something in your life, you can change it, or at least, you can change your perception of it. There is nothing holding you back but you.

STEP TWO: DECIDE TO CHANGE THE DISCOMFORT

The second step in the change process is deciding to do something about the discomfort. Changing requires an active decision to turn the situation around. Without the decision for action, nothing can happen, and things will remain the same.

I love the Chinese proverb that says, "You cannot prevent the birds of sorrow from flying over your head, but you can prevent them from building nests in your hair." If the birds of sorrow are nesting in your hair, you can decide to find a way to get rid of them. All of us, at one point or another, experience sorrow and discomfort in life. It is up to us how we handle those feelings. It is our decision to make. Epictetus, in the first century A.D., phrased it eloquently when he wrote, "People are not disturbed by things, but by the views which they take of them," and, I would add, by the way we decide to handle the discomforts.

Depending on the situation, you may make only one decision to change, or you may end up making many, many decisions to change. For some, the discomfort is so profound, or they become so involved in the process, that one decision is all it takes to stay on the path toward lasting change. For others, many decisions may be necessary.

Decisions to change are not easy to make. They require us to leave the known and the certain, to venture into uncharted territory. Even when the known is painful, many people would rather live with something they know than try something new and different. Many people have told me they stayed in unhappy relationships because at least they knew how to handle the craziness in the situation. It they ventured into other relationships, they might actually be worse off. Living in discomfort seems comfortable compared to the possibility of facing unknowns.

STEP THREE: DELINEATE SPECIFICS OF THE DISCOMFORT

After you make the decision to change something uncomfortable in your life, the next step is to clearly define the problem or problems, to further delineate the reasons for the discomfort. This takes an investigation.

Initially, the discomfort is vague: unhappiness in a marriage, job dissatisfaction, personal restlessness, etc. If you pay attention to it and ask yourself questions about it, the discomfort will further define itself. In a marriage, you might be unhappy about the amount of time your spouse gives you, how he treats you in front of your friends, or how the sex seems to fizzle as you get hot. In a job, your dissatisfaction may stem from working too many hours, not feeling appreciated for your contributions, or working for a boss you hate. In personal finance, your lack of revenue may come from not making enough, paying too much in taxes, or poor investments. Whatever the initial discomfort, it is important to go farther in teasing out its components.

This is necessary if one is to develop a reasonable strategy for change. Let's look at the example of a failing marriage in more detail. First, one or both partners feel *discomfort,* which may take the form of increased arguing or bickering, longing for other relationships, or an increased absence from home. Very often the marriage reaches a crisis point with an affair or a separation before anything is done about the discomfort.

The crisis will bring the couple to a decision point. They may decide to end the relationship, which is a final form of change. Or they may conclude that the relationship is important enough to save, and *decide* to do their best to change it.

In that event, the next step becomes *defining* the specific problems they have with the marriage: not spending enough time together, being treated with disrespect, wandering loyalties, putting parents or children ahead of spouse, sexual displeasure, etc. Before they can develop a reasonable marriage reconstruction program, the couple needs to know what specific things need changing. Without learning the specific causes of the discomfort, there is little chance they can choose a direction for any interventions.

This is a crucial step. Many couples get back together and pretend nothing ever happened between them, that the discomfort never existed. They decide things will be different, but they do not go any farther, afraid of what they might find. They invariably find, however, that when problems get "swept under the rug" the "bulge in the rug" will always be in the room between them. Ignored problems are never forgotten—they just hide out until a later time.

You may need help from an objective third party in delineating reasons for discomfort. Depending on the problem, this can often be done by anyone who understands you and the situation with which you're having difficulty. Self-help groups dealing with problems you experience are often a very good source of information.

STEP FOUR: UNDERSTAND THE REASONS FOR THE DISCOMFORT

After more specifically defining the discomfort, you can move toward the next step in change, which is understanding its source: why the problem exists. Some behavioral psychologists say it is not necessary to understand the reasons problems exist; all that is necessary is a way to change them. I strongly disagree, because if you do not understand why a problem exists, you are very likely to repeat it. You will be unable to recognize when you are headed down a similar failure path.

This is the problem of people who go from marriage to marriage. They get out of one marriage and plunge right into the next one without figuring out what went wrong with the previous relationship. They often believe the other person is the problem, thinking that if they get rid of him or her the problem will go away. They rarely look at their contribution to the downfall of the relationship, and so, without a clear understanding of why the problem existed, they are likely to repeat it.

Let's look at some more examples to further illustrate this process. If you are in business and you fail, how are you going to do better next time if you don't understand why you failed? Which of the hallmarks of self-sabotage are doing you in? Are you blaming others? Being defeated by your failures? Are you poorly organized?

You would hate having a doctor who just treated your symptoms and ignored the cause of your distress. You'd get very uncomfortable if he said, "Well, maybe you have cancer, so we'll give you chemotherapy." That's crazy! If you're going to be treated, you want to understand exactly what problem the doctor is treating and why.

Well, if you're going to change something, it's the same way. You need to understand why the problem exists. For effective understanding, it is necessary to approach identified problems in a thorough, systematic fashion. I call this a "system of inquiry." I ask the following questions to help me understand the origin of problems. (Short answers in parentheses illustrate responses regarding a failing marriage and job dissatisfaction.)

1. What is the general discomfort? (unhappy marriage; job dissatisfaction)

2. What precipitating event or events preceded the decision to change the situation? (a marital separation; getting chewed out by the boss)

3. What specific problems are identified? (spouse remains more loyal to his or her original family; not appreciated at work)

4. How serious is the problem? (the marriage is threatened; may have to quit or be fired from work)

5. What is at stake if the problem is not solved? (terminating the marriage may mean significant depression and losing custody of the children; losing the job jeopardizes income and may seriously decrease self-esteem)

6. When did the problem start? (after being embarrassed in front of friends; after getting passed over for promotion)

7. What was the situation like preceding the onset of the problem? (marriage was always a bit strained; work was very satisfying)

8. In what situation does the problem occur? Is it an isolated problem? Or does the same problem exist in other settings? Has the problem occurred before? (repeat of the previous marriage; this is the first time there has been trouble with the boss)

9. What makes the problem worse? (being around in-laws; deadlines at work)

10. What makes the problem better? (having time away without other pressures; being left to work independently)

11. What have you contributed to the problem? (insensitive to my spouse's need to please his or her family; chronically late on the job)

12. What has the other person contributed to the problem? (spouse embarrasses me to make self look good; the boss treats me like a child)

13. What problems are associated with the primary ones listed? (lack of satisfying sex; no energy to go to work)

14. Can you be objective in looking at the problem? Are you too close to the situation? Do your emotions fit the situation or do you sometimes find yourself acting inappropriately? (anger gets in the way)

15. What feelings are associated with the situation? (disappointment with spouse; hatred toward the boss)

16. Do you know the source of the feelings? (hopes that the marriage would provide the love never felt in childhood are jeopardized; the boss reminds me of father who was impossible to please, so hate him as hated father)

17. Could you benefit from outside help?

18. Is trying to fix the problem worth the necessary effort?

Obviously, these questions are only a general outline to help me get started understanding problems. The questions must be tailored to the individual discomfort.

In trying to understand any problem in which people are involved, we must always consider unconscious motivation. Problems are not always what they appear to be on the surface. I like to compare the unconscious mind to a clean countertop.

At first glance the counter is clean and everything appears to be in its proper place. If we inspect the countertop with a microscope, however, we'll find a whole other world of active, living organisms. It's amazing what we find when we look. Most of the time, if that other, unnoticed world is in harmony with the visible world, things go along without trouble. But if there is trouble in the microscopic life, it will eventually show on the countertop: fungus may grow, rust or decay may appear, hinges may squeak, etc.

If our unconscious mind is in harmony with our conscious world, and that is also true with the other people involved in the problem, it is generally not difficult to figure out the problem. If, however, there is disharmony between unconscious and conscious motivations, it may be impossible to comprehend the situation clearly. At this point, professional help may be indicated.

An unconscious process frequently seen at the core of difficult situations is something psychiatrists call transference. Transference is defined as an unconscious process in which we redirect, or "transfer," feelings and desires from an important individual in our past onto a person in the present. Kevin offers a vivid example of instantaneous transference.

"After I graduated from college, I submitted my resume to a small engineering firm and was called in for an interview," Kevin told me. "When the owner of the firm met me in the waiting room, he looked at me for a minute, then said, 'I know you'll do just fine,' and hired me before we even had a chance to talk. I soon learned, however, that I bore a resemblance to his son who died in Vietnam, which causes a lot of problems in our working relationship."

Transference involves a wide range of fantasies and expectations that we develop on the basis of prior experience, both pleasant and unpleasant, with our parents, significant others, or previous figures of authority. We can have positive or negative transferential reactions.

A positive reaction is exemplified by the employee who bestows omnipotent power on his boss and experiences total dependence on him. This employee might say, "My boss is wonderful! I can go to him with any problem and he'll always have the right answer." The employees' unconscious may be saying, "My boss will take care of me the way my mother did." This form of transference involves regression, compliance, loyalty, and unquestioning obedience. It also frequently gives rise eventually to intense negative transference experiences, because we see that person as "larger than life" and become sorely disappointed when we find out that he is not.

Negative transference reactions are very much at the developmental core of interactional problems. In these situations another person (boss, spouse) unconsciously reminds us of someone who previously hurt or disappointed us (a distant mother, a cruel father, a critical teacher, etc.), and we react toward these people in the present as if they were the person from the past.

The negative transference reaction can be illustrated by the following example: Steve, a bright young chemistry professor, was admired by both the students and faculty of his college for the creative way he taught. But for some reason, he could never find time to fill out the detailed lesson plans required of him by the department chairperson, who happened to be a woman. When, after repeated reminders, she confronted him about his disregard for the paperwork, he became very upset and said, "You just say that because you hate men."

Bewildered, the chairperson probed further into what Steve had meant. He acknowledged harboring silent resentment toward her for some time. In fact, he felt that most women, including his wife, hated men. Yet, as he looked at the facts, these feelings did not seem justified.

Steve eventually decided to begin psychotherapy, in the course of which he discovered that his boss, as well as his wife, reminded him of his mother, whom he could never please. He thought about the fact that his father had left the family when Steve was very young, after which his mother had become very critical toward all men. Steve had spent much of his life trying to overcome his mother's hatred for men, and this had colored many of his relationships with women. He had displaced his negative feelings for his mother onto the department chairperson, causing a covert power struggle over the paperwork. Evidence of this only came to light when his boss took the time to probe Steve's unusual behavior.

The transference phenomena is present in most human relationships, and may help to explain behavior that seems otherwise unexplainable.

There are many other reasons behind interpersonal difficulties, which generalize to cause problems in other situations. These include failed expectations, faulty assumptions, envy, and guilt.

When you know the cause of a problem, you can learn to avoid it or you can find other solutions. Understanding is crucial to change.

STEP FIVE: DETERMINE HOW MUCH CONTROL YOU HAVE OVER THE DISCOMFORT

The next step toward change, after the discomfort, or problem, is understood, is deciding who's in control of the problem. Is it your problem, which you can do something about, or is it someone else's problem, which you are powerless to change?

No doubt, if you're feeling uncomfortable, you have a problem, but is it something that your effort can change? I can't tell you how many people I've seen in my practice who spend inordinate time worrying about things that are beyond their control. They worry about how and when they are going to die, when the next natural disaster is going to strike, what other people think of them, and what their children will be when they grow up. It is true that they have some impact on these events: if they stop smoking, they'll probably live longer; if they move from California to Virginia, there will be less chance that they'll be in an earthquake; if they think before speaking, more people will think them intelligent; and if they provide a loving and accepting home environment, their children most likely will be happy when they grow up. However, they will still not be able to control what will happen, especially when it comes to the behavior of other people.

The wife of an alcoholic, no matter how much guilt she feels, cannot make her husband stop drinking. Only he can do that. She can change her reaction to him if he refuses to change, such as refusing to cover up for him when he is drunk, but she cannot change him. Likewise, a teacher can provide a child with an optimal environment in which to learn, but she cannot force him to learn.

The proverb "You can lead a horse to water but you cannot make him drink" applies to how you solve the problems in your life. You can change the things you have control of in your life. You cannot change things over which you have no control. *The more you realize that you are in control of your life, the more you realize that you cannot control the lives of others.* You can control your response to other people. You cannot control their reaction to you.

After you've identified and understood the discomfort, ask yourself if it's yours to own. If it is, you can do something about it. If it is not, you may be able to change your reaction to the situation, but you are not able to change another person. This is perhaps the most frustrating part of my job as a psychiatrist. I know how to help people change, but, as much as I would like to, I cannot do it for them. As human beings, we each have individual free will. You can pressure others to change, but you cannot make them change.

STEP SIX: DEVELOP A PLAN TO CHANGE

In many cases, if you go through the first five steps, you will solve the discomfort. Understanding alone can sometimes bring about change because obvious solutions become apparent. Or, realizing that it is not your problem may allow you to give up worrying and free you for a more productive use of your time and energy.

If the problem remains, however, Step Six is to develop an effective plan for change. Obviously, this plan must be based on the individual details of the situation. There are, however, some general guidelines that you can use in developing a plan for change.

First, ask yourself if someone else has been faced with the same problem. Most human problems have been dealt with by someone at some time before. If that is the case, find out how the other person solved the problem and then try to adapt his solution to your situation. You do not have to reinvent the wheel.

For several years, I taught a seminar for medical students on "How to Do Medical School." In the seminar I told students to talk to professors, upper classmen, laboratory assistants—anyone who had been through what they were going to go through—to ask how they had survived the process and how they might recommend someone else do it. I also told them to get copies of old exams (if permissible) to learn the kinds of questions asked and how they were asked. I taught them to learn from one of their best resources: those who had successfully been through the process before.

This is true in almost any problem-solving situation. If someone else has had a similar problem and solved it successfully, find out how they did it and adapt their solution to your individual situation. I think this "learning from others" approach is the main reason self-help groups such as Alcoholics Anonymous and Overeaters Anonymous enjoy tremendous success. People who have been through the problem help those with similar problems. *Find out how others solved similar problems.* It takes a teachable spirit to do this. As we will see in the next chapter, being teachable is a major ingredient in the recipe of success.

Second, conscious change is an active process. In order to bring about change in your life, you must take an active role. Some form of activity, whether doing something, writing something down, or talking to someone, is necessary for you to feel in control of the situation once again.

If you're impotent or nonorgasmic, the doctor will prescribe specific exercises for you and your partner to do. If you want to be more assertive, you take assertiveness training. If you want to lose weight, you actively pursue a diet and exercise program. If you want to quit smoking, you actively replace the bad habit with some sort of rewarding activity.

A do-nothing approach never solves problems. Activity, if done correctly, brings about change. Sometimes it hardly seems to matter what you do, as long as you do something with the attitude of self-help. The exercises in this book were developed on the premise that activity is necessary for change.

Third, the plan for change must be flexible. Never lose your individuality in a plan. Always think about ways to adapt it to your personality and your situation. Many plans are rigidly adhered to long after they have proven ineffective. Reevaluate your plan at regular intervals to see if you're on the right track. Be wed to the process of change, not to a specific plan for change.

Fourth, there should be a balance between persistence and alternative planning. Persistence is found in all successful people. At the same time, successful people are flexible. When they recognize they are on the wrong path toward something, they change their path.

You need to find your own balance. The best way I know to strike this balance is to first, before you set out on a path, have all of your options in mind, and form several plans for accomplishing your goals. After you do this, it is easy to persist in one thing if you know you have chosen wisely among the alternatives in the beginning.

Along the same line, mentally rehearsing the events toward change is an important step in the process. Thinking is trial creative action. Successfully imagining the active process of change will have an amazing impact on the process.

The techniques of Inner Tennis and Inner Golf are simply mental rehearsal for playing the way you want to play. Mentally rehearsing the path toward change is an active process that will start you on your way.

STEP SEVEN: CHANGE OCCURS IN STEPS

During the process of change, it is important to keep in mind that change, like success, occurs in steps. After all, it probably took you a long time to become the person you wish to change. Patience and preparation through each step are essential to staying on the path toward change. Good marriages do not happen overnight, successful businesses take time to build, great athletic teams do not just occur. Expecting too much too soon only invites disappointment and failure.

Along the path to change it is important to remember that adequate preparation will save you time and backtracking through unnecessary steps in the future. Nowhere in my own life was this more evident than when I decided to go to medical school.

The first pre-med course I had to take was general chemistry. I had not taken a chemistry class since high school four years earlier, but I thought it was now or never, and went to that class a bit nervous. However, in the first week of the course I was so lost that I thought I was in the wrong room taking a Russian language class. Looking back, the smartest thing I did for my career was to drop that class and, for a semester, take a "dumbbell" beginning chemistry class that gave me a solid foundation and adequate preparation for what I was to encounter. Patience and preparation may delay change for a few months, but it will save you from disaster later on. Change occurs in steps, and being prepared for the first step will enable change to take place more quickly.

The steps to change are not static. I frequently tell my patients that their course of change will be like going up and down a staircase (see diagram below). They will go up several steps, feeling like they've made progress, only to go back one or two steps when a difficult situation arises. They will then make several more steps of progress and them slip back less than before. The slope of the progress, however, is expected to be in an upward positive direction. The down times are easier to handle if they are expected.

Figure 1: STAIRCASE EFFECT OF CHANGE

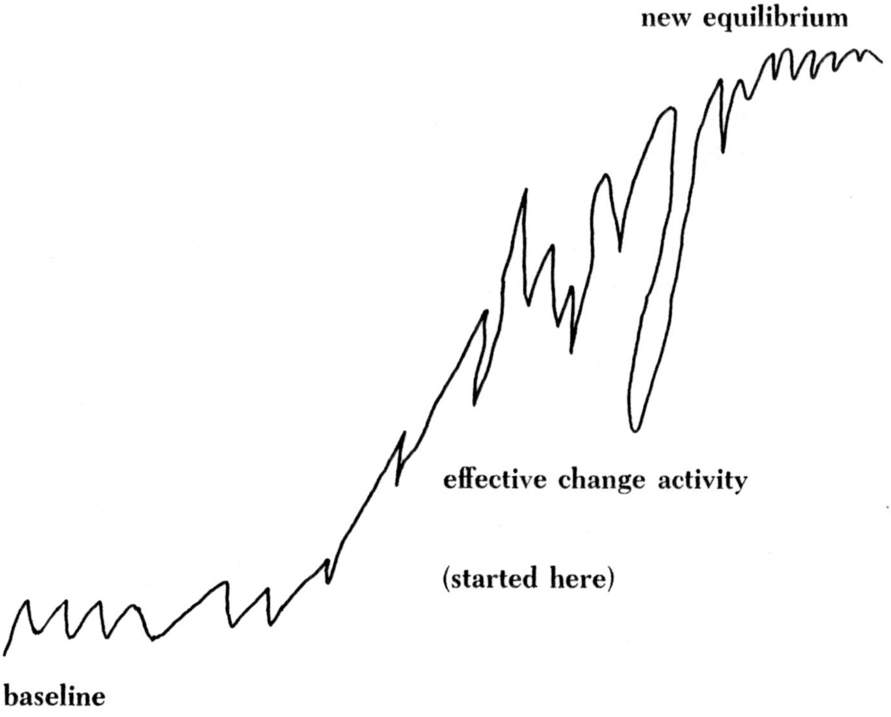

new equilibrium

effective change activity

(started here)

baseline

STEP EIGHT: CHANGE REQUIRES AN INWARD LOOK

The process of change requires serious self-examination. This takes time and often causes a person to withdraw into himself. The story of the butterfly is the most dramatic example of this I know.

Butterflies do not start out as butterflies. They go around looking like a worm with a lot of feet and move slowly from one place to the next. When their biology tells them it's time for a change, they are only too glad to oblige. They then get off alone, form a hard shell (called a pupa or a cocoon) around themselves, and literally go inside of themselves to make a miraculous change.

The time the change requires depends on the nature of the future butterfly. It may take only weeks to change, or it may require months. While making the change, they do not make any decisions about the outside world. They just work on changing themselves. During the change they are oblivious to the goings on around them; they are too busy with their own metamorphosis.

The change is worth the wait. I'll always remember my son's excitement when he placed a monarch cocoon in a large bucket and patiently waited for something to happen. When the day of change finally came, Anton heard a rustling noise in the bucket and went out to see a beautiful gold and black butterfly waiting to be released to the world.

In therapy with children, I often draw a picture of a caterpillar and have them explain to me what happens to it. They all know that caterpillars turn into butterflies. I then ask them to take the picture home and hang it in their rooms. I try to have them identify with the small creature's ability to turn into something beautiful.

I often compare the process of psychotherapy to the caterpillar-turned-butterfly story. People come to me feeling down and out. Their lives are not what they want. They want to change. Doing that, I tell them, will take serious effort on their part, and they will have to look inside themselves for most of the answers. I can guide them, but I can't do it for them. The psychiatrist is like an incubator; he can provide a conducive atmosphere for change, but the most important process occurs within his patient.

The effort required for lasting change is often so intense that many patients are unable to do much in the world until they are well into the process. Many psychiatrists recommend that patients hold off making important life decisions (divorce, job changes, etc.) at the beginning of the therapeutic process, because settling time is required to gain perspective on the changes being made. Any change will cause you to go inside yourself; the degree will depend on the kind of changes you wish to make.

STEP NINE: PRACTICE WHAT YOU'VE LEARNED

One of the final steps in the change process is putting all you have learned to work in your day-to-day life. I know many people who have a lot of head knowledge about themselves, but who go on sabotaging their lives as they did when they began the process of introspection and change.

Change will not occur through knowledge alone. It comes from knowledge, persistence, and practice. Self-esteem can't be built overnight, for instance. People working on this often find that the old feeling of "I'm not worth it"—the very thing they want to change—is an inhibitor of change. They find it easy to revert to old ways. But this is the wrong time to give up. Instead, keep reminding yourself that you *are* worth it.

At this practice stage of the process, it is time to let things from the past remain in the past and work on changing the present and the future. The Gospel of Mark in the New Testament describes this: "No one puts new wine into old wineskins; otherwise the wine will burst the skins, and the wine is lost, and the skins as well; but one puts new wine into fresh wineskins" (Mark 2:22). Lasting change comes about when you practice the new knowledge and feelings you have learned instead of continuing old self-destructive patterns of thinking and acting.

STEP TEN: CHANGE NEVER STOPS

Finally, change never stops. The world and people around us change constantly. We need to be flexible enough to change with them. Our path through life is never straight; it runs around corners, up stairs, down dark alleys, and beside the paths of others. We need to be constantly on the lookout for things in our life that are changing and, if we decide to go along, to direct a new path for ourselves. Taking time to observe your life is the only way to ensure that you're at least on the path to where you want to be.

13

Three Examples of Change

Using the process of change described above, let's take a detailed look at three examples of successful change.

Don, a lieutenant colonel in the army, was in serious danger of losing his military commission. He was one hundred fifty pounds overweight by the army weight standards, and he was given six months to make substantial progress toward meeting the standards or face separation procedures.

1. CHANGE REQUIRES DISCOMFORT—A REASON TO CHANGE

Don's discomfort about his weight had been there for some time, but he was never forced to do something about it. His discomfort, however, reached crisis proportions, because his military career was the most important thing in his life.

2. DECIDE TO CHANGE THE DISCOMFORT

Don, with the Department of Defense's help, made the decision to change. He could have chosen to get out of the service, but he decided his career was more important to him than food.

3. DELINEATE SPECIFICS OF THE DISCOMFORT

Delineating the problem for Don was not difficult. He ate large quantities of high-calorie food and he got very little exercise.

4. UNDERSTAND THE REASONS FOR THE DISCOMFORT
Don, through serious introspection, found that he ate more when he was depressed. He remembered that whenever he was sad as a child, his mother would feed him, setting up the association in his mind between food and mother's nurturing. He attributed his sedentary life-style to being too busy at work, although later on he admitted that it was just easier to go home after a long day at work than to run or go to the gym.

5. DETERMINE HOW MUCH CONTROL YOU HAVE OVER THE DISCOMFORT
Don realized that although the army was the one making an issue of his weight, it was his problem. No one could lose the weight for him.

6. DEVELOP A PLAN TO CHANGE
Don took a multidisciplinary approach to his weight loss. He saw a nutritionist to learn about the best and safest ways to diet, he saw a psychiatrist for hypnotherapy, and he joined Overeaters Anonymous for support from other people who would understand what he was going through.

7. CHANGE OCCURS IN STEPS
Don lost four pounds per week for a month, the he lost two pounds per week for three months, for a total of forty-three pounds lost over four months. Although still very overweight, he was hooked into the process and felt very good about being in control of his life.

8. CHANGE REQUIRES AN INWARD LOOK
He found that in order to keep up the weight loss regimen, he had to dramatically change his life. Don no longer visited the bar every Tuesday and Friday. He stopped eating lunch at the deli. And he stopped eating his meals in front of the television. He had to go inside himself to change his life. He now spent hours at the gym, and found that although he still hated running, he did enjoy long brisk walks along the river.

9. PRACTICE WHAT YOU'VE LEARNED
Through practice, persistence, and the support of people who cared about him, Don was able to lose eighty pounds in six months. This convinced the army that he took his weight reduction program seriously. In the following year he lost the remaining seventy pounds.

10. CHANGE NEVER STOPS

Don knows that his success is tenuous. He sometimes craves large amounts of food, but he knows that if he lets himself slip back, he may slip a long way. He continues to attend Overeaters Anonymous meetings, and he gets satisfaction and strength from helping others lose weight.

Stephanie had been depressed most of her life when she came to my office. She complained of feeling hopeless and helpless, and said that she often wanted to die.

1. CHANGE REQUIRES DISCOMFORT—A REASON TO CHANGE

Her discomfort had been present for as long as she could remember. It was only after she began to seriously consider suicide that she became frightened, because she knew her husband would be unable to adequately care for her four children.

2. DECISION TO CHANGE THE DISCOMFORT

Even though she felt hopeless, she had a friend who had been successfully treated for depression. Stephanie decided she had nothing to lose, and set up an appointment with me.

3. DELINEATE SPECIFICS OF THE DISCOMFORT

Stephanie was able to delineate her troubles. After all, she had been carrying them around with her for many years. She felt that she could never do anything right. Everything she tried ended in disaster. She went through three and a half years of college, only to marry and drop out of school several months before graduation. She married a man who seemed to resent her intelligence, and she subsequently kept her aspirations down to avoid threatening the marriage. And she had much difficulty with her children, constantly struggling with them over homework or household chores.

4. UNDERSTAND THE REASONS FOR THE DISCOMFORT

Understanding the origins of her depression was also not difficult. Her overprotective parents had continually given her the message that she was not good enough, and they had insisted on being too involved in every decision she made. When they thought she was a little overweight, they put her on a strict diet, and she was severely punished if she did not comply. Any attempt by her toward independence was put down with statements about her inability and her lack of appreciation for all her parents did for her. It is not surprising that she had married a man whom she could likewise never please. The very negative parental tapes played inside of her head daily: "You would be nothing without us." She believed them, and on her own, she acted as if her life were worth nothing.

5. DETERMINE HOW MUCH CONTROL YOU HAVE OVER THE DISCOMFORT

Initially, in psychotherapy, she tried to give me control of her life. She asked me to make decisions for her about her children, her finances, and her relationship with her husband. I told her that she was perfectly capable of making these decisions for herself and, if she wanted, I would help her talk through them. After several months she began to take control of her life, realizing that if her life was to change, she would have to change it. After all, if I did it for her, it would be just like her parents doing it for her—the last thing in the world she wanted to happen.

6. DEVELOP A PLAN TO CHANGE

We developed a plan of twice-weekly psychotherapy that included connecting up thoughts and feelings from the past with current situations in her life, cognitive exercises to help her restructure the way she thought about her role in situations, self-hypnosis to give her more control over her body, and dream analysis to synthesize all she was learning. Each session was tailored to her needs at that particular moment.

7. CHANGE OCCURS IN STEPS

Change occurred slowly, and there was initially some regression— after all, people are depressed for depressing reasons—but, looking back, positive change took place in a stepwise fashion throughout the two years I saw her. Stephanie lost her self-destructive urges and began to believe in herself. She still had down times, but, as therapy progressed, these became less and less frequent. The change progressed because Stephanie persisted in coming to her appointments even when she wasn't in the mood, persisted in doing the prescribed exercises we designed for her, and was patient enough to know that change does not happen overnight.

8. CHANGE REQUIRES AN INWARD LOOK

During the first year of therapy, Stephanie withdrew into herself. She was preoccupied with the past and very angry at the messages that had been given to her by her so-called loving parents. As her depression began to lift in the second year, however, she had more energy for her family and was able to forgive her parents, realizing that they were acting within the chains of their own pasts.

Like many spouses, Stephanie's husband resented her seeing a "shrink," and wondered what she was telling me about him. The resentment increased as she became more independent from him, and, although I encouraged her to stay with him until she had a better handle on her life, her husband left her. He was unable to tolerate the changes she was making in her life. She was able to let him go, saying, "My life is not worth the marriage. If I revert back to how I used to be, I'd surely kill myself."

9. PRACTICE WHAT YOU'VE LEARNED
Every morning Stephanie remembered what it was like when she felt depressed. She would then go through the steps that led her out of the depression, firmly saying to herself that she had given up the negative parental voices from the past and that she was now her own parent and needed to take care of herself the way a good parent would care for her. She was worth it.

10. CHANGE NEVER STOPS
Like Don, Stephanie knew that if she didn't take care of her mental health she could slip back into the old mode of self-defeating behavior. When she left therapy, she told me that leaving was not the end of her therapy, but rather it was the beginning of a new phase of it.

Most psychiatrists are introspective. Let me close this chapter with an example of change in my own life.

In high school I was a very mediocre student, graduating with a 2.8 grade point average. At the time, it seemed my life was going nowhere, so I decided to join the army to get some direction. During my time in the service, I decided I wanted something good for my life, and, for me, that would require a college education. The transition from mediocre student to magna cum laude medical school graduate went as follows:

1. CHANGE REQUIRES DISCOMFORT—A REASON TO CHANGE
Until I decided to do something specific with my life, my mediocre grades never bothered me that much. However, when I decided to

go to medical school, I knew my school ability needed to be overhauled or I would never get near my goal.

2. DECIDE TO CHANGE THE DISCOMFORT

After getting encouragement from some very special people, I decided to pursue a medical career. After all, I knew most medical school admission committees did not look at high school grades, so I started over with a clean slate.

3. DELINEATE SPECIFICS OF THE DISCOMFORT

I did the first year of college while I was still in the army. I took it slowly, initially enrolling in one class at a time, so that I could get good grades while learning how to be a student—something no one had ever taught me. I quickly noted that my skill in "doing school" was not very good. I had trouble organizing my time. I lacked an overall approach to the classes I took. I often got bogged down in the details of the material, missing the big picture. And I was too embarrassed to ask questions in class.

4. UNDERSTAND THE REASONS FOR THE DISCOMFORT

After I took the time and energy to look at the problems, it was not hard for me to understand why they existed. School had never been important enough for me to spend energy organizing my time or developing an overall approach to my classes. In high school I could get by with studying from test to test, and that was all I had needed at the time. I was also afraid of appearing stupid, because I hated the times in my life when I did feel stupid and did not want to repeat those experiences, so I wouldn't ask questions in class.

Of course, there were deeper reasons for my wallowing in mediocrity. My father, in my mind, was the most successful man on earth. It seemed to me at the time that I could never be as successful as he was. If I tried and failed, I would be right about never measuring up to him. If I never really tried, then I would never really know, which seemed more palatable than finding out that I could never match up. Through his help and the help of some people who believed in me, I began to believe that I could do anything I wanted, and that life was not a competition between my father and me, but rather a place where we could both win in our own ways.

5. DETERMINE HOW MUCH CONTROL YOU HAVE OVER THE DISCOMFORT

I came to learn that I was in control of how I did at school. It was my responsibility to find out the best ways to approach each class, and there were plenty of people to help me if I took the time to ask. My grades were also my responsibility, and if I thought there were unfair test questions or I received an unfair grade, I made it a point to discuss it with the teacher. I was very surprised by the many students who never argued for themselves but just accepted what was given to them.

6. DEVELOP A PLAN TO CHANGE
I developed a plan for each of my classes. Before a class began, I always went to the professor and asked him how he'd approach his class if he were a student (teachers are the best resource). I would then try to talk to someone who had taken the class before from the same teacher and get as much information as possible, including copies of old exams if he had them. When the class began, I worked especially hard in the first part of the class to give myself a solid foundation in the material. And I always went to class, even when I didn't feel like it. I found that most of what is asked on exams is covered in class. I also became a tutor in many of my classes, because I found that the more I was able to help someone else with the material, the better I knew it myself.

7. CHANGE OCCURS IN STEPS
Initially, I was very anxious about school. Gradually, as my performance in college improved, so did my confidence in my abilities. I went from being a very tentative pre-med to a confident medical student. The change occurred in small steps, but through persistence and patience I achieved what I wanted.

8. CHANGE REQUIRES AN INWARD LOOK
In order to change my study habits I went inside myself to discover my weaknesses and abilities. The time it took to get the grades I needed caused me to sacrifice other things in my life, but it was worth it, because I now can do just about anything I want with my life.

9. PRACTICE WHAT YOU'VE LEARNED
After I learned to be a good student, I could not stop there; I had to practice what I learned with every new course in which I was enrolled. As in swimming or riding a bicycle, however, the more I did it the easier it became, and soon the way I approached school was second nature. The skill of learning helped me go through

medical school without the headaches some of my classmates experienced.

10. CHANGE NEVER STOPS

For a physician, learning never stops. There are always new techniques, new diseases, and new discoveries to learn about. In fact, the dean of my medical school said that in ten years' time, ninety percent of what I learned there would be obsolete. The purpose of medical school was to teach us how to learn, and for us, the process would never stop.

In closing this section on change, let me leave you with one further idea: CHANGE ALMOST ALWAYS INVOLVES SOME PAIN. I spoke of this when I gave the student address at my college graduation: "I think if the crucifixion of Jesus Christ were to occur today, there would be no way we would let him die in the painful way that he did. First, we would try to convince him to take a few painless cyanide tablets to get the job done: but when he insisted on the way of the cross, we would certainly give him two Valium to alleviate any anxiety or pain, and then make sure that his cross was nicely varnished and comfortably padded. My reason for saying this is that I believe American society is geared to the proposition that all pain is bad. I find, however, that all pain is not bad, and that in many instances pain is a necessary ingredient for personal growth."

Growth and change involve pain. There were many nights when my son was awakened from sleep by pain in his little legs. At first, he cried and needed much comforting to go back to sleep. As he got older, he realized that if he wanted to be tall like his grandfather, his legs would have to grow and sometimes that involved pain. As he grew, the pain became easier to accept. There is a reason for growing pain. Don't avoid the pain—learn from it and move on.

The Individualized Prescription for Success

14

Your Individual Prescription for Success

Every noble work is at first impossible.
—CARLYLE

The recipe for success described here applies to any area of life. The ingredients for success are the same whether you are working on your marriage, your financial status, or your personal growth. The mixture of the ingredients of success may be different in individual situations, but the ingredients are the same.

In the last section I discussed how people change in general terms. This section is your "Individualized Prescription for Success," and is designed to help *YOU* specifically change. For those areas marked out as potential problems by your "Sabotage Versus Success Profile" there are a series of practical exercises designed to help you. Be sure to do these exercises first. As you go through the material for your "stronger" areas you can choose to do those exercises you think might be helpful to you. This book gives you a personalized strategy for self-healing by pointing out those areas most in need of work and by giving you practical and clear solutions.

Nobody ever said change was easy. It is worth it, but it is not easy, especially because it involves working on areas of your life that are probably the most uncomfortable for you. I understand that. The material and exercises that follow are carefully structured to help you through these areas as simply and quickly as possible.

Psychiatrist Toksoz B. Karasu, M.D. lists the three common denominators of change: cognitive mastery (reason), behavioral exercises, and emotional experience. The exercises in this section include cognitive (thinking) assignments to help you understand and reason through those things that have been holding you back. If done faithfully, they will help you acquire and integrate new perceptions, clearer thinking patterns, and enhanced self-awareness. Changing thoughts is a precursor to changing actions.

There are also "doing" or behavior-oriented exercises, because the final measure of change is whether or not the self-sabotaging behaviors change. These exercises offer practical, step-by-step instructions for doing things in a new or different way. Proven formulas, recipes, methods, and instructions are given to reinforce learning through the repetition and practice of new behaviors and to provide tangible applications of change. Changing actions often leads to changing thoughts.

The only thing left from the list for change is emotional experience. That, you must provide. The emotional experience is your investment in this book and in yourself. All of the knowledge and behavioral exercises will mean little if you do not commit yourself to them, if you do not take personal responsibility to make this book work for you.

HALLMARKS OF SELF-SABOTAGE

ATTITUDES OF SELF-SABOTAGE	SUCCESS
1. blames others	personal responsibility
2. lacks focused goals	focused goals
3. expects to fail	expects to succeed
4. counts on luck	prepared for luck
5. repeats mistakes	learns from mistakes
6. rigid/inflexible	creative

WORK HABITS OF SELF-SABOTAGE	SUCCESS
7. unobservant	observant
8. uninformed	informed
9. unprepared/unorganized	prepared/organized
10. trouble making decisions	able to make decisions

11. inability to delegate	delegates
12. impulsive	disciplined
13. overly cautious	takes reasonable risks

INTERACTIONAL SELF-SABOTAGE	SUCCESS
14. inability to communicate	good communication skills
15. surrounded by negative people	surrounded by positive people
16. unable to learn from others	teachable
17. shies away from competition	sees competition as win-win
18. insensitive to others	empathic toward others
19. dependent on others	independent

PERSONAL	SUCCESS
20. stinking thinking	accurate perception
21. fears success	motivated for success
22. emotional disorder (depression, anxiety, drug/alcohol abuse, attention deficit disorder)	mental health
23. lack of energy	energetic
24. lack of integrity	integrity
25. lack of self-confidence	self-esteem
26. gives up easily	persistent

15

Overcoming the Attitudes of Self-Sabotage

"I Am in Charge of Me!": PERSONAL RESPONSIBILITY

Your success starts and ends with *you*. *You* want it. *You* define it. *You* go after it. *You* achieve it, or *you* don't. Only *you* are personally responsible for how your life turns out. Many other people will try to take responsibility for you—your parents, your spouse, your friends, or your coworkers—but in the final analysis, they can only influence how your life progresses, they cannot control it. Only *you* can.

Once you fully realize this first and most important ingredient of success, your life will never be the same. You will stop blaming others for your failures and disappointments and start working on changing yourself to be the kind of person you want to be. As long as you can blame someone else for things not being the way you want them to be, you can comfortably avoid change. After all, "It's their fault." However, when you have no one to blame but yourself, you are more likely to seek change. Not many people feel comfortable saying, "It's my fault."

Now, it is true that life is not fair. We are all dealt a different hand of cards in life. Some hands are very good, some hands are very, very bad. The obstacles we have to overcome are not the same for each person. It is, however, what we do with the hands we are dealt in life and not the initial hands themselves, that determines how we feel about ourselves.

The case of Beth in Chapter One, my patient with chronic schizophrenia, is a tremendous example of this. She had one of the worst possible starts a child can have in life: a mentally ill mother who abused her, and a chronic mental illness of her own. She was able to overcome these obstacles, however, and live in the present without blaming her past—a truly successful character trait. As we have seen, being born into what others might consider a success-producing background (intelligence, formal education, successful parents, and money) may have little to do with whether or not you consider yourself successful.

Many patients in early psychotherapy blame parents or significant others for the troubles that remain in adulthood:

"If only my parents hadn't gotten divorced."
"If only they had spent more time with me."
"If only they had pushed me more."
"If onlys" can go on forever. A patient must learn to forgive these people and understand that parents or others were probably only acting out of their own genes and their own backgrounds. Then he can stop blaming these others for the way his life is turning out and move on to take responsibility for it himself.

I often train my patients in self-hypnosis to indirectly teach them to take more control over their own lives. By learning to have more direct control over their bodies through relaxation, hand-warming techniques, or pain reduction, they learn that they can have more control over their minds as well.

Eric Fromm, M.D. summed up the concept of personal responsibility in his book *Man for Himself* when he wrote, "Man must accept responsibility for himself and the fact that only by using his own power, can he give meaning to his life." You have the power. It is up to you how you use it.

There is an interesting side effect to taking personal responsibility for your life. The more you realize that you're in control of your own life, the more you realize that you cannot control anyone else's life. You become more independent, while at the same time you stop believing you can change other people. You realize that only they can change themselves. Efforts directed toward changing your parents, your spouse, or your boss stop, leaving you more time and energy to work on yourself. Success takes a lot of time and energy.

PERSONAL RESPONSIBILITY EXERCISES

The following set of exercises is designed to increase your sense of *personal responsibility* and your ability to have control over your life. Personal responsibility and self-control are the first hallmarks of a successful person. Without these, one sees oneself as a victim of the world and is unable to take or accomplish any more than the world is willing to give. Personal responsibility dictates that, "If it's to be, it's up to me." It's accepting that you are human and bound to make mistakes. But, when you make them, you learn from them, and you look toward creative problem solving rather than looking for someone to blame. Taking personal responsibility for your life takes supreme courage and can be painful at any age. But the payoff is independence and freedom.

Researchers have demonstrated that it is possible for a person to change the way he perceives himself in the world; i.e., victims can take more control. These "thinking" exercises will work to strengthen your sense of personal responsibility if you commit yourself to completing them. The only person you sabotage by not completing these exercises is you. Are you worth it?

Examine the following sabotage factors, which are typical of a person weak in this area. Circle any that apply to you. Note the corresponding success factor, which is the more appropriate response. Circle the success factors that apply to you as well. Build on your strengths and strengthen your weaknesses.

Sabotage	**vs.**	**Success**
I have a tendency to blame others when things go wrong.		I admit mistakes and think about how I might have contributed to the problem.
I often act and feel like a victim.		As much as possible, I take control over my life.
I dwell on how others have contributed to my problems.		I dwell on ways to solve my problems.
I lament about getting little respect from others.		I realize that for the most part, others treat me pretty much as I teach them to treat me.
I count on luck to get what I want out of life.		I take responsibility for myself and my situation.

I often feel helpless.	I exercise the many choices and options I have in my life.
I am always trying to change other people.	I work on changing myself.
I look to the past to justify the way things are now.	I look to the present and to the future to change the way things are now.
I complain about the ways I am being held back—the system, taxes, traffic, boss, etc.	I concentrate on the things I can do to improve myself.

Do the following exercises in the order given.

I. Identify the Way You Think

For the next week, be aware of your thoughts when something goes wrong—a mistake is made, you have a problem, you have an accident—any situation in which you have a tendency to blame someone else. After you identify an incident such as this, fill in the sheet below. Do this for at least three separate incidents.

Example

1. *What happened?* I got a speeding ticket.

2. *What was my first response to the situation?* Was it to find someone else to blame? "I wasn't going that fast. *They* must have set up a speed trap."

3. *Why is it important to blame someone else?* How does that help? "If I can blame the police officer, then it is easy to first try to talk him out of the ticket. If that doesn't work, it is then OK for me to be nasty to him."

4. *Am I uncomfortable if I can't find someone to blame?* "Yes. That means it's my fault. And who likes to admit anything is their fault?"

5. *Is it OK for me to make a mistake in this instance?* "No. My insurance will go up, because this is my third ticket in a year."

Your Turn:

1. What happened?

2. What was my first response to the situation? Was it to find someone else to blame?

3. Why is it important to blame someone else? How does that help?

4. Am I uncomfortable if I can't find someone to blame?

5. Is it OK for me to make a mistake in this instance?

II. *Change the Way You Think*

You can learn to talk back to your automatic "blaming others" habit of thinking. I've set up a double-column technique to help you retrain your thoughts. In the first column, write down your automatic thought when a problem comes up, and in the second column, write down a rational response. Here are some examples to help you get started.

Blaming Others	**Personal Responsibility Response**
I'm late for my appointment. It's my wife's fault I overslept.	I can't honestly blame my wife because I overslept and am late for the appointment. If being on time is important to me, I will set the alarm to ensure I get up and accept responsibility for my timeliness.
I told the staff to rotate the merchandise and the job isn't done. They never do anything right. Their failure to follow orders is the reason sales are down.	When I notice the staff hasn't completed a job, it's my responsibility to follow up on it, so they learn to do their jobs completely. The reduction in sales probably has nothing to do with the staff not following orders. Sales fluctuate every day.
My husband always makes me feel unhappy because he acts so nasty toward me.	My husband cannot make me feel anything without my permission and cooperation. If my husband acts nasty to me, I can choose to talk to him about it; I can make it clear to him that if he doesn't

change his ways, he'll lose me; I can end the relationship; or I can continue to feel miserable. It's my responsibility how I choose to feel and how I allow other people to treat me.

Your Turn:

Blaming Others	Personal Responsibility Response
1.	
2.	
3.	
4.	
5.	

III. *Basic Training for Personal Responsibility*

Each time this week you catch yourself blaming others for something that is happening to you, STOP. Immediately stop the blaming. Think about how you contributed to the situation, and immediately work on ways to solve the problem. Refuse to spend any more energy looking for scapegoats. Look to yourself and others for answers, for ways to solve problems. Stop blaming yourself, stop blaming others. It is wasted energy.

Every time you're tempted to blame someone else, but don't— give yourself a big pat on the back. You're on your way to taking control of your life.

Impact Statements

Write out the following impact statements and tape them up in places where you're most likely to see them (on the bathroom mirror, refrigerator door at home, on your desk at work, etc.). This way they'll constantly remind you that *you* and only you are responsible for you.

I have stopped blaming other people for how my life is turning out.

I take responsibility for my own actions.

I cannot change anyone but myself.

I solve problems instead of assessing blame.

Others treat me the way I teach them to treat me.

I am not helpless; I have choices and options.

THE ROAD MAP TO WHERE YOU WANT TO BE: FOCUSED GOALS

The man without a purpose is like a ship without a rudder—a waif, a nothing, a no man. Have a purpose in life and having it, throw such strength of mind and muscle into your work as God has given you.

—Carlyle

As I wrote in Chapter One, many people who sabotage themselves feel like failures but, at the same time, they have no idea what would make them feel successful. Their motivation is unclear and their goals are ill-defined and invariably, when they try to get out of their rut by establishing new goals, comfort gets in their way. These people, when they define success for themselves, often define it in vague or unreachable terms, which makes it hard for them to know where they are on the road to reaching their goals. They say things that lack a specific definition, such as "I want happiness, contentment, self-fulfillment, wealth, or good fortune."

Successful people are clear about what they want, and they also have a good idea of how they are going to get it. They do not depend on luck or fate to help them decide what their fortunes will be or how their lives will turn out. They depend on themselves. It seems that they follow a clear pattern: They take responsibility for themselves, they begin to understand what motivates them, and then they begin to chart a course of action that will bring them along a path toward where they would like to be.

People who have clear goals have taken the time to understand what they want out of life, and they have thought about how to get it. It is amazing how little time most people spend thinking about and planning for their lives. More thinking and planning generally go into renting video movies, choosing summer vacations, or organizing Christmas shopping than into planning one's life.

Certainly planning your goals is not something you do once and set in concrete. You need an ongoing process in your life of thinking, information gathering, refining, and doing, much like what you would use in planning for any major trip.

First, *you decide to go somewhere,* such as from Washington, D.C., to Los Angeles. Then, *you determine the method by which you will reach your goal,* say driving cross-country in a car. Next, *you get a layout of the journey and plan your trip;* you get detailed maps of the country and begin to figure out the route you wish to take.

After you have the goal mapped out, *you then decide on the skills and supplies you'll need.* On our trip to Los Angeles this will include the ability and license to drive, food, emergency equipment, plenty of cash, etc. If you're smart, *you'll prepare for the possible things that might go wrong along the way.* For the trip, this might include preparing for car trouble, bad weather, detours, or thieves.

You then set a date and head out. If you start out too fast, driving too many miles in one day, you may fall asleep at the wheel and *stop the trip dead. If you start out too slow, you might not reach your goal before you run out of interest or money.*

Being too rigid about your goals might also get you into trouble. Saying to yourself, "I must drive 300 miles today," when there are tornadoes in the path, may also stop your trip dead. On a cross-country trip, as on any trip in life, *we must constantly ask ourselves where are we, where do we want to be going, and is this the best route to take?* The routes may need to change, depending on the weather, road conditions, or interests of the people who are making the trip. The initial goals may need to give way to other goals as the driver obtains new information. Otherwise, the rigidity of staying strictly on course may cause us to miss significant opportunities.

I don't know many rational people who would take such a cross-country trip without extending planning. Yet I know many people who do not spend even that much time charting a course for their lives. It is sad, because how can you get anywhere if you don't have an idea of where you want to go or how to get there?

Successful people have clear goals in the three major areas of their life—personal, relational and work. To set goals in each area, I use the W5H approach: who, what, when, where, why, and how.

1. WHO: You. You are the person setting the goals for you. As I have discussed many times now, you are the person responsible for your life. Any goals that are going to work for you must be set by you. Many people will try to make their goals your goals, but in order for you to spend the time and energy reaching goals, you eventually have to accept them as your own.

Knowing yourself is the first order of business in setting reasonable goals. Take time to inventory your assets, abilities, and liabilities. You may set yourself up to fail if you plan goals that depend on areas you are weak in. Plan around your strengths, not weaknesses.

For example, Bob was dyslexic (that is, he had trouble reading). As a counter reaction to this, he was determined to become a mechanical draftsman. The harder he tried to draw and read blueprints, the more frustrated he became. When he realized he was just attempting to deny his handicap, he was able to give up his current course and tap into one of his strengths: relating to people. He became a very successful insurance salesman for a large company.

2. WHAT: After you begin to know your assets, abilities, and liabilities, you can decide on your specific goals—what you wish to accomplish. Again, this needs to be done in the three major areas of your life, and depends on the needs and wants of your particular stage of life (these change as we change). Refer to the chapter on defining success to help you with developing goals. I'm not asking you to play a fictional story game; rather, I'm asking you to think about writing the story of your life, defining it as much as possible in your own terms, not someone else's.

3. WHEN: It is important, in defining goals, to have a specific timetable in mind for when you expect to meet them. This will help give you the drive and incentive to keep moving toward your goals, and also give you a clear idea about whether you're on the right path. You may need to alter this timetable along the way, but an overall plan must include the pace at which you intend to reach the steps toward your goals.

4. WHERE: It is also important to periodically assess where you are in the process toward your goals. Everyone does not start at the same place, nor do all of us move at the same rate toward similar goals. Periodic reassessment of personal, relational, and work goals is essential to stay on a path that moves you toward your needs and wants.

5. WHY: In order to set lasting goals for the important areas of your life, I think it is necessary for you to have some sense of what your life is all about. Think about the philosophy behind your life, be it in a religious orientation, a humanistic or existentialist framework, a biological survival-of-the-fittest struggle, or a self-actualization mode.

Too many people establish goals that are contrary to their belief systems, setting up a conflict between what they want and what they believe they should have. These areas need to be in harmony if the goals you set are going to work.

6. HOW: In the process of developing goals it is also necessary to develop a plan for meeting them, a strategy to put your motives into action. A well-prepared plan is the most essential tool for anyone who wants to achieve his goals. If you want a bank to give you a start-up loan to go into business for yourself, you must prepare a detailed business plan that covers everything from location, production, and marketing to personnel and financing. Management expert Robert Bullock states, "The strongest similarity that I have seen among owners and managers of businesses with relatively serious difficulties is a general lack of planning. Their businesses tend to run themselves. When problems arise, the boss reacts to events—he counterpunches—but he rarely thinks ahead."

Simply stated, planning is determining specific future objectives and then devising methods for reaching them. Without the specifics of "where am I going by when" and "how shall I get there," planning becomes merely wishful thinking.

Following the W5H plan will help you prioritize your time and give you a clear framework to guide your actions and interactions.

GOAL-SETTING EXERCISES

We ought to be interested in the future, for that is where we're going to spend the rest of our lives.

— ANONYMOUS

The following set of exercises is designed to help you clarify the goals for your life. Without clearly defined and balanced goals, you have no road map to where you want to be, and no standard with which to measure where you are on your life's journey.

Examine the following sabotage factors, which are typical of a person weak in this area. Circle any that apply to you. Note the corresponding success factor, which is the more appropriate response. Circle the success factors that apply to you as well. Build on your strengths and strengthen your weaknesses.

Sabotage	vs.	Success
I take life as it comes.		I take the time to think and plan my life goals.
I set goals that are either too high, without the steps to achieving them, or so low that they fail to stimulate any action.		I establish high goals for myself with identifiable steps toward reaching them.
I have trouble deciding what interests me, often jumping from thing to thing.		I have a clear sense of purpose with a clear idea of where I'm headed.
I define success in vague terms, such as happiness, fulfillment, etc.		I have specific, yet flexible, short- and long-term goals in the major areas of life (relational, personal, work-related).
My goals are unbalanced, too much emphasis in one area at the expense of others.		I balance my goals between my relational, personal, and work-related lives.
I work for other people's goals.		I work on my own goals.

I. *Reread Section One, Chapter Four, "Your Individual Definition of Success."*

II. *The One-Page Miracle*

Make sure you have completed the One-Page Miracle exercise in Section One and that you have posted it where you see it every day. This will help you focus your behavior and actions to help you get what you want.

III. *Focus Your Goals*

Go back to Question Twelve in the worksheet at the end of Section One. In that question you listed three one-year, five-year, and ten-year goals for each of the major areas of your life. Pick one goal from each area (personal, relational, and work-related) in each time frame; that is, choose one personal one-year goal, one personal five-year goal, and one personal ten-year goal. Do the same for the relational and work-related goals: choose one from each time period (for a total of nine). Next, answer the following W5H questions about each goal. Use a separate piece of paper for each goal.

1. WHO: Who is responsible for setting and reaching that goal? Is it internally or externally motivated? That means, is it your goal, or someone else's?

2. WHAT: What exactly is the goal? You need to be as specific as possible. Vague goals won't work because you have no way to measure them objectively. Concepts such as happiness, contentment, or fulfillment are adjectives describing the outcome of accomplished goals. They are not goals in and of themselves.

When you write the specific goal out, phrase it in the affirmative, as if you are certain to reach that goal. For example: "In one year I will be thirty pounds lighter," instead of, "I want to be thirty pounds lighter."

3. HOW: What specific steps do you need to take to reach the goal? This is the information-gathering step to reach your goals. It's your road map. Research the steps to your goals. Never set a goal without having an idea of how you're going to accomplish it. Be flexible, but plan the goal's accomplishment by knowing the specific steps to reaching that goal. If you don't know the steps, ask someone who has accomplished a similar goal for the steps they took.

4. WHEN: Project when you'll complete the specific steps to your goals. Have a timetable in mind. It will give you a means by which to measure your path toward your goals. Again, you need to combine flexibility with good planning.

5. WHERE: Everyone does not start at the same place. Determine where you are on the path toward your goal. Are you starting at the beginning, or have you already been working toward that thing? Mark the road map.

6. WHY: Why is this goal important for you? What is your payoff? How does it fit into your overall life plan? How does it fit into your idea of yourself?

Remember, goals are not just task-oriented. You need to have people-related goals and relaxation-related goals. Your goals need to be balanced!

Example: Work-related Five-year Goal

STARTING MY OWN FLORAL BUSINESS

1. WHO: This is my goal. Something I want for myself. Something that excites me, and that I'll work hard for! But if I am to realize this goal, I must do something about it.

2. WHAT: Specifically, in five years, I will own a successful florist shop in a good location. I will be making a net profit of $50,000 a year, and I will have at least two employees working for me whom I trust.

3. HOW:

a. For several years I will work for one or more florist shops to learn as much about the business as I can. I will work hard so that the owner will think highly enough of me to share what he knows about operating the business.

b. I will take practical business classes (maybe one a semester so that I don't overload myself) at the local community college and those the Small Business Administration offers to gather more information on the workings of a business.

c. I will begin to look at different areas where I'd like to set up my shop. I'll look into the competition already there, the area's opportunity for new growth, traffic patterns, etc. I will also learn the specific desires of the type of customers I'll be serving.

d. I will begin putting together capital for my floral shop. I will save part of my wages for the shop, and will find out about loans and financing from lending institutions, and what I need to qualify for the money. I will also talk about the venture with people I know who might be interested. Planning ahead increases my chances of meeting someone who'll be interested in the business.

e. I will subscribe to the industry trade journal and plan to attend an annual trade show to learn about the latest information and trends in the floral business and to meet other owners.

f. As time draws nearer to opening my shop, I'll write a formal business plan for it and give it to several of the trusted people I've met over the past several years to get their input on it.

4. WHEN:

a. In two to three months I'll have a job in a floral shop with a good reputation.

b. Within one month I will talk to the business counselor at the community college or the SBA to find out what classes would help me reach my goal. I will enroll in one for the upcoming semester if possible.

c. Within the first six months I'll begin asking the owner of the shop more about the workings of the business.

d. Within the first year I'll begin to talk more about my plan to family members, friends, and others to get their feedback, and to plant some seeds for future investors in the business.

e. Within the first year I will begin to put away ten percent of my gross income to save for the business venture. Even though that won't cover all the start-up costs for the business, it will show the bank or other investor that I'm serious.

f. After the first year I'll begin to look into areas where I'd like to set up my shop, to become familiar with upcoming possibilities.

g. As soon as possible, I'll subscribe to the industry trade journal, and after two years I'll attend a floral trade show.

h. In the third year (I'll have learned a lot by now), I'll write the formal business plan and get feedback on it.

i. From then on I'll be seriously looking for locations and opportunities to start the business. I'll also be on the lookout for trusted hard-working people to work for me.

5. WHERE AM I:

I'm just starting out on the path to opening my own business. I have a lot to learn. But I will do it. I already know I like floral arranging, because I've been doing a small business of that in my home. So I'm not a complete novice.

6. WHY:

There are several major reasons why I want to open my own shop:

a. I eventually want to be my own boss. I want to be the one in charge.

b. I want to have more income potential than I will have if I work for someone else.

c. I enjoy creating arrangements and doing things in a different way. I'm excited about the possibilities the floral business will give to my creative expression.

d. As a businessperson I'll be able to provide a service to the community, be involved in employing other people, and down the road I can look at the possibility of expansion.

Now: On a 3 x 5 card, summarize the major W5H points to your goal, using several highlighted words to illustrate the major points. Then in red, highlight the next step you need to take to reach that goal—not the final step, but the next step—and the time it will take to accomplish that. Once you reach the next step, rewrite the card to highlight the step after it. In this way you'll be constantly reminding yourself of the goal and the next step to reaching it.

After you fill out the W5H formula for the nine goals you choose, file them in an easily accessible place. Take the summary 3 x 5 cards you filled out and put them up in a place where you can look at them every day. Read through them every day. Revise them as often as necessary.

Impact Statements

Write out the following impact statements and tape them up in places where you're most likely to see them (on the bathroom mirror, refrigerator door at home, on your desk at work, etc.). This way they'll constantly remind you of your goals, so that you can focus your energy on them instead of on things that have little meaning for you.

I am responsible for reaching my goals.
I balance my goals between my personal, relational, and work life, in order to be a happy, healthy person.
I will focus my time and energy on my goals.
I match my actions with my goals.

IMAGINEERING: THE EXPECTATIONS AND ATTITUDES OF SUCCESS

As long as you have life and breath you start again.
—SMALL BUSINESS OWNER WHOSE BUSINESS HAD JUST BURNED DOWN

After goals and plans are made, successful people expect to accomplish their desires. They are not born with this expectation; over the years, they have developed an attitude of success.

The expectation of success is a very powerful force by itself. Skilled physicians have known for centuries that positive expectations play a crucial role in the outcome of many illnesses. Until 100 to 150 years ago, the history of medical therapeutics was largely that of the doctor-patient relationship and the "placebo effect" (placebos being inert substances that have no physiologic effect on the problem). Actually, most of the treatments by physicians back then would have been more harmful than beneficial to the patient, if it weren't for the recuperative powers of the human organism supported by the belief in the healing powers of the physician's prescriptions.

The benefits of the placebo effect are determined by the expectations and hopes shared by the patient and the doctor. Action, ritual, faith, and enthusiasm are the important ingredients. Jerome Frank, M.D., after studying the psychotherapeutic process, concluded that the belief of the therapist in his treatment and the belief of the patient in the therapist were the most important factors in a positive outcome to therapy.

Although a placebo is a substance that is considered pharmacologically inert, it is by no means "nothing." It is a potent therapeutic tool, on the average about one-half to two-thirds as powerful as morphine in relieving severe pain.

It is now recognized that one-third of the general population are placebo responders in clinical situations relating to pain, whether the pain is from surgery, angina, cancer, or headache. It is very clear that placebo responses are not simply a result of the patient fooling or tricking himself out of the pain. Placebo administration can produce real physiologic changes.

Some of the physiologic pathways through which the placebo effects work have been identified. In a 1978 study done by a University of California research team, it was found that the placebo effect of pain relief in dental patients could actually be blocked by administering these patients naloxone, a drug that neutralizes the effects of morphine in the body. From this study and others, it has become clear that the belief in pain relief stimulates the body to secrete its own pain relieving substance, called endorphins, which act in the same manner as morphine, only they are much more potent. Belief can cause change.

Child rearing is another area in which expectations influence outcome. Every day I come into contact with parents who, through frustration and poor feelings about themselves, expect their kids to grow up and wreak havoc on the world. I've had more than one mother tell me that when her Johnny came out of the womb, he had a mean look on his face, and that he was just waiting to grow up so that he could cause her trouble.

At first I didn't believe what I was hearing. Why would a mother give those feelings to an innocent newborn? After all, was Johnny supposed to have a pleasant expression on his face after being squeezed through a narrow canal for ten hours and then being slapped on the bottom? These parents don't feel very good about themselves, so they project their negative feelings onto the child.

Expectations also affect employer-employee relationships. Many bosses establish initial impressions about employees that stay with them throughout their employment, even if those impressions were based on erroneous assumptions. For example, Blair was late for work his first day at the bank. He was a single father and his daughter had been sick the night before. Now even though he hadn't missed a day of work in his previous job in over a year his new boss still felt he was irresponsible and was overly critical of him from the start.

Those who expect to fail, or expect others to fail, often set up situations so that they do fail. They do not prepare themselves adequately; they take ludicrous risks, act impulsively or act so negative that it's impossible for them to succeed.

Those who expect to succeed set themselves up to win. And if this positive expectation is mixed appropriately with the other ingredients of success, action will occur along the right path.

Expecting to succeed at a task is essential, but be wary of the positive-thinking priests who preach a positive mental outlook by itself. Many people have told me that after leaving a positive thinking seminar they are pumped up and ready to make their first million dollars. That emotional high, however, is usually gone in a few days. When the positive mental attitude is mixed with the other ingredients of success, it adds excitement and energy. When it is applied in a vacuum, it is often no better than a shot of heroin. It makes you feel high for the moment, but the problems are still there when the buzz wears off.

The most effective tool I've found to help people improve their attitudes and increase their expectations is mental rehearsing, or imagineering. I have them imagine themselves reaching their goals with all of their senses. If the goal is better sex, I have them imagine it, as they want it, with all their senses. If their goal is to make an outstanding presentation at work, I have them give each step of the presentation in their minds just as they would want to give it.

In sports, mental rehearsing is becoming a standard practice for professional athletes. They imagine themselves making the golf shot, hitting the home run, or intercepting a pass before they walk on the field or right before they hit the ball, step up to the plate, etc. A marathon runner I know said she never thought that she could run a marathon until she heard about mental rehearsing. She tried it, and after six months she ran her first twenty-six-mile marathon. As you believe, so shall you act.

POSITIVE EXPECTATIONS EXERCISES

When you expect to fail, your subconscious mind acts to set up conditions under which you eventually do fail. You might, quite by "accident," forget to do things essential to your task, however small, and then say to yourself, "See, I knew it wouldn't work."

Your negative expectations have been programmed into your mind over a long period of time. They have a hypnotic hold over what you can and cannot do in your life. The following exercises have been designed to uproot the negative mindset and expectations that hold you back. These exercises are some of the most powerful in the book. If you do them seriously and consistently, you'll notice a dramatic change in your outlook and attitude. This will have an impact on all areas of your life.

Examine the following sabotage factors, which are typical of people weak in this area. Circle any that apply to you. Note the corresponding success factor, which is the more appropriate response. Circle the success factors that apply to you as well. Build on your strengths and strengthen your weaknesses.

Sabotage	vs.	Success
I generally expect that I'll fail.		I expect to win.
I expect to be taken advantage of.		I expect to get the best deal available.
I anticipate that I'll be unable to learn new things.		I know that if I try, I can do what I set out to do.
I think failure, then go about making myself right.		I see myself succeeding at tasks before I do them.
I am a pessimistic person.		I am a hopeful person.
When things go well, I wonder when they'll turn sour again.		I feel good when things work out.
I have trouble believing in anything.		I believe in myself and those around me.

I. Imagineering/The Power Within

We all have a Power Within—a natural power source that most people never tap. It is found within you, within your imagination, within your ability to perceive things as you want them to be before they really are that way. Your powerful mind can be harnessed for your benefit, rather than using your expectations to hold you down, as in the past.

There are very specific steps to unlocking this power for you. To do this effectively requires relaxation and a focused mind. First, it is important to practice the relaxation exercise below to put you in the right frame of mind to use this power. Set aside two to three ten-minute periods the first day and just go through the following six steps.

Relaxation:

1. Sit in a comfortable chair with your feet on the floor and your hands in your lap.

2. Then, pick a spot on a wall that is a little bit above your eye level. Stare at the spot. As you do, count to twenty. Notice that in a short bit your eyes will begin to feel heavy and feel that they want to close. Let them. In fact, even if they don't feel like they want to close, slowly close them anyway as you get to twenty.

3. Next, take a deep breath, as deep as you can, and very slowly exhale. Repeat the deep breath and slowly exhale three times. With each breath in, imagine taking in peace and calmness, and with each breath out, blow out all the tension, all the things getting in the way of your relaxing. By this time, you'll notice a calm come over you.

4. After that, tightly squeeze the muscles in your eyelids. Close your eyes as tightly as you can. Then slowly let the muscles in your eyelids relax. Notice how much more they have relaxed. Then imagine that relaxation spreading from the muscles in your eyelids to the muscles in your face . . . down your neck into your shoulders and arms . . . into your chest and throughout the rest of your body. The muscles will take the relaxation cue from your eyelids and relax progressively all the way down to the bottom of your feet.

5. After your whole body feels relaxed, imagine yourself at the top of an escalator. Step on the escalator and ride down, counting backward from twenty. By the time you reach the bottom, you'll be very relaxed.

6. Enjoy the tranquility for several moments. Then get back on the escalator riding up. Count to ten. When you get to ten open your eyes, feel relaxed, refreshed, and wide awake.

To make these steps easy to remember, think of the words:

Focus (focus on the spot)
Breathe (slow, deep breaths)
Relax (progressive muscle relaxation)
Down (ride down the escalator)
Up (ride up the escalator and open your eyes)

If you have trouble remembering these steps, you may want to record them and do the exercise as you listen to the tape.

When you do this the first several times, allow yourself plenty of time. Some people become so relaxed that they fall asleep for several minutes. If that happens, don't worry. It's actually a good sign—you're really relaxed!

When you've practiced this technique a few times, add the following steps:

Visual Imagery:

Choose a haven—a place where you feel comfortable, a place that you can imagine with all your senses. I usually "go" to the beach. I can relax there, and it calls up beautiful imagery for me. I can see the ocean, feel the sand between my toes, feel the warm sun and breeze on my skin. Smell the salt air and taste it faintly on my tongue. Hear the sea gulls, the waves, children playing. Your haven can be a real or imagined place. It can be any place where you'd like to spend time.

After you reach the bottom of the escalator imagine yourself in your very special haven. Imagine it with all of your senses for several minutes.

Imagineering:

This is where the fun starts. After you've gone through the relaxation steps and have imagined yourself in your haven, your mind is ripe for change.

Begin to experience yourself as *you* want to be. Not as you currently are. But as you *want* to be. Plan on spending at least twenty minutes a day on this refueling, life-changing exercise. You'll be amazed at the results.

During each session, choose one goal to work on. Stay with that goal until you can imagine yourself reaching it, going through each of the steps required to reach the goal. For example, if your goal is to own your own business, see yourself in that business with all your senses. See the office or shop. Interact with your customers. Smell the environment around you. Feel your desk. Sip a cup of coffee in your chair, savoring the taste and aroma, etc. Experience your dream. Make it real in your imagination, thereby beginning to make it real in your life. Or, if a goal is to improve your relationship with your spouse, lover, or children, imagine the relationship as you'd want it to be. Imagine it in as much detail as you can.

Remember the Steps:

Relaxation—Visual Imagery—Imagineering

The way to improve your expectations is to first imagine the situation as you want it to be, instead of, as you have been, imagining the worst.

II. *Mental Rehearsing*

Rehearse each challenging task mentally. Before any difficult or important situation—a job interview, a public presentation, a sail-boat race—most peak performers run through their desired actions in their minds over and over. Famous golf pro Jack Nicklaus, for example, never takes a golf shot without first mentally visualizing the precise trajectory of his swing, the flight of the ball, and the spot where it will land.

Nearly all of us daydream about important upcoming events. But idle daydreams won't get you very far unless you focus them on the exact activity you'll be doing—in other words, put yourself through a mental workout. This mental workout is found in the concepts of the very popular programs of Inner Golf and Inner Tennis. In fact, many professional athletes religiously use their mental workout concept to improve the quality and consistency of their game.

Likewise, many famous professionals use mental rehearsing to strengthen their chances for succeeding at their tasks. One amazing story comes from China. A pianist, imprisoned for seven years during the Cultural Revolution, played as well as ever soon after he was released. His explanation: "I practiced every day in my mind."

Any time you come to an important situation for yourself, mentally go over the steps to success. See yourself succeeding in the situation. Rehearse in as much detail as possible what you will be saying or doing, and imagine how you'll feel after you have successfully completed the task.

Mental rehearsing has a double benefit. It will increase your expectations of succeeding, *and* it makes you better prepared, thereby increasing even more your chances for success.

Impact Statements

Write out the following impact statements and tape them up in places where you're most likely to see them (on the bathroom mirror, refrigerator door at home, on your desk at work, etc.). This way they'll constantly remind you of the power your expectations and unconscious mind have over your life. You can be in control of your expectations or they can control you.

> Before I do something, I imagine myself succeeding at it with all
>   my senses.
> I am an imagineer.
> I believe in myself and my abilities.
> I believe that I can have a positive impact on others.
> I am worth others having a positive impact on me.
> We act to fulfill our expectations for ourselves.

CHANCE FAVORS THE MIND PREPARED: PREPARATION

Successful people are prepared to accomplish their goals. They take the time before they come to a situation to think about it and prepare for it. They also prepare others for how their actions might impact them.

Did God start by creating man? No. In the beginning, God created the heavens and the earth. Then He proceeded to create the day and the night, the sun, the moon and the stars, the land and the sea, the forests and the gardens, the fish, the birds and the mammals. He took into account all that was necessary, and He prepared extensively for His ultimate purpose on earth: the creation of man.

Whether or not you accept the above description of our genesis is not the point. What is important is that preparation is paramount to accomplishment, and with a solid foundation, goals become achievable; without it they're impossible.

So where do you start? Where else but at the beginning. If you want to be a writer, you need to learn grammar and vocabulary. If you want to be successful at business, you need to acquire basic math and accounting skills. And, if you want to be a physician, you need to start with basic chemistry and physics.

To carry this point even further, it is necessary to start at the beginning of the beginning. I know this sounds redundant, but this simple principle will save you many hours of frustration and stress. It is essential in medicine, for example, to know what is normal before you can understand what is abnormal. It is also important if you are going to enter into a new relationship to have some understanding of the give and take required between people to make a relationship work.

Thinking is trial action. Think about what you are going to do; mentally rehearse the steps to your goals over and over so that you can begin to understand what could go right and what might go wrong. Successful actors rehearse their lines many times. They rehearse them in different ways to find the most effective presentation for the material. They then rehearse their lines in front of the director to get his input into the scene. Likewise, it is smart for all of us to mentally rehearse our steps to success, first by ourselves, then with the help of others who can give us a different perspective. When you go for job interviews, for example, prepare for whatever questions might be asked. Ask others who have gone through the process what it was like. You could write out the possible questions and answers, and role-play the interview with a friend or family member.

The principle of preparation may delay your plans by a few months, but inadequate background and preparation are one of the main reasons people fail at tasks they set out to accomplish. A great chef would never think of shortchanging the preparation time necessary to make a great feast. Neither should you shortchange the preparation to your goals. Remember,

---

Preparation is paramount to accomplishment.

Another aspect of preparation that often goes overlooked in the steps to success is, how will your actions influence others? Any time there is a significant change in one member of a family, it always affects the other members in one form or another. I have treated many families with a variety of presenting complaints, and it is amazing how after I help one member overcome his or her difficulties, another member begins to have a problem. People reach an equilibrium with those around them. When one person changes, his relationships invariably change as well. Becoming successful will no doubt change your relationships, particularly if you've been surrounding yourself with negative people. You may note that you have a cheering section to stimulate more success, or, more likely, you may notice people trying to hold you back. Prepare yourself for either response and prepare others for the changes you are about to make.

PREPARATION EXERCISES

Nothing is particularly hard if you break it down into small jobs.

—HENRY FORD

Lack of preparation increases anxiety and markedly decreases effectiveness. Adequate preparation has several components. These include mentally rehearsing each step of your task, obtaining appropriate prerequisites, practicing or rehearsing for the task, structuring time, fighting procrastination, and preparing others for your actions.

The following set of exercises is designed to help you strengthen your steps to being better prepared, thereby increasing your chances for success, as chance favors the mind prepared.

Examine the following sabotage factors, which are typical of people weak in this area. Circle any that apply to you. Note the corresponding success factor, which is the more appropriate response. Circle the success factors that apply to you as well. Build on your strengths and strengthen your weaknesses.

Sabotage	vs.	Success
I am often caught unprepared for my tasks.		I am prepared.
I go into important situations without much forethought.		I spend time before important events, planning and writing down major points to be covered.

I put things off until the last minute.	I get things done right away.
I cram for tests or get projects done hurriedly, sacrificing quality.	When I want to do something well, I spend adequate time practicing and rehearsing it.
I am impulsive.	I think things through before I do them.
Anxiety paralyzes me from preparing for my tasks.	I combat anxiety by using the energy to prepare for the task.
I use lack of preparation as an excuse for failure.	I prepare adequately and accept the outcome.

I. Mental Rehearsing: Thinking Is Trial Action

The first step in adequate preparation is to mentally rehearse each step you need to take to accomplish your goal. Visualize exactly what needs to be done, what you need to do, and what you need to get others to do for you. Going through this mental workout will help you perform better, and by its very imaginative nature will increase your expectations of success and thus your actual chances for successful completion of your task.

1. Choose a task you have to accomplish today. (This can be anything from making dinner to giving an office presentation.)

2. Take several minutes, close your eyes, breathe in and out slowly three times and then imagine yourself (use all your senses) step by step successfully doing the things necessary to accomplish that task. To do this, ask yourself the following questions:

What tools or ingredients do I need to accomplish that task efficiently? How do I get what I need?
Can another person or persons be helpful to me in completing that task?
How much preparation time is necessary for the activity?
Are there people who will be affected by my actions? Do I need to prepare them as well?
What could go wrong? How can I prevent those things from happening?

3. After you've mentally rehearsed the steps to accomplishing your task or activity, write down the preparation steps you imagined. As you do, ask yourself:

What steps can I add that will improve my preparation and thus improve my chances for success?

What steps can I delete that will save me time without sacrificing effectiveness?

Do this for several days on day-to-day matters, then go through this mental workout for some of the more major goals you have for your life. *The more you do this, the more valuable this powerful tool will become.*

II. *Prerequisites:*

For success in any task, it's important to have the necessary tools, materials, ingredients, skills, or training needed to complete it. Many classes in school, for example, require prerequisite classes, so that students will enter the class adequately prepared and not "over their heads." In preparing for any task, ask yourself if you have the necessary prerequisites to get the job done the way you want it done.

Before doing tasks important to you, ask yourself what prerequisites you need. Get in the habit of thinking, do I need specific tools, special materials, extra ingredients? Do I need more training or increased skill to be able to do the job better? In short, what do I need to help me accomplish my tasks in a more efficient and productive manner?

III. *What's the Next Step Exercise*

"What's the next step?"

If you keep this phrase in mind, you'll be on your way toward beating the feeling of being overwhelmed by your tasks. Too often it feels as if there is just too much to do. This feeling is characterized by thought statements such as, "It's just too much. I'll never get finished."

After you've mentally rehearsed your tasks or goals and gathered the adequate prerequisites, ask yourself, "What is the next step to accomplishing it?"

This question will help you break out of the "overwhelmed" group of self-saboteurs. It will help you break down your goals or tasks into pieces you can manage, things you can control.

It's important to have an overall plan or goal for the task, but it's just as important to know the next step you need to take to reach it.

1. Choose a task you have to accomplish today and write out the steps you need to take to accomplish it on a 3 x 5 card.

2. Then circle the very first step you need to take in red. Hint: This is a good point at which to mentally rehearse the task.

3. After you complete that step, cross it off. Then circle the following step, and so on. Do this until you finish the task. This way, your task is broken down into steps that make sense and enable you to be in control of the situation.

IV. *Talking Back Exercise*

Part of preparation is talking back to the negative thought habits that say, "You will fail anyway, so why prepare?"

You can take action on your own behalf: Train yourself to write down your critical, self-defeating thoughts that sabotage your preparation; and practice talking back to them to take away their power.

Automatic Thoughts	**Response Talk Back**
Why should I take any training? I'll just get passed over for promotion.	How do you know? You can't read the future. But you can set it up so that you won't be promoted if you don't get the extra training.
Why study for the exam? I don't understand the material and won't get a good enough grade anyway.	Study what you can. What you don't understand you can ask the teacher about. But first you need to know what you don't know. Break it down into steps.
Nobody appreciates me; why should I do the best I can do? I can get by with minimal preparation.	Your low self-esteem is beating you up. Even if no one really does appreciate you, which is most likely a distortion, you need to appreciate yourself. The better prepared you are for the things important to you, the easier it will be to appreciate yourself.

Add your own automatic thoughts and back talk responses.

1.
2.

V. Procrastination: Eight Ways to Beat It

The following is a list of ideas for defeating the greatest enemy that stands between you and adequate preparation: *procrastination*.

1. Consciously fight procrastination. The sooner you do it, the sooner it will be done. If you can do it now, then do it now.

2. Break down overwhelming tasks into small tasks. This happens on assembly lines every day. Remember, "A journey of a thousand miles begins with one step."

3. Do a start-up task now! Go to the next step you need to do to accomplish that goal and do it. Just getting started will increase your momentum.

4. Make a wager with someone. Use your competitive nature to your advantage. I do this most effectively when I want to lose weight. It helps me get going on my diet. First, I find someone who also wishes to lose some weight. We then agree on a target number of pounds to be lost and set a time limit. If one person makes it and the other doesn't, the loser pays the winner twenty dollars per pound not lost. If we both fail to lose the weight, then it costs us each twenty dollars per pound, but it's sent to an agreed-upon charity. So far, it's worked for me every time.

5. Give yourself a reward. Tell yourself that after you finish a difficult task, you'll reward yourself with something special you want.

6. Do unpleasant tasks first. That way, you'll have the more pleasurable ones to look forward to. If you save the unpleasant tasks for last, you'll have little incentive to get to them.

7. Tell someone else the date that you'll finish by. Putting your word or reputation on the line is often a potent kick in the rear to get started.

8. Think about how you'll feel once the task is done. Anticipating the sense of accomplishment will help spur you on.

Impact Statements

Write out the following impact statements and tape them up in places where you're most likely to see them (on the bathroom mirror, refrigerator door at home, on your desk at work, etc.). This way they'll constantly remind you of the importance of preparing sufficiently for your tasks.

Thinking is trial action.
Preparation is paramount to accomplishment.
Before I do something, I go through a mental workout and imagine the steps to my goals.
Do I have the necessary prerequisites?
What's the next step?
Do it now!

MAKE MISTAKES COUNT FOR SOMETHING: LEARN FROM FAILURES

> *If I had a formula for bypassing trouble, I wouldn't pass it around. Wouldn't be doing anybody a favor. Trouble creates a capacity to handle it.*
> —OLIVER WENDELL HOLMES

Abraham Lincoln built a lifetime of accomplishments out of defeats. Look at his record.

He lost his job in 1832.
He was defeated for the Illinois legislature in 1832.
He failed in business in 1833.
He was elected to the Illinois legislature in 1834.
His sweetheart died in 1835.
He had a nervous breakdown in 1836.
He was defeated for speaker of the Illinois legislature in 1838.
He was defeated for the nomination of Congress in 1843.
He was elected to Congress in 1846.
He lost the renomination in 1848.
He was rejected for land officer in 1849.

He was defeated for the Senate in 1854.

He lost the nomination for vice president in 1856.

He was defeated again for the Senate in 1858.

He was elected president in 1860.

Failure Is Not Fatal. Not Trying Is!

Failure is a part of everyone's life. No one starts out walking in life; it is months before we even learn how to crawl. It is not failure that holds people back; it is their attitude toward failure and their fear of it. Toddlers don't give up when they fall; they take their bruises and try again. Anyone who has had small children knows that despite many failed attempts at mobilization, most children go very quickly from crawling to walking to running to climbing up to places they shouldn't.

It is arrogant to think that we are perfect and we will never fail. We are not programmed with the answers; we learn them. We get the right answers by learning processes and observing our errors along the way. Successful supervisors do not get angry when their employees make mistakes. They say, "Don't be afraid to make mistakes; learn from them. Just don't make the same one twice. Observe what you do and you'll always improve."

How supervisors deal with the mistakes of their employees often determines the quality of the employees. When people go to work and they expect to be yelled at or belittled, their fear and anger get in the way of them doing the best they can. When they go to work and know that they will be taught to learn from their mistakes in a positive atmosphere, they relax and are more likely to produce good work.

Be a good teacher for yourself and those around you. Maturity is being able to learn from the mistakes you make in a positive atmosphere.

How we learn from mistakes is a trait we learned in childhood. What happened when you made a mistake as a child? When you spilled something at the dinner table or you did poorly on a test? Were you berated and yelled at for the mistake or were you encouraged to learn something from it?

One of the most critical lessons a parent can teach a child is how to learn from mistakes. Too often as parents we are super critical of ourselves when we fail, and that attitude then transfers to how we treat our children when they fail at something.

In order to help our children feel good about themselves we must help them to be competent. Of course, competent people make mistakes. The difference is that they have the ability to learn from them and move on to other things rather than to beat themselves up for it.

For example, think about the four-year-old child who spills orange juice at breakfast. Many parents, who might be in a hurry to get off to work, would get stressed by the delay in schedule and take their frustration out by yelling at the child. The child feels incompetent and the next time he tries to pour juice he'll feel anxious and tense—making him more likely to spill it again.

Parents need to focus their energy on helping their child learn from the mistakes he makes. So instead of yelling at the child for the spilled orange juice, I recommend that you teach the child how to clean up the mess and then take him over to the sink and have him pour ten glasses of orange juice. In that way, he's gone from making a mistake to learning two skills: cleaning up a mess and pouring juice. He's gone from feeling clumsy and stupid to feeling competent.

In order to raise healthy children, and be healthy adults, it is critical to teach them how to learn from the mistakes they make and to give them a framework for problem solving.

LEARN FROM YOUR FAILURES EXERCISES

A man can fail many times, but he isn't a failure until he begins to blame somebody else.
— JOHN BURROUGHS

The fear of failure may be preventing you from trying. When you do fail, you may do everything you can to not think about it, and thus end up repeating the same mistakes. Success involves many failures and lessons along the way. It's all in the perception. When you fail, you can say it's because you're a worthless human being who'll never do anything right; or you can tell yourself that everyone fails and makes mistakes, that the success factor is whether or not you learn anything from them. You never win at anything unless you try, and you never learn unless you become a student.

The following exercises are designed to help you perceive your mistakes and failures differently—in a way that lets you learn from them and make them work for you, rather than against you.

Examine the following sabotage factors, which are typical of a person weak in this area. Circle any that apply to you. Note the corresponding success factor, which is the more appropriate response. Circle the success factors that apply to you as well. Build on your strengths and strengthen your weaknesses.

Sabotage	vs.	Success
I make the same mistake over and over again.		I learn from failure and mistakes.
When I make a mistake, I tend to shy away from similar situations in the future.		When I make a mistake, I analyze what went wrong so that I can learn from it.
The fear of failure prevents me from trying.		I try, try again, if I don't succeed at first.
When I make a mistake, I berate myself for it, rather than learn from it.		Failing at something stimulates me to try again until I get it right.
When I fail at something, I try to forget about it, because it hurts too much to think about it.		After the initial disappointment of failing at something, I find new ways to master it.

I. What Mistakes Have You Made?

In each of the major areas of your life, list at least one significant blunder you have made, preferably more.

How did you respond to those failures? Place the relevant numbers of the following statements next to the mistake. List the lessons you can learn from the mistakes you've made.

1. I learned from it.
2. I berated myself for it over and over.
3. I blamed someone else for it.
4. I did everything I could to forget about it.
5. I repeated the failure.
6. It was painful, but I got through and learned along the way.
7. I stayed away from similar situations in the future.
8. The mistake stimulated me to look deeper to do it right.

Personal (emotional, physical, spiritual)

example: I let myself get fat. (#2,3,4 above) I can learn about how I got that way; my triggers for overeating (I had lots of practice); and that I don't like being fat so I'll change it.

Relational

example: For the second time I married someone who always works. (#1,5 above) I can learn the need to know someone thoroughly before I commit to marry them.

Work-related

example: I became lax about promptness and was passed over for promotion. (#3,4,5 above) I can learn that many people regard promptness as a sign of responsibility, and instead of blaming others for what I did, take responsibility for changing the behaviors that hold me back.

Always look for something to learn from your mistakes.

II. *Perfection Is Arrogance*

Expecting to be perfect, to never make a mistake, is arrogant. It's assuming that you're different from everyone else who has ever lived. Stop expecting more from yourself than you're capable of. In order to help you get over having to be perfect, I want you to make three mistakes this week!

1. Give someone the wrong amount for a purchase you make. Give them a few cents less. If they don't notice it, point it out to them with embarrassment. If they do notice it, apologize and pay the difference.

2. Try a new sport this week. Any time we try something new, we're bound to have a shaky start. (Hit golf balls, take a tennis lesson, go to the baseball batting cage, etc.)

3. Try a new video game at your local shopping mall. No one I know gets them right the first time.

III. *What Can You Learn from Your Mistakes?*

Change your attitude. This week, every time you notice that you fail at something, however big or small, write it down in one column, and in another column write down at least one thing you can learn from the failure. Stop berating yourself for your mistakes; learn from them so they aren't repeated.

Failure/Mistake	STOP BLAMING — What Can I Learn?
Traffic ticket	Slow down
Fight with spouse	Can be more sensitive next time
Had too much to drink at a party	Will not drink at the next party, or ask someone to tell me when it looks like I'm getting out of control
Lost temper at a customer	Become more aware when I'm losing control so that I can defuse the situation or walk away before it gets out of control

Impact Statements

Write out the following impact statements and tape them up in places where you're most likely to see them (on the bathroom mirror, refrigerator door at home, on your desk at work, etc.). This way they'll constantly remind you of the need to learn from your failures instead of being defeated by them.

Failures, although not fun, are stepping stones to success.
Like a toddler learning to walk, I learn from the falls I take.
It is a real mistake to not make mistakes count for something.
Don't be afraid to make mistakes; learn from them. Just don't make the same one twice.
When I don't learn from my mistakes, I am bound to repeat them.
I am only exempt from failure if I never try, which also exempts me from success.

A DIFFERENT LOOK: CREATIVITY

Being creative is having the ability to look at common things in an uncommon way; to take a different approach; to discover our other selves.

Inside all of us are many personalities. There is the manager, who handles the day-to-day necessities. The lover, who handles intimacy. The judge, who oversees the decisions we make. The prosecuting attorney, who tries to convict us of real or imagined crimes. The comedian, who helps us not to take ourselves too seriously. And many others, including our artist, who helps us create beauty and newness in our lives by seeing, hearing, or touching things in a different way.

Unfortunately, many people have come to equate creativity with madness, using the painter Vincent van Gogh and others like him as examples. Current medical research, however, teaches us that the healthier we are, the more creative we are likely to be, the less rigid and more able to let our other selves out to play.

Psychiatrist Daniel Offer, M.D. studied several hundred teenagers to see what characterizes "normal" adolescence. He described three distinct patterns of psychological growth: turbulent, sporadic, and continuous. He then gave the ink blot test to the young people in his study and found that those with the healthiest growth pattern, i.e., the continuous growth group, gave the most creative and unusual responses to the cards. Creativity correlated with health.

Successful people are able to let their other sides out. They do not fearfully guard what is inside. Rather, they are able to find ways to give expression to their artist within. There are innumerable ways to do this. Some do it by writing, some by painting or sculpting. More frequently, people let their creative sides out in relationships, in creating at work, or in recreation. They are able to take a new look at common situations.

Creativity does not take genius. It takes willingness to look at common things in a different way; to explore all of the options available to you, conventional and unconventional; and to try new ideas, even when you're not sure if they will work out.

Creativity best occurs in the context of the other ingredients of success. It is much easier to be creative about finances, relationships, or inner feelings if you take charge of the situation, become informed, prepare for the task, learn to observe, and so on.

Creativity and adaptability are very close concepts. Advertising is an obvious example of the need for creativity and adaptability. Ken Roberts, who made several million dollars in mail order publishing in 1989, said, "If an ad works, great! Continue it. If it bombs, and you have a product you believe in, redo it, and redo it until it does work. Sticking with a bomb is dangerous. I had to redo the ad for my book several times before it took. But when it took, wow, did it go!"

Remember studying the American Revolution in school? What was one of the major reasons for the British defeat? They were unable to change as the situation warranted. Even though they had superior weapons and numbers of soldiers, their warfare methods were outdated. They fought the American Colonists in a very regimented, stylized way that had worked for them in other wars. However, their previous military success calloused their egos against change, and even toward the end of the war, when defeat was closing in on them, they still fought the feisty rebels with lines and regiments of soldiers, instead of changing their tactics to the guerrilla warfare of the Colonists. They were unable to change, so they lost.

The same idea holds true for relationships. People change. We all go through developmental periods in our lives. Unless we understand this about ourselves and the people we are involved with, the relationships most likely will turn sour and bring pain instead of joy and comfort.

Jerry Lewis, M.D., director of Timberlawn Psychiatric Hospital in Dallas, Texas, published a landmark study several years ago on the characteristics of a healthy family. At the top of the list he cited the family's ability to adapt to new situations and new developmental stages. They do not react to crisis by fighting or blaming each other for the trouble. Rather, they first look at alternative ways to handle difficult situations. For example, if a family was faced with a long-distance move, the parents did not spend much time lamenting all the losses they would experience, such as friends and familiar surroundings. They would focus instead on the positive aspects of their new home. Even though moves are difficult for everyone, adaptability of the parents influences how the children respond, which in turn influences how the family does as a unit.

As we will see, adaptability needs to be balanced with persistence. Rapid change or adaptation may be just as dangerous as never changing. Experience mediates flexibility and persistence. When you are unsure of the course to take, gather information from the experienced mind.

CREATIVITY AND ADAPTABILITY EXERCISES

Creativity occurs in all areas of life, not just the arts. It's defined here as being able to look at common things in an uncommon way. We all have the capacity to create this newness and change in our worlds when necessary; we only have to take the time to look for new and different ways to approach our lives. Creativity requires looking for new alternatives and new solutions to problems. These new solutions are based on our past experience, current information, and visions for the future.

Examine the following sabotage factors, which are typical of a person weak in this area. Circle any that apply to you. Note the corresponding success factor, which is the more appropriate response. Circle the success factors that apply to you as well. Build on your strengths and strengthen your weaknesses.

Sabotage	vs.	**Success**
I feel helpless in difficult situations, being unable to find new solutions to old problems.		I actively seek new options and new alternatives for old problems.
I feel anxious when I do things in a different way.		I often ask myself how things might be done differently.
I have difficulty compromising, unless I'm pushed into a corner.		When a problem arises I am able to compromise.
Once I make a decision, I stick to it no matter what.		I reconsider decisions if unforeseen disadvantages develop.
I resist change.		I encourage change for self-improvement.
I am controlled by habit.		I approach each situation open to the alternatives.
I handle problems in old ways even when they haven't worked in the past.		I look for new ways to solve problems or situations.
I get upset when something unexpected changes my schedule.		I tolerate, sometimes even enjoy, changes in routine.
I am stubborn, set in my ways.		I am firm in my goals, but flexible in the means of achieving them.

I. Where Are You Stuck?

In order to increase your creative skill, you must first identify the areas in your life in which you feel particularly stuck or uncreative.

For each of the major areas in your life, list problems where you continue to operate in the same unproductive ways, where you have been unable to find new or creative solutions. Examples are given below in parentheses.

Personal life:

spirituality: (I have a wishy-washy faith, and that really upsets me.)
emotional life: (I feel like I'm on an emotional rollercoaster. It seems like I'll never get off.)
physical life: (I keep telling myself I'm going to start an exercise program, but I never get around to it.)

Relational life: (I continue to distrust my spouse, even though he or she has never given me reason to.)

Work-related life: (It seems no matter what I do I remain stuck in a low management position.)

II. *Alternatives: What Can You Do to Change Things?*

For each item you listed in the above exercise, list as many alternatives as you can think of to change those situations. The more alternatives, the better. Then, from those alternatives, choose one to implement. Begin this today.

For example: I always fight with my spouse in the same way. Things I can do differently:

1. *Listen* before I jump in to get my point of view across.

2. *Stop blaming* him or her for all the troubles in my life.

3. Start conversations by saying how much I love him or her, instead of calling him or her names.

4. Try to really *understand* the other person's "beef" before I fight back.

5. *Stop assuming* the worst, or jumping to conclusions before I have the information.

6. *Stay and talk it out,* instead of leaving in disgust when I get tired of it.

7. *Stop holding grudges.* Realize that, like me, the other person is not perfect, and sometimes is in need of forgiveness.

8. Be very clear about how his or her behavior affects me. Deal with addressing the behavior instead of attacking the other person.

9. Show more love myself, hoping that my positive attitude will rub off in the relationship.

10. Focus on positive things I like more than the negative things I don't like.

11. Look for compromises, and win-win situations.

III. Do Things Differently/Change Your Routine

The following exercises will help you become more flexible and more adaptable. Take a look at your day. Are you locked into everything you do? Choose three things to do differently this week. Begin your flexibility program by being more flexible.

1. Go home a new way from work.

2. Do your shopping on a different day of the week.

3. Spend five dollars on video games.

4. Eat at a different restaurant. Better yet, try a food you've never tried before.

5. Make love in a different way.

6. Change your hairstyle.

7. Get a facial or a massage.

8. Take your boss out to lunch.

9. Try a sport you've never tried before.

10. Take a class in a subject you know nothing about.

11. Learn new cooking recipes.

12. Do some volunteer work—see how good you'll feel when you help others.

13. Go to a park by yourself and just swing on the swings.

14. Try a different shampoo/soap/shaving cream/razor/tooth paste/perfume/cologne.

15. Go to church, or a different church.

16. Read a book on meditation.

17. Take your spouse out in the middle of the week.

18. Go to an opera or symphony.

19. Join a self-development group.

20. Spend time reading the dictionary. Learn a new word each day.

21. Take time out each day to strengthen a special relationship—spouse, lover, child, friend.

22. Make a new friend—call up someone and ask him or her to do something with you.

23. Contact an old friend you haven't talked to in a while.

24. Submit a new idea at work; maybe even one you've thought about for a while but were too embarrassed to mention because you thought no one would be interested in it.

25. Forgive someone you hold a grudge against.

IV. Relaxation-enhanced Creativity

A relaxed mind is more capable of creative energy than a mind cluttered with the events of the day. Take special time each day to relax, clear your mind, and get beautiful images of where you'd love to be. Once in such a place, ideas and associations will come to you that will help you see things in a different way that is likely to benefit your life. In a way, this relaxing imagery will help you discover the artist that lives within your soul.

To meet this internal artist and creator, go through the following steps.

1. Set aside ten to twenty minutes each day to go through your relaxation exercise.

2. Sit in a comfortable chair, with your feet flat on the floor.

3. Pick a spot on the wall, a little above your eye level. Stare at that spot and count slowly to twenty. As you do this, you'll notice that your eyelids begin to feel heavy and want to close. Let them close.

4. Then imagine yourself floating and drifting to a very comfortable place of your choice. As you go there in your mind, the image will

become clear to you. Once there, imagine the place with all your senses. See what is there; hear, feel, smell, and even taste the air of your special place.

5. Next, imagine a very wise person coming toward you. Listen to what he or she tells you. Ask questions, listen for answers. When there are no answers forthcoming, just walk in your special place and enjoy it. Answers will come. Patience may be necessary.

6. After the time you set aside is up, count to three and open your eyes. Tell yourself that you feel relaxed, refreshed, and full of energy to face the rest of the day. Once a week or so, it's a good idea to spend extra time in your special place, just working on ways to look at difficult things in different ways.

If you do this on a regular basis, you'll notice that your general level of tension will decrease, and that you'll have your own special place to look at things differently.

Impact Statements

Write out the following impact statements and tape them up in places where you're most likely to see them (on the bathroom mirror, refrigerator door at home, on your desk at work, etc.). This way they'll constantly remind you of the need to be creative and to look at common things in uncommon ways.

I do not benefit from sameness. I look for opportunities to see things in a different way.
I look for alternative ways of handling difficult situations.
I look for alternative ways to handle routine situations so that they don't become difficult or boring.
I take the time to be alone with myself, enhancing my ability to hear my creative inner voices.
Staying the same is in my best interest if it's working for me, but I need to change when change is needed.

16

Overcoming the Work Habits of Self-Sabotage

SEEING WHERE YOU LOOK: OBSERVANT

He who does not open his eyes must open his purse.
—GERMAN PROVERB

In the first day of my pathology class in medical school, the professor took a container of urine and dipped one of his fingers into it. Most of the students then watched with disgust as he apparently put that same finger into his mouth. As it turned out, he had actually put another finger into his mouth, hoping that some of us would catch what he was trying to do. He was teaching us to be observant.

Certainly, being observant is one of the most crucial skills a physician needs to acquire. He observes body posture and facial expressions during conversations with his patients; he observes with eyes, ears, smell, and touch during physical examinations; and he observes body fluids and tissue during laboratory exams. He uses all of his senses in observing and evaluating his patients.

Physicians are trained observers. That is also what you need to be in your daily life if you are going to master the skills of success. You need to be a trained observer. You need to observe yourself and your environment.

The ability to observe oneself is not an inborn natural trait. Most people see what they want to see about themselves, or filter personal information through their negative mindsets. Either way, they distort the facts. I spend much time in psychotherapy teaching my patients to see themselves in a more objective fashion, which is not hard to do when they are motivated to learn about themselves.

Observation allows gathering of more accurate information that they can use to their advantage. Information emerges about what they are truly like, what they are good at, what they are not good at, what they desire, and what they don't want. Observing yourself in as objective a way as possible will give you needed information on your journey into yourself.

When I was on the speech team in college, the members of the team did our speeches in front of a videotape camera so that we could have visual and auditory feedback on our performances. What we saw as we observed ourselves on tape was often embarrassing and disheartening. "I don't sound like that, do I?" or, "I need to stand up straighter," we moaned and groaned as we watched our tapes. But it was the most effective way for us to change and mold our performance to the best we could do. In the same way, many corporations are finding value in videotaping employees at their jobs to give them objective feedback on their job performances. Self-observation, as mentioned earlier, is essential to the process of change.

Likewise, you also need to observe your environment. When somebody has accomplished goals similar to the ones you are reaching toward, you need to observe them to see what it is about them that makes the difference.

Apprentices in all fields of study spend millions of hours each year watching the masters in their field apply their craft. Lawyers, physicians, teachers, politicians, craftsmen, and many others spend time and have organizations designed to facilitate learning from the great teachers. Professionals flock to conferences of this sort hoping to gain added insight into how they can better perform their tasks.

Observation decreases the assumptions we make. By directly observing the life situation we find ourselves in, we can hopefully avoid making incorrect assumptions.

Being observant is not a skill you are born with. Rather, it is something you develop through the years. This book is based on the premise that you have the capacity and desire to observe yourself and your situation in a reasonably objective way. One way to increase your self-observational skill is to choose several commonplace examples and ask yourself how others who know you might view you in that situation. Before you explain away or discount the answer you get, take some time to think about the response and what validity it may have for your life. Without the ability to observe yourself and your situation, any change is hard to make; with this ability, great change is possible.

BECOMING MORE OBSERVANT EXERCISES

Observational skills are essential to learning anything, whether the learning is about yourself, your relationships, or your work. Observation takes time and a willingness to see what is before your eyes and to listen to what you hear. The following exercises are designed to help you increase your observational skill and ability.

Examine the following sabotage factors, which are typical of a person weak in this area. Circle those that apply to you. Note the corresponding success factor, which is the more appropriate response. Circle the success factors that apply to you as well. Build on your strengths and strengthen your weaknesses.

Sabotage	vs.	Success
I miss out on a lot; many things seem to get by me.		I am aware of what goes on around me.
I often jump to conclusions, assuming things to be true without having all the facts.		Before drawing any conclusions, I take time to assess the situation from all standpoints.
I have trouble learning from others, which is often due to my inattention to them. I'm too busy to notice the needs of those I love.		After watching an expert do something I want to do, I find that my own ability is improved. I pay attention (observe) to the needs of those important to me.
I find it hard to spend time alone with myself, listening to what is going on inside of me.		I am able to spend time alone, observing and learning about myself.
The emotional turmoil in my life prevents me from objectively looking at or observing things in my life.		I take the time to observe people who have accomplished the goals I am interested in to see how they did it.

| Others tell me that I don't listen to them. | When someone is talking to me I make an effort to really hear what they are trying to say. |

I. *Take Time to Observe Yourself—Review Your Day*

The first step to becoming more observant is taking the time each day to work on it. Set aside five to ten minutes of quiet time at the end of every day to review what happened to you during that day. Briefly, review in your mind what happened from the time you got up to your review time.

When you come to difficult situations you faced that day, focus on them. Ask yourself what happened. What could you have done differently? What will you do if you are faced with a similar situation in the future?

Use this special review time to make sense of the day's happenings and to begin learning to observe yourself on a daily basis.

Many people keep diaries to help them observe and reflect on their lives. Consider doing this for a period of time to see if it would be of benefit to you.

II. *Take Time to Observe Those Who Have What You Want*

Learning to observe also means learning to observe others, particularly those who have accomplished the goals you wish to accomplish.

For each of the major areas of your life, list at least one person whom you know personally who has accomplished the goals you're after.

Personal life (who appears to have the following personal characteristics you admire?)

    spiritual:
    emotional:
    physical:

Relational life (who appears to have the kind of relationships with their spouse/lover, children, and friends that you admire?)

    spouse/lover:
    children:
    friends:

Work-related life (who has accomplished the kind of goals you'd like to accomplish in your work-related life?)

type of work:
position:
income:
accomplishments:

Go back through the list in your mind and ask yourself how these people accomplished their goals. If you don't know, ask them. If possible, spend more time with them, so that you can observe and learn from them. If you're looking for a good marriage, it's much better to spend time around people who have good marriages so that you can learn from them, rather than spending time with those who have poor marriages, because you learn from them as well.

III. Take Time to Observe Those Who Don't Have What You Want

Along the same lines, learn to observe those who have failed to accomplish what you want out of life. You can then avoid some of the traps they have fallen into. We do not have to make all our own mistakes.

For each of the major areas of your life, list at least one person whom you know personally who has not accomplished the goals you're after.

Personal life (who appears to lack the following personal characteristics you admire?)

spiritual:
emotional:
physical:

Relational life (who appears to lack the kind of relationships with their spouse/lover, children, and friends that you admire?)

spouse/lover:
children:
friends:

Work-related life (who has not accomplished the kinds of goals you'd like to accomplish in your work-related life?)

type of work:
position:
income:
accomplishments:

Go back through the list in your mind and ask yourself what you've noticed about that other person that may cause him to sabotage himself. How does he do himself in, so to speak?

IV. Stop Assuming—Get the Facts

One of the most powerful enemies of accurate observation is assuming things to be true without the actual evidence. You need to fight this temptation. It sabotages observation.

Think about three people you don't like. What actual evidence do you have that makes you not like them: Don't bother with hearsay evidence or circumstantial, but list hard evidence: dates, incidents, conversations, etc. Don't use your own feelings as evidence, because feelings often lie or are projections of our own feelings of low self-esteem.

1.
2.
3.

Many people are surprised by the lack of actual information they have on those they dislike. Get rid of the assumptions in your life. They do you no good and, in fact, hold you back.

V. Observe a Problem

To further your observational skills, observe one problem behavior for a week. The problem behavior can be in yourself or in someone close to you. The following steps will prove helpful to you.

1. Choose the behavior, one that in some way negatively affects you; either in yourself or in someone close to you. This behavior can be anything from losing your temper, your children bothering you while you're on the phone, or your spouse giving you hostile looks, to being chewed out by the boss. The behavior you choose should be one that occurs fairly frequently.

2. Take a notebook, sit down for a moment, and try to decide exactly what it is about the behavior that bothers you. Then write it down. For example, your spouse's hostile looks might bother you because you know it indicates that a fight may be brewing, and you have to walk on egg shells.

3. Decide how you would change that behavior. That is, what you would like to see in place of the negative behavior. Determining the behavior you want gives you a goal to strive for.

4. Next, take your notebook and start recording every time you or the other person exhibits the behavior. In your notes, you should record what you or the others were doing when the negative behavior started. You should also write down exactly what happened, and the reaction and feelings of those who witnessed the behavior. Do this until you have several recordings of the negative behavior.

5. After you have recorded several of these incidents, sit down with your notebook and re-read your notes. This will help to show what mistakes you might be making in the situation, or how you may be contributing to the behavior of others.

6. Finally, write down ways that you can behave to help change the situation. What can you do? How can you react differently in the situation? Look for alternatives!

VI. *Ways to Increase Observational Skills*

Choose one or two a day to work on.

1. Pay closer attention to the people around you. Try to stop daydreaming when you're with them.

2. When talking with others, listen for information that's useful to you.

3. Make frequent eye contact with those you talk to. This will help increase their attention to you and your attention to them.

4. Whenever possible, repeat back to others what you understand them to be saying ("I heard you saying. . . . Am I right?") to clarify the communication.

5. Stop assuming or inferring things to be true before you observe the actual evidence for it. Don't assume someone is mad at you because he hasn't talked to you at a party—something may be going on with him. Go up to him and start a conversation to find out what is what.

6. Stop placing value judgments on things before you have all the facts. For example, don't automatically disregard someone because of his political party or religious affiliation.

7. Try not to compare; this distorts perception by mixing in information from the past. Saying things such as, "You're just like your lousy father who left us," will do little to help you understand or observe a child.

8. Avoid hasty judgments and generalizations. By not judging too quickly we can keep ourselves less rigid and open to observation.

Impact Statements

Write out the following impact statements and tape them in places where you're most likely to see them (on the bathroom mirror, refrigerator door at home, on your desk at work, etc.). This way they'll constantly remind you of the need to strive to become more observant of yourself and the world around you.

Accurate observation leads to correct correlations.
In order to change, I need to pay attention to myself, my interactions, and the world around me.
Assuming gets me nowhere.
I observe the people who do things right to learn from them.
I spend quiet time each day to reflect upon and observe my inner self.
I take time each day to observe the needs of those I love.

I KNOW! I KNOW!: INFORMED

I use not only all the brains I have, but all the brains I can borrow.
—**Woodrow Wilson**
If you spend fifteen minutes a day on something for a couple of years, you'll be an expert.
—**Albert Einstein**

The most informed people are not always the most successful, but *successful people are always informed*. Success in any area, be it personal, relational, or financial, requires substantial and accurate information. Psychologist Abraham Maslow noted that what you do not know has power over you, whereas knowledge brings choice and control. Ignorance makes choice impossible. With the proper information, realistic goals can be chosen, workable plans can be formed, and reasonable risks can be taken. Information is power.

You can have all of the motivation, planned goals, positive thinking, and best intentions in the world, but without the knowledge to go with these, you will surely fail. This is true in any example I can think of. I would never send my car to a mechanic who didn't know his stuff nor would I invest in a stock or money market fund before finding out as much as possible about it.

Yet many people make serious decisions, ones that may have lifelong impact, without gathering the proper information. Do you know anyone who got married after only knowing someone for a few weeks? I know many people like this. I meet them mostly in my office, when they come for marriage counseling.

Successful relationships, like personal or financial success, are based on information—information related to motivation and goals. In counseling teenagers about sexual matters, I strongly emphasize this point. Before they give in to their sexual desires, I ask them to think about what they want and what the other person is really after: Does the sex bring them closer together? Or, is it being used by one of the partners to feel more like a woman or a man? Is one of the partners being used so that the other can brag to his or her friends about "the conquest"? Or, is the sex being used to make someone else jealous?

Having this information, not only for teenagers, but also for adults, is crucial to understanding a relationship and preventing future hurts and disappointments. Look at just one more example of the importance of being informed.

In order to be successful in business, retail buyers find out three things about a product before they purchase it for their stores: price, quality, and service. If a product does not meet those standards, successful buyers won't stock it in their stores. These buyers spend hours talking to salespeople, poring over market reports and order books looking for the merchandise with the right price, quality, and service

The examples of the need for knowledge and information could go on and on, but the point is simple. If you want to be successful at something, you must be adequately informed about it. Information is essential to success. Information is power.

One last word on being informed: It is also important to know what you don't know. Too often, people get into trouble through expecting themselves to know everything about everything. No one, no matter how smart, can know everything. That is why there are so many different specialties in medicine. The trouble occurs when you think you know something you don't.

Ignorance is not knowing something.

Stupidity is thinking you know something you don't and acting on it.

INFORMATION GATHERING EXERCISES

> *My greatest strength as a consultant is to be ignorant and ask a few questions.*
>
> —PETER DRUCKER

The following exercises were designed to help you understand the need for adequate information gathering and to help you get started in finding your best information sources.

Examine the following sabotage factors, which are typical of a person weak in this area. Circle any that apply to you. Note the corresponding success factor, which is the more appropriate response. Circle the success factors that apply to you as well. Build on your strengths and strengthen your weaknesses.

Sabotage	vs.	Success
The fear of appearing stupid or bothering others prevents me from asking questions.		I find ways to ask questions whenever I want or need to know something.
I expect I should know how to do everything.		I ask others for help when I'm in doubt.
I get myself into trouble for thinking or assuming I know something when I really don't.		Before I assume something to be true, I take the time to find out.
I act impulsively, if not recklessly.		Before making a decision, I take the time to gather as much infor-

	mation as possible about it, including finding out my options.
I am often unaware of how and where to find information	I know my sources of information.
I accept hearsay evidence.	I check things out first.

I. What Information Do You Need?

The first question you need to answer about information is, "What information do I need?" In order to answer this question, it's important to go back to the goals you have for yourself (either through the One-Page Miracle or through Questions Eleven and Twelve at the end of Section One) and re-examine the steps you need to take to reach those goals.

If you are clear on the steps to reach your goals, then the information you'll need will be clear.

For now, choose one short-term goal you have for yourself, e.g., to lose ten pounds in two months.

Answer the following information questions about that goal (example answers in parentheses).

1. What information do I need on this goal?
(What is the safest and fastest way to lose the weight so that it doesn't come back?)

2. Who has this information?
(This information can be found in a multitude of places: nutrition and diet books; magazine articles about weight loss; diet centers; other people who have effectively lost weight, either those I know personally or those in a support group setting; and my family physician.)

3. How can I get this information?
(For this example, all I need is to ask. I probably know several people who have gone on successful diets. I can ask how they lost the weight. I can even join a support group and not only get the information they have, but also get their support in losing the weight.

I can ask my physician, especially if I'm very overweight or I have a concurrent medical problem that'll be affected by the weight loss.

If I'm in good health, I can study the books available at the library or bookstore, but before I take their word as gospel, I'd be wise to check out some critical reviews or consumer report evaluations about the different diets, because some really can be dangerous.

Also, if I have trouble with my willpower, I can pay a diet center to evaluate my specific condition and give me all the information I need. I can give up some of my money to help motivate me.)

After you've done this for the one goal you chose, go back and do three other goals in the same way, asking:

What information do I need?
Who has the information?
How can I get the information?

II. *Know Your Information Resources*

1. Odds are that other people are your best resource for finding the information you need. Think of the three major areas of your life—relational, personal, and work-related; list three people in each of these areas from whom you think you could benefit by asking them questions.

Knowledgeable Relational People:
("relational" meaning between people, such as couples, parent-child, friends)

1.
2.
3.

Knowledgeable Personal People:
("personal" meaning self-related, i.e., physical, spiritual, or emotional)

1.
2.
3.

Knowledgeable Work-related People:
("work-related" meaning job, career, school, home-management, etc.)

1.
2.
3.

2. The print media is also a powerful source of information: newspapers, books, popular and professional magazines, trade journals, pamphlets, etc. The best place to find them is generally the local public or university library. They have most of these resources, and they can get almost anything you need.

a. Do you know how to use the library? If not, your next exercise is to go to the nearest library and *ask* the librarian to show you how to use it.
If you really do know how to use the library, do you have a current library card? If not, get one!
b. For the next thirty days spend ten to thirty minutes a day skimming through the local or city newspaper.

Specifically, cut out at least one article a day that relates to your personal, relational, or work-related goals. Underline the important points the article makes. Then, file the article in a folder marked "personal," "relational," or "work-related" goals.

In just a month you'll notice not only that you have more information than before, but that you've also learned what a valuable resource the daily newspaper can be.
Warning: The newspaper can also be a time drain. Skim the newspaper to see what looks important for you. But be careful of trying to read it all.

3. Professional and personal seminars and workshops are another excellent way to find information you want and need. Depending on your goals, look in the local newspaper or the appropriate trade publication, and, if possible, attend a seminar or workshop that interests you. The extra contacts you make may be very helpful for you along with the information you gain.

4. Group support activities are another powerful source of information. Groups come together for almost every purpose imaginable, from babysitting coalitions or trade associations to problem-solving support groups like Overeaters Anonymous. Consider becoming part of a group so that you'll be able to gather more information about your goals through its members. Don't let the fear of meeting new people frighten you away from valuable information.

III. *What Holds You Back from Asking Your Questions?*

The fear of appearing stupid or of bothering someone holds many people back from asking questions. In order to take advantage of all the information resources you have, however, you *must* be able to ask questions. The following exercise is designed to help you get over the fear of asking for help.

Every day for one week, ask at least three different strangers the time. Also, go up to at least one person a day and ask for change for a dollar.

Along with this, write down each time during the week that the fear of appearing stupid or bothering someone else held you back from asking your question. Then answer the following questions about that incident.

1. What was the situation?

2. Was it appropriate to ask that question in that environment? If not, why not?

3. What was the worst thing that could happen if I had asked that question?
Never forget: Asking dumb questions is a lot better than being ignorant.

Many people also hold themselves back by assuming that they know more than they do, or by expecting themselves to know everything. They are almost ashamed to ask for help. Whatever the underlying reasons for these thoughts, it is now time to change them. They hold you back. They do you no good. We need other people, and other people need us.

Try to identify areas of your life where you assume things to be true, when you really don't know. Then make a strong conscious effort to find out the accurate information.

V. KEY NOTE:

Always carry with you a pencil or pen and paper to write on, or a tape recorder. This way, when you have questions that for some reason you can't ask, you can write them down and get the answer later. Or, if you are exposed to important information, you can record it for future reference. Never be without some way to preserve valuable information and ideas!

Impact Statements

Write out the following impact statements and tape them up in places where you're most likely to see them (on the bathroom mirror, refrigerator door at home, on your desk at work, etc.). This way they'll constantly remind you to gather adequate information on the tasks you wish to accomplish, so that you won't sabotage yourself with ignorance.

> The most informed people are not always successful, but successful people are always informed.
> What I do not know has power over me, whereas knowledge brings choice and control.
> Information is power.
> If I want to be successful at something, I must be adequately informed about it.
> I ask the questions; I get the answers.
> I'll give others the information they need about me so that they won't assume things to be true.
> My fear of being ignorant overcomes my fear of asking questions.

THINGS ARE IN THE RIGHT PLACE: ORGANIZATION

> *Organizing is what you do before you do something, so that when you do it, it's not all mixed up.*
> —CHRISTOPHER ROBIN IN A.A.
> MILNE's *Winnie the Pooh*

Your brain is organized in very specific cellular patterns bathed by a delicate balance of precious chemicals. When the cellular patterns or the chemistry of the brain are upset, either temporarily by a few cocktails or permanently by head trauma, thought patterns may become disorganized and your ability to function will be immensely impaired.

In a similar way, many people sabotage their chances for success by having a disorganized approach to their goals. They approach situations and goals haphazardly, and then they wonder why things don't work out for them. Successful people are organized.

Certainly, successful people are not all organized in the same way, but they know their own method of organization or, at least, they are in contact with someone who helps them organize the material important to them. Successful people have an organizational structure for themselves, their time, and their tasks.

Unfortunately, organization is a bad word to many people. After all, it does contain twelve letters, and thus must be worth at least three vulgarities. However, learning to organize yourself, your time, and your task can make your life more profitable and much easier.

Organizing yourself, at first, will take some time. If you're like most people, you just go from day to day accomplishing what you need to for that day and moving on to the next day. Take a minute to step back from the rat race. Get out your goal list (if you haven't made one by now, now is a good time) to see if the way you spend your time is matching up with the goals in your life. If not, why not? Why are you spending your energy on things that are not important to you?

Success takes significant time and energy. Do you spend time doing repetitive things that have little meaning, like watching the news two or three times a day, or being addicted to TV sports or daytime and nighttime TV soap operas?

When they have free time, successful people use it to their benefit. Waiting is a part of life, and you can regard it as wasted time, or as a gift of extra time. Whenever I go somewhere where I might have to wait, such as a dentist's appointment, I always carry some work to do in case my appointment is delayed. Likewise, when I spend time in traffic, I also use the time productively by listening to professional tapes, dictating an article or a chapter in a book (I get some weird looks from people staring at me while I carry on in my car), or catching up on the news so that I won't need to watch it later on.

However you decide to spend your time, make it productive for you. Look at what you do now and ask yourself, "What benefit am I getting, or what benefit are others getting, from me spending my time in this manner?" If the answer is no benefit, find something more productive to do with that time.

A word of caution: don't assume that I'm anti-relaxation. I'm anything but. Exercise, recreation, and relaxation are essential to a balanced life. We all need our batteries recharged in order to function at peak efficiency. I am, however, against wasting time. The more efficient we are with our time, the more time we actually have for relaxation.

"Budget" is another bad word for those of you who classify yourselves as free spirits. I'm not that fond of it myself, but I know that when I'm becoming unorganized with my time or my finances, putting myself back on a budget helps me give the structure I need to become organized.

Organization also involves knowing where needed information is stored and how to put your hands on it quickly. If, for example, cutting your income taxes were a goal, it would be very important to organize the tax information you gather through the year so that when it comes time to do your return, all the information will be readily available to you or your tax consultant. An unorganized approach to storing this information could cost you a lot of money, even if you had taken the initiative to learn about tax-cutting strategies.

If we have boxes and boxes of information, but this information is in disarray, it is likely to have the same fate as all the notes we took in school. For unless you took time to systematically file and organize your notes from school, if you're like most of us, you'll never have the energy to go back over them to make them useful to you. Isn't it depressing to think of all those hours wasted taking notes you'll never use again? Unless we organize the information in our lives, the time we spend gathering it is often wasted.

Some of you will balk at such a systematized approach to life, but I submit that the more organized you are, the more time you'll actually have to be spontaneous and creative. Creativity is not enhanced by disarray; rather, it is enhanced by order.

ORGANIZATION EXERCISES

By being poorly organized you often waste precious time, effort, and energy on repetitive or unproductive activities, leaving little for what is truly important to you.

Organization is the structure needed to successfully complete your goals or tasks. Think of it as an investment: at first you will put in significant time and effort to become more organized, but the payoff will be much more time *and* increased productivity.

The ultimate purpose of this set of exercises is to give you more time for more important things, whether it's starting your own business, spending more time with your family, or rafting on the Colorado River. If you follow these exercises faithfully you'll notice that the more organized you become, the more time you'll have to reach toward your important goals. The more effectively you organize your day-to-day activities, the less time they'll take you—or take from you.

Before you can take an organized approach to your time, your relationships, or the other things in your life, you must first take an organized approach to yourself.

Who are you?
What are you all about?
How much time do you have?
What is the best use of that time?

As you begin this set of exercises, make sure that you've completed the goal-setting exercise at the end of Section One. It's impossible for you to become more organized if you don't know what's important to you!

Examine the following sabotage factors, which are typical of people weak in this area. Circle any that apply to you. Note the corresponding success factor, which is the more appropriate response. Circle the success factors that apply to you as well. Build on your strengths and strengthen your weaknesses.

Sabotage	vs.	**Success**
I hope that things will be in their right place.		I take the time to organize myself and my time.
I do what I feel should be done at the moment, instead of organizing tasks in logical order.		I often ask myself, "What's the best use of my time?"
I waste a lot of time looking for items because I did not initially put them in their right places.		I know where things are and what needs to be done next.
My unorganized approach often causes me to be late for appointments or turning in projects or assignments.		In getting a job done, I start early so that I can finish with time to spare.
I am always busy without ever seeming to catch up.		I do one thing well at a time.
Others intrude on my time.		I have a clear fix on my goals and don't get distracted.

I. Ways to Help Organize Yourself

Here are some hints that organization experts give on organizing yourself, your time, and your goals.

   1. *Always* carry a notebook and a couple of pens or a tape recorder with you wherever you go. This way you'll be able to write down what you need to do and ideas as they occur to you. At night, keep these near your bed to record important thoughts or ideas that may come to you right before you go to bed, in the middle of the night, or as you wake up in the morning. That's when many creative ideas come to people.

2. Schedule similar tasks together, such as errands, appointments, maintenance or phone calls.

3. Write down a time limit for the different tasks to be performed.

4. Consider your personal effectiveness cycle. If possible, schedule your most important activities for the hours when you are at your peak.

5. Don't get bogged down in low-value activities.

6. Learn to say "no." Spend your time doing things that are consistent with your goals.

7. Delegate as much as possible to others (more on this a little later).

8. Watch out for the great time thieves: procrastination, indecisiveness, regrets, fear of failure, and worry. Research shows that more than ninety percent of things people worry about never materialize.

9. Keep a To-Do list of the important tasks you need to get done that day, that week, and "in the near future." Redo this list as necessary. Relying on this list is more accurate than relying on your memory.

10. List the next step to reaching your major goals (personal, relational, and work-related) at the bottom of your To-Do list. Keeping these in mind is the key to reaching them.

11. Be prepared for gifts of time. Always carry some work or relaxing things to do with you for times when you may have to wait: before doctor's appointments, in traffic jams, etc. Likewise for the time you know you'll have, such as in traffic, on an airplane, or commuter train. Use the time to your advantage by listening to professional tapes, taping a letter, listening to the new books on tape, or in any other way you can think of. *Change your perception of this time from dead or wasted time to productive time for you.*

12. Cut unwanted calls short. Unwanted or unsolicited calls waste a lot of time. I often start conversations by saying something like, "I only have a minute..."

II. *Inventory Your Time*

With your goals in mind, the next step is to inventory how you spend the time in your life. It's much like finding out how you spend your money. Time, like money, has intrinsic value, and there's only so much of it alloted to you. Although inventorying your time will take a good deal of time and effort, this information is crucial to being able to organize it.

1. For seven days, inventory how you spend your time, all of your time, in half-hour increments. This may seem like an overwhelming task, but it's not. Keeping track of this information should take about a half-hour per day. It's only after you find how you do spend your time that you can decide how to use it more efficiently.

2. Then list the forty or so most common ways you spend your time, and the time taken per day and per week for each. Personalize this for yourself. An example would be:

INDIVIDUAL TIME SUMMARY CODES

ACTIVITY	TIME PER DAY	TIME PER WEEK

Personal

   grooming
   eating
   sleeping
   physical exercise
   spiritual time
   leisure time
   radio
   TV
   hobbies
   reading
   shopping for self
   other

ACTIVITY	TIME PER DAY	TIME PER WEEK

Relational

time with spouse/lover
time with children
time with family together
time with friends
   (also include phone
   and commuting time)
letter writing
shopping for others
religious activities
group activities

Work-related

commuting to and from
meetings
telephone calls
reading
paperwork, letters
seeing customers
teaching
on-the-job travel
drop-in visitors
other

Maintenance

cooking
laundering
housecleaning
yardwork
household maintenance
grocery shopping
other shopping
paying the bills
car maintenance
other

3. Place a star by the activities that match your short-term or long-term goals. Remember, you have personal goals, relational goals, and work-related goals. Things such as relaxation, personal grooming,

and time with your children are very important to balancing your goals. Are you spending time pursuing those things important to you? If not, why not? *make time!*

4. Which activities do not relate to the goals you have for your life? Why do you do them? Are they necessary? Can you replace them with activities that'll help you reach the goals you have set for yourself?

5. Which things can you delegate? What can you get others to do for you or help you do?

6. What activities are a waste of time? What can be done to prevent or reduce wasting time in the future?

7. How do you let other people waste your time? How can you reduce or eliminate that in the future?

8. Is the time you spend balanced between your personal, relational, and work-related goals?

III. *Everything in Its Place Exercise*

The last step to organizing your life is to organize the things in your life, "things" here meaning your home, your office, your desk, files, etc. When you put things in the right place initially, there's a good chance you'll be able to find them later on.

Organization means different things to different people. To some, an organized desk top is clean, with the most important material to be done next in the center of it. To others, their desk appears to be a mess, but they know where things are and what needs to be done next. Either way, the two most important things are *knowing where things are and what the next step is*.

For those who are novices at organization, I'm going to recommend a clean-desk approach. The important thing to remember, however, is not neatness—it's that you know where things are and what needs to be done next. Use what works better for you. Organizational basics (for homes, offices, desks, garages, etc.)

1. You are responsible for where you put things. If you're not organized, don't blame others for where you misplaced something!

2. Think before you organize. This is what organization is all about: thinking things through logically before you act.

Don't do things just because someone else does it that way.

Don't do things just because you have done them that way before. Think before you act. If it doesn't make sense, question it.

It's easier to keep stumbling along in the same way as before—but it's not generally in your best interest.

Take the time initially to think and plan how you'll do something. Doing it as before is a form of self-sabotage, particularly if it didn't work before.

3. Discard unnecessary things. Ask yourself how often you'll use it, is it worth the space it takes up, and what's the worst thing that will happen if you don't have that thing. If you'll replace it, then keep it. If not, and it doesn't have real sentimental value to you, discard it.

4. Sort things into useable groups. Keep related things together. This will help you discard things you have duplicates of.

5. Take the time initially to put things away properly; this will save time later on.

6. If you're not sure where to begin organizing a certain area, ask someone who has organized a similar place in a manner you like.

7. Always be on the lookout for ways to improve your organizational structure.

8. Do it daily.

IV. *Three More in Its Place Exercises*

1. For seven days, put away everything you take out right after you use it.

2. Reorganize your desk (or the most important workplace you have), utilizing the principles above.

3. For seven days, clean off your desk top (or workplace), leaving the most important thing you need to do next in the middle of the desk.

Impact Statements

Write out the following impact statements and tape them up in places where you're most likely to see them (on the bathroom mirror, refrigerator door at home, on your desk at work, etc.). This way they'll constantly remind you that the more organized you are, the more time you'll have to pursue your other goals, and the more efficient you'll be in doing that.

> Organizing my time and my tasks will give me more time.
> I often ask myself, "What's the best use of my time right now?"
> I start each task with a plan.
> I often ask myself, "What is the next step to completing my task?"
> I'll start early on important tasks to get them done with time to spare.
> Everything has its place.

IT'S MY TURN TO DECIDE: ABLE TO MAKE DECISIONS

No decision is right until you make it right.

You are the chief executive officer of your life. As such, you daily make a whole host of decisions and non-decisions that affect and direct the way your life operates. How you direct this decision-making process correlates with whether you see yourself as being in control of your life or as being controlled by others. Active decision makers are in charge of their lives. Passive recipients of others' decisions take what is given to them.

People who sabotage themselves have trouble making decisions. They let opportunities pass them by because they do not understand the decision-making process, and they feel inadequate to make difficult decisions. On the other hand, successful people intuitively understand the process of deciding, and they use this process for their benefit and personal growth.

Making decisions based on clear goals, asking the right questions of the right people, exploring alternatives, taking action, and getting feedback are integral ingredients in our recipe for success. Here are the six steps to making effective decisions:

1. Define the question to be answered.

2. Gather good information.

3. Get input from those who will be affected by the decision.

4. Establish all the possible alternative decisions.

5. Choose the best alternative and implement it.

6. Establish a system for monitoring progress and modification if necessary.

A decision is a judgment, a choice between alternatives, rarely a choice between right or wrong. A good decision is the best decision at the time based on the information you have.

When decisions are crucial, as they are in relational, personal, and career choices, it is essential to treat decision making as a systematic process which, when properly applied, increases the probability of successful outcomes. A number of such systematic decision-making models have been developed. Although they vary in sophistication, the steps are basically the same.

Let's examine each step of the decision-making process through the example of changing jobs.

1. Define the question to be answered. The question to be answered in this situation is clear: "Is there a better opportunity for me elsewhere?" But better opportunity can be defined further, for instance as more money, increased job satisfaction, increased control or say in the workplace, or a position closer to home.

2. Gather good information. There are many ways to gather information on changing careers. This can be done by talking with employment firms, looking through help wanted sections of trade magazines or talking with friends or acquaintances in other companies. The more information you have, the easier your decision.

3. Get input from those who will be affected by the decision. In a decision of this magnitude it's essential to get feedback from your spouse, children if a move is involved, and even your employer (although the timing of telling your employer can be very tricky).

4. Establish all the possible alternative decisions. It's often best to list each option with its pros and cons as a way to decide between them.

5. Choose the best alternative and implement it. When you choose between the alternatives, realize that you've made the best decision at the time. Do everything you can to make it work.

6. Establish a system for monitoring progress and modification if necessary. If you decide to change jobs, monitor the decision to see if you were right. Evaluate it in light of any new information you may gather.

As another example, let's look at the question of divorce. I'm frequently asked: "How do I know when to leave?" Even though this is a very complex question, I encourage people to go through this same decision-making process.

1. What is the question? "Should I stay or go?" There are many feelings behind this question. Typical ones include: "I don't feel appreciated. I don't feel loved. My opinions don't count. As far as I know, I only have one life, and I want more than I have now."

2. Gather information. Marriage partners have a tremendous amount of information about each other. However, they are often blinded by their hopelessness or hurts, saying that after so many years of marriage they know things won't change.

The fact is, they really don't know unless they try. Marriage and family counselors help couples gather the information on whether or not change may be forthcoming. They report helping more than fifty percent of the couples they see. Because divorce is so painful, even to the spouse initiating the breakup, I almost always recommend counseling, even if a reconciliation does not appear likely. I at least want people to learn from the situation so that they are unlikely to make a similar mistake in the future.

3. Talk to those affected by the decision. It is very surprising to hear people tell me they had no idea their spouse was going to leave them. True, they probably weren't paying close attention; but if someone is very unhappy in a marriage he or she needs to spell it out for the spouse. That way, the spouse can try to work things out or refuse to change. Either way it gives the unhappy partner crucial information.

4. Establish the alternatives. Before decisions like this are made, I encourage people to think about all the options they have: counseling, encounter groups, time together away from the children, legal separation, and divorce.

They also need to think about what life will be like when separated: the financial situation, living situation, custodial issues for the children, new dating situation.

5. Make the best choice. After gathering information, talking to the spouse, and exploring all of the alternatives, it's time for a decision. That decision can range from taking time to gather more information (e.g., in a counseling situation) to divorce.

6. Monitor feedback and alter decisions when necessary. Even after the decision to stay or go is made, feedback on the decision continues. Some ex-spouses undergo clear changes or see changes in their former partner (e.g., the alcoholic who stops drinking), allowing them to get back together. As another example, if the decision was to enter therapy, progress or lack of it will be felt.

We make decisions every day that have an impact on the flow of our lives. Not all decisions are as monumental as the ones we make about career or marriage. However if you remember your goals and the steps to reach decisions, you will make choices that are in your best interest.

The decisions any of us make will not always be right. But the successful person has an objective method for making decisions. Subsequently, if the decision fails, it gives you a systematic way to go back through the decision-making process to see what might have gone wrong. As we've discussed, successful people learn from their errors. Being able to understand the decision-making process will help you understand and learn from your errors.

DECISION-MAKING EXERCISES

The inability to make effective decisions causes many people to miss exciting opportunities, and also fosters dependence on others, allowing others to make difficult decisions for them.

By faithfully doing the exercises listed below, you'll learn an effective decision-making system that will serve you well for major and minor decisions alike. No longer will you feel more comfortable leaving your decisions up to chance, fate, or a "hard, cruel world." Your decisions belong to you—keep them yours!

Examine the following sabotage factors, which are typical of people weak in this area. Circle any that apply to you. Note the corresponding success factor, which is the more appropriate response. Circle the success factors that apply to you as well. Build on your strengths and strengthen your weaknesses.

Sabotage	vs.	Success
I let circumstances decide. I let the opinion of others hold me		I take control to decide. I seek input from others, but decide on

back from making the decisions I want to make.	my own.
I have trouble making decisions.	I have a systematic approach to making decisions.
I miss opportunities because it takes me too long to decide to act on them.	My decisions are clear because they are goal-oriented.
I make impulsive decisions and then worry over them.	Before making decisions I take time to gather information on the options available to me.
I sometimes alienate important people in my life by making decisions that affect them without consulting them.	I am sensitive to those affected by my decisions.

I. *What Decisions Do You Make?*

Before you go through this decision-making system, it's important to be clear with yourself about what important decisions you have to make.

Think about each of the major areas of your life. What decisions do you have pending? List as many as you can think of, including minor as well as major decisions.

Personal:
Relational:
Work-related:

II. *The Decision-making Process*

Initially, choose several of the minor decisions listed above and, on a separate piece of paper, answer the following questions about them.

1. Define the question to be answered. What is the anticipated goal of this decision? How does it relate to your overall goals?

2. Gather information. What information do you need to make an effective decision? How can you gather it?

3. Will anyone else be affected by the decision? Get input from those who will be affected. (That doesn't mean allow them to make your decision; it only means get their input.)

4. Establish all the possible options or alternative decisions. What options and choices do you have? List the pros and cons of each option side by side to make an adequate comparison. This is a key step. The more options you can generate, generally, the easier the decision will become.

5. Choose the best alternative and implement it.

6. Establish a system for monitoring progress and modification if necessary. Since decisions are made with the best information at the time, it's important to be aware of future information as it becomes available. Monitor and change the decisions you make as more information becomes available.

After you've applied this process to several minor decisions, work through it with more major ones. You'll be amazed how this structure helps clear your mind.

III. *Two More Thoughts*

1. Remember to make choices that are in line with your overall goals. As your goals change, so must your decisions. When goals conflict, think about balance. For instance, a decision to gain a promotion at work might conflict with a goal to become closer to your family. These might be balanced successfully by deciding to give up an old habit that is not as important, such as watching television.

2. Just because things have always been done one way in the past doesn't mean that is the way they should always be done. You don't know why things were done in a particular way to start, so there is no sense continuing something unless you understand the rationale for it.

Think before you decide. Decisions are often based on how others did it. Make your decisions based upon information, not what others do. Their actions may be misleading.

Impact Statements

Write out the following impact statements and tape them up in places where you're most likely to see them (on the bathroom mirror, refrigerator door at home, on your desk at work, etc.). This way they'll constantly remind you of the decision-making process, thus helping you to make quicker, more effective decisions that are consistent with your goals and desires.

I make my own decisions.
When decisions I make affect other people, I get their input.
No decision is right until I make it right.
These are the steps to effective decision making:

1. Define the question to be answered.
2. Gather information.
3. Get input from those who will be affected by the decision.
4. Establish all the possible options or alternative decisions.
5. Choose the best alternative and implement it.
6. Establish a system for monitoring progress and modification if necessary.

RECRUIT OTHERS TO WORK FOR YOU: DELEGATION

> *I don't have to know how to do it. I need to know who does it best.*
>
> —HENRY FORD

If you want a job done right, don't do it yourself unless you are qualified to do it! Knowing the limits of your ability and the limits of your time will help you live longer and accomplish more. Knowing your limits will also lead you into the next ingredient in our recipe of success: delegation. You do not have enough time, energy, or expertise to do all you want in life. However, if you use other people's time, energy, and expertise to accomplish your goals, you have a fighting chance.

In reality, we are a society of delegators. Someone else raises our food, builds our houses, makes our clothes, teaches our children, and buries our dead. Yet, even with all that, many people still spend far too much time doing repetitive tasks that have little value in the scheme of their lives. We rarely see successful people doing repetitive tasks that someone else could do. They hire someone to do it. Also, it is rare to see them do things they aren't qualified to do. They hire someone for those jobs, too.

The key to successful delegation is knowing your time and ability limits. This takes observation on your part, but if you can accomplish your goals in dramatically less time, then the time it takes to observe yourself will be well rewarded. Concentrate your efforts on those few projects that have the highest payoff per investment of time and energy.

Questions to ask yourself about delegation are:

Am I the person best qualified to do this job?

What is my time worth?

Can someone else do this task while I am more productive at something else?

What benefit do I get by doing this task?

Does it fit into the goals I have set for myself?

Do I find myself doing routine jobs that others could do or be trained to do?

(This separates the hirers from the hirees.)

Sometimes people keep busy with repetitive tasks to ward off anxiety. Their unconscious mind rationalizes that if they are always busy cleaning the house, doing the books, or gathering details it will keep away the unacceptable thoughts they might have. They have no time to create goals or plans for reaching them. This obsessiveness prevents them from delegating and helps them make up all the excuses they use to do it all themselves. Watch out for the do-it-all syndrome. It inhibits creativity and will leave you too tired for success.

In summary, delegation is:

• having someone who is more qualified perform the task
• staying away from repetitive tasks others can do for you
• teaching others to do the things you don't want to do or don't have time to do
• something that gives you more time to work on your priorities
• a willingness to give up the need to control everything (having to do everything yourself is a form of control).

DELEGATION EXERCISES
Breaking Do-It-Yourself-Itis

Change "If you want something done right, do it yourself," to "If you want something done your way, do it yourself."

Details are important to the successful person; repetitive tasks are not. Success takes time, but not the kind in which you get bogged down doing things that are unnecessary for your goals, or doing things that others could do better for you. Do-it-yourself-itis causes you to be so busy with routine matters that you don't have time to accomplish the important steps that will bring you closer to your goals.

Successful people know what they can do well, and they concentrate their efforts on these tasks. They also teach others how to do things to their liking and *let them do it* so that they'll have more time for other things that are more important to their goals.

The goal of these exercises is to teach you that you have limited time, energy, and expertise; but, through using others' time, energy, and expertise, you open unlimited opportunities and potential.

Examine the following sabotage factors, which are typical of people weak in this area. Circle any that apply to you. Note the corresponding success factor, which is the more appropriate response. Circle the success factors that apply to you as well. Build on your strengths and strengthen your weaknesses.

Sabotage	vs.	Success
I spend time doing things that have little meaning toward major goals in my life.		I often ask myself, "What is the best use of my time?"
I have to do everything myself, never being satisfied with another person's work.		If possible, I stay away from repetitive tasks that others can do.
I believe I should be able to do everything myself.		I use other people's time, energy, and expertise to help me with my goals.
I spend time on low-value activities.		I concentrate my efforts on those projects that provide the biggest payoff for me.
I don't delegate because I can do it better.		Maybe I can, but I realize it is more important to me to focus on things I can't delegate.
I fear others may pass me by, so I withold delegating for the sake of controlling them.		I allow others to grow to their ability. We both win.

I. What Activities Can I Delegate?

Think about each of the major areas of your life (personal, relational, work-related). List the repetitive tasks you do that you think you can delegate to others. Suggestions are in parentheses.

Personal   Since this is personal time, it's hard to find things to delegate to others, but remember you can delegate to things as well as people, such as buying an exercise machine you can use in the office or at home to save time from going to the gym or spa. Also, you may be able to find others to do some of your personal shopping for you—a favor you could return later. Or, you may delegate educational or spiritual material to cassettes you can listen to on your way to work. The more things you can delegate in your personal life, the more time you'll have for a personal life. List others:

1.
2.
3.
4.

Relational   This time is very special, so you have to be careful about what exactly you do delegate. No doubt you need quality time with those close to you, but you don't need to do repetitive chores. For example, you can think of delegating tasks such as picking up the kids from school or sports practice by carpooling, sharing chores around the house, the shopping, working on the committees at church, etc. Some of these things you want to do, and you include them in your goals. Watch out, however, for the relational time drains that aren't in your goals. List others:

1.
2.
3.
4.

Work-related   Divide and conquer: perhaps one person in the office can take charge of one thing while you take charge of another area. Other work areas include commuting (carpooling), paperwork (the computer), ordering, telephone work, answering mail, attending meetings. Delegate these whenever possible. List others:

1.
2.
3.
4.

Note: In the margin to this exercise a friend wrote, "Thanks. I just realized I spent three hours going to office supply stores when I could have phoned in my order and had it delivered. Next time!" Use delegation to your advantage.

II. *The Professor Exercise*

In order to delegate effectively, you must teach others how you want things done. Teaching is the first step to delegation. Look at the items you listed above to delegate in your personal, relational, and work-related lives; then teach at least one person a day how to do one of the things on the list. Teach them the way you want them to do it. At the end of seven days, you should be able to delegate seven more things than you could before.

1.
2.
3.
4.
5.
6.
7.

Jenny, a woman who had a home business, wrote, "I know this is good. It took me three hours to teach my 14-year-old to enter business expenses in my computer data base. Now I have more time, and he has a valuable skill and earns money—which I deduct as a business expense—and he uses the money for things I would have had to buy him!"

III. *Do It Now*

Out of those items you listed to delegate, delegate at least one of them a day for the next seven days. These can be from the items you taught others how to do to your liking, or from the list that didn't require any teaching.

1.
2.
3.
4.
5.
6.
7.

IV. What's In It for Me?

Perhaps you need to look at delegation in terms of advantages and disadvantages. This can be done as in the following example.

Disadvantages of Delegation	Advantages of Delegation
They won't do the work right and I'm responsible.	Delegating part of this task will give me extra time to complete my own work, and since I'm responsible for the quality, I'll follow up to ensure the work meets specifications.
If I have the children do the dishes, they'll probably break some.	The children can learn to be careful, and while they're doing the dishes, I can pick up the den. Then we'll all have more fun time.

List your own thoughts and counter-thoughts.

V. Get Off Your "But" Exercise

"I really should delegate, but..." Your "but" may represent your biggest obstacle to effective delegation. The moment you think about delegating a task, you give yourself excuses in the form of buts. If you really want to delegate, you'll have to learn to move off your "but." You can use a two-column zigzag method to debate the issue in your mind.

"But" Column	"But" Rebuttal
I really should teach a subordinate how to complete this task, *but* there just isn't time.	If I teach someone else how to do this, next time it comes up there will be someone trained to do it and I'll have more time to do other priority items.

But they probably won't do the task right.	It's my responsibility to see the task is completed properly, and if I take the time to teach them, they'll learn to do the job right. They may even improve on the way I do it.
But if they do it wrong, I'll end up doing it myself; then I'll still be behind and no better off than I was before.	If I never give someone a chance to learn, I'll never have extra time to do and learn new tasks. I'll always be playing catch-up.
I'll delegate part of my next assignment.	I have to start sometime; so it might as well be now.

VI. Other Delegation Guidelines

1. Give the job to the person who can do it best. Selecting the right person is most of the game. The best is not always the cheapest, nor is it always the most expensive: check out your resources. Check references and the previous work they did.

2. Make sure those doing the task have the right training and tools. Remember, preparation is paramount to accomplishment.

3. Make a special note to clearly and accurately communicate the exact nature and scope of the delegation. Clear communication leads to clear action.

4. Always give credit to those who do the job. Positive reinforcement is the most powerful motivator of human behavior. This will increase the quality of future work.

5. Help others learn to delegate. Don't give them meaningless tasks, and use their talents wisely.

6. Delegate the right to be different. Allow things to be done in new and creative ways. It may save you money or time in the long run. Use others' time as well as their creativity.

7. Follow up. Delegation does not free you from responsibility. Follow up to ensure things are being done properly.

Impact Statements

Write out the following impact statements and tape them up in places where you're most likely to see them (on the bathroom mirror, refrigerator door at home, on your desk at work, etc.). This way they'll constantly remind you to delegate all you can to give you more time and energy to spend on the really important goals you have for your life.

I ask myself, "Who can do the job best?"

I don't have to do everything myself—it's not in my best interest.

I frequently ask myself, "What is the best use of my time right now?"

I am aware of my own limits and delegate when I can.

I concentrate my efforts on those projects that have the most payoff for me.

If I want others to do things for me, I will first take the time to teach them how I want it done.

KEEPING ON YOUR PATH: DISCIPLINE

Like organization, discipline carries a negative connotation for many people. As children we associated it with punishment; as teenagers we related it to conforming with the system; and as adults, we often think discipline means we have to do something or we will feel guilty about it later on. Rarely do we associate it with freedom or creativity, although many reluctantly correlate it with success.

Freedom, creativity, and discipline, however, have much in common. They go together as reinforcers of each other. Discipline is being able to delay immediate wants and keep on the track of establishing this foundation. After a solid foundation is established, there is more time and more freedom to create.

Take heart. Those of you who have read this far into the book have a considerable amount of discipline. Apply what you are learning. You are on your way. Keep it up.

DISCIPLINE EXERCISES

Discipline is following through on what you start out to do, whether it's for yourself or others. Mixed with flexibility, it's a hallmark of almost every successful person I can think of. They have staying power. They don't sabotage themselves by jumping from project to project, or relationship to relationship. They hang in there.

Discipline is also patience. It's thinking before you act, and it's having the willpower to work and wait for better things down the road. It is recognizing that it is a bad deal to exchange current comfort for later disappointment.

Examine the following sabotage factors, which are typical of a person weak in this area. Circle any that apply to you. Note the corresponding success factor, which is the more appropriate response. Circle the success factors that apply to you as well. Build on your strengths and strengthen your weaknesses.

Sabotage	vs.	Success
I start things with enthusiasm, but become bored or disappointed with them in a short period of time.		I bring things to completion by following through with what I start, no matter how I feel.
I often find myself going from project to project, never seeming to stay with something for very long.		I am patient and persistent in pursuit of my goals.
I have trouble remaining committed to the major goals I have for my life.		Once I start something or commit myself to something or someone, I follow through.
I often say or do things without thinking.		I listen to my conscience and become informed before I act.
I have discipline for one area of my life, but not for the other areas.		I am able to balance my time and commitments.

I. *Identify Your Weak Areas*

In order to acquire more discipline in your life you must first identify the areas in which you have trouble following through with things and the areas in which you act impulsively. List those for each of the major areas of your life. Examples are given below in parentheses.

Personal life:

—spiritual (I lack the follow-through to go to the church of my choice every week, even though I tell myself I'm going to get involved.) Add your own:

—emotional/behavioral (Even though I promise myself not to talk too much about myself at parties, it seems that I do more talking than listening.) Add your own:

—physical (I often overeat, even though I tell myself not to beforehand.) Add your own:

Relational life: (It seems I fly off the handle at the slightest provocation; or, I always resolve to spend special time with my children, but somehow I never seem to get around to it.) Add your own:

Work-related life: (Doing things quickly so that I can just be done with them often gets me into trouble. Or, impulsively talking back to the boss has almost gotten me fired several times.) Add your own:

II. *Reward Yourself for Discipline*

Before you come to a difficult task that you generally want to avoid, but know avoiding is not in your best interest, set up a reward system to help yourself get it done on time. To set up this system, *decide beforehand on a reward that will help motivate you.* It can be anything from a special concert, a new dress, or a new golf club to a night out with your friends. Then, after you've followed through with your task, make sure you follow through with the reward.

This technique worked well for me when I was in college. I told myself that if I could put in four good hours of studying I would then take myself out for some dessert with one of my friends. That way, I had something to look forward to, I got through the studying, and when I went out later on I didn't feel guilty about it—I could enjoy my reward. I'd earned it.

List three tasks in which you have trouble following through. (For example, balancing checkbook.)

1.
2.
3.

Now list at least five rewards that will help motivate you to follow through. (For example, play with the dog.)

1.
2.
3.
4.
5.

Have the discipline to follow through with this positive reinforcement system.

III. *Thinking Is Trial Action*

Impulsiveness causes nails to be driven into many coffins. It starts many fights, ends many relationships, and drains many bank accounts. You need to fight the impulses that hold you back.

Thinking is trial action. Taking some time to think things through before you act will slow the impulses that threaten to hurt you or those close to you. Some ideas to help you harness your impulses into productive energy are:

1. Before you act on the spur of the moment, go quickly through the decision-making process I wrote about in the section on decision making (memorize this process).

This decision-making process can apply to things you say, things you buy, and the way you act in certain situations. It will slow down impulsiveness and enhance your work in your own best interest.

2. Mentally rehearse the action or words you'll say before you do or say them. This may only take five seconds, but it may have a powerful impact on your behavior.

3. When you have an impulse to say or do something that may be harmful to yourself or others, take ten slow deep breaths, and rethink the situation before you do anything.

One way to look at discipline is as a positive commitment to yourself. It's a statement that you're worth the time and effort to succeed.

Impact Statements

Write out the following impact statements and tape them up in places where you're most likely to see them (on the bathroom mirror, refrigerator door at home, on your desk at work, etc.). This way they'll constantly remind you of the need to foster self-discipline in your life.

I follow through on the things I start.

I work and wait for better things down the road.

I have harnessed my impulses, and now work in the best interest of my goals.

I take the time to practice and prepare for the important tasks I do.

SANE CHANCES: TAKES REASONABLE RISKS

Reaching for anything worthwhile in life involves some risk: loving another person—for disappointment might occur; venturing into business— nine out of ten businesses fail within ten years; searching for the truth—you may not find it. Not to risk, however, is to forfeit success.

Every person risks something every day. Ours is not a life with guaranteed outcomes. Crossing the street, driving in a car, riding in an elevator, eating in a restaurant, and many other common activities of daily life may all be risky.

There are many things we can do, however, to enhance our chances of success, such as looking before crossing the street, wearing seat belts, riding only in elevators that appear sound and eating in restaurants that have been inspected by the health department. But we can never be sure of the outcome.

Often the more the payoff, the more risk is involved. Any area of life that offers the internal rewards of success requires risk. But, as in the everyday risks we take, there are things we can do to lessen the risks and increase our chances for success, however we define that for ourselves. Before any weighty risk is undertaken, ask yourself:

1. What is the risk: Be clear with yourself what you are risking by the action (e.g., self-esteem, money, physical harm).

2. What are the potential advantages to undertaking that course of action? What is the cost-benefit ratio? If the cost outweighs the potential benefits, what are the alternatives to the behavior?

3. Does the risk fit into your overall goals? Or are you taking risks, such as driving dangerously, that have nothing to do with what you want out of life?

4. Is the behavior risky to anyone else? Who else could get hurt or disappointed if the venture fails? Is it worth risking something that is not yours, such as other people's money or reputations?

5. Is there something you can do to reduce the risk?

To illustrate risk-taking decisions, let's look at several examples.

Asking someone for a date can be very anxiety-provoking, depending on your attitude toward rejection.

1. *What are the risks?* You can be turned down. It has happened to all of us, and is part of life. But for someone who bases his self-worth on whether or not she'll go out with him, possible rejection keeps him from ever asking. I guess the other risk is that she might go out with you. Any new relationship involves risk.

2. *What are the advantages?* Advantages in this situation include companionship, conversation, warmth, and the possibility of something special. The alternatives of not asking those you like for dates is that your friends will fix you up—you'll spend your time with their choices instead of yours—or that you'll continue being lonely.

3. *Does this fit into your overall goals?* Most people have the goal to be relational, to share their lives with other people. This is very hard to do without helping people enter your life by inviting them.

4. *Will it be risky to anyone else?* By asking someone out, you place them in the position of having to choose whether or not to go out with you. How risky that is to them depends on the kind of person you are.

5. *Are there ways to reduce the risk?* Obviously, in a relational setting, the more you find out about a person, the more you can reduce the risks when it comes to asking for a date. For men, I have found that if a woman truly likes her father, you have a better chance she'll like you; that is, she doesn't begin with a negative mindset about men. The opposite is generally true for women as well; that is, men who like their mothers usually have a more positive attitude toward all women.

Another example of risk taking occurs in starting a business. Statistics from the Small Business Administration (SBA) show that the risk of failure is greater than the potential for success. Successful business owners understand the risk before they venture forth.

1. *What are the risks in starting a new business?* You could lose all of the time, money, and effort you put into starting up a business if it fails. If the successful person lost it all, however, that would not be the end of his ambition, and he would start again.

2. *What are the advantages?* Business owners do not want to work for anyone else. Going into business for themselves gives them the opportunity for personal satisfaction, financial independence, self-expression, community involvement, and a legacy for their families. The alternative, working regular hours for regular pay, is not an attractive alternative.

3. *Does it fit into their goals?* Personal and financial independence are goals of most business owners. Having a successful business gives them the opportunity to be what they want to be.

4. *Is it risky to anyone else?* Owning a business takes a great deal of time and effort. I remember my father working sixteen hours a day, six days a week, and then some on Sunday. He needed the support of my mother to hold his family together. If he didn't get that support, he risked his family. Most successful business owners are in the same position: without family support their success is much more difficult.

5. *Are there ways to reduce the risk?* According to the SBA, error on the part of the operator, owner, or management is the cause of approximately ninety percent of all business failures. The other ten percent include economic conditions, fraud, neglect, and disaster. Being knowledgeable is a clear way to reduce risk.

The riskiest thing I have done in my life is to become a father. Some might think this a strange example of risk, but I know many of you parents will be able to relate to what I say.

Our children are a product of ourselves and the person we love most in this world. As such, they are natural extensions of love, and we invest much of ourselves in them. When they are happy, we are happy. When they are sick or sad, we worry. When their behavior is bad, we get angry because we think their behavior is a reflection of our parenting. The greatest joy I have in life is being able to love and be loved by my wife and children. That is not without risks.

In the summer of 1986 a very tragic event in my extended family brought this point painfully close to home. My Aunt Barbara and Uncle Bill and my two cousins, Robbie, age sixteen, and Gregg, fourteen (my godson), were driving from Los Angeles to Palm

Springs for vacation. While they were on the freeway, a tractor-trailer carrying crushed cars got into an accident on an overpass above them. The truck hit the rail and spilled all the crushed cars onto the freeway below, striking their car, killing Robbie instantly, and critically injuring Barbara.

Even though I had seen death many times in hospitals, including the tragic deaths of children, I had never truly understood the pain that parents who lose their children experience. I have watched with sorrow the pain in Robbie's family, knowing that his death is something they'll never be able to understand or put behind them. They have lost part of themselves.

Very often since the accident I have held my own children and wondered about the risks in their lives. I would like so much to engulf and protect them with my care, but I know that I have to teach them to face the risks of the world on their own as they grow up. Their lives, like all our lives, involve risks of living and dying, happiness and sadness, successes and failures. To know the joy of being a parent is also to know risk that no other risk can match.

TAKING REASONABLE RISKS

> *It is only by risking our persons from one hour to the next that we live at all.*
>
> —WILLIAM JAMES

Anything worthwhile in life involves some risk, either to self-esteem, health, relationships, or finances. To shun risk is to remain stagnant and never grow beyond your present state. Reasons behind avoiding risks involve fear, memories of past failures, and an unwillingness to risk comfort.

On the other side of the coin, however, are those who take dangerous risks which have little to do with the goals they have for their lives.

The following set of exercises is designed to help you think about whether or not the risks you take in your life relate to your life goals. Also, it will help you break out of the fears that have been holding you back, giving you a formula to help you make sense of the risks you need to take.

Examine the following sabotage factors, which are typical of people weak in this area. Circle any that apply to you. Note the corresponding success factor, which is the more appropriate response. Circle the success factors that apply to you as well. Build on your strengths and strengthen your weaknesses.

Sabotage	vs.	Success
I am overly cautious, refusing to take chances even when the odds are on my side.		I am able to take reasonable risks.
I take big risks to make others think highly of me.		I actively look for ways to reduce the element of risk.
I take risks that are dangerous to my health and welfare.		I refuse to jeopardize my or others' safety. There are other goals or other ways to achieve them.
I make impulsive decisions without adequately thinking out the risks involved.		I think of the risks as well as the benefits to the decisions I make.
The risk of failure prevents me from trying.		I accept the risk of failure as a condition of succeeding.

I. What Risks Do You Take?

There are positive risks and negative risks in life. Positive risks are chances you take to enhance your personal growth: for example, trusting another person in a relationship to increase your sense of belonging and connectedness, or investing in the stock market to increase your financial worth.

Negative risks have no growth potential. These include being abusive or neglectful toward those you love—for they may leave you; drinking and driving; smoking; and impulsive financial investments.

Think about each major area of your life. What positive and negative risks do you take in those areas? Write as many as you can think of. The questions provided are there to give you ideas to consider. How do these risks relate to the overall goals you have for yourself?

PERSONAL RISKS: (spiritual, emotional, physical)

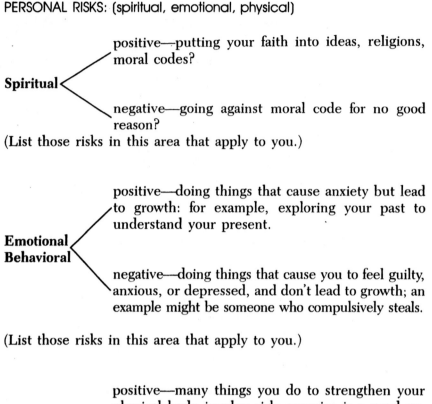

Spiritual

positive—putting your faith into ideas, religions, moral codes?

negative—going against moral code for no good reason?

(List those risks in this area that apply to you.)

Emotional Behavioral

positive—doing things that cause anxiety but lead to growth: for example, exploring your past to understand your present.

negative—doing things that cause you to feel guilty, anxious, or depressed, and don't lead to growth; an example might be someone who compulsively steals.

(List those risks in this area that apply to you.)

Physical

positive—many things you do to strengthen your physical body involve risk; exercise is a good example, since it risks injury.

negative—smoking, overeating, drinking/drugs, driving at dangerous speeds, dangerous sports, etc.

(List those risks in this area that apply to you.)

RELATIONAL RISKS: (spouse/lover, children, relatives, friends)

Positive—becoming vulnerable to enhance your sense of belonging and connectedness; risking rejection.

(List those risks in this area that apply to you.)

Negative—behaving in an abusive, neglectful, or suspicious manner; inviting rejection.

(List those risks in this area that apply to you.)

WORK-RELATED/FINANCIAL RISKS: (job, career, business, home management, financial management, etc.)

Positive—changing careers for more opportunity, putting in extra time to be noticed (of course, the risk is that you may not be noticed); starting or expanding a business; doing things differently at home to improve organization or efficiency; financial investments.

(List those risks in this area that apply to you.)

Negative—stealing at work; doing less than is expected of you; making hasty investments; letting things go at home; not adequately supervising your employees' work.

(List those risks in this area that apply to you.)

II. *The Reasonable Risk-taking Process*

With the foregoing information in mind, answer the following risk-taking questions for each of the risks listed (this will take some time, but in the long run it will be very helpful to you).

1. *What is the risk?* Be clear with yourself what you are risking by the action (e.g., self-esteem, money, physical harm).

2. *What are the potential advantages* to undertaking that course of action? What is the cost-benefit ratio? (Here you may want to use a side-by-side listing technique comparing the advantages and disadvantages.) If the cost outweighs the potential benefits, what are the alternatives to the behavior? If there are no advantages, as in negative risks, why do you take them?

3. *Does the risk fit into your overall goals?* How? Or are you taking risks that have nothing to do with your overall goals in life?

4. *Is the risk dangerous to anyone else?* Who else could get hurt or disappointed by the action? Do you have their permission to risk for them?

5. *What can you do to reduce the risk?* Come up with a plan that allows you to continue with the positive risks you listed, while at the same time decreasing those risks. If you need more information on the risk, do you know how to get it?

III. *Take A Risk*

A good first step for people not used to taking risks is to take some! I've seen amazing transformations in people after they were encouraged into taking that first step. At fist start with some of the small risks you've been avoiding, then build your way up to bigger ones.

Before you do, go through the risk-taking process above. It will free you to take a risk this week. You may fail. That's OK as long as you learn from it.

Impact Statements

Write out the following impact statements and tape them up in places where you're most likely to see them (on the bathroom mirror, refrigerator door at home, on your desk at work, etc.). This way they'll constantly remind you of the need to take reasonable risks in your life, while at the same time helping you eliminate those risks that don't fit into the goals you have for your life.

Reaching for anything worthwhile in life involves some risk.
The risks I take relate to my goals.
In making decisions I weigh the risks as well as the benefits.
When I'm faced with a risk I ask myself:

1. What is the risk?
2. What are its advantages?
3. Does this risk fit into my overall goals?
4. Is this risk dangerous to anyone else?
5. What can I do to reduce this risk?

17

Overcoming Interactional Self-Sabotage

"THIS IS WHAT I HEAR YOU SAYING": GOOD COMMUNICATION SKILLS

Clear communication is the best way to fight interactional self-sabotage and is a key to success in almost any area of life. Too often in personal or business relationships we have hopes and expectations that we never clearly communicate to others. As a consultant to organizations and businesses, I've found that the underlying problem in employer-employee disputes was often a lack of clear communication. In over half the cases, when the communication problems were improved other problems were also quickly resolved.

For example, Billie Jo was an administrative assistant who was frequently angry at her boss. He would give her general guidelines for projects and then become irritated with her when the work wasn't done to his satisfaction. Because of his gruff manner she was too afraid to ask him specific questions about the work. Billie Jo began to really hate her job. She developed frequent headaches and neck tension and was constantly looking for another job. A friend pushed her to tell her boss about her frustrations. The friend said, "If you're going to quit anyway you have little to lose." To her surprise the boss was receptive to her direct approach and encouraged her to ask more questions about the projects he assigned.

255

Here are six keys to effective communication in relationships.

The first key is to have a good attitude and assume the other person wants the relationship to work as much as you do. Too often people become caught up in their own anger and disappointment and they unknowingly set things up to turn out poorly. Having a good attitude can set the mood for a positive outcome. I call this having "positive basic assumptions" about the relationship.

Second, state what you need clearly and in a positive way. Most people are too wrapped up in themselves to think about what's going on with you. In most situations being direct is the best approach. But how you ask is important. You can demand and get hostility, you can ask in a meek manner and no one will take you seriously, or you can be firm yet kind in the way you ask and get what you need. How you approach someone has a lot to do with your success rate.

Third, decrease distractions and make sure you have the other person's attention. Find a time when the person is not busy or in a hurry to go somewhere.

Fourth, ask for feedback to ensure that the other person correctly understands you. Clear communication is a two-way street and it's important to know if you got your message across. A simple "Tell me what you understood I said" often is all that is needed.

Fifth, be a good listener. Before you respond to what people say, repeat back what you think they've said to ensure that you've correctly heard them. Statements such as "I hear you saying..." or "You mean to say..." are the gold standard of good communication. This allows you to check out what you hear before you respond.

Lastly, monitor and follow up on your communication. Often it takes repeated efforts to get what you need. It's very important not to give up.

COMMUNICATION EXERCISES

Clear communication is key to effective relationships. The following is a series of exercises designed to help increase your skill in communicating with others.

Examine the following sabotage factors, which are typical of those weak in this area. Circle any that apply to you. Note the corresponding success factor, which is the more appropriate response. Circle the success factors that apply to you as well. Build on your strengths and strengthen your weaknesses.

Sabotage	vs.	Success
Getting my point across in a discussion is so important that I often do not fully hear the other person or I have trouble understanding their point of view.		I am able to keep quiet long enough in a discussion to get the other person's point of view.
I often jump to conclusions before I completely hear out the other person.		I am good at checking out things I do not understand.
I either clam up or become very emotional in an argument.		I am able to assert myself even in emotional situations.
I'm often not clear in my communication with others.		When I do not understand something someone else has said, I ask them to repeat or clarify their words.
When I'm listening to someone talk to me I often become distracted.		When I have important talks with others I will decrease the distractions in the room.
I have trouble establishing eye contact when I talk with others.		I establish frequent eye contact when I talk with people.

I. Listening

Clear communication requires active listening. Below are some common obstacles that get in the way of listening, followed by ways to get around them.
Common Problems in Listening (Identify those that apply to you and those you need to work on.)

1. Not being in a position to hear, either because you are too far away from the other person, or the other person is talking too softly.

2. Being distracted by the environment: too much noise from others or the outside, poor room temperature, poor lighting, etc.

3. Criticizing a speaker's delivery or appearance. Sometimes people get hung up on a speaker's voice, mannerisms, dress, or some other external factor, causing them to miss out on the message the speaker is trying to convey.

4. Listening only for things to criticize or argue with, particularly if you don't agree with the speaker to begin with.

5. Starting to think about your own responses before you've fully heard what the speaker wishes to say. Many people actually turn off shortly after a speaker begins, remembering only the point they wish to make themselves. Keep an open mind.

6. Getting bogged down in the details without getting the big picture of the conversation. This creates a tendency to take things out of context.

7. Faking attention; pretending to listen when you're really thinking about something else.

8. Failing to provide the speaker with feedback. When we listen, it's crucial to provide the speaker with feedback, even if it's only our attentive facial expression. Without feedback, speakers have a tendency to lose enthusiasm for what they're saying, which decreases their effectiveness.

Improving Your Listening Skills

1. Prepare yourself to listen
—stop talking; you can't listen while you're talking.
—put other thoughts and concerns out of your mind; give the speaker your full attention.
—get closer to the speaker or ask him to speak up. Hearing is a prerequisite to listening.
—decrease distractions and allow as few interruptions as possible.
—prepare yourself for the topic by thinking about it in advance.
—develop a desire to listen by realizing that the other person has something important to teach you if you're only willing to learn it.

2. Start listening immediately. Don't wait to begin paying attention to others. Their first few sentences may be crucial to the whole conversation. Missing the beginning of a conversation may be like missing the beginning of a movie; you may never catch up with what's going on.

3. Listen for something you can use. You can learn something from everyone.

4. Concentrate on what's being said instead of judging the speaker's presentation or appearance.

5. Just because you disagree with someone, don't turn them off completely. Listen with an open mind. Listen for something useful. In order to reasonably defend our own position, we must understand the opposite point of view. If you think someone else is in "left field" most of the time, take advantage of the time they're not.

6. Listen for the big picture of what's being said. Listen for the major themes, instead of just facts with no framework in which to put them.

7. While you're listening, responses to what's being said will enter your mind. Write them down or mentally note them in some way so that you can come back to your point later. By doing this, you can then pay attention to what else is said, instead of just concentrating on getting your response into the conversation.

8. Don't fake attention. If you can't listen right now, say so.

9. Provide feedback (verbal and nonverbal) to the speaker so that he'll know you're paying attention and understanding what's being said. Feedback also involves asking questions to clarify what's said (more on asking questions a bit later).

For the next week, pick at least three of these nine suggestions and put them into practice.

II. *The Echo Technique*

The "I hear you saying..." or echo, technique is another important part of communication. It forces you to really hear and understand what the other person is saying. This technique involves repeating back to others what you understand them to be saying. In this way, you check out with the sender whether the message you received is the one you were intended to get.

Communication often breaks down because of distortions between intention and understanding, especially in emotionally charged encounters. Simply saying, "I hear you saying.... Is that what you meant?" can help avoid misunderstandings. This technique is particularly helpful when you suspect a breakdown in communication.

Different phrases in using this technique might be:

1. "I heard you say.... Am I right?"
2. "Did you mean to say...?"

3. "I'm not sure I understand what you said. Did you say... ?"
4. "Did I understand you correctly? Are you saying that... ?"
5. "Let me see if I understand what you're saying to me. You said that... ?"

Advantages to the "I-hear-you-saying" technique include:

1. You receive more accurate messages.
2. Misunderstandings are cleared up immediately.
3. You are forced to give your full attention to the other person.
4. Both parties are now responsible for accurate communication.
5. The sender is likely to be more careful with what he says.
6. It increases your ability to really hear the other person and thus learn from him.
7. It stops you from thinking about what you're going to say next so that you can really hear what the other person is saying.
8. It increases communication.
9. It tends to cool down conflicts.

Begin practicing this technique on at least two people every day for a week. See if it doesn't increase your communication abilities and thus your ability to learn from others.

III. Assertiveness: Say What You Mean

Assertiveness and communication go hand-in-hand. Assertiveness means to express feelings in a firm, yet reasonable, way, and to never allow another person to emotionally run over you with his anger. Don't say yes when it's not what you mean. Assertiveness also never equates with becoming mean or aggressive. Here are five rules to help you assert yourself in a healthy manner and communicate in a clear way:

1. Do not give in to the anger of others just because it makes you uncomfortable.

2. Do not allow the opinion of others to control how you feel about yourself. Your opinion, within reason, needs to be the one that counts.

3. Say what you mean and stick up for what you believe is right.

4. Maintain self-control.

5. Be kind if possible, but above all be firm in your stance.

Remember, we teach others how to treat us. When we give in to their temper tantrums, we teach them that that is the way to control us. When we assert ourselves in a firm yet kind way, others have more respect for us and treat us accordingly. If you have allowed others to emotionally run over you for a long time, they will be a little resistant to change. But stick to your guns and you'll help them learn a new way of relating.

Impact Statements

Write out the following impact statements and tape them in places where you're most likely to see them (on the bathroom mirror, refrigerator door at home, on your desk at work, etc.). This way they'll constantly remind you to communicate effectively.

I am able to keep quiet long enough in a discussion to get the other person's point of view.
I am good at checking out things I do not understand.
I say what I mean.
When I do not understand something someone else has said, I ask them to repeat or clarify their words.
I establish frequent eye contact when I talk with others.

DAILY POSITIVE INPUT: SURROUNDED BY POSITIVE PEOPLE

Positive people are contagious. That's why so many people feel so good after attending a positive thinking seminar or an inspiring religious service. Those positive effects may wear off quickly when these same people go home to negative environments where they are surrounded by people who do not believe in them, who put them down or treat them as though they will never amount to much. Negative people are also contagious.

This lesson has been taught to me many times. The most striking example is when I decided to go to medical school. I have already told you that I had doubts about my ability to meet admission committee standards. Wanting to enlist the support of people who were important to me, I began telling my friends about my decision.

I told Larry, my speech team coach, who replied that he had a brother who was twice as smart as I was, and who had been unable to get into medical school. "You don't have a chance," he said.

His comment was cutting to the core. I began having more doubts about my ability. But, happily, I spoke with my father, who bluntly told me that I could do anything I wanted if it meant enough to me. "Danny," he said, "you have a good mind. Keep it on your goals, and it will take you wherever you choose. If someone puts down your ability, stay away from him. He will be like a rock around your neck if you let him." What great advice. I avoided Larry as much as possible and concentrated my efforts on my goal. It paid off.

If you surround yourself with negative people, you will feel negative about yourself. That is not to say that it is all their fault. You need to own your feelings and recognize that you have contributed to the negative environment you find yourself in. You get treated in life the way you teach people to treat you. If you sit back and accept being abused, you are responsible for permitting that abuse to be dumped on you.

As I have mentioned many times now, taking personal responsibility for your life is the first ingredient of success. You can teach those around you how to treat you. You do this by giving and accepting positive strokes, and by tolerating nothing less than respect from others. If for some reason those people are unwilling to change, your relationship with them is not worth your life, for truly this negative treatment will shorten your life. Some compelling questions to ask yourself are: Why do I have a need to be treated this way? Why do I set myself up to be around people who put me down? What can I do about it now?

There are many stories of people who become successful to spite those who said they wouldn't make it. Revenge is also a very powerful motivator. A famous sports broadcaster once told me that when he was starting out in the business, one of his station managers told him he'd better learn to cut meat, because he'd never make it as a radio announcer. That spurred him on to prove the manager wrong, which he did many times over.

Let the malcontents spur you on. Don't let them hold you back!

SURROUNDING YOURSELF WITH POSITIVE PEOPLE EXERCISES

The people with whom we spend the most time have a tremendous impact on how we view ourselves and the world around us. They can be a boost that helps drive us toward our goals, or they can be an energy drain that drags us down.

It's extremely important for you to take care of the environment in which you grow. A positive environment is growth-enhancing, a negative one chokes and suffocates growth. In doing the following exercises, remember that you are responsible for the environment in which you find yourself. You can blame all sorts of others for your situation, but until you take control of the situation and mold it into something positive for you, it will not improve.

Examine the following sabotage factors, which are typical of those weak in this area. Circle any that apply to you. Note the corresponding success factor, which is the more appropriate response. Circle the success factors that apply to you as well. Build on your strengths and strengthen your weaknesses.

Sabotage	vs.	Success
The people close to me treat me as if I'll never amount to much.		The important people in my life behave in a positive, encouraging way toward me.
I feel negative about myself after visiting close friends.		I gravitate toward those I feel good being around.
I feel I have to fight the primary people in my life in order to feel good about myself.		I encourage and care for my relationships with those who behave toward me in a positive way.
If I grew up in a negative environment, I continue to surround myself with the same negative input.		Even if I grew up in a negative environment, I do not tolerate being put down by others.
I continue to spend time with people who put me down.		I gain energy and strength from my primary relationships.

I. Inventory Your Interactions

In order to change your interactions with those around you, you must first get an idea of who you spend the most time with and what those relationships are like. List the five people with whom you spend the most time. Then answer the following questions about each of those relationships.

1.
2.
3.
4.
5.

How much time do you spend with each?

In what context or situations do you come together?

Do you look forward to being with that person? How do you feel prior to seeing him or her?

How do they treat you when you're with them? Are they critical, or supportive? Do they make overtly hostile remarks, or do they abuse you in a more subtle way?

How do you treat them?

How do you feel when you're with them?

Are you able to hear what they have to say without being defensive? Or do you always feel you must fight with them to feel good about yourself?

How do you feel when you're away from them?

After you answer these questions, rate how you feel about each of the relationships on a one-to-ten scale, with one being a put-down, abusive relationship, and ten being an uplifting and supportive relationship.

1	2	3	4	5	6	7	8	9	10
− − − − −							+ + + + +		

1.
2.
3.
4.
5.

II. *Identify Your Personal Filter with Others*

Before you can really understand your relationships with others, you must begin to understand yourself. How you feel about yourself has the central impact on how you perceive the interactions with those around you. I discuss the concept of projection under "Perception" a little later. Simply put, projection means that we take our feelings and project them on other people. If we feel bad about ourselves, we assume or project that others feel bad about us as well. Thus, we take their interactions with us in that light.

For the interactions you rated less than 6 in exercise I, write out the specific evidence that shows the negative quality of the relationship: dates, incidents, etc. I want you to look at whether you project your negative feelings onto the relationship, and thus negatively distort the interactions, or whether the other person really acts abusively or negatively toward you. Both responses are possible, both are common. You'll be able to come up with hard evidence for the ones that are abusive and, most often, vague evidence for the ones onto whom you project your low or negative feelings.

III. *Change the Negative Interactions*

We all teach others how to interact with and respond to us. If, by our actions, we teach them that they must respect us or we'll have nothing to do with them, they either treat us with respect or they leave us alone. If we teach them that we'll accept their negative comments or verbal or physical abuse, they may abuse us.

We must show them what we are unwilling to accept. Quite often, low self-esteem gets in the way, and some accept the abuse because somehow they think they deserve it. Well, let me tell you: you don't deserve it!

Once an interactional pattern is established, it can be changed. I've seen this over and over.
Follow these six steps to changing your negative interactions with others:

1. Recognize and be clear about what, specifically, you or the other does to contribute to the negative interaction. Specify incidents, dates, etc.

2. Take responsibility for what you do to add to the negative situation—and change it.

3. Tell people they are important to you (if they weren't, you wouldn't be bothering with them), and that some of the things they do cause you to feel hurt or put down. Be specific: "When you cut me down in front of other people, it really hurts my feelings."

4. Ask them to change. First, tell them how upset their behavior makes you feel, and then ask them to change it. (Often, this is all it takes.)

5. If asking doesn't change the behavior, make it uncomfortable for them to treat you that way, i.e., "If you do that again I'll return your anger with fire—I won't allow you to treat me like that in front of others!" Make it clear what behaviors you'll accept and which you won't. Be ready to back up words with action.

6. If that still doesn't work, raise the heat further. Remember the section in the book on change? In order for change to take place, the person must feel uncomfortable, sometimes very uncomfortable. Often this may mean threatening to terminate the relationship. But, if you're really important to that other person, he or she will change. If you aren't, what are you doing in the relationship? In my opinion, negative relationships take more out of you physically and emotionally than they're worth.

Before you get out of negative relationships, you need more information: Can you change your interactions? Can the other person change his? If others are teachable, you need to teach them how to treat you. Whether you recognize it or not, you've been doing that all along.

If you find yourself unable to teach others to treat you with respect, odds are it's because you believe you don't deserve respect. If that's the case, you may need professional assistance to help you work on your own self-worth.

IV. Decrease the Time You Spend with Those Who Put You Down

If those negative people in your environment are unwilling or unable to change, decrease the amount of time you spend with them. Remember, if your environment is negative, so are you. Obviously, you may not be able to totally eliminate your interactions with some of these people, such as parents or close relatives. But you don't have to spend as much time with them. The time is better spent with those who uplift or encourage you.

Here are some actions to take:

Only call them half as much, or wait for them to call you. If they start in on you, find a way to get off the phone. Spend your coffee breaks with new people.

If you need to communicate with them, write them a letter.

Keep a schedule of things to do, so that when they ask you out you don't say yes out of boredom.

Change your routine, so that you're less likely to run into them.

At the same time, you need to establish new, positive relationships. Often, those who surround themselves with negative people gravitate toward them, leaving healthier, more positive relationships behind. When you meet someone who adds good things to your life, take care of the relationship. Call, be kind, be interested.

Ideas on ways to meet new, more positive people:

Go to five different congregations in five weeks and determine at which one the people make you feel the most comfortable.

Join a support group.

Go to lunch with someone new, someone you may never have thought you'd like to have lunch with; expand your horizons.

Attend a political rally, or even work for a political candidate.

Take a fun class at your local community college or through the adult education program, even if you already have a degree.

Start a hobby you've never tried before, one that includes other people, such as sailing, hiking, square dancing, volleyball or any team sport, model railroading, photography (a good reason to ask practically anyone to pose for you), volunteering for a local service agency. The possibilities are endless.

Buy an adorable animal and take it out. I once had a pet raccoon I used to take to the beach. Many people would stop to ask me about her.

Start doing your laundry at a launderette.

Add your own ways of meeting new people.

Impact Statements

Write out the following impact statements and tape them up in places where you're most likely to see them (on the bathroom mirror, refrigerator door at home, on your desk at work, etc.). This way they'll constantly remind you of the need to surround yourself with positive people, and to teach people how to treat you with respect.

I let negative people spur me on, never hold me back.

I spend time with positive, uplifting people.

I teach others to behave toward me with respect.

I refuse to be abused.

My environment is my life; I must protect it.

ABILITY TO LEARN FROM OTHERS: BEING TEACHABLE

If there is any one secret to success it lies in the ability to get the other person's point of view and see things from his angle as well as your own.

—HENRY FORD

Television's Lieutenant Columbo approached each homicide case as a student. He started without preconceived notions about the guilt or innocence of the suspects, and he asked many, many questions. Whenever the answers to the questions didn't match up with the facts, it led him to ask more questions and do more probing.

His style was to enlist the killer to help him solve the mystery. Columbo would often approach suspects with the suggestion that they might be able to explain something that baffled him. He went about his work in such a nonthreatening and, at times, even bumbling way that many mistook his manner for naïveté and offered their help. He always discovered the murderer.

Dr. Jean Piaget used a method similar to Columbo's to discover how children think. Until Piaget's genius appeared earlier in this century, behavioral scientists tried to fit their preconceived theories to the behavior and thinking of children. Piaget's approach, however, was radically different. He took the position of student when interviewing children; he started with the idea that he didn't know anything about them, and they were his teachers.

After all, he reasoned, who is more qualified than children to teach about the thoughts of children. The children blossomed in this situation. They weren't use to being listened to, and when they were given the opportunity, they spoke at length about their inner worlds, telling Piaget things never recorded before. They told him their ideas about how clouds stayed in the sky, where the rivers came from, how boats float, whether or not the sun could see them and so on. They felt free to talk because he didn't make them feel silly, but treated them like important individuals. He was curious, and he was a willing pupil of their tutelage.

And teach him the children did. He was then able to describe the different cognitive (thinking) stages of development, which to this day remains the definitive work on the ways our thinking processes develop.

Piaget's ability to learn from those who had the information he needed exemplifies a major ingredient for success in any endeavor. In order to learn anything, we must first be teachable. All of the ingredients for success are characteristics that can be learned. The question is, will you take the time to learn them, and will you be a willing pupil, as Piaget was?

Others have so much to teach us, if we will only listen. Do you get so caught up in having to get your own point across in a discussion that you fail to hear what the other person is saying? Be quiet enough to listen! You know what you have to say; learn from others. Get out of the role of having to have all the answers, and be receptive enough to take in the information.

Of course, when I write "Be quiet enough to listen," I don't mean you must *always* be quiet. Don't be too timid to ask questions, which is also very important to the learning process. Engage in the interchange, but be willing to listen.

Also, stay away from the "Yes, but" syndrome, which negates any piece of information or advice anyone gives you. I have spoken to many parents who ask for my advice, but when I give them some, they respond to it with things like, "Oh, I tried that and it didn't work" or "That would never work with Billy, he's not interested in being good." The fact is, even if they did try the advice, it was often an inconsistent or halfhearted try. Listen, ask questions, but most of all, try to really hear what someone is trying to communicate.

TEACHABILITY EXERCISES

Being unable to learn from others is a major sabotage factor. This may take the form of being unable to ask others questions; having to be right in conversations, so that you miss the other person's point of view; having to always counter others' advice; completely turning off those whose opinions differ from yours; or lacking a teachable spirit.

Obviously, you've been able to learn much from others, but this is an area most of us can improve on. The following exercises are designed to help you increase your ability to learn from others, and thus increase your chances for success in any endeavor you undertake.

Examine the following sabotage factors, which are typical of a person weak in this area. Circle any that apply to you. Note the

corresponding success factor, which is the more appropriate response. Circle the success factors that apply to you as well. Build on your strengths and strengthen your weaknesses.

Sabotage	vs.	Success
I expect I should know everything myself.		When I have trouble in an area, I seek out the help of others.
I act like a know-it-all.		I possess a teachable spirit.
I often get caught in the "Yes, but..." syndrome.		I don't always follow advice, but I make sure I listen to get any new ideas that may be offered.
In a discussion, I have to be right or I feel bad.		When I have an important task to accomplish, I ask experienced people for help.
I feel I can't learn from those who are beneath me.		I realize that I can learn from anyone.
Getting my point across is so important that I have trouble understanding the other person's point of view.		When someone is talking to me, I make an effort to really hear what they're saying.
If I don't like something someone else has to say, I turn them off completely.		I am able to learn from those I don't always agree with.

I. *From Whom Can You Learn?*

The first step in improving your ability to learn from other people is to think about who you can learn from. Who has information that could be beneficial to you? For each of the major areas of your life, list at least three people you know who could contribute to your knowledge or help you toward your goals.

Personal (spiritual, emotional, physical)
1.
2.
3.

Relational
1.
2.
3.

Work-related
1.
2.
3.

II. *Ask Your Questions*

Asking questions is another essential in learning from others. If you don't ask your questions, how will they be answered? How will you be able to learn from someone else?

At least one time every day this week, force yourself to ask someone a question you have. It doesn't matter if it has to do with home, work, or your relational life. You need to train yourself to stop sabotaging yourself by not asking your questions.

Also, each time this week that the fear of appearing stupid or of being a bother held you back from asking something, answer the following questions about that incident.

1. What was the situation?

2. Was it appropriate to ask that question in that environment? If not, why not?

3. What was the worst thing that could have happened if you had asked the question?

4. How else could you have gotten that question answered?

Allow the answers to these questions to spur you further in asking the questions you need. Never forget: Asking dumb questions is a lot better than being ignorant!

III. *Refusing-to-Act-Like-A-Know-It-All*

In order to learn, we have to take the position of being a student, to become teachable, to get away from acting like a know-it-all.

Each day this week, catch yourself when you come off as knowing everything about a particular subject. Instead of hearing yourself lecture to someone else, take the time to get the other person's point of view or perspective. Be it your coworker, your kids, or your spouse, catch yourself acting like you know all the answers and begin to learn from them. Ask them questions, clarify what they say using the echo technique, and really listen to them.

IV. Establish a Mentor Relationship

Another very effective way to begin learning from others is to choose a mentor for yourself. A mentor is defined in the dictionary as a wise adviser, a teacher or coach. This person can be someone you meet with regularly or someone whose work you admire in the media. In each of the major areas of your life, choose one person with whom you could establish a mentor relationship (a list of suggestions follow). Then either spend regular time learning from them, or spend regular time reading their works. Learn everything you can from them. Keep a questioning mind and don't take all they say as gospel, but learn all you can from them on a regular basis. When you've learned as much as you can from them, choose other mentors and continue the learning.

Personal   (this might be a spiritual or religious leader, an exercise coach, a nutritionist, or a mental health professional)

1.

Relational   (this might be anyone who has gotten his or her relational life together, a pastor, or a marriage and family counselor)

1.

Work-related   (an example here might be a trusted supervisor, an expert in your field, or someone who has gone through what you wish to accomplish)

1.

The type of people you look up to will tell you a lot about yourself.

Impact Statements

Write out the following impact statements and tape them in places where you're most likely to see them (on the bathroom mirror, refrigerator door at home, on your desk at work, etc.). This way they'll constantly remind you of the need to possess a teachable spirit.

I possess a teachable spirit.
I learn something from others every day.
Acting like a know-it-all gets in the way of my self-development.
I take the time to observe those people who have accomplished the goals I am interested in.
Even if I don't always completely agree with someone, I can still learn from them.

WE BOTH CAN WIN: COMPETITION AS A WIN-WIN SITUATION

Competition is feared by many people who ardently avoid it. They believe the price for losing is not worth the risk. The only competition they know is a game of winners and losers. They have never heard of the competitive game of winners and winners.

When you view competition as a game with winners and losers, someone has to get hurt in the process; someone has to lose, whether in an argument with your spouse or kids, or in gaining a promotion over someone else at work. When our egos have to win, it is often from a need to be better than someone else, which is a sign of low self-esteem.

In the game of winners and winners, no one has to lose. Mutual benefit is gained from the competition. The examples of this are myriad.

Many marriages turn into a game of winners and losers. Think about the last argument you had with your spouse or lover. Did both of you spend time trying to understand the other's point of view? After all, you already knew your point of view. Or, did you spend all your time trying to convince your partner that he or she was wrong and you were right, that you were the winner of the discussion and your partner the loser?

Someone who feels like a loser is not likely to admit your genius and bow at your feet. Rather, if your opponent is like most people he or she will try to find a way to get even with you, by withholding affection from you, making you look foolish in front of others, or taking it out on the kids. Revenge is a powerful motivator of human behavior.

Win-lose situations also abound between parents and children.

"You will do what I say or spend the afternoon in your room," is not an uncommon response to a child's negative behavior. Parents often forget that their child is a developing person who has thoughts and ideas of his own.

Treating children in a win-lose mode—"I am the boss, and you are the one to be bossed"—does little to develop a sense of cooperation, which is the basis of positive competition (win-win). Children generally respond to the win-lose treatment by either becoming more resistant with defiant or passive-aggressive behavior, or retreating from all competition, feeling that they'll lose no matter what. If you want to engender a feeling of cooperation and positive competition in your children, teach them understanding by first understanding them.

I do not mean to say that children should not submit to a parent's authority. They should. Because if you do not teach them discipline, the world will, and not in a loving way. And certainly there are times when parents should say, "Do what I say or there will be consequences." Discipline and cooperation are not polar concepts.

Win-win opportunities also occur every day in the workplace. Many successful corporations have learned this secret. They use employee incentive plans to hook their employees' investment into the corporation. As an employee's investment in his work goes up, so do his productivity, attendance, and cooperation. At the same time, his tendency to steal from the corporation goes down, as he feels like he is stealing from himself.

The recent surge in the growth of the self-help movement in this country is another example of the win-win situation. Self-help groups are based on the premise that by helping someone with a problem similar to yours, you are in essence helping yourself. Experience shows that nothing works better to keep an alcoholic from drinking than for him to help another alcoholic remain dry. Likewise, it has been my experience that no one can help a bereaved parent better than another parent who has also lost a child.

No doubt sometimes we have to face win-lose situations. That is the reality of war, in the absence of negotiated compromise. In marriages, there may be some unavoidable win-lose situations; especially when one partner no longer loves the other, someone will get hurt. And with children, when it comes to drugs or alcohol, parents need to win, to be very firm about what is acceptable and what is not. Likewise, in a free-market society some businesses will fail due to the competition. These are just the facts of living in a survival society.

Whenever possible, however, look for opportunities to put yourself in win-win situations. The results will enhance the efforts of both sides and bring you closer together rather than isolate you from each other.

THE WIN-WIN COMPETITION EXERCISES

Competition occurs in all aspects of life; there's no escaping it. Sometimes we win, sometimes we don't. The best strategy is to use competition to your advantage. The secret to doing this is to look for win-win situations.

Basically, win-win situations are those in which two competing parties help each other to improve, thus increasing the quality of the product and the competition. This is exemplified by merchants who band together in trade associations to learn from each other. The following exercises were designed to help you change your attitude toward competition—from seeing it as a win-lose proposition to seeing win-wins—and for you to engage more constructively in the competition that may be necessary for you to reach your goals.

Examine the following sabotage factors, which are typical of a person weak in this area. Circle any that apply to you. Note the corresponding success factor, which is the more appropriate response. Circle the success factors that apply to you as well. Build on your strengths and strengthen your weaknesses.

Sabotage	vs.	Success
The fear of losing prevents me from trying.		I view competition as a way to improve my skills, rather than a game that just needs to be won.
I stay away from competition even to my detriment.		Competition spurs me on to be as good as I possibly can be.
When someone I know succeeds at something, I feel I've lost out in comparison.		I encourage others to win.
I see competition only as a win-lose situation.		I actively seek win-win situations.

Victories and successes often feel empty to me.	I feel good when I win.
Competition makes me nervous.	I realize my worth is not tied up in my winning.
Losing is a blow to my self-esteem, and may be even harming my relationships with others.	Even when I lose, I learn from competing with others.
I have to win in order to feel superior.	Losing isn't the end of the world, but just a stop along the way.
I envy the success of others.	I encourage others' success.

I. What Competition Do You Engage In? What Do You Avoid?

For each of the major areas of your life, list at least one area of competition you are currently engaged in and one area that you avoid. Examples are given below.

AREAS OF COMPETITION

Personal Life (competition with and challenges to self)

Engaged In	*Avoid*
competing to keep the weight off	competing at sports not good at
competing to keep shopping to a certain time	competing doing hobbies you think you can't do; e.g., sewing
competing to get a project done on time	competing with the negative inner voice, just agreeing with what it says about you instead of fighting back

List Own Experiences

1.   1.

Relational (competition with others in your relationships)

Engaged In	*Avoid*
competing for intimate relationships	competing for friendships
competing to outdo a sibling	competing for power in the relationship
competition to see who's the best at something; e.g., cooking, games	other people when you suspect a competitive relationship
List Own Experiences 1.	1.

Work-related

Engaged In	*Avoid*
competing for customers	competing for lucrative contracts
competing for school grades	competing for career advancement
competing to be the best employee in the boss's mind	competing for the promotion
List Own Experiences 1.	1.

In what ways do the competitive situations you avoid hold you back from getting what you want out of your life, from accomplishing your goals?

Personal
Relational
Work-related

II. *Change Your Perception of Competition*

You must change your perception of competition in order to use it to your benefit, instead of letting fear of it hold you back. To do this, perform the worst/best scenario exercise: Pick a scenario where you're competing with someone you know over something important. List the worst things that could happen to you when you compete, and talk back to them, giving reasons why the thinking is self-defeating instead of self-protecting. The example I'll give from my own life is when I competed with my best friend for grades in medical school.

Worst Thing	Talk Back
He could get a higher grade than I do.	Even though I'd like to be the best, my purpose is to learn as much as I can, not to be better than someone else.
I'll feel inferior if he gets a higher grade.	Depending on beating others for your self-esteem is dangerous. You feel good when you win, but you're back in the pits when you lose.
I'll feel embarrassed if I get a lower grade.	Feelings of embarrassment are less likely if your goals are intact. If your goal is to beat the other person, you feel embarrassed when you lose. If your goal is to do as well as you can, it's OK to lose when you've done your best.
I could lose him as a friend if I beat him.	This is a possibility, if the other person depends on winning for his self-esteem. Be careful how you flaunt your victories.
If I lose I may be unable to start over.	As long as I have life and breath, I can start over.

Add your own:

The worst thing is to make competition a game of winners and losers: odds are that half the time, you'll come out on the bottom. The Best Thing About Competition Is...

   To win at something
   To learn from losing
   To improve skills through the competition
   To help someone else learn through the competition

Add your own:

Making competition a game of winners and winners is the best thing that could happen: odds are that you'll come out on top all the time.

III. *The Double Win*

Win-win situations, or the double win, are key to successful competition. Having to be better than someone else is often a no-win situation. Improving your own skills by helping someone else improve is a win-win situation. When I used to tutor other students in school, I often received more benefit than they did, because it helped me solidify my own knowledge of the subject. Also, when I taught my son to play chess, I taught him to be as good as he could be, so that even though he occasionally beats me, we have great games. It's more competitive that way, and a whole lot more fun. I don't have to be better to feel good about myself. Actually, I feel better when I can help others be the best they can be.

Over the next week, and longer if necessary, help someone compete with you. Choose one activity you compete in with another person (this may be from your list in Exercise I) and share some of your knowledge about that subject with him or her. In doing so, it's likely you'll begin to build a bridge of cooperation that will benefit both of you. An example might be, if you're competing with someone to be the best employee in a section, help that person learn from your knowledge of the job. If he catches on and begins to help you, the section productivity will increase and you'll both be looked upon favorably.

IV. *Face Your Fear: Compete*

In order to overcome fear and sabotage factors, you must face them head-on. This week, compete in something you usually avoid: sports, games, business, social, self. Choose one thing you have stayed away from in the past and go for it. You may lose at it, so be prepared. But it's OK to lose. The world will go on tomorrow. It's not OK to lose and not learn anything from it. And, it's not OK to avoid trying; that will always hold you back.

Competition isn't bad, it's just competition. When your perception of it gets in the way, it's time to change your perception.

Impact Statements

Write out the following impact statements and tape them in places where you're most likely to see them (on the bathroom mirror, refrigerator door at home, on your desk at work, etc.). This way they'll constantly remind you of the need to look for win-win situations and to benefit from competition instead of just having to win at it.

Helping others to change and improve is a way to help myself.
I am on the lookout for win-win situations; I'll be better for it.
Competition is a tool I can use to improve my skills.
When I compete, I don't have to win, but I do need to learn.

BEING SENSITIVE TO OTHERS: EMPATHY

If we could see the sorrows of others, we would be very tender towards them.
                              —Henry Wadsworth Longfellow

We are relational beings. Doing almost anything in life requires us to go through other people. The more smoothly we can do this, the easier the journey.

Relating to others, however, is no easy task, despite having practiced it all of our lives. The problem arises because we all bring our own emotional baggage from the past (the sum of all of our experiences, good, bad, and indifferent) to each new relationship. So instead of two people relating in the here and now, we more often relate to parts of several people in the there and then, mixed with the here and now, which can be a very complicated process. Think of how complicated group behavior can get.

The best way I have found to simplify this interpersonal process is to get outside myself and be sensitive to others, to begin to understand what they may be going through before deciding any-thing about them. This process is called empathy. If you can learn to get outside yourself in relationships, many others will quickly pick up and appreciate your effort to understand them, and in turn they will be more willing to understand you.

Understanding others is the tool I use as a psychiatrist to make a therapeutic alliance with my patients. The therapy would go no-where if they didn't trust me, and they learn to trust me by believing I am there to understand their needs and desires. You do not have to be a psychiatrist or go through years of psychoanalysis to begin to understand other people. Understanding others requires desire, a willingness to observe, and being able to imagine yourself in their shoes for a time. All of this requires practice.

The by-product of understanding others is that when they dump on you, when they treat you as less than human, you can ask yourself what is going on with them. Why do they need to treat you that way? This will help you distance yourself from their negativity and at the same time help you respond to them in a constructive way, rather than in a way that will only perpetuate the conflict. Being sensitive to others helps us protect ourselves.

Assertiveness training was an attempt to teach shy or withdrawn people to express themselves more openly. Mental health professionals know that when a person holds in his feelings he may wreak emotional and physical havoc. Assertiveness training quickly received a bad reputation, however, because the early efforts were perceived as a way of teaching people to get their feelings out no matter who got stepped on in the process. It is necessary to release our inner feelings, but it is also necessary to get these feelings out in a way that others can hear.

Before you tell someone something that might hurt him, think of his reaction to your words. Is there a way you can tell him that won't turn off his attention (which is generally our first reaction to things that hurt)?

In letting out your feelings, it is helpful to address specific behavior, not personalities, and to use "I" statements. "I" statements are phrases that tell someone how you feel. You are the owner of the feelings: "I felt embarrassed when you corrected me in front of the other employees."

These statements are very hard to argue with, because no one can deny what you feel: "When you did that, I felt this." This is opposed to "you" statements, which attack or blame the other person and invite a defense: "You embarrassed me in front of those people."

That's more apt to bring responses like, "I didn't say anything so terrible" or "Well, it's your own fault. If you hadn't..." Blaming others invites retaliation, which is less likely to happen if you are specific about how their behavior makes you feel.

Being sensitive to others involves many other things, including hearing them, treating them in a way you'd like to be treated, not making false assumptions about hidden meanings for their behavior, and never talking down to them or making yourself appear better than they are. Being sensitive to others will open many doors for you. Being insensitive will shut you out from others.

EMPATHY EXERCISES

Empathy (being able to see and feel things from another's perspective) and sensitivity are key to getting along in a relational world. Being insensitive to others not only causes them to avoid you, it can also make them "mad as hell," for which they tend to retaliate when they get an opportunity.

The input from others to our lives is so important that we need to befriend them and utilize their time, trust, and talent, not alienate them. The following set of exercises is designed to help you increase your empathic skills—that is, your ability to get outside of yourself and understand the needs of others. By understanding others better, we not only encourage them to be on our side throughout life, but, in the process, we also begin to understand ourselves better.

Examine the following sabotage factors, which are typical of people weak in this area. Circle any that apply to you. Note the corresponding success factor, which is the more appropriate response. Circle the success factors that apply to you as well. Build on your strengths and strengthen your weaknesses.

Sabotage	vs.	Success
I tend to be insensitive to others.		I treat others the way I would like them to treat me.
I often come off as critical of others.		I make others feel understood.
I don't have the time or desire to understand others.		I can put myself in other people's shoes to understand how they feel.
I have to get "my" point across in a discussion, thereby missing what the other person has to say.		I am able to keep quiet long enough in a discussion to get the other person's point of view.
I often act as if others do not matter to me.		I make an effort to get along with those who are important to my loved ones.
I forget to thank others for kindnesses shown to me.		I am appreciative to those who do things for me.

I. *Mirroring*

Your ability to understand and communicate with others will be enhanced by learning what psychiatrists call the mirroring technique. You can use this technique in any interpersonal situation to increase rapport with those around you.

When you mirror someone, you assume or imitate his body language—posture, eye contact, and facial expression—and you use the same words and phrases in conversation that the other person uses. For example, if someone is leaning forward in his chair, looking intensely at you, without making a big point of it, do the same. If you note that he uses the same phrase several times, such as, "I believe we have a winner here," pick it up and make it part of your vocabulary for that conversation.

This is not mimicry, which implies ridicule; rather, this technique helps set up an unconscious identification with you in the mind of the other person. Attempt to use this mirroring technique at least once per day for a week.

II. *The Golden Rule Exercise*

Another exercise that will help you get outside of yourself and into the feelings of others is what I call the Golden Rule Exercise.

In one interaction per day, treat someone else as you would like to be treated in that situation. For example, if your spouse has a headache when you feel amorous, instead of feeling rejected make a conscious effort to understand and say something like, "It must be awful to have a headache before going to bed. Can I get anything for you?" (This line will get you more in the way of passion than the accusation "You always have a headache!")

Doing this is more difficult than it sounds. But, if you do, you'll learn that relations with others will really go places.

III. *Get-Outside-of-Yourself Exercise*

The next couple of times you get into a disagreement with someone, take the other person's side of the argument. At least verbally, begin to agree with his point of view. Argue for it, understand it, see where he is coming from. Although this can be a difficult exercise, it will pay royally if you use it to learn to understand others better.

In order to do this exercise effectively, you must first listen to the opposing point of view without interrupting. Really listening is difficult, but if you concentrate on echoing back what you heard, you'll be almost there.

Note: What you'll also notice when you do this exercise is that a difficult person will become less difficult. By agreeing with him you'll take the wind out of his sails and deflate his anger. I have seen this technique work wonders. Of course, you don't want to use this technique when there are very important issues at stake.

IV. Stop Criticizing, Start Teaching

How do you feel when someone criticizes you? Or when someone makes you look bad in front of others? Not very good. Think of how you felt the last time someone criticized you. Write it out below.

Now, think of the last time you criticized someone else. How do you think he felt? Write it out.

We're always more like others than you are different from them. It hurts to be criticized. This week, try to stop all criticism.

That doesn't mean to stop correcting people. Unless we teach others how to treat us or how to do their jobs, our personal and professional lives would be a mess. Correction and criticism, however, are different. Correction implies teaching others to do the thing right. Criticism implies judging or finding fault with someone for doing the thing wrong.

Think of three situations where you can constructively teach someone when he has made a mistake without using criticism. Some hints are: Focus on his behavior, never on him as a person; be very specific about what he did wrong; do it as soon as possible to prevent resentment from building up; tell him the good things about him that you appreciate; use a matter-of-fact, conversational tone of voice and manner, rather than being harsh, angry, or sarcastic.

1.
2.
3.

Impact Statements

Write out the following impact statements and tape them in places where you're most likely to see them (on the bathroom mirror, refrigerator door at home, on your desk at work, etc.). This way they'll constantly remind you of the need to be able to walk in another's shoes, to be empathic and understanding of those around you.

I will concentrate on treating others the way I want them to treat me.

In order to understand others I'll keep quiet long enough to be able to truly hear what they're saying.

I will strive to be more appreciative of the gifts others give me.

Before I take it too personally, when someone dumps on me I'll ask myself, "I wonder what's going on with them that makes them act that way?"

I AM ME AND YOU ARE YOU: INDEPENDENCE

As I've noted above, others have a powerful impact on the development of our self-esteem. How they have treated us has an influence on how we treat ourselves. There comes a time, however, when we need to put away things of the past and take charge of our lives in the present. This is maturity. Putting away things of the past also means putting away childlike dependence, with its need for others to make decisions for us and the need for their approval in order to feel good about ourselves.

Dependence is dangerous. It breeds contempt and confusion, and it causes the boundaries between people to become blurred. Statements that exemplify this include:

"If I need you to fill all my needs, who am I when you are gone?"

"If I am successful because of what you have done for me or what you have instructed me to do, isn't that your success instead of mine?"

"If I'm dependent on you for how I feel about myself, then when you're upset at me, for good or imagined reasons, I must be upset as well. Because it is your opinion that counts about me. Not mine." Being dependent on others for all of your needs is, at best, a shaky proposition.

Being independent, on the other hand, being able to make one's own way, is fundamental to the feelings of success. Of course, this does not mean that we do not need other people. We do. And this does not mean that many of our goals and accomplishments are not shared with others. They are. The necessity of healthy relationships has been emphasized throughout this book. We feel best when we can share our lives with others and have them share their lives with us. We are relational beings who need the bonds of human connectedness. Without those bonds, loneliness and isolation set in, paralyzing personal growth.

Being independent means we remain individuals, despite our need for others. We have the understanding that no matter how close we feel to others, how connected we are to our family, spouse, or friends, how like others we are, there is a fundamental separateness between us and them.

Beyond experiencing ourselves as separate from others, independence involves the capacity to function on our own, to function autonomously. Many people sense their separateness, but they rely so intensely on others that independent functioning is impossible.

Independent people are able to set their own goals and initiate activities, rather than only responding to the behavior and expectations of others. The more independently you are able to function, and the more you can rely on yourself for your self-esteem, the freer you will be to be your true self in relationships. This freedom in turn leads to relationships that are more open and more honest. There is a decreased need to feel the hurts others dish out to control you. You can separate yourself from them, or you can choose to be close to them. This separateness allows you the freedom to pursue inner dreams despite what others think, and allows you to be yourself with other people—which, to my mind, is a lot healthier than having to act a certain way to get the approval of others.

INDEPENDENCE EXERCISES

Independence is having the internal feelings of self-esteem, independent of how others treat you at the moment; it is being able to make your own decisions, despite what others may think; and it is pursuing goals you set for yourself, not those set for you by someone else. Independence is not being alone, it is being able to really be yourself when you are with others.

Examine the following sabotage factors, which are typical of a person weak in this area. Circle any that apply to you. Note the corresponding success factor, which is the more appropriate response. Circle the success factors that apply to you as well.

Sabotage	vs.	Success
I depend on others to make my decisions for me.		I make my own decisions.
I need the approval of others to feel good about myself.		I do not rely only on the opinions of others for how I feel about myself.
I am dependent on others in a way that chains me to them.		My independence allows me the freedom to be myself in relationships.
Without the guidance from others I would feel lost.		Even though I enjoy others, I can make it on my own.
After I make a decision, I spend a good deal of time thinking about what so-and-so would say about it.		Instead of worrying about what others would say, I spend my time making my decisions work.
I feel that I have to be what others want me to be.		I have the internal OK to be who I want to be.
I express the opinions I think others want to hear.		I feel free to express *my* opinions.

I. Realization Exercise

It's very important for you to realize that when you're dependent on others for your self-esteem, for the decisions you make, or for your goals, you have let them take a certain measure of control over your life.

Unless you give up control of your life to others, you're in charge. You are in charge of your personal life (how you deal with your spirituality, your emotions, and your physical body), your relational life (who you spend time with, how you treat others, how you allow others to treat you), and your work life (the type of work you do, who you work for, the hours you're willing to put in). Certainly, all our choices have consequences, but we decide on the course we take. Often, the decision is to let others decide for us, or to default by not deciding at all, leaving it up to circumstances.

In what areas of your life have you given up control to someone else? For each of the major areas of your life, answer the following questions:

Who do you depend on for your self-esteem?
Who makes decisions for you?
Whose goals do you work for?

Personal life:

spirituality: do you follow spiritual guidelines and practices because someone else told you to or because it's expected of you? Or do you follow your own beliefs and the practices you choose? Add other questions pertinent to you.

emotional life: who do you depend on for your self-esteem? Can certain others make you feel anxious or depressed? Why? Do you *allow* the pain of your past to influence how you perceive things in the present? Add other questions pertinent to you.

physical life: do you diet because other people think you should? Do you overeat because someone puts the food in front of you? Do you take care of your body the way you know you should, or do you allow others to keep you from it? Add other questions pertinent to you.

Relational life:

Who do you depend on for your self-esteem (spouse, parent, children, friend)?

Who makes your relationship decisions for you (the people you spend time with, what you do, how you treat others, how you allow others to treat you)?

Whose goals do you work for (do you have your own goals for the relationships you're in, or do you allow others to dictate to you)?

Work-related life:

Who do you depend on for your self-esteem (do you always have to please people at work to feel good about yourself, or to feel worthwhile)? Is your work your worth?
Who makes decisions for you at work?

Whose work-related goals do you strive for? Are you busy making a fortune for other people? Are you doing what you want or what someone expects of you?

Look over your answers to these questions. Are you the one in charge of your life? Or have you given up control to others? Have you become dependent on them?

II. *Get Away from Needing the Approval of Others for Everything You Do*

Remember, dependence is dangerous. Unless you are dependent on a super being that will always have your best interest in mind, other people are likely to disappoint you. Thus, being totally dependent on them for how you feel about yourself is dangerous. When dependency needs are too strong, they also breed contempt and confusion. After all, you're never sure where you stop and the other person begins; your identities begin to fuse.

Read the following statements, and list those people in your life to whom these might apply. Then think of a way you can approach these people in a more independent way, without threatening the relationship. This may be hard to do, because others often need to have control over us to compensate for their own low self-esteem. Examples are given in parentheses.

If I need you to fulfill all my needs, who am I when you are gone? (In order for me to have a real sense of myself, I need to spend time working on my needs by myself. That doesn't mean I don't love and need you. I do. But I also have to know who I am by myself. The freer I am to be me, the more I can love and give to you from my heart, instead of doing only what's expected of me.)

If I am successful only because of what you've done for me, isn't that your success instead of mine? (I appreciate the things you do for me. It really helps. But some things I just have to do on my own. That helps me be an independent person, a real person by myself.)

If I'm dependent on you for how I feel about myself, then when you're upset with me, for good or imagined reasons, I must be upset as well, because it's your opinion that counts, not mine. (You may get mad at me; sometimes it's because I've been insensitive; sometimes because you're having a bad day. When I'm insensitive, I want to know about it; please tell me in a way I can hear. When you're having a bad day, I also want to know about it, but not by you beating me up.)

III. *Make Your Own Decisions*

Making your own decisions is an important part of becoming independent. It's likely if you scored low in this area that you were either not allowed to make your own decisions when were small, or you were ridiculed for the independent decisions you made.

In the next week, make at least three decisions independent of what others think or say. Use the decision-making process outlined in Chapter Fifteen. These decisions may relate to major goals in your life, such as starting back to school, or they may be related to the demands of your day-to-day life. In either case, begin to make the decisions you make *your* decisions, instead of letting others decide for you.

List the independent decisions you make this week.

1.
2.
3.

After you make these decisions, don't spend time worrying what so-and-so would say about it. Rather, put your energy into making those decisions work for you.

IV. Initiate Your Own Activity

Being independent, finally, means initiating your own activity, deciding what you want to do and doing it.

For the next week, choose at least one thing you've wanted to do for a long time, then do it. If you wish others to do it with you—great. If you want to do it by yourself, that's great, too. But you decide on the activity, and you follow through with it. You don't need to continue only responding to the behavior and expectations of others. You are capable of initiating activity.

Impact Statements

Write out the following impact statements and tape them in places where you're most likely to see them (on the bathroom mirror, refrigerator door at home, on your desk at work, etc.). This way they'll constantly remind you of the need to be able to think and act independently.

I make my own decisions.

Instead of worrying about what so-and-so would say about the decisions I make, I spend my energy making my decisions work for me.

I am learning to feel good enough about myself that I don't have to depend on others for my self-esteem.

I work on my own goals, not someone else's.

18

Overcoming Personal Self-Sabotage

POSITIVE INTERNAL PROCESSING: ACCURATE PERCEPTION

I once heard the following story: At the turn of the century a shoe company sent a representative to Africa. He wired back, "I'm coming home. No one wears shoes here." Another company sent their representative, and he sold thousands of shoes. He wired back to his company, "Business is fantastic. No one has ever heard of shoes here." They perceived the same situation from markedly different perspectives and they obtained dramatically different results.

Perception is everything. It is the way we, as individuals, interpret ourselves and the world around us. Our five senses take in the world, but perception occurs as our brains process the incoming information through our "feeling filters."

When our filters feel good, we translate information in a positive way. When our filters are angry or hostile, we perceive the world as negative toward us. Our perceptions of the outside world are based on our inside worlds. For example, when we're feeling tired we're much more likely to be irritated by a child's behavior that usually doesn't bother us otherwise.

The view that you take of a situation has more reality than the actual situation itself. Noted psychiatrist Richard Gardner, M.D. has said that the meaning of life is like a Rorschach Test, in which a person is asked to describe what he or she sees in ten ink blots that mean absolutely nothing. What we see in the ink blot is based on our inner view of the world. Our perceptions bear witness to our state of mind. As we think, so do we perceive. Therefore, in reality, we need not seek to change the outside world, but rather to change our inside view of the world. And it is how we perceive situations, rather than the actual situations themselves, that causes us to react.

> If   A is the actual event
>   B is how we interpret or perceive the event, and
>   C is how we react to the event,
> $$A + B = C.$$

Other people or events ("A") can't make us do anything. It is our interpretation or perception ("B") that causes our behavior ("C"). For example, I yawned during a therapy session with a patient. He then asked if I found him boring. I replied that it was important that he asked. I told him that I had been up most of the previous night with an emergency and was tired, but that I found what he was saying very interesting. My yawning was "A"; his interpretation that I was bored was "B"; and his asking me about it was "C." I was glad he checked out my yawn because some patients would have inferred that I was bored and their "C" would have been to leave the therapy session with a negative feeling. When we can allow ourselves to look at the alternatives and challenge our initial negative perceptions, then we're a long way toward emotional health.

Another example of perception is found in an ancient Chinese tale that describes a farmer in a poor country village. He was considered extremely well-to-do because he owned a horse, which he used for plowing and transportation. One day his horse ran away. All his neighbors exclaimed how unfortunate this was. And the farmer replied, "How do you know it's unfortunate?"

A few days later, the horse returned, and brought with it two beautiful, wild horses. The neighbors gathered again and exclaimed how wonderful this was. And the farmer replied, "How do you know it's wonderful?"

The next day, the farmer's son tried to ride one of the wild horses and was thrown and broke his leg. The neighbors sympathized and said how terrible this was. And the farmer replied, "How do you know it's terrible?"

The next week, conscription officers came to the village to take young men into the army. They rejected the farmer's son because of his broken leg. When the neighbors said how lucky he was, the farmer replied, "How do you know this is lucky?"

Again, perception is everything. In approaching the world of people, our perceptions dictate our behavior. Understanding that our perceptions may be different from someone else's will be very helpful in dealing with a relational world.

It is also possible to change how you perceive yourself. One way to do this is to begin treating yourself as a good parent would. When we grow up and leave home we, in effect, become our own parents. We make our own decisions, we live where we want to live, we eat the kind of food we want to eat.

Yet we rarely treat ourselves as a good parent would. When we make a mistake, we often behave in an abusive manner toward ourselves. We overeat, belittle our esteem, and feel hopeless. When children make mistakes, good parents don't belittle or abuse them; rather, they soothe their esteem and help them learn from their mistakes. *Change your perception: be your own good parent!*

I have been writing about the importance of your own perception. Now let's turn our attention to how others perceive you. Again, all of us perceive out of who we are. Others will perceive you out of their own situations. Their perceptions will be different from yours. That's why it is dangerous to get all of your self-esteem needs from others. Invariably, they will disappoint you.

You can, however, have a significant impact on their perception of you by the way you present yourself. Are you sensitive to others? Are you teachable? Do you have a sense of integrity? Do you dress appropriately for the situation? How is your ability to communicate, both verbally and in writing? You can't alter another person's internal filter, but you can alter the information that you put forth. You can work on your relational skills and how you present yourself to others.

PERCEPTION EXERCISES

An accurate view of yourself and the world around you is essential to growth. The following exercises are designed to help you perceive yourself and your situations more accurately and more positively. Changing your perceptions is a major step forward in changing your life.

Examine the following sabotage factors, which are typical of a person weak in this area. Circle any that apply to you. Note the

corresponding success factor, which is the more appropriate response. Circle the success factors that apply to you as well. Build on your strengths and strengthen your weaknesses.

Sabotage	vs.	Success
I tend to make negative things out to be bigger than they are.		I accurately perceive situations.
I have a tendency to overgeneralize negative events; when something goes wrong, I think nothing will ever go right.		I look at positive things in the present without filtering them through the negative events of the past.
I get into trouble by thinking or assuming that I know something when I don't.		I am careful to avoid jumping to conclusions without adequate information.
I take innocuous events too personally.		I judge character based on observation, not assumption.
I think with my feelings; that is, I assume that the way I feel about something is really how it is.		I am able to perceive when something deeper may be going on with those around me.

I. Cognitive Distortions

The first step to changing your perceptions or thinking patterns is to identify the way you do think. *Understand and memorize* the ten cognitive distortions listed in the Distorted Thinking section of Chapter Ten. These are:

1. *Black-or-white thinking:* Everything is all good or all bad.

2. *Overgeneralizing:* One event is viewed as something that will always repeat itself.

3. *Negative filter:* Focusing on the bad in every situation.

4. *Disregarding the positive:* Successes or positive experiences are attributed to chance or "because someone else helped out."

5. *Fortune telling:* Predicting that things will turn out badly even though you have no definite evidence.

6. *Mind reading:* Assuming what another person is thinking before you have checked it out.

7. *Thinking with your feelings:* Assuming the way you feel about something is really how it is. "I feel bad, therefore, I am bad."

8. *Guilt reasoning:* Overmoralizing. "I should have done that. I ought to do this. I mustn't think like that ever again."

9. *Labeling:* Attaching negative labels or descriptions to certain behaviors (such as jerk, idiot, brat, loser).

10. *Personalizing:* Taking innocuous events to have personal meaning.

A. Whenever you notice a self-critical or distorted thought entering your mind, train yourself to recognize it. Write down the thought and then match it to one of the cognitive distortions listed above.

B. After you recognize it, talk back to it. Give yourself a more rational way to look at the situation.

Example:

Negative Thought	Distortion	Talk Back
I never do anything right.	Overgeneralizing	That's crazy. I do a lot of things right.
I'm stupid.	Labeling Disregarding the positive	I may do some things that aren't very bright, but I'm not stupid. I do a lot of things that are smart.
People will think I'm a jerk if...	Labeling Fortune telling	First of all, I can't tell or control what others will think. Secondly, I can't live my life by their standards.
I didn't get the job. I'm no good and no one will ever hire me.	Black-or-white thinking Overgeneralizing Labeling Fortune telling	There may have been many reasons I didn't get that job. I am good. I can develop the needed skills. And there are other jobs I can interview for. One rejection is not

a statement on my whole life, even though it may feel like it.

Buy yourself a notebook. Divide the pages into three columns, as shown above. Then carry it with you wherever you go. Whenever you note one of these distorted thoughts coming in, write it down, identify it, then talk back to it. The power in this method is tremendous. It not only will help you correct distorted perception, it will also help your mood and self-esteem.

II. *Reframing*

Family therapists use a technique called reframing to help families look at their problems in a different light or from a different perspective. For example, when parents bring a child in for counseling, the therapist may congratulate the child for bringing in the family for help—thus shifting the focus from blaming all the troubles in the family on the child to the idea that maybe the child's troubles are a result of a dysfunctional family. This technique helps families stop blaming each other and start understanding and solving the problems.

Trait-reframing is similar. It means looking at a trait or experience that seems to be undesirable and recognizing how the same experience is actually an advantage in a different situation. For example, on a foggy night, Rudolph's red nose—normally a handicap for him—became a terrific advantage. What are handicaps in one situation may be strengths in others.

Try to think of one trait or situation in each of the major areas of your life that you consider a disadvantage, and then try to reframe it as an advantage in another context. Examples are given below.

Personal

Trait/Situation	Disadvantage	Reframed Advantage
Short size	Some ridicule, not as likely to be chosen for most sporting teams	Can fit under the desk in an earthquake

Add at least one of your own.

1.

Relational

Trait/Situation	Disadvantage	Reframed Advantage
Being raised in alcoholic home	Distorted perceptions in relationships, have difficulty trusting, feeling, or expressing feelings	Able to empathize with others

Add at least one of your own.

1.

Work-related

Trait/Situation	Disadvantage	Reframed Advantage
Job requires a lot of paperwork which he hates	Swears and gets irritated when has to do it	Figures out a new, more cost-effective way to do the paperwork

Add at least one of your own.

1.

Never stop reframing. It will train you to be a possibility thinker instead of being someone who finds ways to negate all the possibilities.

For another exercise, think of the major mistake you made this year and reframe it to see the advantages that could come from it.

III. Anti-projection exercise

Projection is attributing your own feelings or thoughts to others. For example, if you feel guilty about something, you may project that feeling to someone else and think they're going to punish or chastise you for the thing *you* feel guilty about.

Projection distorts the way you perceive the world. It hinders clear communication with others, and it prevents clear thinking.

In any situation in which you suspect that you may be projecting your feelings, ask yourself what evidence you have to feel that way. Make yourself gather accurate information before you come to conclusions.

Choose three situations in which you have recently felt strong negative emotions toward another person, then answer the following questions (an example is given in parentheses):

Describe the situation. (I began working with someone new at work.)

What specific feelings did you have? (I had an immediate uncomfortable feeling about the person, such as maybe he was trying to show off.)

What evidence do you have to support those feelings? (He tried to participate in all the discussions with the boss.)

Do you remember anything similar to those feelings in the past? (In a prior job there was a person who often put me down in order to make himself look better.)

If you lack specific evidence for the feelings, think about whether or not you may be projecting your feelings into the situation.

Impact Statements

Write out the following impact statements and tape them in places where you're most likely to see them (on the bathroom mirror, refrigerator door at home, on your desk at work, etc.). This way they'll constantly remind you of the need to accurately perceive situations before you act on them.

I am controlled not by events or people, but by the perceptions I take of them.
Negative situations are changed by positive perceptions.
Reframing is something I do to change the way I think.

FUEL IN THE ENGINE: MOTIVATION FOR SUCCESS

Motivation is what moves us. It is the force that gives rise to our behavior, the gasoline that gets our engines moving. Motivation is the *why* in why we do things.

We are all motivated. The question is, what are we motivated for? Successful people are strongly motivated to achieve their goals. People who sabotage themselves often play out their motivation to fail. We have discussed some of the reasons behind failure motivation. In this section we'll discuss several theories of motivation with an eye toward helping you understand the motivating forces behind your behavior.

Obviously, there are so many whys to our behavior that a few pages could never hope to discuss them all. But in order for us to think about this together, we need a basic understanding of what motivates us as human beings.

The first theory of motivation is actually one we've been looking at throughout the book: *Man is motivated to maintain comfort*. This theory says that we are pain-avoiding and pleasure-seeking animals, and that we will, when faced with alternatives, choose the course of action that will maximize our pleasure, and try to avoid anything that causes us pain.

Unfortunately, we often forget that initial discomfort may be necessary for later success. This is true for almost any area in which we wish to be successful, whether it be in obtaining an education, advancing at work, or being a parent.

Motivation also depends on two other parameters: how we view ourselves and how we view our environment. As mentioned several times before, most often we get the view of ourselves from our childhood experiences. If we were given positive, "you can do it" messages, motivation becomes easier because we believe we can accomplish what we wish. If, on the other hand, we were given the "you are never good enough" messages, motivation is more difficult because we come to believe that no matter how hard we try, we will never succeed.

How we perceive our environment also influences our motivation. Perceptions of our world as a safe and accepting place free us to move on to higher levels of pursuit. Perceptions of the world as a hostile or disappointing place will cause us to seek safety and isolation.

Here again, I must emphasize that some people will get into the trap of blaming their lack of motivation on others or their environment: "You never made me feel good about myself," or, "The world is a dangerous place. How can I be expected to do anything under these conditions?"

No doubt, motivation is influenced by our pasts and by the environment in which we find ourselves, but, quite frankly, no matter what situation we find ourselves in, *motivation remains our responsibility,* no one else's! College students quickly learn that no matter what the circumstances, no one will be there holding their hands or coaxing them to study. They are grown-ups and motivation is their business. If they don't have the get-up-and-go to complete their work on their own, they usually end up leaving college.

In review, so far we have looked at the motivators of comfort, and our perception of ourselves and our environments. As mentioned above, we have many, many motivators to our behavior. Here is a list of other motivators that power human behavior. This list is by no means exhaustive, but it will help you to think further about why you do the things you do.

Other Motivators of Human Behavior

A. Negative Energy Motivators

Fear	•
Hate	•
Envy	•
Jealousy	• These so-called negative emotions are power-
Greed	• ful motivators that have caused world wars.
Prejudice	•
Revenge	•

B. Egocentric Motivators

Power	•
Prestige	• The need for recognition and control often
Pride	• stimulates behavior that is difficult to under-
Passion	• stand.
Control	•

C. Positive Energy Motivators

Faith	•
Hope	•
Love	•
Caring	• These are forces that often motivate behavior
Concern	• in a positive way. Of course, they have de-
Affection	• structive potential as well.
Appreciation	•
Contribution	•
Meaning	•

Egoistic Altruism—Hans Selye's concept of the need to do good to feel good about yourself. Charity organizations thrive because people want to think of themselves as giving and loving.

In developing the motivation of success, it is crucial to be honest with yourself about your own motivators. Get beyond the trap of lying to yourself about the things you really want. Look inside to see what will move you toward your goals, and then hold on to it.

At this point, go back and re-read Chapter Four, "Your Individual Definition of Success." It will give you more information on what motivates you, particularly question seven, which asks whom you would like to be like. After you do this, spend several minutes each day thinking about the specific things that motivate your behavior. In order for you to have some control over the things that motivate you, you must work on using your motivators on a regular basis. It is just like having a friend. In order to feel good about the relationship, you must spend time cultivating it. Cultivate your motivations in the direction of your success.

MOTIVATION FOR SUCCESS EXERCISES

Motivation is an inside job. It is the inner drive that provides the incentive for you to act. It is what gets you out of bed in the morning and through the day. In fact, motivation plays a part in all you do.

Choosing this book suggests you're motivated to change what hasn't been working for you up to this point. That's a positive sign—that you want to better yourself. There are, however, negative motivators that hold you back from reaching your dreams. These include fear of failure, so you may never begin; fear of loss of love, so you may remain in harmful relationships; fear of criticism, so you may be motivated by what other people think; and guilt, so you do what the past is controlling you to do.

In order to use motivation to your advantage, you must first understand what motivates your behavior. The following set of exercises is designed to help you more fully understand your motivation. This will help you to form appropriate goals and channel your energies into more productive and satisfying areas.

Examine the following sabotage factors, which are typical of a person weak in this area. Circle any that apply to you. Note the

corresponding success factor, which is the more appropriate response. Circle the success factors that apply to you as well. Build on your strengths and strengthen your weaknesses.

Sabotage	vs.	Success
I just take life as it comes.		I go after what I want instead of daydreaming about it.
I need someone to push me.		I am a self-starter.
It's hard for me to get going.		I have initiative.
I am plagued by procrastination.		I get things done that are important to me.
I feel afraid when good things happen, wondering when things will go sour again.		I am pleased when something good happens to me.
I am satisfied with whatever life dishes out.		I want to be everything I can be.
I am motivated by guilt.		I am motivated by an inner sense of purpose.
I do what I like, regardless of the consequence.		I do what gets me closer to my goal, whether I like doing it or not.
I often sabotage or fear success.		I work in the best interest of my goals.

I. *Your Individual Definition for Success*

Go back to the worksheets at the end of Chapter Four, "Your Individual Definition of Success." If you haven't already completed questions one through ten, complete them now. If you have, then review and add to them. This is yet another way to help you understand yourself better.

II. *Outline Your Life*

Outline your life up to this point. Take a sheet of paper and number from one to however old you are. List one major positive and negative event for each year. If you do not know much about your earliest years, ask someone who might know. Also write down the major decision points in your life (school, marriage, job, children, etc.). Try to understand why you did or didn't do those things that have been most important in shaping your life into what it is now. Do you see any patterns to your behavior? Are the patterns helpful or harmful? Can you pick out any significant motivators in your life?

III. What's the Motivation for Your Future?

Outline how you want to live the rest of your life. What things are important to you from here on out? You can do this in writing, or you may want to draw pictures or make a collage that illustrates your dreams and hopes. Whichever way you choose, be as specific as you can be.

IV. Fighting the Guilt Motivator

One of the most common negative motivators of behavior is guilt. It causes us to do things in resentful ways and it causes us to resent ourselves. There are many reasons behind feelings of "I am bad because I have not lived up to what I 'should' have done." Briefly, these include: feeling that your negligence caused something bad to happen to someone else ("It's my fault she got hurt"); feeling that you did not live up to your own ideal image of yourself ("I should have known better"); or feeling that your actions fell short of your moral standards or violated your sense of fairness ("I should have reported that income on my tax statement").

The concept of "badness" is central to guilt. Because you did something you regret, you feel like a bad or worthless person. This is quite a different concept from remorse, which is a healthy feeling. Remorse stems rom the awareness that you did something you wish you hadn't, but it does not imply that you are a "bad" person because of it. Remorse motivates you to change. Guilt motivates you to berate yourself.

Are you often motivated out of feelings of guilt? If yes, here are some ways to fight it.

1. Realize that feelings do not have moral value. It is what you do that counts in life, not what you feel. We all, at one time or another, have murderous, rage-filled thoughts. We all have sexual thoughts. It's normal. It's natural. It is actions that determine value, not fleeting thoughts.

2. Fight the guilt by doing something, if rational and reasonable, to correct the things you feel bad about. For example, if you feel guilty for not spending enough time with your children, schedule regular time for them. If you feel guilty about your behavior toward your coworkers, let it motivate you to treat them better. Let the feeling motivate you to improve, not to beat yourself.

3. Stay away from the irrational "should" traps; they are sure pathways to guilt feelings. These are the thoughts that imply you are expected to be perfect, all-knowing, or all-powerful. You are not perfect. None of us is. Accept it. Do your best. Strive to do better. Don't beat yourself because you should have known or done some- thing that was *impossible* for you to know or do. Have realistic expectations for yourself. You'll be easier to live with.

4. Go back to the Stinking Thinking part of Chapter Ten. Each time you are plagued by feelings of guilt, look over the list of cognitive distortions. See which ones are operating to sabotage the good feelings you have about yourself.
Memorize this list.

5. Many people feel guilty but don't know why. This is often because they were raised in a difficult environment, they were physically or sexually abused, or they unconsciously feel that they caused something terrible to happen, such as a divorce between their parents. If you don't know why you feel guilty and this has been a chronic problem, it's worth further investigation to uncover those hidden feelings that have been sabotaging you.

Impact Statements

Write out the following impact statements and tape them up in places where you're most likely to see them (on the bathroom mirror, refrigerator door at home, on your desk at work, etc.). This way they'll constantly remind you of your motivators and that motivation is your business, not someone else's.

Motivation is my responsibility.

I am motivated to _____(fill in the blank)
I am motivated to _____
I am motivated to _____

I am motivated to _____
Am I motivated to maintain comfort, or to achieve my goals?

Say no to the comfort of the moment to reach toward a higher, more satisfying goal!

CLEAR THINKING: MENTAL HEALTH

I remember sitting in classes, during my psychiatry residency, during which we were asked to define mental health. Some said it was being normal, whatever that is; some said it was being able to adapt to new situations; others said it had to do with being mature. Through the years, I have come to use what I call a practical definition of mental health:

> *Mental health is having the ability to work in the best interest of your personal, relational and work life, and to avoid putting yourself in the way of your goals.*

This definition of mental health implies that when someone is experiencing an emotional problem, he will seek help for it; he will take care of himself in the same way he would if he developed a physical problem, which is obviously in his own best interest. This doesn't mean that he'll necessarily seek psychiatric help. There are many other resources, including books, trusted friends, ministers, psychologists, and self-help groups; but he will seek help until he finds what works for him.

Many people ask me how you know if you should seek professional help for emotional problems. I respond in two ways. First, I compare seeking psychiatric care to seeking medical care. If you have physical symptoms such as a cough or chest pain that last for a period of time, you seek help. Likewise, if you have emotional symptoms, such as a phobia, a depressed mood, disturbing repetitive thoughts, or needing a drink to get through the day, that last for more than a brief time, it is time to seek help. The earlier help is sought, the better chance there is for a successful resolution to the problem.

My second response to this question is that if you see a pattern of repeatedly finding yourself in negative situations that you cannot figure out, e.g., persistently being involved in destructive relationships, or always having trouble with the boss, it might be worth the time and money to seek help.

Many people do not seek help because of false assumptions. They think having a mental disorder means they are crazy, or that there is no hope for them. A very small percentage of the typical psychiatrist's practice deals with what might be considered truly "crazy" patients. The three most common types of psychiatric problems are anxiety, alcohol and drug abuse, and depression. They are also the most treatable of psychiatric disorders. Every year new and more effective treatments are found for these.

I often compare mental health to being a good parent to yourself. Around age eighteen we put our parents' authority behind us and, in essence, become our own parents. We make our own decisions, give direction to our lives and become legally responsible for our actions. What kind of parent are you to yourself? Many of the adults I see in my clinical practice are clearly abusive to themselves. They're extremely self-critical, they neglect taking care of themselves, and they allow others to dump on them.

Carol, a twenty-six-year-old mother of two, was abandoned by her mother when she was three years old. She was subsequently raised partially by her father and by an orphanage. She often felt lonely even though there were always people around. In raising her own children, she was confused about what was good for them and had a difficult time disciplining them. Additionally, she was very self-critical and had trouble pushing herself to do things that were good for her. She often felt depressed.

In therapy with her over several months we came to the conclusion that she was missing a very important part of herself: "the good mother." Since her mother had left her early on in life, she was never able to internalize the traits that a protective, nurturing, firm and loving mother gives to her child. She lacked basic self-mothering skills.

Carol had to go back in her mind to imagine the little girl inside of herself. She has begun to re-parent herself. She asks herself, "What do little girls need?" And then she tries to give those things to herself. For example, she knows that good mothers are firm with their children. So when she has a task to complete, such as the laundry, she does not put it off anymore, she goes ahead and does it, which gives her a sense of relief and accomplishment.

Many people grew up in homes with parents who were overly

critical, harsh, or neglectful. As such, a part of themselves has become critical, harsh, and neglectful. Those voices and feelings from the past continue to haunt them. How do you treat yourself? How do you treat the child within you? I think that many of us need to learn how to re-parent the child within.

Here are seven traits of a "good mother"; see if they apply to how you treat yourself.

1. A "good mother" loves her children no matter what. She doesn't always like or approve of what they do, but she always loves them. Do you love yourself no matter what?

2. A "good mother" notices her children when they do things she likes. Her focus is on building self-esteem, rather than tearing it down. When was the last time you noticed something good about yourself?

3. A "good mother" is firm with her children and will push them to do things that are good for them, even if they do not want to do them. Are you good at pushing yourself (in a kind way) to do the things you need to do?

4. A "good mother" wants her children to be independent and encourages her children to have choices and make decisions for themselves under her supervision. Do you feel good about yourself independently, or do you depend on the opinion of others to make yourself feel good?

5. A "good mother" helps her children learn from their mistakes. She does not berate them when they mess up; instead, she helps them look at what happened and figure out what to do differently the next time. Do you learn from your mistakes or just berate yourself when you make them?

6. A "good mother" is *not perfect*. No one can relate to a perfect person, and a "good mother" is someone who is easy to relate to. Do you expect yourself to be perfect and then beat yourself up when you're not?

7. A "good mother" always notices more good than bad in her children. What do you have a tendency to notice about yourself: good or bad?

When we grow up we become, in a sense, our own parents. How we treat ourselves plays a large role in what we get out of life and in our mental health.

Note: If you scored high on the anxiety, depression, alcohol/drug abuse or adult children of alcohol or drug abusers scale, then it is important to obtain a psychiatric evaluation to get adequate treatment for an underlying problem that might be present. The best way to find a competent psychiatrist is to ask your family physician or local medical society. If possible seek someone who is board certified.

THE CAPACITY FOR ACTION: ENERGY

> *1. force of expression, 2. a) inherent power; b) capacity for*
> *action, 3. in Physics the capacity for doing work.*
>   **—WEBSTER'S NEW WORLD DICTIONARY**

No doubt by now you've figured out that being successful at your goals takes a lot of time and a good deal of energy. Success is not something that happens to you overnight. It is something you cause to happen over time. In order to stay on the road you have charted for yourself, you must have the energy to stay with your program.

Gathering information on your energy level is key, because effectiveness at any task declines when you are tired. The amount of energy we have varies from individual to individual. Some people are on the move right after popping out of the birth canal. Some take a long time to get going. Whatever your energy baseline, it is important to maximize all you have.

Many things can drain your energy stores. Briefly, these include physical illnesses, emotional worries, poor diets, erratic sleep patterns, and poor physical conditioning. How do you fare in each of these areas?

The most important thing to remember is that energy is limited. No matter how much energy you do have, it will run out if you do not use it wisely. Focus your energy on the things that are important to you. As I've mentioned, many people spend a good deal of time wasting time. They engage in repetitive, nonproductive activities that have little, if anything, to do with the goals they have set for their lives. By keeping your mind and actions on the things you want, and off the things you don't want, you'll be able to put more of yourself into reaching your goals.

Finally, it's very dangerous to take chemicals to raise your energy level. Substances such as amphetamines, speed, uppers, and excessive caffeine have been reported to cause psychotic episodes. They deplete certain chemicals in your brain related to mood, causing reactive depressions in some people who have taken them for a long time. Natural highs and energy are more satisfying than those delivered from pills.

ENERGY EXERCISES

Energy is the capacity for action.

Lack of energy may come from poor physical conditioning, erratic sleep patterns, a poor diet, bad habits, physical illness, or worries causing an emotional drain. Whatever the cause of low energy, it's in the best interest of a person who often feels tired to investigate and eradicate it. The other ingredients of success will mean little if you don't have the energy with which to implement them.

For those with low energy, the following set of exercises will help you sort out the cause. Once it's identified, you may then be able to correct the problem.

Examine the following sabotage factors, which are typical of people weak in this area. Circle any that apply to you. Note the corresponding success factor, which is the more appropriate response. Circle the success factors that apply to you as well. Build on your strengths and strengthen your weaknesses.

Sabotage	vs.	Success
I often find myself saying, "I don't feel up to it."		I am an energetic person.
I feel blocked or slowed down in getting things done.		I have stamina, energy with staying power.
I allow things to build up because I am just too tired to get to them.		I get things done right away, so they won't build up.
I am too busy to relax.		I spend time relaxing and refueling my energy stores.
I perform important tasks when I am tired.		I maximize my energy cycle.
Others feel drained when they're around me.		Others feel invigorated in my presence.

I. *Explore the Possible Causes*

Fatigue is normal when it's at the end of a full day's work or sustained physical activity. It may also be a consequence of prolonged emotional stress or mental strain. In these circumstances, the cause of the fatigue is usually evident. Chronic fatigue, however, is not a normal state. Its causes must be explored.

As mentioned above, there are several general causes of low energy. Check which of these might apply to you.

Unhealthy life-style (the most common group of causes of chronic fatigue):

1. Poor physical conditioning. A sedentary life-style may be the most common of all reasons behind chronic fatigue or low energy. It's also behind much of the nation's number-one killer: heart disease. Do you vigorously exercise for at least twenty minutes three times a week? A brisk walk will do.

2. Erratic sleep patterns. Our bodies need time to refuel themselves. Although we don't all need the same amount, most of us need between six and eight hours of sleep each day. The more regular your sleep schedule, the better. Note: Depression is a major cause of insomnia. When trouble sleeping lasts more than a week or so, it's a good idea to have it checked out by your doctor.

3. A poor or unbalanced diet. Eating balanced meals is essential to good health and a healthy energy level. How is your diet? Is it planned? Or is it eat-as-you-can? Vitamin and mineral deficiencies may lead to chronic fatigue. Also, overeating may deplete your energy stores, as your body must divert large amounts of blood from your brain to your stomach to digest large meals. A balanced diet is essential.

4. Smoking, excessive caffeine. Both of these are well-known energy stealers. Initially, it may seem that they give you more energy, but that initial boost will be paid for later on. As you know, smoking serves to prematurely harden your blood vessels, restricting blood flow and draining your energy.

Check out your life-style: If any of these energy-draining areas apply to you, fix them. There is so much literature on staying in shape, eating right, stopping smoking, and sleeping, that you can easily learn how to control these problems. Become informed.

Physical Illness:

There are many physical causes for low energy. Some of the more common ones include hypothyroidism, diabetes, anemia, renal disease, and premenstrual tension syndrome.

Check out your health: If you suspect there may be a physical ailment behind your low energy level, see your doctor and get a checkup.

Emotional turmoil:

1. Depression. Clues to this one include weakness, loss of appetite, weight loss, apathy, insomnia, lack of desire to go on, feeling sad or blue, feelings of guilt, a desire to isolate oneself, and suicidal thoughts.

2. Anxiety. Clues here include nervousness, excessive fears, physical complaints for which no basis can be found, panic attacks, or an impending sense of doom. The fatigue appears to lessen through the day.

3. Heavy alcohol or drug use. Clues include withdrawal symptoms, cravings, and unusual behavior on or off the drug.

Check out your mental health: If the clues given lead you to suspect a problem here, again, check with your doctor. He or she will be able to give you guidance on ways to further clarify the problems you're having.

II. *Sixteen Energy-Giving Hints*

1. Take a multivitamin with iron every day.

2. Spend at least ten minutes a day refueling your energy stores by doing something relaxing.

3. Get out of your negative cycle of do-nothingism; change the way you feel by first changing the way you act. When you don't feel like doing something important, do it anyway. You'll find that the more you do, the more energy you'll have to do with, and thus the more you will do.

4. Get between six to eight hours of sleep per night.

5. Eat a balanced breakfast every morning.

6. Seldom eat between meals.

7. Eat more high-fiber foods such as whole grains, fruits, and vegetables. Besides reducing the risk of colon cancer, high-fiber foods help your body regulate sugar better and decrease the chances of diabetes.

8. Shield yourself from the sun. The sun, besides increasing the risk of skin cancer, also causes dehydration, which drains energy as well as water.

9. Keep within ten pounds of your ideal body weight. Ideal body weight for women is often figured by allowing 100 pounds for a five-foot woman and then adding six pounds per inch thereafter. For example, if a woman is five feet three inches, her ideal body weight would be:

	5 feet	= 100 lbs.
	3 inches (at 6 lbs./inch)	= 18 lbs.
total	5 feet 3 inches	= 118 lbs. ideal weight

(Add ten pounds to your ideal weight for a heavy-boned frame; subtract ten pounds for a slim frame.)

Ideal body weight for a man is figured in a similar way: 100 pounds for five feet, and six to seven pounds per inch thereafter. So a man who is five feet ten inches tall ideally should weigh 160–170 pounds. Again, this will vary depending on type of body frame.

9. Exercise continuously for fifteen to twenty minutes three times a week. Brisk walking is great. If there is any question about your health, first check with your doctor.

10. Quit smoking: Live longer. Feel better.

11. No more than three cups of coffee per day.

12. Do not drink more than two alcoholic beverages a day: two regular mixed drinks or one double; two six-ounce glasses of wine; or two six-ounce servings of beer. (Contrary to what many people believe, beer is just as dangerous to your health as other forms of alcohol, and as potentially addictive.)

13. Do things you have to do right away. STOP PROCRASTINAT-ING. When things build up, your energy level goes down!

14. Maximize your energy cycle. If at all possible, do what is most important to you when you are the most effective.

15. Start climbing the stairs instead of riding the elevator. Again, use caution if your health is an issue.

16. Do something you have been dreading. Alleviate the anxiety by facing the dreaded task head-on. Face your fear. This anxiety tires you out and holds you back.

Impact Statements

Write out the following impact statements and tape them up in places where you're most likely to see them (on the bathroom mirror, refrigerator door at home, on your desk at work, etc.). This way they'll constantly remind you of the things you need to be doing to raise and keep your energy level at its peak.

Energy is the capacity for action. I take care of my energy stores.
Without energy, which comes from taking care of myself, little can be accomplished.
I focus my energy on the things that are important to me.
To be able to give energy to others, I first refuel my own energy stores.

BRINGING TOGETHER WORDS AND BELIEFS WITH ACTIONS: INTEGRITY

Honesty is the first chapter in the book of wisdom.
—THOMAS JEFFERSON

The truth is very hard to come by in this world, mainly because there are so many truths around and so many people trying to get you to believe their truths. There is religious truth, scientific truth, psychological truth, economic truth, common sense truth, and so on.

Often, these truths are in conflict. What we end up believing at any time is a matter of faith based on our personal experience. Truth needs to be individually defined. My truths cannot be yours. I can only share what I believe with you; you will assimilate it, along with other experiences, to develop your own belief system.

These belief systems change over time, as you grow, mature, and gather more information. Integrity is living within your belief system over time. It is being consistent with your values, being who you believe you are.

In relationships, integrity is being who you say you are. Nothing more, nothing less. The advantages to this type of honesty are long-lasting. First, as I have mentioned, people behave toward us as we teach them to behave. If our behavior is consistent, others are more likely in turn to treat us in a consistent fashion, in ways we can understand. If our behavior is on and off, it confuses those around us, and they treat us in a confusing way.

Second, when we are living examples of our words, people are more likely to believe that our words will match our actions. In a world of relationships, having others take us at our word is crucial to success.

And third, integrity is contagious. It encourages others to respond to us in kind.

We are faced with the choices of integrity every day. Sometimes we choose for it, sometimes not. When we circumvent our commitments, we cheat not only ourselves, but those who depend on us. When we live up to our commitments, the bonds of trust are strengthened.

One of our commitments in life is to teach those who depend on us, especially our children. Children quickly pick up on and learn about integrity from their parents. I remember my temptation to buy a radar detector after I got a speeding ticket. I looked at detectors in the stores, checked the prices, and was ready to buy one, until I thought about what kind of message that would give my children: "You do what I tell you because I am the authority, but I don't have to play by the same rules." I dropped the idea, and dropped my speed as well.

In psychiatry there is a term, superego lacunae, which means "holes in the conscience." This concept is found in parents who ignore or unconsciously encourage delinquent behavior in their children, which is illustrated by the case of Peter.

Peter was constantly in trouble for fighting at school. Each day when he got home, his father asked Peter if he had gotten into another fight. When Peter said yes, his father would tell him that fighting was wrong, but then would listen to the details of the fight with the utmost interest. When Peter went without a fight, the father didn't make any comments or pay much attention to the boy. We teach others about us by our actions, not our words.

Integrity is bringing a person's words and beliefs together with his actions.

INTEGRITY EXERCISES

Integrity is bringing together words and beliefs with your actions. At first, when I wrote this, I thought: who am I to tell someone about integrity? What a value judgment! This section, however, is not meant to be a value statement. I can't, nor do I have any desire to, tell you what is right or wrong. That's for you to decide for yourself. But I can tell you that when you act in ways contrary to your own conscience, you set yourself up for feeling like a failure, and you thus behave in ways that sabotage your success with others.

Bringing together what you say and what you believe with what you do is a key, not only to success with others, but to self-esteem as well.

The following exercises are designed to help you identify and change those areas of your life in which your words and beliefs don't match your actions.

Examine the following sabotage factors, which are typical of a person in need of a boost in this area. Circle any that apply to you. Note the corresponding success factor, which is the more appropriate response. Circle the success factors that apply to you as well. Build on your strengths and strengthen your weaknesses.

Sabotage	vs.	Success
I have trouble following through on my word.		I live up to my commitments.
My behavior is often unpredictable, confusing those close to me.		I am consistent in the way I behave toward others.
I say one thing when I mean another.		People can trust my word; I mean what I say.
Others don't trust me because of my past record.		I teach others that I am trustworthy by my actions.
I avoid difficult issues, thereby lying to myself about important matters.		I am open and honest with myself.
I feel I have to put up a front in order to be accepted by others.		The person inside me is the same one I present to others.
I spend time covering up lies.		I have open communication with others.

I. *Examine Your Life: Where Are the Discrepancies?*

Examine the major areas of your life (personal, relational, and work-related). Where are the major discrepancies between what you say or believe and what you do? What is it that you do that worries you, that makes you uneasy, that makes you feel guilty? No doubt this means taking a hard, honest look at your life, but that's what we're about. We're about changing those things that hold you back, and getting you to work in your own best interest and out of the patterns of the past that haven't been working for you. Examples are given below.

DISCREPANT AREAS IN MY LIFE

Personal life (spiritual, emotional, physical)

You fail to live up to commitments to yourself; "I'll start the diet tomorrow," or "I'll start that exercise program when I get the time."

You lie to yourself (maybe about an alcohol or drug problem), tell lies to others to appear more important than you feel.

Add Your Own:

Relational life

You say you love someone, yet you put them down, make fun of them in front of others, don't give them your time, or cheat on them.

You fail to live up to commitments to others—spouse, children, friends (be as specific as you can be).

Add Your Own:

Work-related life

You fail to live up to business commitments, promise to deliver more than you can.

You don't give your best; you sabotage others' tasks to make yourself look better, put up a front, cheat on taxes.

Add Your Own:

II. Change the Discrepancies: Develop a Plan

For each of the areas you listed above, develop a plan to change the discrepancies: commit yourself.

It's in your best interest. Commit yourself to yourself, your relationships, and your work. In your plan for change include:

1. A clear statement of what you do that is not consistent with your words or beliefs.

2. Its impact on you.

3. Its impact on others.

4. At least two ways to change the inconsistency.

5. The consequences or benefits of change.

6. A date to put the plan into action.

Example:

1. Statement of discrepancy: I tend to shoot down Bob in meetings even when his ideas are good, because I don't like him and he seems to be the boss's favorite.

2. I feel guilty afterward, and wonder if I sounded petty.

3. I worry that it might have a bad affect on our work environment.

4. a. I can stop myself when I find myself doing it and try to contribute just what I really think in the situation, no matter what Bob says.

   b. If I have trouble changing by myself, I can talk with a counselor for a few sessions to see why Bob irritates me so much.

5. I'll feel less guilty and better about my own performance at work. I will have more integrity.

6. I'll start today.

III. *My Words Match My Actions*

For this week, and hereafter, make a commitment to match your beliefs and words with your actions. This will help combine the person you are on the inside with the one you present to others, making you feel more like a whole person instead of the split or impostor personality you often feel.

   More things to do:
   In your personal life: respect yourself by accepting your humanity, forgive your wrongdoings, and learn from your mistakes.
   In your relationships: remember that love is an action verb, not just a feeling. TODAY, love the important people in your life with your actions as well as your words. Show love by giving them your time and your respect.
   In your work life: respect your employer, job, or business by giving your best effort, and living up to your commitments.

Would you take counsel with a fat dietician, a broke financial advisor, a cussing minister? Unfortunately, the old saying, "Do as I say, not as I do," haunts all of us from time to time; but is that how you want to live your life? Do you convey that message to others? You can't fool anyone but yourself with empty actions.

Impact Statements

   Write out the following impact statements and tape them in places where you're most likely to see them (on the bathroom mirror, refrigerator door at home, on your desk at work, etc.). This way they'll constantly remind you to match your words and beliefs with your actions—to work on integrating the person on the inside with the one you present to the world.

Bringing together words and beliefs with actions helps to make
me a whole person.
We teach others about us by our actions, not our words.
I live up to my commitments; my word is important to me.
Integrity is also being honest with myself.
I am able to forgive myself and move on.

"BEING ON GOOD TERMS WITH YOURSELF": SELF-ESTEEM

Self-esteem is being on good terms with yourself. It is believing that
you are worth working in your own best interest. It is believing that
you can have a positive impact on others and that you are worth
others having a positive impact on you.

Self-esteem is the internal OK to be who you want to be. It is the
internal voice that is on your side and gives you the encouragement
to press on with your goals. Without a positive sense of self, any
accomplishments, no matter how big or small, will be negated by an
accusing inner voice that keeps repeating "you're no good," erasing
any feelings of success. Self-esteem is a cornerstone in our recipe of
success.

Many psychiatrists say that self-esteem is developed within the
first three years of life. They also say that it stems from how much
parents allow their children to do things for themselves and encourage their abilities. The more children do for themselves, the more
confident they become about their abilities, and the better they feel
about themselves.

I see many children whose parents do everything for them,
including homework, housework, and even picking their friends.
The children often don't view this as helpful. Rather, they get the
message that their parents don't think enough of the children's own
ability, which is why the parents feel they have to do things for
them.

A forty-year Harvard study turned up some startling truths about
self-esteem. Started in an effort to understand juvenile delinquency,
the study followed the lives of 456 teenage boys from inner-city
Boston. Many of the boys were from broken or impoverished
homes. When they reached middle age, one fact stood out: regard-
less of intelligence, family income, ethnic background or amount of
formal education, those who had worked as boys, even at simple
household chores, enjoyed happier and more productive lives than

those who had not. These results are not difficult to explain. George Valliant, M.D., the psychiatrist in charge of the study, said, "Boys who work in the home or community gained competence and came to feel they were worthwhile members of society. And because they felt good about themselves, others felt good about them as well." People who felt best about themselves as adults were made responsible for themselves as children. Children do, so they believe they can do: they believe in themselves.

I do not necessarily believe that self-esteem is solidified as early as age three. But certainly the parental pattern of either letting children do for themselves or always doing things for them is in place at that time.

Other significant people also contribute to a child's sense of himself, particularly grandparents, teachers, coaches, and any other person who becomes important to him. Children very often idealize important adults, and early on they develop an image of the ideal person they'd like to be like.

Initially, the ideal persons are the parents. It is very common to hear four- and five-year-old children say they want to be like their mommies and daddies. As they grow, the ideal person often becomes a composite of many admired and respected people. The closer their sense of themselves is to their image of those they admire, the greater their self-esteem. The greater the distance between their sense of themselves and their image of the ideal person, the lower their self-esteem.

Let's get back to the idea of the inner voice I mentioned above. The way we talk to ourselves is the day-to-day indicator of our self-esteem. We all have many voices inside our heads commenting on our daily thoughts and behaviors. Some describe these voices as part of our conscience, while some describe them as a struggle between the child in us and the parent.

These voices are a synthesis of the strong voices we've heard throughout our lives. If the parental voices we heard were positive, chances are our inner voices will be the same. If they were harsh and negative, it is likely that we'll talk to ourselves in a punitive way. When our self-esteem suffers, our inner voices often take on the quality of a "critic's committee," which runs a nonstop dialogue on how we could have done things better. These voices can often be recognized as specific voices from the past if we take the time to examine them.

I often compare our inner life with its voices to a courtroom battle. On one side there is a group of prosecuting attorneys, accusing us whenever they can, planning self-sabotage. On the other side our self-esteem sits with our defense lawyer who, depending on his skill, is either a large powerful figure or an inept weakling. There is also the judge, who is ultimately the final decider of how we feel about ourselves. In addition, both sides are able to call witnesses to help strengthen their cases.

As you can imagine, there are many possible courtroom scenarios. Those with strong self-esteem have a competent defense lawyer working in their behalf. The prosecutors serve to bring up moral questions that we all need to consider, but they are not harsh or abusive. The witnesses called remind them of their successes and help teach them about the mistakes. The judge sets a compassionate tone that enables continued growth.

On the other end of the spectrum, for those with very low self-esteem, the courtroom is often the scene of a constant assault. The prosecutors are vicious. They repetitively bring up real and imagined crimes of the past, pointing their accusatory fingers at the helpless defendant, belittling him for the minor mistakes of the present, and calling witnesses who should have been long forgotten.

Despite weak objections from the defense, the judge allows the prosecutor's attack to continue unchecked. Outside evidence from the real world that indicates competence and talent is not allowed into this courtroom of destruction. Sometimes the attacks become so harsh that the internal judge actually gives the death penalty, which the defendant carries out so that he can be rid of the prosecutors. This is called suicide.

Most of the courtroom scenes are in between these two extremes. How is your defense lawyer these days? Is he working in your best interest? Or, is he standing by silently while your internal accusers beat you up? He needs to be working for you if you are to work for yourself.

Those who accomplish their goals and feel good about themselves in the process protect and defend their self-esteem. Of course, this also means taking care of those they love, because that is a form of taking care of themselves.

Daily we decide to work for or against ourselves. Are you worth it? Are you on good terms with yourself? What can you do to be at peace with yourself? How can you match the image of who you are with the person you want to be? The answers to these questions will help bring about change.

SELF-ESTEEM EXERCISES

"He that respects himself is safe from others; he wears a coat of mail that none can pierce."
                    —HENRY WADSWORTH LONGFELLOW

When your self-esteem is low, your inner voices tell you that you can't. When it's healthy, your inner voices cheer you on, telling you that you can. Self-esteem is not static. Just because it's been one way through the years doesn't mean it can't be changed. It can. The exercises that follow are designed to help you increase your self-esteem, so that you are able to work in the best interest of the goals you set for yourself.

Examine the following sabotage factors, which are typical of a person needing a boost in this area. Circle any that apply to you. Note the corresponding success factor, which is the more appropriate response. Circle the success factors that apply to you as well. Build on your strengths and strengthen your weaknesses.

Sabotage	vs.	Success
I often feel like an impostor, even when things are going well for me.		I am on good terms with myself.
I mostly think others don't care whether or not I'm around.		I feel that others have a good time when they're with me.
I feel as if my life will be wasted.		I believe that I can have a positive impact on others.
My inner voice sounds more like a critics' committee than anything else.		I find that my inner voices help me to learn from my mistakes, and spur me on no matter what I do.
I spend time wishing that I were someone else.		I have the internal OK to be who I want to be.
I put other people down because it somehow makes me better.		I build others up, which serves to also build me up in the process.

I. Good-vs.-Bad Supervisor/Good-vs.-Bad Parent

In order to change how you feel about yourself, you must first identify how you treat yourself and how you talk to yourself. To do this, make a list comparing a good-vs.-bad supervisor or a good-vs.-bad parent. I'll give you the lists that many of my patients have come up with through the years; add to them through your experience.

Good Supervisor (Good Parent)	Bad Supervisor (Bad Parent)
—supportive	—can't trust
—gives time to teach	—expects you to know things you haven't been taught
—leads by example	—example is opposite of what is expected from you
—positive attitude	—poor attitude toward work
—expects you'll do well	—expects you'll screw up
—pleasant to be around	—a real drag to be around
—feel like you can talk to him or her without being ridiculed	—afraid to talk to him or her for fear of ridicule or embarrassment
—notices particularly good work	—only mistakes are noticed
—can make decisions	—leaves decisions to employees, but doesn't take responsibility for mistakes made
—honest	—dishonest
—predictable	—unpredictable
—communicates clear, reasonable expectations	—gives vague expectations, over-tasks
—gives honest feedback	—no feedback till trouble
—not always serious, can use humor to lighten things	—always serious, never acts like a real person
—admits mistakes	—blames others
—takes time to find out	—jumps to conclusions
—fair	—shows favoritism
—competes with self	—competes with employees
—patient	—impatient, too critical
—allows privacy and space	—intrusive/nosy

Add more traits from your experience:

Now, go back over this list and circle the ways you treat yourself. List the number from the good side versus the number from the bad side and circle it.

good vs. # bad

When we become adults we, in essence, become our own parents and our own supervisors. We have the choice to love and support ourselves, or we can continue in the ways of the past. You are your own supervisor. Choose to be a good one. You are your own parent now. Choose to be what a good parent would be.

II. *Strengthen Your Defense Lawyer*

One of the exercises many of my patients have found helpful to boost their self-esteem is the one I call "Strengthen Your Defense Lawyer." It takes at least several hours to do, but you are worth the time it takes.

To do this:

1. Take a piece of paper and draw out a courtroom scene. Include the judge, prosecuting attorneys, defense lawyers, defendant, court reporter, witness stand, and jury box. This is a drawn representation of the voices in your head.

2. Choose a crime that you mentally accuse yourself of. It can be anything you feel guilty about, or anything you've actually done of which you're ashamed.

3. Put yourself on trial. Actually begin to write out the dialogue of a trial. Have opening statements by the prosecutor and the defense. Call witnesses. Raise objections. At first, notice the strength of your internal prosecuting attorney; after all, it's had practice accusing you all these years. However, as you write out the trial you'll begin to notice the lies your prosecutor tells in the courtroom. He distorts the truth to make you look worse.

4. Strengthen your defense attorney. Instead of the wimp he has been, make him stand tall and defend you with eloquence instead of silence. Hire the best lawyer in the world to help defend you. You're worth it.

5. The only catch to this exercise is that you must win the verdict. You must be on your side.

6. Repeat this several times, until you have sufficiently strengthened your defense attorney.

Some have written two pages of dialogue; I have one patient who wrote forty pages of dialogue. Do what helps you. One person who performed this exercise wrote, "This is fun. I hired a whole gang— Clarence Darrow, Daniel Webster, Melvin Belli, Bella Abzug, and Perry Mason. Then I gave the prosecution Hamilton Burger, who has never won a case, and a guy I used to know who became the worst lawyer ever to pass the bar. Every time old Burger is about to make a point, my old friend trips him up. He forgets to file papers and summon witnesses, too."

After you've done this several times on paper, begin to set up this scenario in your head. Identify your accusing voices (can you match them up to your accusers of the past?), identify and strengthen those voices that root for you and defend you. Our prosecuting attorneys can also work in our best interest. They do that by bringing up important issues we need to look at, but they do it in such a way as to help us learn from our mistakes, rather than beating us up for them. The commentary these inner voices provide on our actions can either enhance or sabotage our chances for success. Train your inner voices to work in your own best interest. After all, they are your voices; put them under your control.

III. Critics' Committee-Busting: Talk Back

Another exercise my patients have found helpful is the Talk-Back exercise. Every time you notice your inner voices putting you down, talk back to them. Don't take their abuse.

1. Keep a notebook with you at all times, titled "Critics' Committee-Busting."

2. Divide the paper of the notebook into three columns. Label the columns: Self-critical Thought, Thought Distortion, and Response to the Lie.

3. Write down the self-critical thoughts as they go through your mind.

4. Write down the thought distortion from the list of ten distortions on pages 98–100 (from Chapter Ten).

5. Add a rational response to the self-critical lie.

6. Do this every time you notice a self-critical thought; have the discipline to follow through.

Examples:

Self-critical Thought	Thought Distortion	Response to the Lie
I went off my diet again; I can't succeed at anything.	Overgeneralizing	Going off my diet one day out of seven doesn't mean I'm a failure. I need to focus on my successes and encourage myself for them.
I never do anything right.	Overgeneralizing	Nonsense. I do lots of things right.
This mistake shows what an idiot I am.	Labeling	Making one mistake does not make me an idiot, particularly if I can learn something from it.
Everyone will look down on me if I'm late.	Jumping to conclusions Overgeneralizing Black-or-white thinking	Some people may be annoyed, but it's not the end of the world. Besides, I really can't control what other people think.

IV. Write Down Your Accomplishments

Write down at least two major personal, relational, and work-related accomplishments. The hard part of this exercise is not thinking of the accomplishments—we all have done at least two things in these areas that we were proud of. The hard part is that you're not allowed to downplay or degrade what you have done in any way.

Personal accomplishments:

1.
2.

Relational accomplishments:

1.
2.

Work-related accomplishments:

1.
2.

Remember, *no downplaying or degrading!* Take them at face value, enjoy them, be proud of them. Stop telling yourself they mean nothing. They mean a lot.

Impact Statements

Write out the following impact statements and tape them in places where you're most likely to see them (on the bathroom mirror, refrigerator door at home, on your desk at work, etc.). This way they'll constantly remind you of the need to treat yourself with respect and kindness.

I talk back to the inner voices that try to put me down.
I am on good terms with myself.
I treat myself as a good parent would.
I often have a positive impact on others.
I am worth others having a positive impact on me.
My inner voices help me to learn from my mistakes, and they
    spur me on to be as good as I can be.

PRESS ON: PERSISTENCE

A big shot is simply a little shot who kept shooting.
—ZIG ZIGLAR

The make-or-break quality of life is not intelligence, not formal education, not background, not money, not luck—but persistence. With it, almost anything is possible; without it, very little is possible. You can have all the other ingredients in the right amount and so on, but if you give up before you complete your task, what good is any of it?

I have a friend who wanted to go to medical school so badly that he applied to thirty-five schools. He got in to one of them. He used to say, "How many medical schools can a person go to at one time?" He persisted to make his dream come true.

I also know an author who received twenty-seven rejections on her first book before it was finally accepted by a small publishing company. She has had two best-sellers since then.

My wife, Robbin, was in love with someone else for the first several months we knew each other. I persisted, however, until I could see a crack in the door to her heart. When she was ready for me, I was there. Persistence allowed my dreams to come true.

Stories like this go on and on. Those of us who achieved our goals weren't lucky. We made our dreams work by not giving up, by persisting.

At times, we all feel like giving up. It is not our feelings, however, that dictate our life. It is our behavior. Many people work when they don't feel like working. Many people act loving when they don't feel love. Many people continue onward when they feel like quitting.

Actions speak louder than feelings. In fact, actions are what lead to changing feelings. As you go through the exercises you may feel like quitting. Don't. The work on yourself will help to change the behaviors that have been holding you back, and changing your behaviors will go a long way to changing the underlying feelings of not being worth it.

The strongest businesses, relationships, and personal faiths did not start out that way. They all started with ideas that turned into focused energy. They went through failures, disappointments, and doubts, but they persisted through to their goals. Heroes of success stories do not give up on themselves. They press on even when they feel like giving up.

As I mentioned in the section on change, there needs to be a balance between persistence and flexibility. Continuing at a task when there is no evidence that it will pay dividends is not being persistent. It is being stubborn. Persistence by itself is like the rest of the ingredients of success: it cannot be isolated. But putting this together with the other twenty-six ingredients finishes the recipe.

Eric Hoffer, in *Reflections on the Human Condition*, sums this up by writing, "At the core of every true talent there is an awareness of the difficulties inherent in any achievement and the confidence that by persistence and patience something worthwhile will be realized."

PERSISTENCE EXERCISES

By perseverance the snail reached the ark.
—CHARLES SPURGEON

Never give up on yourself. You are always worth the time and effort it takes to reach your goals. Persistence, however, needs to be balanced with flexibility. Sticking with something long after its viability is stubbornness, not persistence. The exercises which follow are designed to help you increase your ability to stick with things long enough to bring them to the best conclusion possible, and to help you to never give up on yourself.

Examine the following sabotage factors, which are typical of those who need a boost in this area. Circle any that apply to you. Note the corresponding success factor, which is the more appropriate response. Circle the success factors that apply to you as well. Build on your strengths and strengthen your weaknesses.

Sabotage	vs.	Success
I give up on myself easily.		I am the last person I'd give up on.
I often fail to finish what I start.		I see projects through to the end, provided that finishing them is in the best interest of my goals.
I start things that prove too difficult to finish.		Before I start something I take time to think it through.
If I fail at something I'm likely to give up.		I try again, if at first I don't succeed.
It is too much trouble for me to follow through on the dreams I have for myself.		I continue to work on my dreams, even though reaching them may be years away.
I often don't follow through on the resolutions I've made to myself or others.		I keep the resolutions I've made.
Self-help programs have not worked for me because I have failed to follow through with them.		I get benefit from many sources because I follow through with recommendations when they make sense to me.

I. In What Areas of Your Life Do You Give Up Easily?

In order to stop giving up easily on yourself, you must first identify the areas where you lack persistence. Think of the three major areas of life; list those areas of your life where you give up easily. Examples are given below.

Personal life:

spirituality: (I often give up on God, unless I'm in a jam.)
emotional life: (When I get anxious I just leave a situation, rather than tough it out.)
physical life: (I have given up on trying to lose weight.)

Relational life: (I'm going to leave my spouse. It will never work out.)

Work-related life: (No matter what I do at work I won't advance, so why try anymore?)

For those areas you listed, ask yourself the following questions:

1. How important are these areas to your overall goals?

2. What reasons do you give yourself for quitting? Now that you know about distorted thought, are they rational?

3. What can you tell yourself to help you persist through your weak areas?

Example: Brad, who wrote professionally as a second job, received five rejection letters for a magazine article he had written. He was ready to put away the article even though he believed it had merit. Brad had a tendency to give up on his writing.

1. How important is this area to your overall goals? Very important. Brad wants to be able to quit his job and write for a living.

2. What reasons do you give yourself for quitting? Now that you know about distorted thought, are they rational? Brad tells himself that no one will ever publish anything he writes, even though he has been published twelve times, and that he just doesn't measure up. Of course this is distorted thinking. His "fortune telling" and "overgeneralizing" bring his mood down to the point where he feels like quitting something he loves.

3. What can you tell yourself to help you persist through your weak areas? On a rational level Brad knows that sometimes it takes ten or twenty submissions before he gets an article selected for publication. If he really believes in it he needs to persist through the rejections and not take them as a statement on his personal worth.

II. Who Do You Know Who Follows Through?

Who do you know who follows through on their goals? List them for each area of your life. How do they match up in these areas? Do they get what they want? These people have a valuable lesson to teach you. Spend more time with them.

Personal life:
spirituality:
emotional life:
physical life:
Relational life:
Work-related life:

Ask these people to spend some time talking with you about some of their accomplishments. As you talk, ask about any setbacks or problems the person faced, how he or she reacted, and then how the problems were solved. Listen carefully for cues to how this person thinks and feels when faced with a discouraging situation.

It would be most helpful if you could tape record the conversation, or take notes during it. If you can't do that, at least make notes immediately after the conversation, playing back as much as you can remember in your mind.

Next, go over the conversation again, either in your notes or on tape. Look for the differences in how the other person felt about problems and handled them compared to the way you would feel and act in similar situations. This exercise can be very valuable in helping you pinpoint self-sabotaging thoughts and behavior in contrast to the ways successful people persist until they reach their goals. In fact, the more times you repeat this exercise, the more you'll learn. There's no reason ever to stop doing it, although as you gain experience and success, you don't have to record every conversation.

III. *What's Your Excuse to Quit?*

There are as many reasons to quit as there are people. Excuses are reasons to give up trying. You must have one when you give up. Which excuses do you use to hold you down? Circle those from the list below that apply to you.

It's his/her fault.
I always fail.
No one believes in me.
I keep making the same mistakes. I'll never learn.
I don't want to be successful. It makes me feel bad.
If only I had started when I was younger.
I never get the breaks.
I should have been more prepared.
I just can't commit myself to it.
I don't know if that's what I want.
I never saw it happen.
I have no energy; maybe tomorrow.
I know I'll fail if I try.
I got caught up in the details.
I can't look at things differently. I've been like this too long.
I can't change.
I want it now, but now never comes.
I just can't decide.
It's too risky.
No one knows any more than I do.
What do you think? I just never know.
You'll hate me if I do that, won't you?
I'll let you guys compete. That way I won't lose either one of you
    as friends.
I'm just going along with everyone else.
I don't care what you think. I'll do it my way no matter what.
It's too hard. I give up.
The lawn mower broke. (What's that got to do with it? Nothing.
    One excuse is as good as another.)
Add your own special excuses:

Throw your excuses away. They do you no good. They hold you back. They sabotage your life. Take responsibility for following through with what you start.

IV. *When You Feel Like Giving Up—DON'T!*

At least once every week, when you feel like giving up on yourself, someone else, or one of your projects—DON'T! Just once keep going. Go the extra mile. Learn to develop persistence by persisting.

V. *Become-the-Squeakiest-Wheel Exercise*

One form of persistence could almost be called "pest"-istance. Sometimes it takes a pest to right a wrong. This week you are to become a squeaky wheel. Think of an existing situation in which you are owed something, or want something (a bank has messed up your account, or you need to return some defective merchandise). By the end of the week make them know who you are. Phone, write, visit, call the radio station, write your Congressperson . . . whatever! Go on the attack.

Never mind what they may think of you. You don't need their approval, you need a settlement. They will probably respect you for it anyway, which makes for a far better relationship than being a doormat or a "nice" person.

Impact Statements

Write out the following impact statements and tape them in places where you're most likely to see them (on the bathroom mirror, refrigerator door at home, on your desk at work, etc.). This way they'll constantly remind you of the need to foster self-discipline in your life.

We all feel like giving up at some point. But it is not my feelings that dictate my life; it is my behavior.
I refuse to use excuses to quit.
I never give up on myself.
As long as I keep trying, I have a chance.
It is not my talent or charm that pulls me through; it is *me* that pulls me through.

19

Live Life in Real Time

"Real time" is a science and computer term that I like because it describes how to live life. We are much more effective when we live in the present, in "real time," rather than allowing our past fears and hurts to control our actions. Living in "real time" requires us to be intensely focused on our present and future goals and to live each moment as a special part of our existence. I hope this book has brought you closer to living life in "real time."

The concept of "real time" also forces us to realize that there is limited time. There is only so much time for us to accomplish our goals and it's important that we spend that time and effort on things that really matter to us. Too often we spend our time trying to please others or on activities that have little value (such as excessive television).

When we know what we really want out of life and we are effective in our approach, then we give ourselves the best chance of reaching our goals. This is the essence of "conscious living." Unfortunately, most people live an unconscious life in which they go from problem to problem or situation to situation without asking themselves what's really important to them. Their lives miss direction and form and it may take the tragedy of an accident or a serious illness to shake a person out of his unconscious or automatic way of reacting to the world.

What's important to you? What do you want in your relationships with your spouse, lover, children, or friends? What do you want at work? What do you want for your finances? What do you want for your health? Does your behavior help you reach your goals or does it push you farther from them? These are the major questions to ask yourself.

Living life without regrets will give us the energy to look forward rather than be burdened by the past. Too often people say things like: "Where did the time go... How did the children grow up so fast... I can't believe I let the opportunities slip away." Looking backward is a waste of time because we cannot do anything about it.

"Real time" living involves taking responsibility for our actions, being focused on our goals, being present and aware of our interactions with others and utilizing our time on things that matter. Anything less is living in the realm of the unconscious.

In closing, I will share with you a very successful exercise from my course, "The Sabotage Factor." It's called "Make A Personalized CHANGE Tape," and it's based on the major premises of the course book. After you make the tape, listen to it every day. Many people have told me that this tape is one of the most valuable parts of their treatment. Don't shortcut yourself here. You have been programmed or in a sense "hypnotized" into believing you can't change those things that are holding you back. The first thing to change is your negative belief system. In order to do this make your CHANGE tape in the following way.

1. Use a tape recorder that will clearly record your voice. Use *your* voice on the tape. Change is going to occur within you, so you must get used to listening to your own voice.

2. When you first begin taping, record your full name. Introduce yourself to the new you. Use your name often in the tape.

3. Tell yourself to sit in a comfortable chair, loosen all tight clothing, and let yourself feel relaxed all over.

4. Then, tell yourself to pick a spot on the wall, a little above your eye level, and stare at it. As you do, count slowly to twenty. When you get to six, twelve, and eighteen tell yourself to feel the heaviness in your eyelids. And when you get to twenty, tell yourself to slowly let your eyelids close. If you find your eyes wandering, that's OK, just bring them back to stare at the spot.

5. Next, on the tape, tell yourself to take three deep breaths, each time exhaling very slowly. Say, "with each breath in I just breathe in relaxation, and with each breath out I just blow out all the tension, all the things that interfere with my becoming as relaxed as possible."

6. After that, tell yourself to tightly squeeze the muscles in your eyelids: "Close your eyes as tightly as you can. And then, slowly let the muscles in your eyelids relax. Notice how much more they have relaxed." Then progressively tell yourself to imagine that relaxation spreading from the muscles in your eyelids, to the muscles in your face... down your neck into your shoulders and arms... into your chest and throughout the rest of your body. The muscles will take the relaxation cue from your eyelids and relax progressively all the way down to the bottom of your feet. Some like to imagine themselves in a warm tub, some liken their relaxed muscles to a limp wet rag. Use what works for you.

7. Next on the tape, describe a place where you feel comfortable, your special haven so to speak, a place that you can imagine with all of your senses. Your haven can be a real or imagined place. It can be any place where you'd like to spend time. Describe it on the tape, using all of your senses, in as much detail as possible.

Then say, "As you listen to the rest of the tape, imagine yourself walking in your haven, looking and exploring its inner reaches."
—These first few steps should take about five to ten minutes to go through.

8. After you go through these initial steps, read the following statement into the tape recorder.

"Now that I feel very relaxed, and very comfortable... I feel physically stronger and fitter in every way. With each breath in, I just breathe in strength... with each breath out, I blow out the weaknesses that hold me back. Day by day I feel more in control of my life... increasingly able to do what I enjoy doing, rather than what other people think I should be doing. If others approve of what I do... Great... but I can no longer base my life on the goals of others... I develop my own goals and focus my energy on them. I know deep down what makes me happy, where I belong... I now have the strength to follow through with my dreams.

"I expect to succeed at whatever I set out to do... and I see myself succeeding before my effort... I program myself for success. That doesn't mean that there won't be failures. Everyone fails at one time or another—everyone... expecting myself to be perfect is arrogance. On the other hand, I expect myself to learn from my failures... it is the only way to make them valuable to me. No longer will I have to make the same mistakes over and over. I learn from the mistakes and move on. I also strive to learn from others... we live in a relational, teaching world... and I am a willing pupil. Acting like a know-it-all does not help me in any way... learning from others always has the potential for expanding my horizons.

"In a similar way I am a more informed person... When I have questions I ask them. I am always on the lookout for new and different information. I prepare for my tasks, setting myself up to win, instead of putting off my tasks and setting myself up to fail. Organization is becoming more second nature to me... I realize that when I put something in its right place initially, I'm more likely to find it when I need it.

"Making decisions is no longer a mystery to me. I am first clear with myself about what is actually to be decided, gather adequate information on it, talk to those affected by the decision to get their input, see my options, and then decide on the thing based on the goals I have for myself. I am thus able to take reasonable risks, while being able to avoid taking risks that are dangerous for me.

"Every day I strive to become alert... more wide awake... more energetic. I am becoming much less easily tired... much less easily fatigued... much less easily discouraged... much less easily depressed... much less easily anxious. Every day I am more deeply interested in what I'm doing... in whatever is going on around me... in the people around me. I work smart as well as hard, focusing my energy on the goals I have set for myself. I delegate when I do not need to do a task, or if someone can do it better for a better price. I am also more observant of situations and people around me, truly seeing what is there to see and listening to what I heard.

"Starting now, I am able to look at common things in uncommon ways. I act and think more creatively. No longer do I have to solve problems in old ways that have not worked in the past. Creativity is not the prerogative of artists, it is part of all humans... I do not have to stay in any rut, unless I choose to stay in it. Day by day I am also more flexible... more adaptable... more willing to change as change is needed. At the same time, I am more disciplined... less impulsive... I keep the words, "Thinking Is Trial Action," in the front of my brain, and refer to them every time I wish to do something that may not be in my best interest.

"I realize now that I am a product of my environment... If my environment is negative, so am I. I teach others, by my actions, that they need to treat me with respect, and in turn, I treat them as I wish to be treated. I also spend time with those who uplift me and believe in me. I surround myself with positive people. On the same note, I focus my energy on being more empathetic with those around me. I am now able to get outside of myself to understand the feelings of others...and I am willing to see things from their perspective as well as from my own. No longer am I afraid of competing with others...it is great when I win...but I can learn new things from any situation. Competition spurs me on to be as good as I can be.

"With ever-increasing frequency, I accept myself and others as we are, instead of how I think things should be. I compromise when necessary...and I now refuse to let the accusing inner voices have free reign over how I feel about myself. I am in control of me...and I live with inner voices that help and uplift me, rather than ones that try to tear me down. I fight the negative voices within whenever they appear.

"Gradually, I find less and less need to worry about future problems and dangers, many of which are quite imaginary and silly when I really think about them. I am increasingly able to determine the real dangers about the things I fear and to determine the reasonable probabilities of their occurrence. Most of the things we worry about never happen...I am now able to mobilize my anxieties into energy by preparing for the other tasks I need to do, thus decreasing my overall anxiety. Every day I find myself successful in overcoming the anxiety that holds me back.

"Every day, the irrationalities of the past influence my life less and less. I reject the idea that the traumas of the past need to have powerful importance in my life. I live in the present...I have choices in the present. My life is not dictated by what happened when I was young...I can overcome the past, the excess baggage that has been weighing me down.

"I never give up on myself. I give my best effort toward reaching the goals I have set for myself, and no matter what, I keep pursuing the dreams in my life. I am flexible enough to change as change is needed, but I believe in my ability and I never give up on me."

9. Now, on the tape, tell yourself to count backward from ten, and say that as you do so, you will feel more awake, more alert, and full of energy to do whatever you wish to do. When you get to zero, open your eyes, stretch, and get up and walk around the room.

The total time of the tape will be from ten to twenty-five minutes, depending on the pace of your voice, images, and so on.

Now that you have made the tape, listen to it once every day. It is important, the first few times you listen to the tape, that you find out how your body will react to the relaxation. Some people become so relaxed that they doze off to sleep for a bit. If that happens to you, great! Listen to the tape before you go to bed, or when you can catch a nap. Some people find that it takes them a while to be fully awake and alert; they remain very relaxed for several minutes afterward, as if they were waking up from sleep. If the tape affects you that way, you want to make sure that you're clearly awake before you do anything that requires full concentration, such as driving a car. Others can listen to the tape anytime, anywhere, and feel a relaxed kind of energy flow through their body.

The most important thing is that you listen to your tape every day. You can change the content of the tape to emphasize particular weak areas. Or, you can change it in any way that you think will be beneficial to you. This is *your* tape. Use it to strengthen *your* life.

Printed in the United States
17894LVS00002B/102